HUNGRY FOR IT

Books by Fiona Zedde

BLISS

A TASTE OF SIN

EVERY DARK DESIRE

HUNGRY FOR IT

SATISFY ME
(with Renee Alexis and Sydney Molare)

SATISFY ME AGAIN
(with Renee Luke and Sydney Molare)

Published by Kensington Publishing Corporation

HUNGRY FOR IT

fiona zedde

KENSINGTON BOOKS
http://www.kensingtonbooks.com

KENSINGTON BOOKS are published by

Kensington Publishing Corp.
850 Third Avenue
New York, NY 10022

All Kensington titles, imprints, and distributed lines are available at special quantity discounts for bulk purchases for sales promotion, premiums, fund-raising, educational, or institutional use.

Special book excerpts or customized printings can also be created to fit specific needs. For details, write or phone the office of the Kensington Special Sales Manager: Attn. Special Sales Department. Kensington Publishing Corp., 850 Third Avenue, New York, NY 10022. Phone: 1-800-221-2647.

ISBN-13: 978-0-7582-1739-4
ISBN-10: 0-7582-1739-0

First Printing: July 2008

10 9 8 7 6 5 4 3 2 1

Printed in the United States of America

Chapter

1

The light in Rémi's office was dim. Shades pulled. Speakers dead. Just the quiet of her breathing and the trailing smoke from the glowing red tip of her cigar.

"You did well for yourself here." A voice, only an octave or so above the silence, emerged from the darkness opposite her.

"Thanks. I had some help."

Rémi felt more than saw the shape nod its head. Heard the slow intake of breath.

"So is this a business call, Wynne? Or are you on one of your rare American pleasure trips?"

"You know my business is always a pleasure."

Although she could only make out faint details, Rémi knew that Wynne lay relaxed on the couch by the door, her schoolgirl-thin body clothed in something pretty, maybe even cute. But the woman was a deadly thing, sure to be wearing weapons under those clothes. A gun, maybe. Knives, certainly.

Annoyed, Rémi pursed her lips. "Don't play games, cousin. Why are you here?"

The couch's leather sighed as the slim shape on top of it shifted and laughed. "Always to the point, aren't you?"

"With you, I have to be. Once we get that out of the way, then I can know how to treat you." Despite her cautious words, Rémi remained relaxed in the chair, her own feet booted and crossed on top of her desk. She puffed on her cigar, inhaled the pungent smoke, before blowing it back out into the air. The gray cloud floated toward Wynne.

"I got word that some trouble was going to start. For you."

Rémi paused with the cigar halfway to her lips. "From who?"

"Some guy who thinks you're his rival. It's nothing personal, I assume. He just wants your business."

It was Rémi's turn to nod. That explained why she'd been getting so much shit lately from people she'd always dealt well with. Shipments late or not arriving at all. Fights breaking out, inexplicably, in the middle of a busy night at the club between people she'd never seen before. And she'd heard rumors of a new place that just opened on the beach. Another club that hosted jazz and downtempo bands during the day and early evenings, but turned into a strip club after dark.

"He needs to get his own then."

"This greedy boy already has his own. Now he wants yours."

"Did he hire you?"

Rémi almost smiled at Wynne's insulted breath. Almost.

"I don't make trouble," her cousin said. "I make it disappear. Besides, that *capon* couldn't afford me."

"Good to know." The small muscles in Rémi's belly slowly relaxed. "So this little visit is pleasure then?"

A low laugh. "For now."

For now. Rémi could work with that.

"So I don't suppose you'd want to tell me who this pest is?"

"He's not hiding, cousin. You'll be able to find out soon enough on your own."

Rémi hummed a non-answer around her cigar. An annoyance. She didn't like this game. Frowning, she thumbed a speck of loosened tobacco from the tip of her tongue. "Do you have a place to stay while you're in town?"

"Yes. Thanks for asking." Cloth whispered in the darkness as Wynne stood up. "I'll be staying at Cecile's on the beach. You can reach me there or at my usual number if you need anything."

Rémi couldn't imagine what she might need her deadly cousin for but she nodded anyway. "It's good to see you," she said more out of politeness than truth. As much as she yearned to have family with her here in Miami, she'd rather get a phone call from Bronwynne St. Just than have her in the town where she lived.

Her cousin laughed. When she opened the door, light burst into the office, abruptly illuminating her features. Deceptively soft doe eyes. Sharp teeth flashing white against sepia skin. The lean body in blue jeans and a white blouse with tiny bows on the sleeves.

"Good to see you too, Rémi," she said with the smallest of nods. "By the way, nice review in the *Herald*. If you haven't read it yet, you should."

With a gentle click the office door closed behind her. In the wake of her cousin's visit, Rémi stared at the empty side of the door, brow knitted in thought.

The first time she'd become aware of her cousin was when her parents called her into the family room after school to tell her about the unfortunate Wynne who'd lost both of her own parents in a fire. Her cousin had miraculously become their responsibility while the girl's older sister, Celeste, had disappeared into the wilds of Canada rather than become someone's charity case. Barely a week after the revelation, Wynne was broodingly installed in their house. The girl was pretty, tall in the way of all the women on Kelia's side of the family. And the grief sat on her face like a bruise. Rémi, caught up in her own miseries, had mostly avoided her, but one evening she stumbled into Wynne on the porch. It was an unforgettable encounter.

The wind brought the smell of jasmine and burnt wood swirling onto the porch. Rémi let the door swing shut behind her and saw Wynne flinch. Her cousin turned. Face tear ravaged. Eyes like black holes. This was someone who had lost. This was—

"What would you do if your daddy was dead?"

The raw question rocked Rémi back on her bare heels. "He won't die."

"That's bullshit and you know it."

The fourteen-year-old's curse straightened Rémi's spine and she stood up stiffly on the porch in that scorched darkness. "We don't curse here," she said. "Papa won't allow it."

"My mama burned up. My sister ran away." Tears bubbled up with the words from Wynne's throat. "Everything I had was lost in that fire."

A rope of light snaked from the corner of Rémi's vision. She turned. And gasped. Fire climbed quickly up the birch tree across the lawn.

"Oh my god!"

"Everything you love can burn," Wynne said.

"Are you crazy?" Rémi shoved past her cousin and ran for the garden hose attached to the side of the house, calling "Mama! Papa!"

The grass stung her bare feet with cold. Bits of twigs stabbed at her ankles. Rémi grabbed at the hose, but it slipped out of her hands again and again and again. "Mama! Papa!" Her throat grew hoarse. Her fingers trembled. Finally the hose, wet and muddy from her mother's earlier gardening, stayed in her hands. Water gushed from it and into her face, slapping against her chest, plastering her T-shirt against her body.

Rémi ran with it, finally wetting the grass, eating the tail end of the fire.

"What are you doing?"

Her father appeared at her side, slapped the hose from her hands, and pulled it away. Rémi almost tripped up, tangling in the long green vine of plastic. Kelia dashed by her, a bucket in her hand. Water splashed the smoldering tree. Splashed Rémi. Then the fire was out. Her father, in unbuttoned slacks and bare chest, spun to her, the hose limp and spitting into the grass. His face was hard as a stranger's.

"What did you do?" he hissed.

Rémi shook her head and stammered, "Nothing."

On the porch, her cousin watched them with grief-black eyes, saying nothing.

Less than two weeks later Wynne was gone, leaving behind only a faintly apologetic note telling the Bouchard family not to look for her and that she would be fine.

Over the last few years, Rémi had intermittent communication with her cousin. Communication that left no doubt what kind of occupation Wynne had fallen into after she left Maine. To Rémi's knowledge, they'd never had a hired killer in the family before. She exhaled a cloud of cigar smoke and stared at the door her cousin had disappeared through. Then she reached for the desk lamp, and with a quick twist of her fingers, illuminated the uncluttered surface of her desk. Her eyes winced from the sudden brightness.

In the top of her inbox, newly exhumed from its depths by Wynne, Rémi assumed, was the article her cousin mentioned. It had been sitting on her desk for nearly two weeks now, and she hadn't made the time to read it. Her manager, Elena, said it was a good review and that was enough. Rémi opened the paper.

GILLESPIE'S—A NOT-SO-HIDDEN TREASURE

Walking into Rémi Bouchard's club was a new experience. For a couple of years now I'd been hearing about this place, how hot the clientele was and that it was the happening place to be on just about any night of the week. For these very reasons this reporter didn't feel a need to make a visit. But something on the wind spoke to me and so I found myself stepping through the doors of Gillespie's, expecting the expected. However, from the first breath of jazz-infused air to the last mellow note of the evening, my experience was anything but.

The stellar live band, intimate tables on both levels, the two well-stocked bars and attractive waitstaff aside, what made the experience shine for this reporter was the food: the presentation, flavor, and service of my unplanned three-course meal at the club was four-star quality. From the crisp yet tender circles of calamari to the intoxicating slice of iced rum cake, my dining experience at this jazz club was more than remarkable and very reminiscent of the late Auguste Bouchard's European-style restaurants in Canada and the northeast. Not surprising since the owner of Gillespie's is the renowned chef and restaurateur's older daughter.

Rémi put the paper down, unable to keep reading. Wynne was right, the article was very flattering. What she didn't appreciate, however, was the damn reporter's insistence on linking her business, her hard work, with anything that her father did. Even now, nearly two years since his death and fourteen years since he abandoned her, she still couldn't escape Auguste Bouchard. Just as she'd meant nothing to him, he meant nothing to her. So it was the bitterest irony that since the article came out, linking her and her club to Auguste, they had been overrun with reservations, having a waiting list for tables for the first time since they opened three years ago. At least now Rémi knew the reason for the club's sudden surge in popularity.

"Fuck him." She tossed the review aside.

"That sounds like an interesting proposition."

One of Gillespie's waitresses, Monique, stood in the doorway, delectable in the club's uniform, pin-striped tuxedo-style vest and slim-fitting skirt that showed off her stunning figure.

Rémi smiled. "Not really. What can I do for you?"

She felt Monique's eyes roam over her, a clean and ravenous glance that would have alarmed Rémi if she wasn't used to it. In that glance, she saw herself as clearly as if looking into a mirror: The relaxed weight of her tall and leanly muscled body in the office chair. Her short wavy hair with its tendency to grow out into inky curls that Monique loved to run her hands through, and her skin like the outside of a ginger root. All courtesy of her French father and Black Canadian mother. The waitress's tongue peeked past her full lips and she shifted in the doorway as if something under her skin itched.

Monique had never been subtle where sex was concerned. Whenever she wanted it, she wore that desire plainly on her face and all Rémi had to do was take it. Or leave it alone. The other woman never complained if things didn't go her way, just shrugged and continued on as if to say, "Maybe next time."

"Your friends are outside to take you to the airport."

"What? I told them to call me when they were ready."

Monique held up a cell phone. Rémi's. "I think they did."

"Shit. I must have left it in the kitchen."

"Something like that." Monique walked fully into the office, not bothering to close the door. "When will you be back?"

"In four days." Rémi stood up from behind her desk and leaned down to pick up her luggage. "Elena will be taking care of things while I'm away, but you can reach me on my cell if you need anything."

"Anything?" Monique slid the phone into Rémi's inside pocket, boldly touching her breast in the process.

Rémi made her voice cold. "Within reason, of course."

"Of course." Monique stepped back, eyes to the floor.

With her duffel in one hand and the folding leather garment bag slung over her shoulder, Rémi waited at the door for Monique to walk out of the office before locking up behind her. A black limousine idled at the curb. As she stepped into the lush Miami heat, the uniformed driver quickly came to take her luggage and open the car door for her.

"Thanks," Rémi murmured absently to the suit-clad woman, giving the curved backside a passing glance.

"You work much too hard," Sage said from the bright confines of the car.

Rémi buckled herself into the seat and smiled tiredly at her friends. Sage, not bothering with her seat belt, poured herself a glass of champagne from a nearly empty bottle. In dark jeans and a white tank that showed off the black tribal tattoos that curled the length of one arm and sunk into the skin of her throat and neck, Sage looked something like Maori warrior. Until she smiled, showing off pretty teeth and the feminine warmth in her face.

Her girl, Phil, blew Rémi a kiss from her sprawl on the opposite seat, looking pleasantly drunk although it was barely two in the afternoon. On her, the matching outfit of low rider jeans and white tank was sexier. Tighter. The diamond stud in her navel and gym-hardened abs pressed against the shirt.

"Yeah, I thought we'd pick you up from home, not work." Her nose wrinkled as she said the last word.

"There were a few last-minute things I had to do," Rémi said. "No big deal. Now I can focus on the party and Dez's wedding. Plus whatever else might come along."

Phil grinned. "Hm. I'm hoping for lots of 'whatever else.' Do you think Victoria has any hot relatives who might show us a real nice time?"

"Even if she doesn't, I'm sure you'll find someone to entertain yourselves with," Rémi said.

"True that." Sage chuckled.

The car pulled away from the curb and Rémi, unable to help herself, glanced beyond the tinted windows to look at her club. Even at two o' clock on a Thursday, traffic through the wide black double doors was already thick. Gillespie's was more than "work." It was her livelihood. The main reason she could play with her friends and not go crawling back to her family for money. Without it, everything in her world would collapse, and it was always a surprise whenever the realization hit that her friends didn't know that. But they'd never had to worry about money. Probably never have to. Rémi didn't have that luxury. Not since the day she came out to her father and burned all those bridges behind her.

She reached for the champagne. "So what time do we land in Montreal?"

Chapter

2

Rémi had a strong feeling that a threesome with the brides was out of the question. The thought made her smile. Never mind that she and bride number one had often indulged in such excess. There was no way that Desiree Nichols was going to share her woman, especially the one she was about to get legally hitched to.

She stood at her friend's wedding, basking in her nostalgia. Dez looked nice in her tux and her femme bride was a firecracker in a red froth wedding dress with its deep cleavage and off-the-shoulder lace sleeves. If anybody deserved a wife like this one it was Dez. They'd gone through a lot to get to this place, the quiet little chapel in Montreal where the families and close friends of both brides watched with equal parts pride and disbelief. Rémi had been there for most of their courtship, saw the sparks that flew between them, but never thought in an infinity of years that her friend would pledge monogamy for always. *But that just goes to show what I know about love,* Rémi thought with a twist of her mouth.

The minister seemed to sense it in the couple in front of him, though. In his white robe and golden sash, he gazed benevolently down at Dez and Victoria as if they were his own children being sent off in the world together.

"Now you will feel no rain, for each of you will be shelter for the other," he said, gray head nodding first at Dez then Victoria. "Now you will feel no cold, for each of you will be warmth to the other. Now you are two persons, but there is only one life before you."

From her position behind Dez, Rémi noticed the tears overflow Victoria's eyes. They ran, unashamed, down her face. She looked across at her future partner as if all the answers to her life's questions lay in the woman before her. Dez's jaw shook. Rémi put a steadying hand on her best friend's back and felt its tremor.

This was real commitment. Something strong and undeniable that had taken over her friend, like a fever, or destiny. Envy pricked behind Rémi's breastbone. Against her will, her eyes moved from Dez's dark-suited back, drifting to the attentive figure in white sitting in the front pew. Delicate but resilient, this woman was everything that Rémi had ever wanted. But she had never dared to ask. Had never been ready to ask.

The red pillbox hat on top of white-streaked curls bowed as the woman dabbed at her tears with a white handkerchief. Was she remembering her own wedding years before or the husband who left her in an otherwise empty bed? Did she long for someone to take his place, to be better at loving her than he was? Rémi swallowed thickly then looked away.

Just in time, because the minister concluded, smiling. "May happiness be your companion and your days together be good and long upon the earth."

That was Rémi's cue to present the ring as best woman. She took the platinum band from her vest pocket and held it out. Dez's hand shook as she accepted the ring.

"As a ceaseless reminder of the promise you have made to each other, these rings also speak of the oneness you now experience as partners."

The women exchanged rings with equally trembling fingers.

"And now repeat after me."

The minister recited the vows, and Dez and Victoria solemnly repeated them, staring into each other's eyes. With their "I dos" still echoing in the air, he faced the congregation.

"Because they have so affirmed, in love and knowledge of the other, so also do I declare that Desiree Nichols and Victoria Jackson are now life partners. Wife and wife."

A breath left Rémi's throat. It was done. The congregation of over two dozen rose to its feet in the same moment, applauding. The sound thundered in Rémi's ears.

After the ceremony and showering of white rose petals, Rémi stood back, watching the newlyweds receive their congratulations on the front steps of the church. They looked good together. Dez tall and handsome-pretty in her tux, a more butch Jada Pinkett Smith, and Victoria, a voluptuous visual feast with her curly hair twisted into a baby's breath–dotted topknot with a few loose curls around her round face. Their smiles looked almost too big to be contained.

Sage and Phil had already disappeared somewhere, probably to have sex in one of the church's back rooms. Rémi wasn't worried about them. When her friends were done they'd find her. Maybe at the reception where there would be drinks, dancing, and more congratulations.

"Did you ever think you'd see a day like this?"

Claudia appeared from behind a fall of rose petals the flower girl had just thrown at one of her friends. In a body-skimming white skirt suit that emphasized her narrow waist and the red camisole peeking from beneath the jacket, she was the sexiest mother-of-the-bride Rémi had ever seen.

She bit her lip against naughty thoughts. "Not really. Our Dez was the last person I thought would ever get married."

"I know. But this happiness suits her." Claudia smiled.

"Yes, it does."

Cheers erupted as a white limousine pulled up.

"I think that's our ride. Are you ready?" Rémi offered her arm to Claudia, half surprised when the other woman took it, insinuating her green apple scent into Rémi's senses.

They got into the car on the opposite side from the church, giving Dez and Victoria time to pose for pictures and wave at friends they would see at the reception in only a few minutes. Although Claudia sat on the seat opposite her, Rémi swore she could still smell the other woman on her, feel the shift of skirted thigh against hers. She took a deep breath. This weekend might be longer than she thought.

At the reception in the hotel, Rémi tried to keep her distance from her best friend's mother. Although the later the evening grew, the less certain she was as to why. She'd known Claudia for years. Had lusted for years. There was no reason why an event as simple as a wedding should test her control this much.

Claudia had the second dance of the evening with her daughter after offering a small and gracious toast to the happy couple. Dez's twin, Derrick, did the same, although he had a wealth of complimentary things to say about Victoria, and a few warnings for his sister. All in all, what Rémi expected.

The small hotel ballroom, decorated with splashes of red and white, was well turned out for the reception. Long tables with room for all thirty guests, a delicious three-course meal that seemed to satisfy every palate, and alcohol flowing freely enough to loosen even the most uptight of matrons. Victoria's parents had taken care of everything.

"Good luck," Rémi said to Dez as the two women stood at the bar watching the whirl of bodies around the dance floor. "Not that you'll need it. The two of you belong together."

Her friend, relaxed and smiling in her dove gray suit, patted Rémi on the back.

"Thanks, man. I want to make her happy. That's it." She flashed that irresistible Nichols grin of hers, the one that had landed her into trouble—the good kind and bad—since she hit puberty.

"That's a great place to start, although obviously I wouldn't know too much about those kinds of things."

"Your time will come soon enough."

As the two women watched, Victoria finished her dance with Derrick in a twirl of red tulle and immediately began looking around for her new wife.

"I think that's your cue," Rémi said.

Dez grinned again before walking away. Rémi followed with her eyes, a cool spot in her chest. Jealousy. Not the purest emotion, but she'd never been accused of having an abundance of those. She wanted what her friend had. Not Victoria, of course, although it would have been nice to test those waters. A lascivious smile found its way to her mouth. What she wanted was someone she could love like that. Someone she could lust for like that. Unbidden, the memory of Claudia surfaced.

"I would ask what—or who—put that look on your face, but I don't want to be embarrassed."

Rémi smiled at the cheeky little thing who addressed her. "You don't strike me as the type to embarrass easily."

The redhead with the look of Veronique, Victoria's mother, pursed her plump mouth and smiled. "Depends on what day you catch me."

"And what kind of day is this?"

"It's too early to tell." Her pale green eyes flickered over Rémi's tall frame. "I'm Cecile." She offered her hand. "Victoria's cousin."

"Rémi." She didn't bother giving her relationship to the other bride. It was fairly obvious who or what she was since she was the one who had stood by Dez during the ceremony and presented the ring for Victoria's finger.

"I know." Cecile smiled again. "Care to dance with me?"

Why not? "Sure."

As she stepped out on the dance floor with Cecile, she caught Claudia's eye. The older woman meaningfully looked between her and the girl. Rémi felt herself blush, although she didn't know why. Actually, she did. Claudia's look made her feel guilty. If Cecile was willing, and it seemed like she was more than, this evening had its own inevitable conclusion. Rémi held the shorter woman close as they began to move in rhythm to the opening strains of Meatloaf's "Paradise by the Dashboard Light." Caught off guard by the song, she laughed out loud.

Chapter

3

Rémi walked through the doors of the hotel, leaving the crisp fall of the city outside. The soft amber ambiance, dripping crystal chandelier, French renaissance settees and baroque décor. Her boots clicked against the antique floors. As she passed through the lobby, the intermittent mirrored paneling reflected her image back at her—tousled hair, lazy-lidded eyes, crumpled tuxedo jacket, and the shirt unbuttoned at the throat. She looked a little high, a little hot, and a lot available. Not bad.

Rémi slipped into her room then, without breaking stride, outside to the balcony facing the St. Lawrence River. The clean air seared through her lungs, even more bracing the second time. Stars glittered faintly above the city, no competition for the ribboning lights on the bridge and in the skyscrapers with their illuminated windows. Traffic roared dimly behind her. She knew Claudia was out here. For the past few nights around this time, long after most people were in bed, even in this vibrant old city, she heard her treading softly on the wide balcony outside their shared suite of rooms.

She'd wanted to go out and share the night with Claudia, but that struck her as strangely wrong. She didn't want to intrude on the older woman's quiet, although the company would have been nice. *More than nice*, Rémi thought, remembering the smell and feel of Claudia from earlier that day at the wedding.

"Are you coming to join me tonight, Rémi?"

She smiled sheepishly, though Claudia couldn't see her face. The weed from earlier had made her mellow, while the smell of the stranger she'd introduced to her latest fucking technique and the pleasure of having a double-jointed lover had almost faded from her fingers and skin. She wanted to be sure that Claudia didn't smell any of that. But what if she did?

"Sure, Mrs. N."

She sprawled out on the long bench next to the older woman, propping herself in the corner to better watch Claudia, who sat with a blanket covering her from hips to toes. She smelled like apples.

"How was your date?"

Rémi felt herself blush. It hadn't been so much of a date as it was a fuck and run.

She'd never been to Canada before, but something about Montreal's landscape and weather reminded her of Boothbay Harbor and of the family she no longer had. The feeling wasn't quite nostalgia, really, just a prickling in her chest that made her uneasy.

The best thing for it had been that pretty cousin of Victoria's who'd smiled at Rémi like she recognized her. Their "date" was long—a walk on the St. Lawrence River that took them to the woman's high-rise apartment, then a brisk round of fucking that left Rémi breathless and safely amnesiac. The drinks and weed they had afterwards were just a nice perk. Then Rémi left. She didn't want Dez to think that she abandoned her or Claudia. And so she was back. But Claudia seemed in no danger of suffering from loneliness. The newlyweds were more than likely in their hotel room inventing new ways to fuck each other comatose. But back to the question at hand.

"My date was fine."

"I'm sure it was." Claudia's delicate nostrils flared, and Rémi blushed again. She felt like the other woman could tell with that one delicate sniff everything that she had done that night. The scent of the night's fisting, smoking, fingering, and fucking lay on her like a filthy cloak she longed to throw off. Rémi wanted to apologize, and barely held herself back from it.

She shifted uncomfortably at Claudia's side until the other

woman's hand landed on her thigh. "It's okay." And she smiled again.

Just like that it *was* okay. Rémi smiled back and relaxed on the bench.

Once, when Rémi was very young and very drunk, she'd thought about having Claudia. It wasn't a specific fantasy, just a thought. A what-if idea of tasting Claudia's lips to sample their sweet curve and inhale the fresh green apple scent that always seemed to cling to her. Rémi was very drunk. But the idea had been so sweet. It stayed with her past the next day's sobriety and the next and the next. That was eight years ago. And the thought of tasting apples still made her lips tingle.

"Did you enjoy the wedding?" she asked Claudia.

"Of course. It's not every day that I see my popular little baby commit to someone so lovely. They're both very lucky, and I had a good time watching it all come together."

Rémi nodded.

"But I know you'll miss her." Claudia's eyes lay gently on Rémi.

"That's true. She and I have been through a lot together."

"So I hear."

Rémi looked at her. "I don't even want to know what and from whom."

"Good. Then I won't tell. I wasn't planning on telling you anyway." Claudia chuckled. She shifted under the blanket then glanced at her companion. "Do you mind it I—" she made a motion to the empty space between them.

"Go ahead."

"Thank you." Claudia swung her blanketed legs up and shifted until she lay with her legs almost fully stretched out on the bench. Her toes brushed Rémi's slacks. "Even though it's a little chilly out here, I could easily fall asleep sitting here. It's so peaceful."

"It's a beautiful city." Rémi glanced at the steady lights below and the winking stars above.

Claudia laughed. "But it's no Miami. Is that what you were thinking?"

"Maybe." Rémi flashed her smile.

"It feels a bit like New England to me. The mist and the smell. Very hypnotic."

Rémi glanced at her. So she wasn't the only one. But for her the memory of mist and lobsters wasn't quite so pleasant.

Claudia's feet shifted on the bench. "Oh, I'm sorry."

"About what?"

"I just thought about it. New England. You don't have very many good memories of up there, do you?"

"They're okay. Nothing to write home about, but certainly not nightmarish either." Rémi shrugged.

"That's good. I wouldn't want you to have a sleepless night because of me."

"Not from mentioning New England, you won't." Definitely not from that. On impulse she lifted Claudia's feet and laid them across her lap. The burgundy velvet and lace blanket with its trailing fringe splashed across the black cotton of her slacks. Warmth from the other woman's feet and legs slowly seeped into her thighs.

The bench felt warm at her back. The cool beauty of Claudia at her side and the sparkling light off the sky of Montreal gave her another kind of high. She felt at peace, yet strangely more stimulated than she had been earlier that night with the girl's—Cecile—pussy riding her clenched fist and squeezing in perfect time with Rémi's pulsing clit. Rémi sank even deeper into the chair. So, this was contentment. She looked at Claudia again and smiled.

Chapter

4

From the stage at Gillespie's, Cassandra Wilson held the audience in thrall, her smoky voice wrapping around the hearts and ears of everyone in the room as she sang her hypnotizing version of "Time after Time." Rémi sat in her office overlooking the club and its dimly lit stage. She'd sent Claudia an invitation on a whim to come see the jazz diva at the club, but hadn't gotten a response. Rémi was disappointed. But she didn't want it to ruin her night. It would be better for her to be downstairs socializing with the people who made her club a success night after night but she didn't want to go down there just yet. Her eyes darted once again to the entrance of the club, hoping to see Claudia.

With Dez sailing the high seas for a month on her honeymoon, Rémi knew that Derrick would probably want to spend as much time as possible with his mother. After the cancer, he still thought of Claudia as fragile. They all did, including Rémi.

She leaned back against her desk with her hands in her pockets, her mind firmly on Claudia. She didn't know what she had initiated in Canada. *If* she had initiated anything. All she knew was that the mostly dormant feelings she'd had for her best friend's mother had flared up even more powerfully than ever. She didn't know if it was the wedding or the fact that the older woman's beauty had pierced through her at a particularly vulnerable time. When she was high and just come from sex, anything could happen. Then again, Rémi thought with a smile, she was always vulnerable to Claudia.

It had been an effort hiding her feelings from Dez in the beginning. Then as Rémi grew older, she learned to hide it in the open. No one thought she was serious when she brought Claudia flowers or raved about her cooking or went to visit her for no reason. Now, after too many years of wanting, she was about to make things complicated.

Cassandra's voice trailed off to enthusiastic applause and whistles. Someone threw a scattering of red roses at her feet and she smiled graciously, picked one up, and brought it to her nose. The band began the opening strains of "Tupelo Honey," and the crowd went wild with cheers again.

Something made Rémi look toward the door. She smiled. Claudia looked gorgeous even in the dim light of the club. A simple cream sheath hugged her slight body, made her seem like nothing less than an angel as she made her way through the club to find herself a table for her and her son. That was going to be impossible. All the general seating tables were taken on both levels of the club.

Rémi made a quick call, and one of her bouncers appeared out of the shadows to show Claudia and Derrick to the table that Rémi had reserved. She released the tense breath she had been holding since the beginning of the night. It didn't even matter that Claudia had brought Derrick. At least it wasn't one of her banker boyfriends that she was being seen around town with these days. Rémi checked her reflection, running hands through her short curls, before leaving the office.

Her friends, minus Dez, were at their usual table. They sat quietly, for the most part, paying attention to the beautiful woman on the stage and the magic she created in the room. Phil sat in Sage's lap, almost purring as her girlfriend stroked her back. Nuria leaned forward in her chair as she watched the stage. Her fingers circled the rim of her nearly empty martini glass while her eyes roamed the stage and the crowd around her. Rémi noticed that she paid special attention to the table a few feet away from her on the right.

She must have seen Derrick walk in with Claudia. Ever since Dez announced her involvement and subsequent engagement to the woman she was now married to, at least in the eyes of the Canadians and a few American states, Nuria noticeably shifted her interest to the twin. She wasn't at all subtle in her attentions, and none of her friends cared one way or another. After all, they were pretty much all of the live and let live school of philosophy. As long as you aren't hurting anybody, sure, go ahead and get yours. Derrick was attractive enough. He had a handsome face, a slim and muscular body, and a respectable bank account. In short he was a biological penis-wielding version of his twin sister.

Rémi sat at her friends' table. Nuria turned to give her a moist smile and an Opium-scented hug. Her cleavage was on impressive display tonight. Rémi gave the lifted and separated breasts a cursory leer to let her friend know that her efforts weren't wasted.

Sage greeted her with a distracted look. "That woman is pure nitro," she said, staring at the stage. "Do you think she's into some company tonight?"

"I doubt she plays that way," Rémi said.

"Too bad."

Rémi cocked an eyebrow at Sage. "I doubt she has any regrets."

Phil grinned and shook her head. Rémi stayed with her friends for a moment longer before getting up to make the rounds. Although most of the club's patrons were wrapped in the spell Cassandra wove on the stage, they noticed when the owner took the time to stop at their table and inquire about their comfort. Many came to Gillespie's for some of the best live jazz in Miami and the flavorful, unique spins on classic dishes served up by its beautiful four-star chef. But a lot of people also came to Gillespie's to see its owner.

Before the review in the *Herald*, many of the patrons of the club came out to see one of Miami's rare gems, the celebrity club owner and model. On any given day in the city, one just had to look up to see one of the three billboards that boasted Rémi's image. Her unconventional beauty and look of unmistakable power were used to sell high-end men's shoes, watches, even cigars. A few years ago when she was starting to get worried about money, Rémi agreed to be the local face of an exclusive jeweler who wanted to reach a certain type of client. With Rémi's help, he reached those clients. Still, the club owner didn't know where the fame came first, her sporadic modeling, or from owning Gillespie's, the sexiest pre-party place on the beach.

Rémi waited until Cassandra Wilson and the band took a break before she approached Claudia's table.

The older woman greeted her with a wide smile. "I wondered when you'd grace us with your presence, Ms. Celebrity."

"I *am* a busy woman about town, you know," she teased before shaking Derrick's hand. "Good to see you, Derrick."

"Rémi." The polo shirt he wore under his blazer, a rich shade of red, complemented his complexion and reflected the color in his full lower lip. Nuria must be salivating nearby. "The place is great," he said. "I've been here a few times but I had no idea you owned it."

"You must have come in for the music or the food, then. That's good. I'll take that. As long as you came in."

Since there was room for only two at the table, Rémi found herself hovering. She clasped her hands behind her back. "Are you two enjoying yourselves?"

"Absolutely." Claudia's mouth curved in a smile. "Thank you for the invitation."

"No problem, Mrs. N. Please consider yourself my guest anytime you're here. You can even come up to my office and say hello if you like." She felt stiff and formal standing over them and offering the invitation when all she wanted to do was press the back of Claudia's hand to her lips and inhale her scent.

"Derrick. Mrs. Nichols."

All three turned at the sound of Nuria's voice. She walked blithely through the packed bar, her cleavage making the way for her. Derrick was definitely paying attention.

"Hello, Nuria." Claudia stood up to greet the other woman.

"No, no. Please don't stand up. I just wanted to come over and say hello since I just noticed the two of you sitting over here." She crouched between the two people sitting at the table so they could all be at the same level, using her hip to effectively nudge Rémi out of the way. "I'd love to buy you a glass or bottle of whatever it is that you're drinking."

Claudia laughed. "Not a bottle, Nuria. Please. I'm just having a glass of the house white, but my son is a Scotch man."

Nuria signaled over the waitress and ordered them refills on her tab. She bobbed up and down in her generosity, and Derrick had no choice but to notice her bountiful assets spread out before him like another option on the menu. Rémi met Claudia's eyes over their heads and smiled. The older woman's eyes sparkled with mirth. It was fairly obvious what Nuria was up to. Rémi reminded herself never to be that blatant or desperate. She cleared her throat.

"Cassandra is about to go back on, so I'll see everyone later." She took Claudia's hand in hers and held it briefly. "As always, Mrs. N. A pleasure." Rémi nodded at Derrick then left her friend to her games.

She didn't know what she had expected from Claudia, but she knew that she didn't get it. Maybe it was Derrick's presence, maybe it was the stares pressing at her from all sides. Whatever it was, she didn't want to be caught like that again. She wanted to get Claudia to herself. She wanted to go on a date with the woman.

Chapter

5

"What the fuck was that?"
Rémi's eyes darted, following the flash of black as it scurried across the floor and disappeared behind the large stainless steel refrigerator. "Tell me that's not what I'm seeing right now. Someone tell me."

She looked up, meeting the horrified eyes of her kitchen staff, all except for Rochelle, who chased after the rat, her white apron flapping behind her, the chef's hat tumbling off her dark head to the floor.

"That's not possible," Rochelle wailed, trying to push at the refrigerator. "There's no way that thing should be in here."

"Carlos, call the exterminator, now!" Rémi looked at her watch. "Fuck!"

It was nearly three hours until they opened for the Friday afternoon rush leading into their normally busy weekend. This was complete bullshit. Rémi turned on her heel and stalked out of the kitchen, tugging her phone from her jacket pocket.

"Elena." She forced calm into her voice when her manager answered the phone. "Can I see you in my office now, please?" Rémi didn't wait for an answer. A few minutes later, a brief knock sounded on her office door before Elena poked her head around it.

"You wanted to see me?"

Rémi gestured her inside and Elena closed the door, concern knitting her brow as she walked into the office to claim her customary seat on the couch.

"Why are there rats in my kitchen?"

The manager stopped her progress across the room. "What?"

"Why are—"

Elena put up her hand. "Sorry, I heard you. But that's not possible. We just did our inspection, and Sam was just here less than a month ago," she said, naming the owner of the extermination company they used.

"I think he missed something."

"No." She shook her head. "We've always used Sharpe's Exterminating. There's no way that they missed something like that. But"— she raised her hand again as Rémi opened her mouth to speak—"I'll call them again. If you saw rats, they need to come back out."

"Get another company. I'm not taking any chances."

"All right. Whatever you want. But I'm telling you, they didn't miss anything."

"Sure. Whatever." Rémi waved her hand in dismissal. "Just get it done."

Without watching to see Elena leave, she turned away, shoving her hands in her pockets in frustration. This was the last thing that they needed. The absolute last. Beyond the wide glass wall, the club lay quiet, but Rémi felt as if she could see through the walls to the kitchen, the filthy rat dropping its shit all over her clean floors and counters. In the food. She believed Elena. They'd used Sam for years now with not one problem. But what was the other explanation? A dull pain blossomed behind her forehead.

A low chime in her jacket pocket interrupted her fruitless thoughts.

"Am I interrupting something?"

Claudia's voice on the other end of the line immediately rebooted her brain, and she sank into the sofa before her desk, her body loosened into some semblance of relaxation.

"Not at all, Mrs. N. What's on your mind?"

It had been nearly a week since Claudia's visit to the club. In that time, she'd examined her resolution to ask the older woman out on a date. The more she thought about it, the more possible it seemed.

"I'm having a little get-together here at my house this afternoon. Can you make it? I know that it's short notice."

"I can make it." Rémi took her lighter out of her pocket and turned it over in her hands. It was platinum and had her name engraved in script on its bottom. One of the many presents Dez had given her over the years. "Thanks for thinking of me." She flicked the lighter open. Closed it. Opened it again.

"We always think about you." Rémi idly wondered who the "we" referred to and how often they thought about her. And how. "By now, you're practically one of the family," Claudia finished.

Family. Hm. "I have a few things to take care of at the club, but I'll drop by afterwards. Is that all right?" With a twitch of her thumb, a sharp blue flame shot from the lighter.

"That's perfect." Claudia said. "See you then."

"Okay." As Rémi hung up, someone knocked at her door. *If I want Claudia, I have to quit smoking. Cigarettes and cancer survivors don't go well together.* She closed the lighter and put it back in her pocket.

"Come."

Elena's head peeked around the corner of the door, but she didn't come in. "Carlos found another rat."

"Fuck." *Maybe I'll quit tomorrow.*

Rémi's headache grew with each passing hour until finally at five, when the doors opened and customers began walking through them, her head felt like an abused warning drum. She stood looking down into the bowels of her club, watching the tables and barstools slowly fill. This was how she loved it, crowded and thick with noise. Low hum of conversation and sparkling laughter on both levels of the club while the speakers wove mellow jazz through the air.

A flicker of unexpected movement by the main door caught her eye. Two men in suits. One with a notebook under his arm, the other a look of distaste on his face. The hostess, Melina, smiled pleasantly enough at them, but her body language was all terror. Rémi stiffened. When the young girl held up a finger, asking for a moment, before she picked up the phone next to the reservation log, Rémi was less than surprised when her cell phone rang.

"The health inspector is here to take a look at the place." There was a slight tremor in Melina's voice. "Do you want to give the go-ahead for that?"

A cold sweat shuddered over Rémi's skin. Did she want to give them the go-ahead? Shit. She wanted to tell Melina to show them the other side of the door. But if they had to come back later, they would make the club pay dearly for that inconvenience.

"Welcome them in. But call Elena first and tell her what's happening."

Rémi closed the phone. Feigning a calm she did not feel. This was too tidy. First the rats, then a health inspection. On the same day? There wasn't that much coincidence in the entire world. Was this the danger Wynne talked about? Anger surged like poison through her veins. Who was this trying to fuck with her life? With shaking hands, she rolled down the sleeves of her shirt, put on her jacket, and left the office.

"Gentlemen," Rémi approached the two men with a smile, holding out her hand. "I'm Rémi Bouchard. Welcome to my place of business."

Both men smiled pleasantly enough, but she felt an air of expectation around them. The one with the notebook shook the offered hand and returned her smile, introducing himself as Henry Caballo and showing his credentials. The other only shook her hand, looking as if he wanted a wipe off his own after he did so.

"What brings you here, and on a Friday evening too? We had an inspection barely six months ago."

"This is a surprise inspection, Ms. Bouchard. Sorry for any inconvenience this might cause you. I wanted to do it earlier in the day, but my colleague was insistent on doing it tonight."

"Not a problem. As you can see, I have many customers here tonight. If you can carry out your business without disturbing them, I'd be most grateful."

"We'll try our best."

Again, the other man remained silent. Rémi kept the smile on her face and gestured ahead of her through the crowd that shifted around them.

"Thank you, Melina."

The hostess gave Rémi a trembling smile before turning back to the growing line of customers.

The inspectors looked through every inch of the club, paying special attention to the kitchen, the bars, and the back lot with the Dumpster. With a cold fist pounding in the pit of her stomach, Rémi accompanied them each step of the way, smiling, giving them access to everything that they wanted as they asked for it. The kitchen staff glanced up as the men walked in, but looked thankfully unconcerned and went about the business as usual of managing the kitchen's organized chaos. Pasta boiled on the stove. Aimee, the pretty sous chef with the plum purple skin and long fingers, rhythmically chopped garlic on the cutting board while Rochelle put the finishing touches on the meals ready to be served. Each looked in turn at Rémi with a comforting smile. When Henry Caballo knelt to look behind the refrigerator, Rémi flinched but kept her smile firmly in place. Two hours later the inspection was finished.

"I think I almost had a fucking heart attack tonight. Twice." Rémi collapsed into the couch, fingers twitching in their need for a cigarette.

Elena perched her backside on the desk and smoothed a hand over her already neatly twisted hair. "Everything was already taken care of by the time they came. Carlos found two more rats. Although it could've been the first one and his sister." Her mauve lips tightened. "He tossed their carcasses in a bin far up the street. Right after that Sharpe's cleaned the place up and did another inspection."

Rémi dropped her head back against the arm of the sofa and put a hand over her eyes. "Let me guess. He saw no evidence of long-term rodent activity. It was as if they just showed up one day."

Elena's eyes widened in surprise. "How did you know?"

"A shot in the dark."

"Is something going on that I should know about, Rémi?"

"Maybe. I'll let you know when I know. In the meantime, just keep a more careful eye on everything and everyone around here. Pay particular attention to strangers."

"Are you serious? Everybody around here is a stranger to me most nights."

"Yeah, I know it's a lot but that's what has to be done for now."

"Okay. You're the boss."

Rémi chuckled. "Right. And don't you forget it."

When Elena left she went to her desk and booted up the computer. Searching the Web with narrowed eyes and venom in her veins, she didn't get up until she had an address and a name. Matthias Anderson. Rémi called her manager.

"Elena, I'm gone for the rest of the night. If anything happens, call. No matter what time."

Then she jumped on the bike and went on the hunt.

The club was right on the water. Prime real estate in Miami that anyone with the means would happily kill for. Riding up to the squat, single-level building, Rémi idly wondered if Matthias Anderson had bumped somebody off to take control of the property. At barely eight o'clock, the parking lot was already full, with a uniformed attendant pointing cars toward what looked like an overflow lot. All the windows of the building were reflective. No matter how much anybody from the street looked, they wouldn't be able to see anything inside.

Rémi parked her bike next to three others near the entrance and sat back on the seat, watching the customers flow in and out of the door. The clientele was nothing extraordinary, mostly men from any ethnic background under the Miami sun, dressed in jeans or slacks and blazers, ready to unwind after a long day at the office or at home. The few women walking through the doors were stiletto femme types, holding onto their boyfriends' arms or strolling in groups of three of more. Some of them obviously would be working there later on in the evening.

Rémi took out a piece of peppermint gum and folded it into her mouth before getting off the bike. At the door, the muscled door-man looked her up and down with nothing more than curiosity in his face before grunting the entrance fee. She gave him the ten dollars without comment and walked past. Inside was an orgy of mirrored walls, naked girls bouncing on clear four-inch heels, and infatuated men holding their thick wads of cash in their hands. Top 40 music, heavy with bass, pumped from the club's speakers.

"I'm looking for Matthias Anderson," she said to the first eye-level woman she saw.

The woman, cleavage set up high in her red shelf bra and long legs bare below the black fringe of a skirt, gave Rémi the same treatment as the doorman but pointed her with a feline smile and thrust of a narrow hip down a dimly lit hallway. Rémi's knock on the door with the plaque that read "office" yielded a deep, "Come in."

Rémi didn't know what she expected, but it wasn't the pale fig-ure behind the desk. An angular face, illuminated by the security monitors showing shifting images of the club, turned lazily toward her. Thick, closely cut white blond hair framed that ageless face. He could have been thirty-five or fifty-five. And Rémi suspected he had genetics to thank for that, not surgery.

There was nothing handsome about the man, but his electric green eyes burned with intelligence, and the hands that rested on the desk looked strong. The man before her had everything. His two-thousand-dollar suit, manicured nails, neatly trimmed mustache and beard. The ease with which he wore his body and the room made that clear. In the darkened office, she sensed the presence of at least two other people. Rémi kept the door open.

"Matthias Anderson?"

"What can I do for you, Ms. Bouchard?"

Her eyebrow arched at his obvious familiarity with her while she remained in the dark about who he was.

"If you know who I am then you must know why I'm here."

"I have my suspicions," he said. "But I'd rather you tell me. I don't like guessing games much."

"I don't like games either myself. Of any sort."

"Your life must be very boring."

Rémi felt her jaw twitch. "Are you trying to sabotage my business, Mr. Anderson?"

"I'm not *trying* to do anything to you or your business." Amusement crawled into his voice. "But if you feel like you can't handle the responsibility of owning such a successful club, I'll happily take it off your hands."

"My hands are very capable. Thanks for your concern." Rémi's shoulders shifted under her jacket. "Your hands, however, I don't want anywhere near me or my business."

The shadows behind her shifted. She smelled leather. Heard a heavy breath come closer. Rémi put her hands in her jacket pockets.

"One thing I can't stand is a presumptuous *woman*"—his eyes moved scornfully over her—"telling me what I can and can't do. You must not value that pretty face of yours very much." Anderson fingered the letter opener on his desk.

He gestured to someone behind her and Rémi tensed. Maybe it hadn't been the best idea to come here alone.

"Frank, Todd. Please escort Ms. Bouchard from my club." He looked at her again. "Don't ever come back here again with threats against me."

She blew out the breath she'd been holding even as two men, both smelling strongly of battling colognes, firmly took her arms and turned her away from Anderson's desk. Pain rippled through her shoulders at their rough handling.

"I don't make threats," Rémi hissed. "Only promises. Stay away from Gillespie's. I won't tell you again."

Frank and Todd, one blond and the other a redhead, but with the same thick necks and wearing identical black suits, dragged her toward the door.

"Or what? You'll fuck me into submission?" He laughed, a low, choked sound that bowed him over his desk like he was having some sort of attack. "I've seen how you operate in this town. You're nothing but a paper doll. Pretty to look at but useless. What I want, I'll take. And there isn't a damn thing you can do about it."

Frank 'n' Todd guided Rémi out of the office, looking for all the world like concerned, gentlemanly escorts to the few who cared to look their way. They shoved her out a side entrance into a blushing hot Miami dusk. The stink of the alley—piss, rotten food, sun-heated cum—choked the breath in her throat. Rémi gagged. Her boot heel caught on a piece of cracked and jutting concrete.

The Dumpster's blue steel shell thumped as she stumbled against it, barely saving herself from falling. The adrenaline surge savagely through her. The punch to her kidney cleared her thoughts. Quickly. She ducked and leapt away, only to stumble into the second muscle bag who batted at her face, ricocheting pain into all her bones, all the way down her neck. Rémi dropped to one knee and slammed her fist up, catching the blond hard between the legs. His balls jellied under her knuckles and she winced, jumping out of his path as he howled—the first sound out of his mouth all night—and fell to his knees on the damp and dirty pavement. She panted.

The goon fumbled for something in his jacket. Fuck! A gun. Not good.

"I wouldn't do that if I were you, Frank." A cold voice cut between Rémi and her would-be killer.

Wynne stood just to Frank's left. Except for the Glock, its deadly length extended with a silencer held firmly in her black-gloved hands, all of her was hooded in darkness. "Pick up your friend, turn around, and go back into the club." Her voice was a steady blade. "Don't let me repeat myself."

After only a moment's hesitation, Frank did as he was told, helped the whimpering Todd to his feet then stumbled through the black door into the club.

"Nice job, cousin," Wynne said after the men disappeared. "But you might want to pack something a bit more effective than your fists next time."

"Thanks. I'll remember that."

Rémi straightened, adjusted her jacket around her suddenly trembling shoulders, and started walking away from the club and her cousin. She didn't even want to think about why Wynne appeared in the alley when she did. Although Rémi was grateful for her presence. Very grateful. She glanced briefly back, but her cousin was nowhere in sight.

The motorcycle was right where she left it. After dropping the keys twice, Rémi finally started the engine then cruised out of the busy parking lot. She didn't realize where she was going until the familiar outline of Claudia's house rounded the corner and the bike pulled into its driveway.

The modest-sized Spanish-style house with its two levels and two-car garage was the perfect place for a two-income family—a successful lawyer and tenured university professor with their two point four children—to live. Through the years, Rémi had found herself outside that door wishing that her own family lived somewhere like this. Somewhere normal with a pool and the sounds of a mother cooking. Not a maid always threatening to quit or perfectionist papa with more passion for his job than his family.

Instead, she had to content herself with being the "point four" child. The extra one at dinner who couldn't stay at her own house, although it was on the beach and she had the whole place to herself.

She had been very happy to call this Coconut Grove house her second home, imagining that Claudia Nichols belonged to her too. Imagining that she would one day ring the bell and the lady of the house would throw open arms around Rémi and welcome her into a comforting warmth she never had to leave. She rang the doorbell and waited.

"I didn't think you'd make it," Claudia murmured as she opened the door. Her eyes flickered over Rémi's face and she gasped. "God! What happened to your face?" Cool fingers brushed Rémi's cheekbone.

"Bad judgment." She winced at Claudia's touch, then instantly wanted to feel it again.

"Come in. Let me get you some ice for that."

Before Rémi could tell her not to, Claudia went quickly down the hall, leaving Rémi with no choice but to close the door behind her. She dropped her helmet and jacket on the sofa before following. In the kitchen, Claudia moved efficiently between the pantry, fridge, and sink, dispensing ice from the stainless steel refrigerator into a sandwich bag, then grabbing a dishtowel to hold the ice with. She turned and nearly bumped into Rémi.

"Oh! I didn't realize you were so close."

Rémi steadied her, grasping her thin arms, holding Claudia's warmth briefly against her body.

"Sorry."

"It's okay." She gave Rémi the bagged ice, eyes patting over Rémi's face with concern.

Rémi smiled self-consciously. "Thanks for this." She held the bag against her cheek. "Although you didn't have to. Looks worse than it is." The cold seeped immediately into her face. With the ice against the bruise, she felt the swelling. Felt the pain.

"Was this a fight over a woman?" Claudia stared narrowly at her.

"Well, um . . ." but she must have hesitated too long. The other woman shook her head.

"Oh you girls!"

But her chiding seemed automatic, not something she was truly invested in. She leaned back against the sink and watched Rémi's face. Instead of looking away, Rémi watched her in turn. Claudia looked almost like a creature from another world, eyes large and shining, cap of white-streaked black hair in small curls around her face. Her slender body was clothed in a white V-neck blouse and black yoga pants. Claudia's bare feet seemed vulnerable and small against the black-and-white check tile floor. Now that the adrenaline had subsided, unblocking her senses, Rémi became aware of the soothing rhythms of Boney James coming from the living room stereo.

"So, did I miss the party?" Rémi asked.

Claudia shook her head again, seeming to fight the childish urge to roll her eyes. "Yes. Everyone's already left but you can help me clean up." She finally smiled. "There's plenty of food."

"That's just what I wanted to hear." She experimentally took the cold and seeping bag away from her face. Already, the bruise felt better.

"Come," Claudia led Rémi back through the living room and out the sliding glass doors to the deck.

From the light glowing from under the pool's surface and through the windows of the house, Rémi saw there was only a little bit of a mess; paper cups stood, some half empty, others not, on the wooden railing. Paper plates littered the surface of the small glass table near the pool while the barbeque grill still released its smoke. But there was nothing cooking on it.

Stepping over the wooden slats of the deck, Rémi stumbled. She grabbed the railing to stop herself from falling completely on her face.

"Are you doing all right, Rémi? Did that girl mean that much to you?"

Her mind staggered back to what happened before she appeared on Claudia's doorstep. "I'll be fine, Mrs. N. Just a small misunderstanding. Nothing that can't be cleared up."

She put aside her ice pack and mechanically began to pick up the litter on the deck and around the pool, all the while keeping up a light patter of meaningless talk. And Claudia indulged her, watching her with concern even as the last of the trash was being bagged and dumped into the large black bin at the side of the house.

When she got back from putting away the trash, Claudia had a plate of food for her, a glass of what looked like lemonade, and a smile laced with comfort.

"Come sit by the pool with me," she said. "I feel like putting my feet in the water."

Rémi sat on the deck chair, the food—barbeque chicken, baked beans, and roasted corn—on the glass table next to her, the lemonade with ice clinking against the glass, cooling her palms. She watched as Claudia rolled her pants up to her knees and slid her feet into the pool with a low sigh.

"I'm happy you were able to come over." Claudia's gaze remained on the rippling surface of the water. Her legs stirred up tiny waves as she moved them slowly back and forth. "Even with your drama." She looked over her shoulder at Rémi. "Just be careful when you play with those women out there." Her mouth twitched. "I hear they're vicious."

Rémi nodded, but said nothing. She wanted to tell Claudia what really happened, but the words eluded her. This whole business with Anderson seemed so sordid and dirty. She didn't want any of it touching the other woman.

Claudia's gaze gently met hers. "If you ever need to talk with me about anything, Rémi, anything at all, my door is always open to you. Don't forget that."

"I never have." Rémi put the lemonade to her lips and drank until the glass was near empty. The tart flavor of limes—not lemons, she realized—washed over her tongue, entwined with the sweetness of the raw cane sugar Claudia preferred to use in her kitchen. A bit of pulp, fat with juice, burst between her teeth.

"Good." Claudia's smile flared as brightly as a flame. And just as beautiful.

A wordless breath escaped Rémi. This was why she'd come here.

And just that quickly she was tired of moping, tired of waiting for who knows what to happen. There was more to come, but she was here. *Here.* She picked up her glass and walked to sit beside Claudia at the pool's edge. The older woman watched as she pulled off her boots and socks, rolled up her pant legs, wiggling her pale toes first before plunging them into the water. She winced at the surprising cold.

Rémi dragged a towel off the deck chair behind her and spread it on the ground so she could lean back onto her elbows without scraping up her skin.

"So, Mrs. N., how was your barbeque? Knowing you, I'm sure it was scandalous." Rémi waggled her eyebrows. "Please tell all."

Claudia leveled an arch look at Rémi for the sudden turnaround, but she played along. "It went well," she said. "Derrick came with his girlfriend. Eden brought her husband and a few mutual friends from the university. It was nice. There were other people your age for you to talk to if you had come."

"I'm not only interested in people my age," Rémi murmured. Her feet wavered beneath the pool's surface next to Claudia's. Not quite touching. Not quite estranged.

"You're such a darling." Claudia's hand landed briefly on her thigh in a series of pats before drifting away.

Hardly, Rémi thought as she watched the black pants stretch over Claudia's hip and curve of her bottom, allowing herself to be distracted from the afternoon's madness. She would take care of Anderson. Rémi didn't quite know how yet, but she would. He wasn't going to get the best of her. She didn't come this far for some random asshole to take it all away.

"I see people my age at the club all the time. When I come to your place, I expect something different. Barbeque instead of foie gras." Her smile teased. "White wine instead of bubble gum."

She lay fully back against the towel, lifting her feet out of the water and propping them on the edge of the pool.

Suddenly Claudia laughed. A surprisingly girlish giggle that made Rémi smile. "You are a terrible flirt, you know that."

"Does that mean I'm terrible at it, or I'm so *terrific* that you're *terrified* you'll get taken in by my dangerous charm?"

Her warm chuckles cascaded down on Rémi's ears, and she felt a shift in the air beside her, heard a splash and trickle of water as Claudia lifted her legs out of the pool and lay down beside her.

"You are terrific, there's no doubt about that."

"Of course."

"Do you know"—Claudia murmured, close enough that Rémi smelled the faint sweet traces of barbeque on her breath. *Chicken, maybe?*—"that you have webbed feet?"

Rémi's eyes flew open as surprised laughter tumbled past her lips. "After all these years you're just now noticing that?"

"Maybe I've never been this close to you before."

Rémi spread her toes wide, felt the subtle webbing stretch. She dropped her feet back in the water, still smiling.

"Maybe."

Chapter

6

Rémi took the day off from her responsibilities at the club to take Nuria to a birthday brunch. It had been a while since the two of them had had any time together, and her friend said as much as they sat across from each other at Nuria's favorite Brazilian restaurant, taking bites from each other's plates and drinking caipirinhas. With her dreadlocks curling around her face and throat and the wicked glint of her labret stud punctuating the deep red of her mouth, Nuria looked fantastic.

"You look like the birthday present, not the birthday girl," Rémi teased, flicking Nuria's chin with a playful finger.

"Birthday girls should always look ready to be opened," she said with a growl.

"Ha! Just don't get into any trouble tonight. You know how you can get."

Sounds of the restaurant swirled around them. The low-voiced conversations of other diners. Clink and tinkle of cutlery against china. Here and there, the gentle thud of plates being placed on tables. Sunlight leaned, golden and friendly, against windows revealing the passing parade of people on the boardwalk just outside.

Nuria's eyes glinted. "Dez got me a gift."

"Trouble?"

"I think so." She tugged a chunk of beef from the skewer across her plate and bit deeply into it. A line of juice escaped her mouth, and her tongue darted out to catch it.

"Are you going to take it?"

"Definitely."

Rémi laughed. Ice cubes clinked as she swirled the remnants of the caipirinha in her glass. "Why am I not surprised?

"You and I know trouble's not so bad. Especially when you have it in your bed tied up on its belly and whimpering your name."

Rémi put the glass to her mouth and snared an ice cube with her tongue. "I'll remember you said that."

After brunch, she dropped Nuria off at her place then headed back to her own, intent only on taking a nap then working out at home before heading back to Nuria's for her birthday party. But her friend's words about trouble—and they were *so* true—kept echoing in her head. The trouble she wanted to get into took the shape of Claudia. But would it be worth the potential loss of a friendship?

At the condo, she sat in a warm pool of sunlight on the stairs and stared out through the windows. But for once she didn't see the spectacular Miami skyline carved against an azure sky or the meditation garden below her window, with its gently waving trees and white rocks. She saw Claudia and Dez, her best friend. She saw trouble. Still, Rémi knew what her decision was. Had known it when she'd walked out to that balcony in Montreal and seen the older woman sitting there on that bench, waiting for her. Rémi just hoped she could live with its consequences when the time came.

She picked up her cell phone and punched in the number.

"Did I catch you at a bad time?" she asked when Claudia answered.

Rémi heard something, a roughness or cough in the other woman's voice when she answered the phone. Claudia cleared her throat.

"No. Now is fine." She cleared her throat again.

Rémi squirmed against the stairs, even though, obviously, Claudia couldn't see her. "Would you come to dinner with me tomorrow night?"

She didn't know what to expect but it wasn't the immediate, "Yes. I'd love to."

"Oh. Okay."

Claudia laughed weakly. It was a new, almost rusty, sound, as if she hadn't laughed all day. Or all week. "What time and what should I wear?"

Rémi's surprise slowly began to give way to excitement. Her heart pounded even more heavily in her chest. "Seven o'clock. And anything you want."

"Even my sequined gown from senior prom 1976?"

"If you want," she murmured, answering the tease. "As long as you're comfortable."

"That's the best offer I've had all month."

A pleasant, glowing warmth blossomed in Rémi's chest. "Good. I'll see you at seven tomorrow then."

"Seven o'clock."

Rémi held the warm phone to her cheek even after Claudia hung up. She said *yes.* Rémi could barely believe it, but Claudia had said yes.

For as long as Rémi had known what desire was, she desired Claudia. She remembered clearly the day that desire was born. Not because it was such a momentous one but because she had masturbated to the memory of it more times than she could count. It was because of that day she knew some women—and Claudia in particular—received real and visceral pleasure from putting their lips around chocolate-covered strawberries.

Rémi found out about Claudia's passion by accident. One day she came over to see Dez after school and walked in on Claudia over a plate of the strawberries. The woman had made sounds that Rémi never heard a woman make before. At least not outside of her father's porn videos. Rémi felt herself get wet. And swallowed to get rid of some of that sudden excess moisture going in her mouth.

"Good afternoon, Rémi."

Claudia seemed nonchalant about the effect she was having on the fifteen-year-old. Rémi already had a massive crush on her, thinking that Claudia was the most beautiful woman she'd ever seen off the pages of a fashion magazine. Here in the flesh, her loveliness was much more potent than any movie star or *Penthouse* pet spread, especially as she sat at the kitchen bar in her long white skirt, pale yellow blouse, and buttercup sandals. The last bite of a dark red berry slid between her lips just before her moist tongue appeared to lick away a bit of chocolate from the corner of her mouth.

"Hey, Mrs. Nichols," Rémi managed to croak before dashing upstairs to meet Dez. She never told her best friend about her crush, although over the years she had alluded to it, hoping that those hints would somehow prepare Dez for what Rémi was undoubtedly going to do.

At three minutes to seven the next evening, Rémi rang Claudia's doorbell. She answered the door with a surprised smile.

"You look very nice, Rémi."

"Thank you."

She had chosen the look with care. Something that spoke of maturity yet was fun enough for her to wear without feeling out of place. The black suit with its mandarin collar, white shirt peeking from the collar and cuffs, and spit-shined boots did the trick. She left the spurs at home tonight.

But her mature suit didn't save her from stuttering like a kid in Claudia's doorway. Her date looked amazing. Three platinum chains of descending length lay against the smooth skin at her throat, rivaling the flash of diamond studs in her ears. Her strapless red dress highlighted her gorgeous glowing skin, making it very apparent to Rémi's eyes how far she had come after her bout with the cancer. She'd gained some of the weight back and didn't seem quite as fragile as before. The smooth shoulders rising out of the dress begged for intimate caresses that Rémi was more than happy to provide.

"Y—you," she forced her unexpected stammer under control. "You make that dress look stunning."

Claudia smiled again, then with her little red bag clutched in one hand, pulled the door shut behind her. "Whenever I'm having a bad day, I'll definitely be calling you up. You always know the right thing to say to make a woman feel her best."

As the older woman brushed past her at Rémi's request to head for the car, a hint of scent teased her nose. L'Air du Temps. The antique perfume, with its notes of jasmine and sandalwood, reminded her briefly of her French aunt on her father's side who used to visit the family in Maine. Rémi had always associated the scent with timeless elegance. Watching Claudia walk down the path toward the truck with her narrow backside rocking gently from side to side as her heels clicked rhythmically on the sidewalk, Rémi began to associate the scent with lust. Contained and cultivated. Laying in wait. She swallowed, then walked quickly after Claudia to open the door for her.

"So where are we heading?" Claudia asked once Rémi started the truck and they were driving out of her quiet neighborhood.

"One of my favorite places. I hope you'll like it too."

"We'll see." Her eyes twinkled in the cozy confines of the Escalade. She leaned back in the sighing black leather seat and shifted her long legs.

"You can put on some music if you want," Rémi invited, gesturing to the CD player below the navigation display.

"No, it's fine. I like hearing you talk. Thank you."

Claudia smiled at her. She was having trouble with her senses. Every shift the woman made in the seat, every whisper of the leather, Rémi smelled her. She smelled the floral perfume anointing her flesh. And she smelled *her*. That undeniable woman scent that made Rémi want to burrow under her clothes to find the source.

"Do you like Indian food?"

Of course she did. It wasn't a real question since Rémi had made it her business to know almost every intimate thing possible about Claudia. Indian was one of her favorites. Second only to Jamaican food and anything with well-made rice.

"Yes, I do," Claudia said. "As long as it's not that place near Riverside Park. They need to shut it down, the food is so awful."

Rémi chuckled. "No, it's not that one." Thank God. "It's actually south Indian and very, very far away from that part of town."

When they pulled into the parking lot almost twenty minutes later, Claudia looked out the car window with surprise. The old-fashioned building with its very old-world Indian charm immediately captivated her. "Great! I haven't been here before."

"Good. It's vegetarian. I hope you don't mind."

"No. Not at all. It's very appropriate for a first date." Her eyes danced. "Even if I eat like a pig, I'll still seem virtuous for all those greens."

"And don't forget the potatoes." Her mind skated over the words "first date," afraid to look at them too closely. "Essential to fattening up the ladies."

After they parked, Claudia took Rémi's arm like it was the most natural thing in the world. She looked carefully around the specially cultivated garden that framed the path from the parking lot to the restaurant itself. Statues of round-breasted and multiarmed goddesses sat in serene contemplation of the beauty around them. Dark fish moved beneath the water of the pond while gently scented flowers waved their bright heads in welcome.

"I love this place already." Claudia gently squeezed Rémi's arm. "Thank you for bringing me here."

If Rémi had her way, the older woman would be thanking her all night, but. . . . "Thank you for coming," she murmured.

The inside of the restaurant was as elegant as the exterior, though with the early evening crowd also much less formal. There were as many tables with giggly college girls as there were romantic-eyed couples, or solitary diners. When the hostess came to seat them, Rémi asked for a table with a view of the garden. They shared the long padded bench with pillows that gleamed and slid beneath their hands like sari cloth.

When the menu came, Claudia happily pounced on it. From those visits to her house when she and Dez were children, Rémi remembered Claudia voraciously eating at dinner, elbows bracketing entire plates of crab legs, or chicken wings, and even salad. She'd always lived with her senses. The cancer had made her less so, but now that she was well, Rémi wanted to see her eat extravagantly again. Her passion for life had been one of things that drew Rémi to her, and that often translated to a passion for food.

"Everything looks wonderful," Claudia said, glancing quickly at Rémi before looking again at the burgundy leather-bound menu.

"Then order everything. Whatever you want."

"Ha!" Claudia looked at her again. "If you'd said that to me before the cancer, you'd have regretted it. Back then I could have eaten my way through an entire Norwegian buffet and still kept going."

"In that case, it's good for that hot little dress of yours that you can't chow down like you used to, but"—Rémi nodded at the approaching waiter—"you can try. If you can't finish it all, there are always doggie bags."

"Hm, I like this little arrangement already."

The waiter set down their water and a bottle of wine with one glass, then leaned over attentively to take their order. Claudia took Rémi up on her invitation. When the waiter came back with the food, the plates took up the entire table and then some.

Rémi laughed at Claudia's delighted expression. "Take these away, please," she said to the waiter, handing him the elegant little silver platter holding various condiments as well as the candle that Claudia had exclaimed over as they sat down. After that they had room for everything.

"I don't think we'll be hungry after this."

Rémi had been looking forward to the food almost as much as the pleasure of Claudia's company. This south Indian restaurant really was her favorite, the place that she only took her friends to or herself when she wanted a quiet moment with good food. She pulled the masala dosai close to her and tore off a piece of the decadent concoction—potatoes, onions, curry and other knee-weakening spices wrapped in one of the universe's most miraculous inventions: fried bread. The dosai sank and parted under her teeth before releasing its bounty of potatoes and curry over her tongue. Rémi groaned in appreciation. Her fingers were moist from handling the bread. She rubbed her thumb and index finger together, enjoying the oily slide between them.

"Is it that good?"

"You don't have to ask. Just try it for yourself."

The other woman seemed caught in an agony of indecision, staring at the bounty before her and not knowing where to start first.

"Here," Rémi said, tearing off a bit of her flat rice pancake and its contents and holding it toward Claudia's mouth.

Rémi's brain almost short-circuited when Claudia's mouth closed around her fingers. She hadn't really thought about that. She really hadn't, although it seemed so obvious. The inside of Claudia's mouth was warm. Hot. And wet. And a low groan, an unstoppable one, slid from her lips as Claudia sucked the food between her lips before drawing back to chew.

"You're right. This is . . . really, really good."

Yeah. And I would be good too. I'd be very good to you. Inside you . . . The feel of Claudia's mouth still occupied her. Her fingers still hovered in the air near the other woman's mouth as if she was waiting for another . . . something. She licked her suddenly dry lips.

"The batura. You should . . . you should try that dipped in the tamarind sauce."

But Claudia was reaching for something else. The gobi manghuriani, pretty bushes of breaded cauliflower marinated in a flavorful brew of garlic, ginger, chili, and soy sauce. At the first bite she almost came undone.

"You have converted me for life," she said, chewing very slowly with her eyes closed. "I'll never go to another Indian restaurant again." After a few more moments of blissful chewing, she opened her eyes. "Ever."

"I've heard that before," Rémi murmured coyly, reaching for the batura.

"Really, I swear. This is the best that I've ever had. And I'm not even vegetarian."

"Neither am I. And you don't have to convince me. I've been coming here for years."

That was the last thing that Rémi said for a while. The batura bread, with its crunchy, fresh-from-the-fryer-of-heaven taste brushed with the tangy, sweet tamarind sauce, was the closest that Rémi came to having an encounter with the angels. Claudia was having her own divine experience as she sampled one dish after another, each, by the look on her face, more delicious than the last.

"I'm going to have to run about fifty miles in the morning to burn this off," Rémi said after she lay back in her chair, replete.

"You go ahead. I'll be in my bed still basking in the afterglow of this wonderful meal." Claudia sighed. "Thank you so much, Rémi. This is one of the best meals I've had in a while."

"My pleasure."

She sipped from her glass of chardonnay, watching Claudia curl into the seat beside her. The older woman had slipped off her shoes and now lay with her head back, smiling. Her necklaces sparkled above her modest cleavage, catching the low overhead light. Behind her the restaurant garden lay awash in moonlight. The lightly swaying plants, the patina-covered bronze statue of the goddess Lakshmi on her lotus blossom, the fountain gurgling silently into the fishpond. All this Rémi could see beyond this woman. But Claudia was the most beautiful. She sipped her wine again.

When the check arrived she silently paid it, although Claudia craned her head trying to see the total.

"For the next time when I come, I want to see how much all this is going to run me." She gestured to their small mountain of takeout boxes.

"Right. I hope you won't be trying to eat all that by yourself. And I don't think I'd approve of you bringing anyone else here."

"Not even Desiree?"

Rémi appeared to consider, not bothering to hide her small smile at the mention of her best friend. "Maybe."

In the parking lot, Claudia wanted to fight over the takeout. "Please take it home so I won't be tempted to eat it all."

"I thought that was the point, remember; we're fattening you up."

Claudia shook her head. "No, we're not." Her look was stubborn.

"Fine. We'll leave the food at my place."

Claudia looked smug.

"If you don't mind though," Rémi said, starting the engine to the truck, "let's swing by my place to put the stuff in my fridge. I don't want it smelling up the truck."

"Sure." Claudia buckled her seat belt.

At the condo, she parked in the garage and invited Claudia up while she put the food in the fridge. They rode the elevator in comfortable silence.

"This is nice. Somehow I expected you to be in a place similar to Dez's. Big with lots of room for"—Claudia wrinkled her delicate nose—"playing."

Rémi smiled, thinking about all the games she and her best friend had played over the years, but never at either of their houses.

"Do those games disgust you?"

Claudia seemed to think about it for a moment. "I don't know."

"Just to let you know, whatever Dez did, whatever I did, we were always safe."

"That's good to know." She looked at Rémi, nodding as the elevator opened.

Rémi unlocked the heavy olive green door and invited Claudia to walk in with her. She slipped quietly past Rémi, graceful and sure, with her purse held loosely in both hands in front of her. L'Air du Temps teased Rémi's nose again, and she barely stopped herself from reaching out. She turned on the lights instead.

"This is unexpected," Claudia said.

Rémi swept her eyes around the condo, trying to see the space through Claudia's eyes. During the day the condo was flooded with natural light. It flowed in through the two floor-to-ceiling windows that slid back completely to give access to the terrace. She (her mother, actually) had the good timing to get one of the corner penthouse condos with a view of the city and easy access to her rooftop patio with its Jacuzzi, barbeque grill, and a table usually set for five.

"Is where I live more or less than what you thought?" Rémi asked.

"It's simpler. And there are no pictures of naked women. I at least expected that."

"Please. I can see that anytime I want. I have other pictures."

Claudia dropped her tiny purse on the couch. "Can I look?"

"Please."

While she took off on her self-guided tour, Rémi brought the leftovers to the kitchen. Having never learned to cook, she didn't spend too much of her time there. It was where she kept her liquor, made her coffee, and occasionally had her friends over for small, catered parties. It was a large room with a stainless steel fridge and a gas stove that Dez had exclaimed over once or twice. But it was mostly for show.

Rémi kept a vase of fresh Gerbera daisies on the pristine white dining table. The cupboards were always stocked with cups, plates, and whatever else normal people used in a kitchen. Track lighting and the frosted cupboard doors that allowed the pretty arrangement of the things inside to be seen made the place suitable for a *House Beautiful* photo shoot. Rémi turned off the lights and went to find Claudia.

She found her at the foot of her stairs, looking up. "Every moment," she said as Rémi came up behind her, "you surprise me."

Claudia stood framed in the moonlight glowing through the tall windows. Rémi felt her breath catch. The silver illumination bleached color from Claudia's dress and it was simply her, neck arched up, one hand at her throat, the other caressing the fragile bones of the upraised wrist.

"Those are beautiful."

She stared up at one of the massive paintings on either side of the stairs leading up to the bedrooms, workout room, and office. The one that held her attention was an abstract of an infinitely petaled flower endlessly unfolding to reveal even more layers, more beauty. The unfurled petals trembled in their red and yellow flame, while below a graceful aurora borealis of blues and greens and whites flared up, higher and higher, embracing the flames making the flower glow even hotter. Its companion piece was its opposite in color flow, the same flower, only this time with blue, green, and white petals chased and surrounded by yellow and red flame.

"I didn't know you liked flowers, Rémi."

"I don't like them," Rémi said with the smallest of smiles. "I love them. It's not very . . . uh, butch of me, but I like what I like."

"I see that. You have really excellent taste."

"Thank you."

They glanced at each other, and Claudia looked away, smiling.

"Would you like a drink?" Rémi asked. She felt like clearing her throat, but she thought that would make too much noise and break whatever fragile mood lay in the room with them.

"Yes. Fruit juice if you have it."

"I do."

After she'd learned about Claudia's cancer diagnosis and subsequent recovery, Rémi had made it a point to learn everything she could about the healing process, including the best foods to eat in order to help keep the body cancer free. Once she'd decided on her course of seduction, she'd gone out and bought as many things that she knew Claudia would need and want to eat (at least those things that didn't need cooking). She was glad she'd never developed the habit of smoking in the condo. She didn't want even the most minute threat to Claudia's health to exist here.

Rémi poured two tall glasses of guava juice and turned to take them into the living room when Claudia walked into the kitchen. She strolled around the built-in dining table with room for five, trailing a ringless finger along the pristine white edge. Eyes nearly black with amusement, she inspected the open, elegant space.

"You don't cook, do you?"

Rémi smiled. "Not even a little bit." She gave one of the glasses to Claudia and leaned back against the bar to watch her. "Dez cooks here sometimes. When she and the others want to have something here, they do. But I cater, or do takeout from the club most days."

"But surely you can't eat three meals a day from Gillespie's, no matter how wonderful the chef is."

"Rochelle takes care of me."

Claudia smiled. "I bet she does."

Rémi laughed. "Not in that way, I swear. The woman is happily married to her husband for . . . oh, I dunno, years and years. She doesn't need or want my attentions."

Claudia sipped her juice and said nothing. Only the teasing light in her eyes gave away her real thoughts on the matter.

"I'm not that bad you know." But Rémi laughed, spoiling the righteous indignation act. She shook her head. "Come out to the terrace with me."

Claudia sipped her juice and followed Rémi outside. The Miami night was gorgeous. City lights glittered and the scent of the ocean rose up, a perfect complement to the breeze lapping gently at their bodies. Claudia leaned against the railing, smiling into the night.

"I can't say again how glad I was to get your invitation to come out with you. Even before you called, it had been a long day."

"Want to talk about it?"

"Not really." She lightly brushed Rémi's arm to lessen any possible sting in the words. "Your company is doing more than enough."

Rémi nodded. She hated the idea that Claudia might be having any sort of hardship. After what she'd been through lately, she needed to have an easy time of it. Rémi put the glass of juice to her lips and stared thoughtfully at the other woman. Whatever was just said seemed to have propelled her back into the mood that she had been in before Rémi called her this morning. Her smooth brow furrowed and she glowered at the Miami city lights as if they'd personally done her wrong.

"Dez tells me you're back at school this semester." Rémi sat her glass down on the table nearby and straddled a lawn chair. "Are you teaching French lit again, or just language?"

Claudia turned. The look on her face said that she knew what Rémi was doing, but with a light shrug, she allowed the distraction from whatever was troubling her.

"I've jumped back into my full schedule. Four classes, literature and language both. Why? You want to take some more classes with me?"

Rémi blushed. She looked down between the sprawl of her legs. "Maybe."

Claudia's question was an abrupt reminder—did she really need one?—of just how far her crush had taken her after that fateful day of the strawberries. Not only had she ended up at the same school that Claudia taught at, Rémi also took her classes. All of them. Even the basic French class that taught pronunciation. It wouldn't have been so obvious and laughable if Rémi didn't already speak French. Until she was fourteen, she'd spoken it at home with her parents and sister. Even when her mother had run away with her children to Miami to escape Auguste Bouchard's stranglehold on her life, Kelia

Walker-Bouchard kept up Rémi and Yvette's second language until no one knew which was native to the young girls, English or French.

Rémi shook her head and smiled, finally able to make peace with the foolishness of her youth. "Come sit with me, and tell me about school."

They talked quietly on the terrace until Claudia, curled up in the lawn chair next to Rémi, began to lightly shiver from the suddenly enthusiastic breeze.

"Let me get you a blanket," Rémi offered, standing up.

"That would be lovely, thank you," Claudia said, then as Rémi turned to go inside she stood up too. "No, wait. I think it's time for me to go." She rubbed her hands up her goose bumped arms. "It's already after midnight. I'm sure you have other things to do besides babysit me."

"I hardly call this babysitting." Rémi said. "I'm enjoying your company."

"Still, I think I should go."

Rémi opened the glass doors and allowed Claudia to go inside first. She'd forgotten how easy it was for the other woman to feel the cold. Although it was nearly the end of August, the night breezes off the ocean were already crisp. Claudia's strapless temptation of a dress, though incredibly sexy, was no protection against them.

"Come inside," Rémi murmured, as Claudia passed beneath her arm. "I'll make you some hot tea before you go."

In the kitchen, she put on the teapot and sat down at the table with Claudia. She could have put a cup of water in the microwave, but this way she was guaranteed the older woman's company for a bit longer.

"You don't have to go, you know," she murmured, fiddling with a silver container of Darjeeling tea.

"I know, but any moment now this old woman might fall asleep on you and cut your evening short."

"This is our evening, not just mine." She shifted the canister between her hands again. "Oh, by the way, is Darjeeling okay with you?"

Claudia took the tea from Rémi's hands then opened the container to smell it. She closed it. "Do you have any passionfruit?"

"For you, yes."

When Rémi stood up to steep the tea, Claudia walked to the fridge. "I don't know why," she said, "I'm a little hungry."

"It's all that shivering you did outside."

Claudia chuckled, reaching into the recesses of the refrigerator. She brought out one container and replaced it with another until she finally found what she was looking for. The container of tamarind sauce opened with a satisfying pop, and she grinned, sitting down with slivers of paratha. She put her finger in the sauce and licked it off. "This really is *too* delicious. The perfect midnight snack."

Rémi set Claudia's honey-sweetened tea near her hand and got a beer from the fridge for herself.

"Since you tempt me with honey and spices," Claudia said, inhaling the indulgent smell of the tea, "I might as well make myself comfortable."

"Come make yourself comfortable in the sitting room, if you don't mind. I don't spend much time in the kitchen, and it's kinda creeping me out."

"Maybe you should learn to spend some more time in the kitchen. Have you ever thought about learning to cook?"

"No."

Claudia chuckled. "Come, sit beside me."

Rémi sat, not knowing what to expect. She was used to being in control. Women did what she wanted, when she wanted, how she wanted. They didn't tell her what to do. She took a sip of her beer. Claudia looked at her, still smiling. Her gaze lingered on Rémi's face. Rémi could feel the eyes like an actual touch, skimming over her eyes, her cheekbones, her mouth. Was she imagining it? Just when she thought she would explode from wondering what the hell was going on, Claudia stood up. She nuked the bread in the microwave for about fifteen seconds before scooting back into position beside Rémi.

"You look so serious." Claudia murmured, as if it were the worst possible crime. "Taste this."

She dipped the warmed bread into the cool tamarind sauce and offered it toward Rémi's mouth. Without thinking, Rémi opened her mouth. The bread wasn't as good reheated, was her first thought. The second thought had nothing to do with her brain. Claudia's scent, her delicate perfume, and her own womanly smell, licked at Rémi's senses. As Claudia leaned close, offering another bite, a dollop of the sauce fell from the bread to her fingers and palm. Rémi's eyes zeroed in on the earth-colored moisture against the pale flesh. Her lashes fluttered down to hide her eyes as she moved forward to accept what Claudia offered.

Rémi bypassed the bread and went straight for the finger. She raked her teeth across the delicate surface, and Claudia gasped, so softly that Rémi had to lean even closer to hear it, then suck the finger into her mouth before it could completely escape. She soothed the previous hurt, forming a trough with her tongue and sliding the finger into it, back and forth until her panties were wet and a vibrating moan shook her throat. Her eyes fell closed. She was vaguely aware of the tamarind-coated bread falling from Claudia's hand to somewhere under the table.

Claudia wasn't pulling away. The knowledge of that made Rémi's knees weak, and made her bold. She went for the palm next, licking down the long finger into the center of her hand. With all logical thought obliterated by her desire, she licked the tamarind sauce away, sucked at the surface until the hand curved around her cheek, trembling. She smelled like honey and spices, like bread and, of course, that sauce. Her teeth sank into the soft skin and Claudia groaned Rémi's name. At last. God. At last. The pale flesh ended at the delicate wrist and Rémi followed it, nibbling and kissing her way up Claudia's arm to the dip of her elbow.

"Rémi . . . stop."

Her tongue flicked at the delicate crease. Her nose greedily drank in Claudia's scent.

"Please."

That last word was her undoing. She stopped, head resting on the slope of Claudia's arm, just near her breast. Rémi could hear the frantic gallop of Claudia's heart, and it made her glad. The other woman wasn't immune to her. And she hadn't pulled back.

"I've wanted to touch you for so long," she said, still with her head resting near Claudia's heart. "So long." Rémi released a sigh and stood up, finally able to meet Claudia's eyes.

They were startled, pupils dilated to swallow nearly all the lustrous brown of her irises. Desire. They were the shape of desire. For her. But she wasn't going to push it.

Still breathing deeply, Rémi stood up. "Come on. I'll take you home."

The ride to Claudia's house was a silent affair, with both women lost in their thoughts. Memories of Claudia's flesh, of it yielding sweetly beneath her teeth and tongue, made Rémi clench silently in the truck beside the object of her desire. An old Gregory Isaacs love song played quietly in the Escalade as they rode back to Coconut Grove. As the twenty minute drive neared its end, Claudia shifted in the seat for the millionth time beside Rémi, but still said nothing.

"Sorry, I made you uncomfortable," Rémi said, nearly whispering the apology.

"You didn't."

But she had. There was no easy conversation. No effortless talk between them. All Rémi felt was her desire and her clumsiness. She'd never been this inept at seduction before. It never required this much effort. Then again there had never been this much riding on her technique before. Silence reigned in the truck again.

They pulled into Claudia's drive and Rémi got out, walking with her to the front door. As the other woman looked in her purse for keys to open the door, Rémi tried again.

"Claudia."

The other woman stopped the seemingly fruitless search through her purse and looked at her.

"I don't want things to change between us in that way. I want to still be your friend and the person to distract you from your worries. Awkwardness between us would kill me."

"You should have thought of that before you touched me, Rémi."

Rémi closed her eyes at the unexpected pain that lanced through her chest. But regrouped.

"Did you enjoy it?"

She really wanted to ask if it made her wet, if her nipples had gotten hard under that pretty red dress. But Rémi had seen that evidence for herself. She had seen the stone hardness, felt the labored breath against her face. She knew well the face of want.

Claudia's eyes fluttered down and she sighed. And found her keys. "Yes, I did," she said and opened the dark oak door. As she turned to disable the security system on the wall, the telephone rang.

"Give me one second," she said and dashed into the house to get it. Her heels made a musical sound against the hardwood as she went.

At Claudia's breathless greeting to whoever was on the phone, Rémi slowly closed the front door behind her. She walked into the house that was more familiar than her own, through the split hallway that to the left led to the swimming pool and deck, and to the right opened up into the house. Except for the addition of a few small pieces of furniture, its cozy arrangement hadn't changed very much. In the sitting room with its warm furnishings—a deep chocolate sofa and sectional with matching footstools scattered around. The coffee table and the neat arrangement of books and magazines and a few academic journals. Various pieces of black art on the cream-colored walls, and the large window overlooking a garden that always had flowers in bloom.

Claudia walked back toward Rémi with the cordless phone tucked into the space between her cheek and neck as she took off one high-heeled shoe, then the other. The normally smooth skin on her forehead was puckered in a frown.

"The wedding was over a week ago," she said into the phone. "And you didn't even send a card. What's wrong with you?"

Rémi turned from her contemplation of the unlit fireplace. "I can go," she mouthed to Claudia.

The other woman shook her head and gestured for her to sit before returning to her conversation. "Warrick, I swear you've hurt her for the last time. . . . No. It doesn't matter what—"

Rémi tried not to listen, but not very hard. According to Dez, Claudia still carried a torch of some kind for her ex-husband, who was now remarried and living in California. Dez hadn't talked about her very absent father too much other than to say that Derrick seemed to be following nicely in his footsteps. And that Claudia wasn't as over him as she would like. At the moment, she didn't sound very enamored of him.

"What do you mean you've been trying to call me all night?" Claudia sat in one of the velvet chairs by the garden window. She reached over to grab her purse as she spoke then took out her cell phone. The display lit up as she read whatever was there. "I was busy." Silence. "Yes, it was a date."

Rémi smiled and looked away. This was good. This was *very* good.

"Tell me what you want, Warrick, so I can get on with my evening. That's none of your business." She sighed. "Get to the point or I *will* hang up on you." Then, "Okay. Okay. That's fine. Just call me when you get here. I'm sure I can arrange to meet with you at some point in my busy schedule." Her mouth twisted in irony, but it wasn't at all conveyed in her voice. "Good night." She pressed a button to end the call and turned to Rémi.

"Sorry about that."

"It's fine. I kept myself occupied." She stood her hands in her pants pockets, watching Claudia fairly vibrate with frustration. Not the kind that Rémi would prefer, but frustration nonetheless. "Do you want to talk?"

Claudia chuckled tiredly and shook her head. "My ex-husband is an ass."

She stretched out her feet to the footstool and leaned her head back in the chair. "That's all it is. Nothing more. Nothing less. I just tend to let myself get a little too emotional where he's concerned." She sighed.

Rémi nodded, though Claudia didn't see her with her eyes closed. So Warrick was still a big part of her life. Not only was she planning to meet up with him next time he came to town, her emotions were still on his yo-yo. Reaching a decision, Rémi sat down on Claudia's footstool, sweeping the bare feet into her lap as she did so. They were delicate beneath her hands, like small birds. She began to massage them.

Although she felt Claudia's startled eyes on her, she didn't stop. The soft feet with their surprising blue nail polish slowly relaxed beneath her fingers until Claudia's gaze fell away and her head rolled to the back of the chair. Rémi slid her fingers between each of the slender toes, massaging the delicate skin of her feet as well as the soles. She cupped the heel in her palm and slowly, firmly manipulated the flesh until Claudia was sighing softly in her chair. A woman she'd dated briefly was a reflexology teacher and taught Rémi a lot about the feet and the points that linked to areas on the body. With sure strokes, she relaxed Claudia, had her purring in her chair; then she began to do something else.

She stroked the delicate bottoms of her feet, lingering on the areas leashed to the neck, waist, tailbone, and belly until Claudia wriggled in her seat, relaxation and stimulation working in tandem. Rémi could smell her. The scent of her pussy, wet and warm, flowed from between her legs, unencumbered, she thought, by underwear. She swallowed. After one final and deep caress, she stood up.

"I'll leave you to it."

Claudia's lashes lifted to look at her. The eyes were liquid with desire. But Rémi could see that she didn't know why. After all, it had been a simple foot massage. Right? Rémi smoothed a hand down the front of her shirt, over her trembling belly. She wasn't exactly unaffected either.

"Don't get up. I'll lock the door behind me."

"No, I'll see you out." Claudia made to stand, but Rémi put an insistent hand on her shoulder.

"I know where the front door is," she said. "Relax, Mrs. N. I'll see you later."

Claudia subsided beneath Rémi's touch and lay back in the chair with a soft laugh. "At this point, you might as well call me Claudia. Don't you think?"

Rémi thought of the scent that rose from under her red dress. She'd been "Claudia" in her mind for a long time. She smiled and nodded.

"Good night, Claudia."

Chapter

7

Her pussy was wet and wide open. The ass, firm and round, glowed a particular shade of brown that had long since been Rémi's favorite. That lovely ass tapered down to sleek thighs that spread and knees bent so beautifully as the woman knelt on the bed. Rémi pulled off her jacket and dropped it on the chair before rolling up her sleeves and undoing the buttons of the shirt. She liked the fine cotton on her skin. How it lightly caressed her bare nipples and the sensitive flesh of her belly.

A fine layer of sweat already covered her skin from her night's work. But she wasn't finished. Casting an eye over the built-in shelves before her, she tried to decide just how she would reward the woman in her bed for her patience. And how to reward herself. The lowermost drawer caught her eye and she smiled. It had been a while since she used that.

The woman in the bed, Monique, made a low noise when she heard the drawer open. She was bent doggie-style in the bed, her arms bound behind her in twin leather wrist-cuffs. A long chain, suspended from a bolt in the ceiling and looped through the cuffs, held her wrists up over her naked back. The pretty blue silicone ring sticking out from her ass danced in the air as she squirmed. Monique moved on the bed, a strangled moan working its way past the ball gag in her mouth. The gag ball poking from between her burgundy-painted lips was a pale blue and made her look even more delectable, like she was swallowing the sky. Her thighs dripped with her pussy juice, thick and plentiful from where Rémi had played with her, teased her hole and clit until the woman was moaning and begging to come. Rémi didn't let her.

It was after one o'clock, and she had gone to Gillespie's just to make sure that everything was going fine in her absence. And it was. But she was a little distracted. The scent of Claudia's pussy and the way she had moaned under her hands made Rémi burn. If only she had reached under that red dress, touched that cunt that was steaming for her. Steaming and hot for a touch of Rémi's mouth. Or her fingers. Or both. Just the thought of it made Rémi's mouth go dry. Her pussy wet.

But Claudia wasn't ready for her. Monique was.

The slim waitress intercepted Rémi on the way to her office, smelling of sex in the leather corset and miniskirt, her permed hair caught in a French twist. She said she wanted to play tonight, and Rémi's nostrils flared. This was just what she needed to distract herself from Claudia. They'd played together occasionally, nothing serious, but Rémi always liked how Monique could take whatever she had to give without complaining. Even better, she always asked for more.

She didn't complain when Rémi had simply nodded without speaking, none of the usual small talk and pleasantries. The invitation was her open hand and a tug into the dark chamber of her office. Without turning on the lights, they made their way to the bedroom at the back of the office, beyond a small set of stairs and behind a thick, soundproof door. The room was originally meant just for sleeping, but Rémi hadn't slept there in a long time. Its king-size platform bed was used for play. A set of wide, built-in shelves above the bed held a display of instruments for every possible pleasure and pain. The drawers just below the shelves kept the smaller items—butt plugs, anal beads, vibrators, nipple and clit clamps, and batteries, everything that an inventive woman might need to prolong or begin a session meant to last deep into the night.

Rémi stroked Monique's ass then reached past to retrieve one of her old favorites from the drawer above the bed. It had been washed and slid in nearly pristine condition into its Ziploc bag weeks ago and not been used since. But she was ready for it again. More than ready.

The woman on the bed squirmed at the sound of Rémi's zipper being released and lowered. She stepped out of pants, still leaving the shirt on. Her pussy was well lubed. Had been since the first of Claudia's moans began almost four hours ago. She rubbed the smaller end of the double-ended dildo back across her wet slit, teasing her own opening, then up to skim her clit. In the bed, Monique wriggled her ass and stared in the mirror above the bed, watching Rémi tease herself with the big dildo before slowly easing it inside. The silicone already felt warm in her fist as she teased her clit again, this time with the nearly flat middle section of the toy. She slid a condom onto the seven inch length thrusting out from her body, black and glistening. Monique was going to get fucked tonight.

Although she couldn't move in that position, the woman tried her hardest to back her ass up to get it closer to Rémi and her bobbing dick. She didn't need to try. Rémi brushed her wet pussy with long fingers, stroking the thick wet lips with a gloved hand. Monique wriggled and groaned again. The sound could have been made by anyone, and Rémi wanted it to be so. The memory of Claudia was so vivid in her mind that she could easily imagine it was the older woman bent over in her bed, wriggling in pleasure and anticipation of her touch. She gagged Monique because she didn't want the other woman's voice—a rough New York growl—to interfere with the fantasy of Claudia's Florida-softened contralto sighing the notes of satisfaction beneath her.

She slammed the dick inside the waiting pussy and groaned at the answering sensation in her own body. *Yes.* Monique grunted under her and pushed back, meeting Rémi's hips stroke for stroke. The metronome motion sped up until she was thrusting hard and deep inside the upturned pussy and a growl rumbled continuously from her throat. *Yes.*

As they fucked, the chain holding Monique's wrists captive rattled and swung. Monique's face pushed back and forth into the sheets, and Rémi's back and ass heated and slid with their own sweat. Claudia's name was building in her throat. Fuck. Fuck. Fuck. She swallowed it, focused instead on the sweet ache in her pussy, the thick energy building inside.

Groans. The music of flesh on flesh connecting. The sound of the wet pussy swallowing her dick, her grunts and growls of impending satisfaction. Monique's sweat-slick hips slid under hands, but she dug into the flesh even more, gripping her tightly, slamming into her hips, pushing, sawing until the woman's guttural cry burst past the gag and Rémi could feel her pussy undulating, swallowing more of the dick as she came. Rémi didn't stop. She slid a gloved hand over the other woman's clit, guiding her up another summit, making sure her pleasure lasted. Because Rémi wasn't done yet.

She massaged the slick clit, feeling her own orgasm rise, that tightening in her belly, that deep throb in her pussy that signaled everything. *Fuck.* She grasped the hips tighter as she felt her own peak, as the light was beginning to burst behind her tightly closed eyelids. It took her over, bent her hard over the shuddering entity, her body on fire, her face hot, pussy imploding. Monique gasped under her.

Still moving her dick inside the trembling woman, Rémi circled the clit harder and harder, then shoving abruptly, deeply inside, she pulled at the ring at the entrance of the woman's ass. The anal beads slid free in one steady movement. Monique reared up in the bed, heedless of the chafe on her wrists from the cuffs, her pleasure taking her far beyond pain. Her lust-contorted face was gorgeous in the mirror, a mixture of drool and tears flowing freely down her chin and throat as she came again.

Rémi lightly stroked her sweat-soaked back, slowly moving inside her to bring her down from the orgasm. Monique's body sagged into the bed, and the chain rattled above her. Rémi unbuckled her wrists, allowing her to fall into the soft cotton sheets, then scooted back to remove the dildo from her body. Rémi sighed as the light aftershocks of pleasure ricocheted through her. The silicone dildo fell to the sheets with a soft plop.

Monique moaned and shivered softly on the bed. With a low

groan, Rémi eased down beside her and unbuckled the ball gag, tossing it beside the dildo.

"Thank you," Rémi breathed in Monique's ear.

The other woman smelled strongly of sweat and sex, and of Rémi. She wiped at the corner of Monique's mouth with the sheet. Monique laughed softly.

"No. Thank *you*, sir."

Rémi laughed and relaxed against the sheets. If she listened hard enough, Rémi could hear the quiet laughter and voices of the night's patrons. She'd left those speakers on, the ones that fed the noises of the club into her office. She'd left the bedroom door open too.

At almost three in the morning on a Thursday, the night was still just getting started for some. Although Gillespie's was the pre-party spot for much of Miami, some of the laid-back crowd happily stayed at the jazz bar until it closed its doors at five a.m.

The live music part of the evening was over. Now it was just quiet background jazz from the club's speakers, drinks, and good company. Elena would take care of everything. It was time for Rémi to go home and enjoy the rest of her evening. She looked over at Monique, whose heavy-eyed stare was still fixed on her. The woman licked her lips. But Rémi was through playing with her for the night.

She brushed her thumb over Monique's damp mouth and smiled. "I have to go. It's my night off."

The other woman looked disappointed, but she took the hint and stood up to get dressed. Rémi put her own clothes on, cleaned the toys, and put everything back in order until Monique was dressed and waiting hesitantly by the door. She picked up her keys and gestured toward the door.

"Ready?"

Chapter

8

Rémi was pleasantly worn out from the night before, the muscles in her arms, back, and thighs singing with faint pain. Straddling her bike at a stoplight, she stretched, further waking up the body that didn't get nearly enough sleep.

After leaving the club, she'd lain awake thinking about Claudia, wondering what it would have been like to have her instead of Monique. And even after sleep came, Rémi had twisted in the sheets, restless, only to wake up much too early, again thinking about Claudia. The woman absorbed her nearly every waking moment.

As the light turned green, she wondered where to take Claudia next and how to show her that Rémi was the one for her. But maybe that was asking too much right now.

Ah, but if you don't ask, you won't get. She chuckled and stepped harder on gas, sending the powerful black Harley growling past the slow-moving Nissan truck in front of her. Rémi could already see the roof of Novlette's Café up on the left. She put on her turn signal and waited for traffic to thin on the other side.

When she walked into the restaurant, she didn't have to look around to find her friends. They were, predictably, on the terrace, taking advantage of the slow Monday morning crowd to sit at one of the prime spots in their favorite restaurant. The group of three already sat in various poses of ennui at the table overlooking the glittering blue water of Biscayne Bay.

"Hey." Rémi sat in the only remaining chair, spreading her smile around the table. "What's going on?"

"The usual," Sage said with a crooked smile. "We stopped by the club last night but you weren't there."

"Night off," Rémi answered.

"But," Nuria's wicked grin materialized, "I heard Monique was up in your office. I'm sure it wasn't to complain about how you treat your employees."

Sage sniggered. "I don't think complaining is something she'd ever do in Rémi's presence. Word is you always leave that little pain slut satisfied."

"I do my best," Rémi murmured. She slid her helmet and gloves under the table, still smiling.

Phil stirred from her contemplation of her coffee cup. "So what was it, stud? Your night off or on?"

"Definitely off. I had a date. Afterwards, I came over to check on the place, and then—"

"What? You had a date?" Sage's mouth dropped.

Rémi never referred to one of her women as "dates." She hung out, had appointments, met up with some people, but didn't really date. Hadn't since college.

"Don't tell me you're going the Dez route. I couldn't take it if both you and she hitched up and left us poor pitiful singles to play alone."

"Speak for yourself, honey," Phil said. "We're not single."

She and her girlfriend enjoyed a very open relationship. They fucked whoever and whenever, within the specific and often too-complex rules of engagement. The two women lived together, but that didn't stop them from bringing people home and having parties of varying degrees of abandon on their shared property.

"But you act like you're single," Nuria said. She looked especially luscious today, Rémi noticed, as if she'd spent her entire birthday weekend soaking herself in pleasure. Which she probably had.

"So?" Sage said, reaching over to grab a menu. "You would too

with so many gorgeous women—and decadent ways to enjoy them—
out there."

"No, I don't think so."

"Not me."

Nuria and Rémi both spoke at the same time, and they looked at
each other in surprise. Then shook their heads, grinning.

"Do you ladies know what you'd like?"

The waitress appeared at Sage's side, ostensibly smiling at the
whole table but in reality looking right at Rémi. Half the waitstaff
was in lust with her—male, female, and in between—and often
rushed in tandem to service the table with whatever the women
might need when she was around. Nuria looked at Rémi, fully expecting her to order first and give the little waitress a thrill.

She obliged her with a smile, rattling off her order without looking at the menu. Rémi knew exactly what she in the mood for today.
The waitress licked her lips once before turning to take Sage's
order. Phil rolled her eyes and snickered.

When the waitress was gone. Sage turned to her friend. "I could
easily hate you."

"Don't hate me because I'm beautiful."

The entire table groaned.

"But back to this date of yours."

"There's nothing much to it. I met up with someone nice; then
we went our separate ways at the end of the night."

"And you fucked the shit out of someone else. She mustn't have
been that nice."

"Or maybe she was too nice." Sage's eyebrow rose. "You know,
didn't want to give it up on the first date. I've heard of women like
that."

"A dying breed," Rémi murmured into the inquisitive silence.

No one wanted to drop the subject of Rémi's mysterious date,
but since nothing was forthcoming, the three women gave a collec-
tive shrug. No one ever said no to Rémi. Ever. So this was something they were sure to speculate on when she was gone. Rémi gave
a mental shrug of her own. There was nothing to tell about her date

with Claudia, and even if there was, they wouldn't be hearing the details from Rémi's lips.

When the waitress came back with their food, with two eager members of the waitstaff to help carry the heavy load, the friends adjusted themselves around the table. Rémi's double order of crepes, fresh strawberries, and whipped topping was, of course, laid out first. Then Phil and Nuria's platters of steak, eggs, and seasoned potatoes. And last, Sage's traditional Jamaican breakfast of ackee and saltfish, green bananas, and dumplings with the steam still rising off the food. She rubbed her hands together in anticipated pleasure.

Rémi took her pleasure more subtly, but it was no less profound. The crepes were heaven on her tongue, the way that Claudia would feel. The way that Rémi would make her feel. She smiled and reached for a strawberry.

"Does anyone know when Dez is supposed to come back from her honeymoon?" Phil asked after the proper moment of silence in respect for the wonderful food the women were eating had passed.

Knives and forks skated across the white plates. Full mouths hummed around food.

Sage swallowed first. "Why? Do you want to join in for a little threesome?"

"You know she's not down with that kind of thing anymore," Rémi said.

"A shame." Phil really did look sad, as if the idea of monogamy was a thing to be mourned.

"But true. She's in love." Nuria sneered the last word.

"Don't be a bitter bitch, Ria." Phil nudged her friend's shoulder with her own. "You can't get *everything* you want."

"I don't see why not." Nuria pouted. "I almost had her, though."

Her friends didn't bother to correct her.

"I did." She insisted.

Sage laughed. "Whatever you say, princess."

Rémi speared the tender pink heart of a strawberry with her fork. "Well at least you still have a chance with Derrick."

"I know he wouldn't mind tapping that ass."

"I know *you* wouldn't mind tapping that." Rémi pointed her fork at Nuria.

"Do you think he'd let you bend him over?" Sage cocked her head in mid-chew.

Nuria shook hot sauce over her eggs and potatoes. "Hm, that's an interesting image."

"Do you think he'd take it like a man, or beg you to stop?" Sage was getting carried away, and no one was about to stop her.

Phil looked up and across the restaurant. "This is your chance to ask him. Here he comes."

"With his latest piece," Sage said.

Phil smiled, exchanging a look with her girlfriend. "And she's very hot."

"Very." Sage snickered. "Oh. My bad. That's his mother."

Rémi couldn't help it. She twisted around in the seat to watch Derrick and Claudia walk out to the patio of the restaurant. The older woman had bleached her hair. Now it was all white and hugged her scalp in thick curls. The combination of the black lashes, eyebrows, and youthful face with Claudia's silver hair was stunning. Rémi let out a slow breath.

"Claudia looks really good," she said before she could help herself. She picked up a strawberry and stuck it into her mouth before she could say anything else. Like correct herself and call Claudia "Mrs. N." like she used to. But her friends didn't seem to notice the slip; they only murmured in agreement.

"Dez really lucked out swimming in that gene pool," Sage said around her food.

"Derrick!" Nuria called out, causing her friends look at her. "What?" she muttered under her breath as the person in question looked around the restaurant then started walking toward their table when he noticed them. "I'm just trying to be neighborly."

Rémi grinned. "Right." She wondered when the guy would put Nuria out of her misery and just fuck her already.

"Morning, Nuria." Derrick greeted the pretty Dominican woman with a polite smile that did nothing to disguise his attraction to her.

"Hey, there," she greeted him in her sex kitten purr.

"Hey, Derrick."

"What's going on?"

"Good to see you."

The other three women were at their politest. But when Claudia walked up behind Derrick, the warmth became more genuine. Her smile bathed Rémi in affection before she looked at the other women at the table.

"Good morning, girls."

"Why don't you sit with us, Mrs. Nichols?" Phil suggested, smiling at Claudia.

The older woman smiled then looked at her son. "I'd love to if Derrick doesn't mind."

She and Derrick sat between Nuria and Phil, giving Rémi a chance to watch her during the entire meal. She watched and remembered. Last night had been a test to see if Claudia could feel for her anything that Rémi felt. The desire. The respect. The yearning. The older woman felt all that. But would she let Rémi touch her?

"We were just talking about Dez," she said.

Claudia looked at her. "What about?"

Rémi pursed her lips and smiled, but Sage answered the question for her.

"The usual. We're happy for her, and we wonder how long this thing with Victoria will last."

While they talked, Rémi signaled the waitress, and she promptly came over with two more menus and silverware for the additions to their party. After getting the new drink and food orders, the girl dashed back to the kitchen.

"I think chances for the longevity of that relationship are good," Claudia said.

"Why?" Nuria asked.

"Because they're so different," Claudia answered between glances at the menu. "They provide each other with things that the other lacks."

"I could agree with that," Derrick said. "Dez is a little slutty. A lot lazy. And Tori is the complete opposite."

"Slutty?" Rémi looked at her best friend's brother. "Why do you say that? You don't like sex?"

"It's not that I don't like sex, but I do believe that my sister has gone to hell with the joke. To say that she likes sex is an understatement."

Nuria jumped in. "Sex is a natural expression of the exuberance of life, of one's desire to be a part of other people. You don't agree with that?"

Derrick seemed startled by the question. "Of course I agree with that, but I think there are other ways to go about celebrating the 'natural exuberance of life.' "

"True." Nuria's look was impish and sly. "But what's more fun?"

Rémi thought of all the ways that she and Claudia were different. Too many to count. Her eyes flickered up and tangled in the other woman's. Rémi hoped that everyone at the table was caught up in the discussion to notice how she wasn't able to keep her eyes off this woman. She almost sighed with relief when the waitress came back with Derrick and Claudia's food, distracting her too-intense gaze. Rémi picked up her fork and refocused on her plate.

Chapter

9

The students streamed out the classroom door and past Rémi. She waited until the stream slowed to a trickle of one or two eager-looking freshman girls before poking her head in. The knobs of Claudia's spine pressing against a black turtleneck dress as she bent over her desk greeted Rémi's gaze. And below the wide black belt encircling her tiny waist lay the slight curve of her bottom, thighs elongating to legs, tiny ankles, and high-heeled shoes, three inches of sexy that made Rémi's mouth go dry. Claudia straightened. The contrast of her white hair with the black dress was perfect.

"Hi, Rémi." She smiled, looking pleased, Rémi noted with relief, instead of stalked.

"We didn't get to talk very much at brunch a few days ago, so I came by on the off chance that you could have lunch with me."

Claudia raised an eyebrow, looked pointedly at her watch.

Rémi walked farther into the classroom. "I know it's after four. A late lunch."

The other woman smiled. "That actually sounds wonderful," she said, shouldering her thin briefcase and bringing an armload of books against her chest. "But I already have plans."

Rémi's footsteps faltered. *Oh.*

"Derrick is taking me out to dinner in an hour or so." She bumped

Rémi's arm. "But you can buy me a smoothie to tide me over until then. I haven't eaten a thing since breakfast." She inclined her head toward the door. "Come on. There's a place by the quad that has some healthy blends." Then, as if remembering Rémi's fondness for rich foods, she laughed. "And some not so healthy ones, too."

Rémi bought their smoothies and Claudia led her to a long field of grass sheltered occasionally by trees hung with threads of Spanish moss that waved timidly in the late afternoon breeze. Despite the chill in the air, a dozen or so students were spread out under the trees and in the full glare of the sun.

Claudia found an unoccupied tree for them and sighed as she sat down between two massive roots shooting from the foot of the banyan tree, leaning back into its embrace.

"This is perfect," she said, plucking off her shoes. Her toes stretched and wriggled in the bed of grass.

Rémi sat down. She silently passed Claudia her drink, aware of the nervousness trapping whatever words she had behind her teeth. Clearing her throat, she moved her tongue over dry lips.

"I like your hair," Rémi finally said. She put the bright green straw to her mouth and sucked the creamy pineapple and coconut mixture into her mouth.

"Really? Thank you. I was initially worried that the white might make me look old." Claudia made a face. "But I already had all those gray hairs at the front anyway. I felt it was the more noble route to take rather than dying the whole thing black."

She pried the plastic cover from her smoothie cup and placed it beside her in the grass. With a plastic spoon, she dug into the pink mound of pureed ice and fruit.

"It's very"—the word "sexy" hovered on her tongue, but she tucked it away for later—"elegant."

"Elegant," Claudia echoed. "It's a much better word than 'geriatric,' that's for sure." She chuckled and spooned some of the smoothie into her mouth.

"Never that," Rémi shook her head, suddenly tongue-tied.

She wanted to say so much. Brilliant things that would make

Claudia fall instantly and madly in love with her. Witty things to make her laugh. But all Rémi could do was watch the other woman slyly from beneath her lashes, take in the gorgeous symmetry of the face and figure held in the loose embrace of the banyan tree.

"You know," Claudia murmured, breaking the silence, "seeing you outside my office today reminded me of old times. When you were one of my students." She smiled. "You used to bring me the biggest apples."

Rémi groaned, laughing. "And mangoes, and oranges, and cherries." Then she said it. "I had the biggest crush on you back then."

"I know. It was hard to miss."

She froze inside her skin.

Claudia stopped with the spoon pressed to her bottom lip. "I thought it was sweet. You helped me to feel good about myself when everything else in my life seemed bent on doing the opposite."

"As long as you didn't feel a need to get a restraining order." Rémi tilted her head, quirked the side of her mouth. "Although I'm not sure that would have stopped me."

"Youthful passions are very strong," Claudia agreed.

"And the not so youthful ones as well."

Claudia held her cup in her lap, balanced in her upturned palm. "Rémi. I'm old enough to be your mother."

"But you're not my mother. I already have one. She's in Maine. Mothering has nothing to do with what I feel for you."

Claudia looked at her. "It's not that I'm not flattered by your attention, Rémi, I am. But you have to know that this won't go anywhere. It can't."

"Why not?"

"Well for heaven's sake." She laughed as if was the most obvious thing. "Just open your eyes."

"Yes," Rémi said. "Open your eyes. Look."

She lay back on her elbows in the grass and crossed her booted feet, willing Claudia to really *see* her. She knew that she looked good in faded jeans and the thin, man-tailored shirt lightly covering her breasts and the flat plane of her belly. The rays of the sun, filtered through the swaying leaves of the overhanging tree, made the shirt almost transparent, showing clearly that she wasn't wearing a bra.

"I'm not asking for your hand in marriage." She grinned. "At least not yet. But I would like the chance to court you and show you that I can make you happy if you give me the chance to."

Claudia's lashes flickered as she stared at Rémi, the smoothie still held in her palm. Melting.

She never said yes. She never said no. They'd walked on the tightrope of possibility until Derrick's phone call came and his silver Lexus eased into the parking lot near where they sat. But Claudia's eyes had taken quick sips of Rémi, as if she couldn't help herself, while they talked about other things. Rémi felt those eyes, felt them touch her mouth, her skin, her breasts through the thin shirt. Her blood raced, but she tried to show no sign of it. She would wait, Rémi decided, and see.

Chapter

10

Days later, Rémi still hadn't heard from Claudia, but she hoped. She understood that falling into a relationship with her daughter's much younger and *female* best friend wasn't an idle thing for Claudia to do. Still, she wished the older woman would hurry up already so they could get to the fun stuff. She grinned, imagining exactly what "fun stuff" they could get into together.

With her motorcycle helmet and gloves gripped in one hand, Rémi got off the elevator in the lobby of her building and turned right past the front desk to go to the mailboxes.

"Ms. Bouchard." The concierge caught her attention the same moment that she registered the softer, less familiar voice.

"Rémi."

She turned around and her eyes collided with an identical pair. Rémi stopped.

"This young lady says she's here to see you. I wasn't sure about—"

"That's okay, Clive. I know her."

It was impossible that Clive didn't realize that they were related, the girl looked so much like Rémi it was disconcerting. Still, she appreciated his vigilance in not just letting anyone into her place.

"Thanks," she said to the concierge.

The girl in the chair stood up. Rémi knew that she was nineteen. That they shared parents and a last name, but that was all.

Her sister looked every inch a Bouchard. Olive skin, wavy hair a wild explosion around her face and shoulders, and a mouth that even at rest seemed on the edge of a smile.

She was Rémi's femme equivalent, and though the thought should have made her smile, it didn't. She'd gotten so used to being without a family that Yvette's presence was . . . disturbing.

"I've been waiting all morning for you," Yvette said.

The last time she'd seen her sister was almost eight months ago, when her mother had summoned her home for a strange sort of reunion that Rémi had to ditch earlier than planned. It had been disconcerting to be with family she hadn't seen in so long. Especially her sister Yvette, whom she remembered as a gap-toothed five-year-old before Rémi had seen her briefly during their father's funeral nearly two years ago.

"You should have told me you were coming," Rémi said.

"I did. I left a message on your phone a week ago to let you know. Didn't you get it?"

Apparently not. Rémi stared at her sister, her face carefully blank. "I'll be right back."

Keys in hand, she walked slowly to the bank of mailboxes. She wrestled the wide stack of letters, catalogues, and bills out of the metal enclosure. Did their mother know that Yvette was here? Stupid question. Rémi locked the box and went back out to the lobby.

"Come on."

The girl picked up her rolling suitcase and backpack then followed Rémi into the elevator. On the fifth floor, the doors opened and they walked down the hall to her unit, still without speaking. Rémi had left the stereo on this morning. Had left it repeating the new Damian Marley album that she'd recently become obsessed with. A few motions of her fingers over the control panel built into the wall by the door and the reggae was replaced by Yo-Yo Ma's soothing rendition of Bach's *Cello Suite # 2*. She put her helmet and gloves on the low shelf below the control panel and sighed.

"Does Mama know that you're here?" she asked.

Yvette pulled her luggage into the living room and parked it near the couch. "No."

"Of course not." *Fuck.*

Rémi didn't have a relationship with her mother, to say the least. When Rémi was fourteen, her mother ran away from Maine and her father with her and Yvette. The three of them had thrived in Miami after being under the thumb of the tyrannical but financially generous Auguste Bouchard. But after a year of fresh air, unconditional hugs, and life in the sun, Auguste managed to seduce his wife back to Boothbay Harbor. At fourteen, Rémi decided she was old enough to stay in Florida by herself while Kelia Walker-Bouchard and Yvette went back to their gilded prison.

During her stay in Florida, her mother had made sure that Rémi had everything she needed by way of money and occasional supervision from her sister, Jackie, who lived in North Miami Beach. She even bought Rémi the condo where she lived. Kelia never understood why Rémi couldn't go back to live in Auguste's house, or worse, why she felt the need to come out to him when she knew how conservative, republican, and homophobic he was. Not at all the typical Frenchman that he seemed to most who knew him. She suspected that her father never knew that Kelia was still funneling money to her, even after she turned eighteen. Even now.

"You can put your things in the spare bedroom at the far end of the hall," Rémi told her sister, pointing beyond the kitchen, "but tomorrow you have to leave."

"I don't want to go. It's not my fault you didn't check your messages. If you want I can call Mama and tell her that I'm here with you, but I'm not leaving."

"Why?"

"I need someplace to be that's not home or school."

"Did you drop out of school to come here?"

"I'm taking a break. I already told them I won't be back until summer semester."

"And how long were you planning on staying here?"

Yvette crossed her arms over her chest. And smiled. "As long as you let me."

"Right."

Rémi picked up the phone and punched in her mother's number.

Although she'd only used it once in the past fourteen years, she'd already had it memorized. When a little boy answered the phone, she flinched. She'd forgotten. Not long after Kelia had gotten back to Maine, Auguste had gotten her pregnant. The boy's name was René.

"Bon nuit." She automatically slipped into French at the boy's greeting. *"Pouvoir je parle avec votre mère?"* May I speak with your mother?

"Who may I say is calling?"

"Mathilde." For some reason, Rémi gave her middle name.

"Yvette is here," she said without preamble when Kelia answered the phone. "She says she won't leave. I'd like you to come and get her."

Her mother's silence was telling. She didn't want to get her child. Rémi was hit by a sense of déjà vu. Kelia chose to leave her in Miami and go back to her pig of a husband.

"She doesn't want to be here," her mother said. "Please let her stay with you. I don't think we can do anything for her here."

Rémi almost slammed down the phone, but instead murmured a polite, "Of course," and quietly hung up.

Clenching her jaw, she sat on the couch to pull off her boots and socks. The thin, long-sleeved shirt followed, leaving her in a white tank top and faded jeans.

"I know she doesn't want me in Maine right now." Yvette emerged quietly from the spare bedroom around the corner. "I'm asking questions she doesn't want to deal with."

"Like what?"

"Like why she left you by yourself and came back to Daddy when you were obviously too young to be here by yourself." Yvette shook her hair back, probably an unconscious habit, sending the thick waves moving around her face and shoulders.

Rémi sighed. It was a question that she'd asked for years, silently, but had never gotten the answer to.

"Are you hungry?" she asked.

"No, I ate at one of the restaurants earlier." When Rémi had been having brunch with her friends at Novlette's.

Rémi sighed again and scraped fingers through her short curls. What did she do to deserve this?

Yvette sat beside her on the couch, propped her chin on her fist to stare at Rémi. "I saw the billboard on my way from the airport. Do they pay you for that?"

"Of course."

"Is that the kind of watch that you wear?"

"No, but they gave me one for free. I hocked it for a motorcycle." The girl smiled weakly.

A part of Rémi wanted to just leave the girl to her own devices, let her find her own entertainment in the condo. There was enough to do, enough books to read. The Jacuzzi worked, and the pool downstairs was sparkling and clean. But Yvette had all that in Maine and more. Well, maybe not the sunshine, but that was only a matter of a few months.

"Come on. Let's go up to the roof."

Rémi grabbed a beer from the fridge and a soda for Yvette; then they went outside to the balcony and up the white-railed stairs leading to the rooftop balcony with its expansive view of the city. She gripped the railing as she stepped up on the roof, the white concrete surface instantly warm under her bare feet.

The sun was brilliantly white, stripping away any darkness from Rémi's own corner of the roof. Partitioned on one side by tall white planters and the thick, decorative shrubbery that grew out of them, the Jacuzzi took up fully a third of the rooftop space. It flashed blue under the bright afternoon sun from its raised dais, the four white steps that Rémi often joked led to wickedness and vice. The thing was built for five, but it had held eight comfortably enough.

She walked past the Jacuzzi to one of the three lawn chairs spread out beneath wide umbrellas. The chair took her weight with a slight groan.

"Sit," she said to Yvette. "Relax."

"Thanks."

Although she had been too wrapped up in her own emotions to notice it before, the girl was tense. It mustn't be too easy for her to dump herself on a virtual stranger. And, abruptly, Rémi remembered it wasn't so much that she had fallen in love with Dez and her family, it was just that she didn't want to go back to the hell she knew in Boothbay Harbor. The teenage Rémi hadn't been able to understand why her mother would even think of leaving their new life in Miami for the cold, possessive love Auguste Bouchard threw at her in Maine. By saying that she wouldn't leave, Rémi was trying to force a hesitant Kelia to stay. Even back then she hadn't been able to beg.

"So what's going on?" She took a sip of her beer. "Since I can't get rid of you, you might as well tell me why you're here." She hoped that whatever Yvette was dealing with in Maine was as simple as longing for her older sister.

"Gee, thanks for the welcome."

"You're lucky I don't just throw you out on your ass. Message on the voicemail or not, I did not invite you stay with me." Her sister flinched, but Rémi continued. "I've been alone for a long time. Don't expect me to feel warm and fuzzy about you all of a sudden."

Yvette looked down at the space between her sprawled legs. "I didn't do anything."

Rémi got the feeling that was something she always had to say in her own defense. It had the unpleasant ring of familiarity to it. She bit her tongue to stop herself from apologizing. Then.

"I know. I'm just asking what happened. Not blaming." Rémi swallowed the slightly bitter Mexican beer.

Yvette looked at her, a quick brush of her eyes, before she looked away. When she looked back at Rémi, she was ready.

"I almost forgot that I had a sister until you showed up in Maine last year. Daddy made us all forget you. I couldn't understand that. I don't know why it happened or how."

"I'm a dyke." Rémi's casually said words hid the hurt her father's cruelty caused. But some of the anger burned through.

"That's stupid. I can't believe Papa would be like that. It's not like you killed somebody. You're his daughter."

The passionate insistence in Yvette's voice brought Rémi's head up sharply. "Don't tell me that you fuck women too. The rest of the family would just love to blame for me for that."

"No, I'm not into girls like that. I tried it. Not my style." Yvette showed her teeth.

Her sister was all bravado and show. Much like Rémi was at nineteen. Still, her eyebrow shot upwards at Yvette's words. She took another sip of her beer to hide her smile.

Was this why the girl was considered so bad? Because she did and said as she liked? An unfortunate and completely predicable side effect of Auguste's rigid control was rebellion. Rémi's eyes flickered over her sister.

Yvette had probably tried every drug known to man and beast. Sex she'd obviously already had. The girl's body was ridiculously beautiful. She wore it with the careless grace and ease of someone who knew exactly what it was capable of. Her jeans fit her lithesome figure well. The T-shirt showed off her effortlessly toned arms, generous breasts, and flat belly with a slight bump at the navel, which Rémi assumed was some sort of piercing. Yvette had probably completed the parental nightmare with horrendously inappropriate friends. Maybe even a motorcycle gang or two. Kelia hadn't been prepared for that.

With Rémi's defection, she'd been spared the worst of it. The five thousand dollars a month allowance she'd kept coming after running back to Maine hadn't soothed Rémi's resentment. But with paying for her college education, the condo, and nearly all of her other expenses, Rémi had at least given the appearance of being pacified.

"Sorry about the way things turned out with Mama," Rémi said. "I can certainly understand all of it. But you can't stay here indefinitely."

"Don't worry. I don't want to be here forever. Like I said before, I'll be back at Brown in the spring. Right now, I just want to get to know you, not interfere with your life."

"I see," Rémi said. And she did.

Later, while she dressed for Gillespie's, pulling a thin leather belt through the loops of her black slacks, Rémi's hands paused. Noises floated from downstairs. The television murmuring. Plates gently tapping against each other in the kitchen. It had been a long time since she'd lived with anybody. Years. Not since her mother left. Yvette's presence served as a distracting reminder of how alone she had been. How completely abandoned by family until Dez had enfolded her into the Nichols clan. Buckling her belt, Rémi strode to the door and firmly closed it on Yvette's noises.

But it wasn't as easy to shut the thoughts from her mind.

On the drive to the club, she listened to her messages again, paying particular attention to the one from Elena that she'd been too distracted to listen to earlier. Elena asked her to come in tonight even though Sundays weren't her usual nights to be there. But needing an excuse to be away from the living memory in her condo, Rémi had just put on her clothes and left without questioning why. On the voicemail, Elena's usually warm tones sounded brittle, the words carefully uttered as she spoke them quickly into the phone.

She hoped that it was nothing serious. Elena had been her manager since Gillespie's opened three years ago, and she did an excellent job that helped to make the place what it was now—popular and successful. Her particular brand of sex appeal, fair-mindedness, and hard work made her well liked by nearly everyone at the club.

"Can we talk in your office?" Elena asked as soon as she saw Rémi.

In her black skirt, purple silk shirt, and with her hair neatly pinned at the back of her head, the petite Nicaraguan woman blended in with the club's stark sensual and old-world décor in a way that immediately identified her as part of Gillespie's without alienating her from any of the customers she came in contact with.

Rémi nodded. "Sure. Come on up."

She led Elena through the bustling club preparing for its Sunday night customers, up the stairs and into her office. She sat on the couch and invited her manager to do the same.

"What's on your mind?"

Elena sat down, smoothed her skirt over her thighs, took a deep breath. Her hands trembled. Up close, without other eyes on her, Elena seemed ready to break down. Tinges of gray had crept under her dark gold skin and the muscles around her eyes were pulled tight. There seemed to a lot on the other woman's mind, but Rémi waited.

"I'm having some difficulties at home." She cleared her throat and folded her hands across her knees. "It's very embarrassing and unfortunate. Believe me, I wouldn't come to you with this unless it was very bad. I won't—I can't." Elena squeezed her eyes shut and looked down. Shadows crept into the space between her jaw and throat before she looked back up at Rémi and continued. "I want to keep my job, but I need to stay at home and take care of some things for a while."

In the years they had worked together, Elena had never asked Rémi for any favors. She did her job well, never brought drama to the club, and remained absolutely professional in her dealings with everyone at Gillespie's. There must be something very serious going on at home if she was asking this now. And Rémi was willing to support her through it without asking the very private woman to reveal her obviously personal business.

"That's no problem. I'm sure we can take care of things here while you're gone. How long do you need?"

Elena's lashes flickered down then back up again. "A month. Maybe two."

Her eyes widened. That was much longer than she'd expected. But. . . . "Try to make it as close to one month as possible. Okay?"

Elena shook with relief. "Okay." A trembling sigh. "Okay."

"I'm assuming that you want to take your leave as soon as possible, so just take the rest of the evening and tomorrow to tell me everything I need to know to do your job while you're gone. If it gets too much, I'll hire someone temporarily, but I don't really see that happening."

"Thank you so much, Rémi." Elena's hands reached out toward Rémi, then pulled back to settle back in her lap. "You won't regret this. I promise."

"No regrets, Elena. Just do what you need to and come back to us. Soon."

When Elena left to get some paperwork and her schedule, Rémi leaned back in her chair, suddenly ridiculously glad for something substantial to occupy her while Yvette stayed with her. Things perhaps wouldn't be so bad after all.

But the rest of the night proved her wrong.

While her manager, between running downstairs to take care of minor emergencies, carefully explained to Rémi the things she needed to do in order to make the club run smoothly while she was gone, her mind wandered. It flitted. To Yvette's presence in her condo. The betrayal she'd felt when her mother chose Auguste over her. Claudia's changing role in her life. And what she stood to lose if things with Claudia didn't work out.

I can't do this, Rémi thought. *I shouldn't.*

She had to leave Claudia alone. The older woman and Dez were the only family she had left in her life. It would be stupid to fuck that up.

Her hand jerked against the desk, spilling Elena's precariously stacked pile of lists and spreadsheets. Papers fluttered from the desk to dark floor.

"Sorry about that." Rémi mentally cursed herself, moved from behind the desk to squat on the floor and picked up the scattered papers.

Elena's eyes, softer with their lessened tension, looked at her with concern. But she knew better than to ask.

Rémi smiled at her in gratitude and stood up. "Let's try this again, shall we?"

She didn't end up leaving the club until well after closing time, six o'clock in the morning and the sky a blushing shade of gray. Feeling tired to her very bones, Rémi climbed into the truck and set herself on autopilot, heading for home. She wearily massaged the back of her neck. Before her, the road stretched, graphite and empty, a soothing counterpoint to the evening of never-ending smiles to be returned, handshakes to be given, needs to be met. Outside her windows, the Miami skyline was soft and dim. Colors on mute, as if she had stepped into a black-and-white photograph. Even the air smelled dull, cool with a hint of the sea's salty tang as it waited for the sun to rise and make it hot again.

The cell phone rang, jolting Rémi from her stupor. She blinked at the unfamiliar number.

"Hello?"

"Somehow I knew you'd be up this time of day."

The laughing voice and accent meant one of three women. Three very delightful women. Despite her tiredness, Rémi smiled.

"Nakamura-san. A pleasure to hear you."

Chance—it had to be her—laughed again. "You *are* good. Letta, Matsuko, and I just got back in town. We'd love to see you."

"And I'd love to see *you*." Rémi's mind flitted briefly to Claudia.

"Oh, good. We were hoping you'd say that."

The sound of animated chatter came at Rémi from the background. A deep-throated laugh. "Can you come by this morning for a bite to eat?"

Rémi's neck popped as she stretched, its muscles protesting over her long night hunched over the desk. "I can come over now for sleep and a bite after. Right now I'm useless for anything but."

"We can take that." Then her voice muffled as if she put her hand over the mouthpiece before a flurry of Italian came out, all too fast for Rémi to catch. "That will be absolutely fine. Let me give you the address of our hotel."

At a red light, Rémi took down the information then continued down Collins heading to the Bal Harbour Beach Sheraton. The last time she had been with the Nakamura sisters, they showed her such a good time that she slept dreamlessly for nearly two full days after. Their charms were certainly not for one lacking in stamina.

"Oh, you look wonderful," Chance Nakamura said when she answered Rémi's knock. In a thin robe that barely covered the top of her thighs, she posed in the doorway, giving Rémi a chance to appreciate her long legs and ready breasts pushing against the cotton, before leaning forward to offer a tight hug. Her short pixie haircut was wet with water, and she smelled like orange juice. "Come in, *bella*."

"We've been waiting for you." Behind her, an exact replica minus the robe but with long hair draped over her otherwise bare breasts, lay across the already rumpled sheets. "But we'll wait even longer since we know that you're tired."

"That's admirable of you." Rémi couldn't tell if this was Nicoletta or Matsuko. The two women wore their hair the same with the only physical difference between the sisters being that Matsuko's clit was pierced. She kicked off her boots at the door and smiled down into Chance's eyes. "Give me an hour or two of good rest, and then you can do whatever you want with me."

"Really?" The last triplet walked in from the balcony wearing a bathing suit. She looked as sleek as an otter in her one-piece tank and with her hair plastered to her scalp and back. "The last time you were the one with the reins." She closed the sliding glass door and walked toward Rémi, leaving wet footprints in the carpet. "We liked that."

With palms against Rémi's belly, she leaned in, the smell of chlorine and her lips hovering close. She rose up on tiptoes to kiss Rémi on one cheek, then the other. "Come in. Rest."

At Rémi's questioning look, she pressed Rémi's hand between her legs. Rémi smiled at her tiredly. "Good to see you again, Matsuko."

The woman laughed. On the bed, Nicoletta moved closer when Rémi lay down. "Hello, darling," she whispered in her melodious accent, compact body sprawling across Rémi's clothed one to cling like a succulent limpet. But Rémi was already falling asleep.

She woke up to sucking. A deep groan pulled her out of a dream and dropped her heavily in the midst of three very hungry women. Only when her eyes fluttered open and she registered the hot mouths on her breasts and on her pussy, did Rémi realize the groan was her own. Naked. She lay naked against white sheets while the three terracotta women—sex goddesses with upturned asses, mouths that licked, sucked wickedly at her nipples and clit, churned her body to hot liquid. She slid her hands into Letta's long hair while the woman nibbled at her breast, nipping at the skin with sharp teeth until Rémi sighed in the bed, brought to awareness by the pain. Across from her, Matsuko played a gentler game, sucking the hard nipple into her mouth and agitating it with her tongue.

Despite the strangeness of it, three sisters who liked to fuck together, Rémi had always enjoyed her encounters with the Nakamura women. In sex, they never touched each other, preferring instead to wait their turn when it came to getting access to Rémi's body, or latching onto their favored part of her (or second favorite) until the other sister was finished. They shared their sex with true pleasure, laughing, teasing, and baring their delicious bodies with an innocence Rémi found refreshing.

Chance crouched between her thighs. She'd recognize that wicked mouth anywhere. It completely covered Rémi's pussy in heat, sucking on her clit. Her tongue diving into Rémi's pussy that had gotten wet in sleep and now throbbed, swelled, wept to feel these beautiful women, their mouths bringing heated pleasure. The sleep gradually fell away until she was aware enough to begin feeling her way to satisfaction. Her hands reaching out for twin bushy mounds, seeking between swollen and sticky lips to find clits and slits attached to women attached to her, who writhed against the sheets as she fucked them lazily with her fingers.

They moaned against her breasts, their voices, rising and falling, a chorus of sex, their pussies moving against her hands, swallowing her fingers that skimmed and dove in their foamy salt seas. Breaths catching, moans rising, Chance between her legs eating her pussy with groaning enthusiasm, her ass wiggling in the air. Fucking the air. The sight of her heart-shaped ass, its pale curve kissed by the sun peeking through the windows, sent Rémi diving gratefully off the edge. She clenched her teeth over a harsh groan, hips jerking against Chance's face.

One of the women came. Maybe it was all three. But Chance sat up, wiping her chin.

"I brought toys," she purred.

It was sublimely mindless. Rémi buried herself in the act of fucking, taking what the women offered, obliterating her exhaustion for something better. Perfect shining awareness of her body as an instrument, even as she strapped the thick red dick to her hips and Nicoletta bent over in the bed on hands and knees, pink tongue licking her own lips in anticipation of Rémi's touch. And Rémi gave that touch. Pussy glistening and open, petulant lips that Letta reached back to spread and pinch.

And the red dick sank in, nuzzled against Rémi's clit, and she was gone. Up to her eyeballs in pleasure and groaning as if her soul were pouring out into the women under her. First Nicoletta, then Matsuko, slamming into hungry cunts that foamed and clutched around her intrusion. When it was Chance's turn, she insisted on fucking face first, looking into Rémi's eyes. She sat on the marble-topped sofa table, legs spread, back against the wall, waiting with thickening pussy lips until Rémi lifted her, grasped the firm globes of her ass, and thrust the dick deep into her already soaking pussy, a hand flat against the wall behind Chance's head, fucking until their sweat ran together like two rivers intent on being one.

Behind them, Rémi was dimly aware of Nicoletta and Matsuko watching and touching themselves, separate but joined together in pleasure. She felt their gaze on her naked back, on the bunch and release of her ass muscles as she fucked their oldest sister, the slam! slam! slam! of the table against the wall. Chance's gasping shouts. Screaming Rémi's name punctuated with inciting words in Italian— Faster! Yes! More! Harder! Do it!—that made Rémi want to keep fucking her forever. Chance was great for her ego. In the midst of the pleasure ravaging in her belly, Rémi laughed.

More than any woman she'd ever met, Matsuko loved kissing. While her sisters lay on the bed, gasping in the aftermath of sex, lethargic like sunbathers, she pulled Rémi down and clambered on top, small and succulent breasts swinging, pussy opening up over the dick Rémi held steady, mouth already seeking. She growled, soft and kittenish. The scent of pussy clung to her face and, hidden in the slightly damp hair, the essence of chlorine and early morning sun.

Matsuko kissed the same way she liked to fuck. Slowly, intently, paying attention to each detail of the flesh she shared hers with. Her tongue licked delicately at Rémi's mouth. Tasted. Her pussy settled around the scarlet dildo, pressing into it so Rémi felt her presence, a hammer of sensation against her clit. It was her turn to groan.

"I like having you to myself, Rémi," she whispered, slowly riding the dick, her lips brushing Rémi's, breasts pressing into breasts. Belly to belly.

And the kind of attention she paid was addictive. Matsuko's ass was like butter in Rémi's hands, churning around the tool that gave her pleasure. Her juice dripped to Rémi's fingers, slick and plentiful. The lush length of her tongue in Rémi's mouth, lips wet and open, the breath huffing like a distant freight train. She rode Rémi slowly but forcefully, sweat between their bellies slipping and warm. Rémi could have forced her to move faster, but she didn't. She allowed Matsuko her leisure, courting the liquid slide of sensation in her own belly until the heat crawled up her chest, engulfed her face, squeezed her eyes tightly shut.

It was an orgasm she saw coming from minutes away. Minutes in which she imagined Claudia's face, imagined that it was her moving like a wave on the jutting red cock. Her gasps, relentless. Her lips like Scotch whisky. The orgasm split Rémi from the inside out, carved out a wide space in her throat for her to call out Claudia's name and mean it.

Rémi shouted into Matsuko's mouth. The girl shuddered on top of her like a small bird, heart fluttering, cooing sounds in her throat. With her body flush and breathless with release, Rémi barely moved when Matsuko sat up, mouth rosy wet and breasts and belly glistening with sweat.

"Thank you," the small woman panted. A pulse beat heavily in her throat.

"Glad I could oblige," Rémi gasped.

She brushed her palms up Matsuko's thighs, the slight curve of her hips, her small waist. Her nipples shrank like late summer strawberries under Rémi's thumbs. The electricity in her body fizzled out and she became aware, slowly, of the wet spot under her ass and the cooling dampness between her thighs. Matsuko, sensing her withdrawal, dismounted and, looking at Rémi over one pale shoulder with eyes soft as love, blew a kiss before disappearing into the bathroom. Her sisters crawled toward Rémi to take her place.

The women lay spooned, like children, naked and exhausted under the sheet that Rémi pulled over them. An existence with them floating in and out of her bed was someone's dream. And as she watched them, Rémi realized that this was no longer *her* dream. Claudia. She wanted Claudia. But she couldn't have her. It was simple as family. The older woman, her warm heart, and her daughter who was also Rémi's best friend were the only family that she had left and could count on. She could take sex from women like these. Willing, passionate women who shared tenderness along with their bodies. Afterward, only afterward could she go into Claudia's house for something beyond the flesh. For sweetness that had nothing more attached to it than a desire for Rémi to be happy.

Quietly, with the sun a blazing amber ball falling outside the window, Rémi pulled on her clothes. The rumpled slacks, thin undershirt, long-sleeved shirt rolled up at the sleeves. She gave the women one last look before she left the hotel suite, pulling the door shut behind her.

At home, Yvette swept her once with an amused gaze. "Long day?"

"Not really." Rémi threw her keys in the bowl by the door and walked between her sister and the flickering television. "I'm leaving again in a few, but I'm taking the bike this time. Feel free to use the car for errands or whatever."

"Thanks."

She felt her sister's eyes on her as she bounded up the stairs, lightly gripping the railing. "I have been known to be generous," Rémi said.

Yvette's laughter followed her into the room. Hours later, showered, dressed, and back at the club, she paused. Twenty-four hours ago, she had been right here. It felt like nothing had changed. Despite her cathartic marathon with the Nakamura sisters, Rémi still felt empty. As if she'd done nothing more fulfilling the last few hours than brush her teeth. There had to be more to it than this.

On the stage below, Sage crooned one of her original songs to the restaurant's early crowd. In her leather pants, white muscle shirt, and miles of tattoos etched over her body, she could have been any rock star. And even as her friend moved across the stage, seemingly singing for everyone within ear's reach, it was obvious to Rémi, watching from above, that she was only aware of Phillida, her woman draped back in her chair watching with a smile of possession. Despite the very unique aspects to their relationship, the two women were happy together.

Rémi shoved her hands in her pockets. Sighed. Pushed away the image that came automatically to her mind in the most inconvenient moments. This, she thought looking down at her friends, was what she wanted for herself. Happiness.

But could she get it with Claudia or was she setting herself up for heartache and an even bigger loss than she was prepared to take? The phone in her pocket rang and Rémi reached for it. Claudia's name flashed across the cell phone screen and she was helpless to the surge of happiness that flooded her chest. But . . . she didn't answer the call. Rémi let it ring until the small beep sounded, her voice mail picking up. *Fuck.*

Chapter

11

The next day, Rémi dialed Claudia's number, but after the fourth ring, she got dropped into the voicemail. She hung up. *That's psycho behavior, Bouchard. She's going to know it's you. Caller ID fucking up the stalker again. Shit.* It had been over a week since Rémi had seen Claudia. Over a week since she'd made the decision not to pursue the older woman. But that decision wasn't an easy one to sit with. At night, at the most unexpected times, her body remembered the feel of Claudia against it. Recalled the smell of her breath. The sound of her voice. The way she asked nicely for something she really wanted. Those memories became too much. Rémi had to call. Just to see how she was doing. Besides, she hadn't returned Claudia's call from three nights before, only sent a message directly to her voicemail letting her know she was managing the club while Elena was away.

She called back. At the second ring, Claudia answered. Breathless.

"Sorry about that. I was getting dressed."

Rémi's eyes fluttered closed at the image of Claudia, her pretty breasts in a bra, something black and lacy, a delicate swell in the A cups, as she bent down to fasten black silk stockings to a garter. Rémi breathed deeply.

"Candy Dulfer will be at the club tonight," Rémi said. "Do you want to come check it out?"

"Oh. Really? That sounds so good." Disappointment leaked into her small pause. "But I can't."

Rémi put one and nothing together. "You have a date?"

"Yes."

"Who is it?" Then she cursed herself for asking.

"No one you know."

Okay. She deserved that. "You're probably right. Have fun anyway, and give the lucky guy my regards." And she closed the cell phone. Then cursed herself for being an idiot. Not smooth at all. Not even a little bit.

Night was approaching. It slid between the cracks of the sun, signs of impending darkness. The skyscrapers emptying of their daytime prisoners, cars speeding toward more comforting destinations, lights flickering on all over the city. Rémi sat in her truck, remembering how Claudia had filled it with her presence and her scent. Tonight, she would do the same to someone else's car. She would tease them with her light laughter, with the way she arched her neck and reached toward the source of her amusement, touching with a careless hand or feather-light fingers. Rémi imagined Claudia kissing her date, this mystery man, and she felt her jaw clench. She forced herself to shake it off. She had to get to work.

The parking lot behind the club was quiet, misleadingly so on some nights. Most people didn't know about this smaller lot that she and club employees used. As Rémi neared the back stairs, she heard the sound of voices raised in argument and other noises, of an instigating crowd that didn't belong at her club.

"Fuck off! I can't believe you did that shit."

"I didn't do anything." The sound of a slap connecting stopped the rest of whatever that person was going to say. "Stop this nonsense right now." The voice came back with a hoarse shout.

"Nonsense? I can't believe you slept with her. She is supposed to be off limits."

Sage and Phillida stood in a loose circle of over half a dozen people, arguing. As the onlookers saw Rémi, they nudged each other, met Rémi's eyes in quick greeting, then walked quickly toward Gillespie's entrance. Sage had her hands wrapped tightly around Phillida's wrists. The muscles in her arms and neck stood out in harsh relief as she tried to keep her struggling girlfriend under control.

Rémi walked toward the couple. "Aren't you guys kinda early? The stage show doesn't start until ten."

Phil glared at Rémi. "Back off. This is none of your business."

Rémi's generous mood vanished. "It actually is my business. Gillespie's to be exact." She glanced around, noticing the lingering pairs of eyes peeking out the club's window. A car pulled up, another employee coming in to work for the night. Aimee, the sous chef, emerged from the small silver Toyota and glanced quickly toward the threesome before making her way toward the building, the hem of her pink skirt fluttering quickly around her knees.

"There's no drama here. None." Rémi looked from one woman to the other to push her point home. "Take it somewhere less public."

"Listen, Rémi—"

Sage cut her girlfriend off. "It's cool. Sorry about that."

"No—" Phil tried to protest but she tugged her hands forward until the two women were chest to chest. She hissed something, and Phil subsided. Then the two women turned and walked quickly into the club.

This was definitely not what Rémi wanted to deal with today. Her friends didn't often fight, but when they did it was a pain in the ass for everyone around them. She scrubbed a hand through her curls and blew out a harsh breath. Women.

She missed Claudia's presence. One of the main reasons she'd invited Candy Dulfer to come was because Claudia loved her music. Dulfer was one of the few modern jazz artists that Rémi was guaranteed to hear when she walked into the older woman's house. Otherwise Claudia preferred the classics like Dinah Washington, Johnny

Hartman, and Billie Holiday. And now she was out on a date with some fucking guy. But Rémi would get over this. She had to.

In her office, she went through one of her many nightly routines, going over the accounts and employee evaluations with a sharp-eyed diligence she trusted to no one, not even Elena. Once finished, she prepped for the night. Found the right clothes to wear in her massive closet hidden in the bedroom at the rear of the office.

When she was at Gillespie's it was mostly a show. She was a version of herself that burned hotter, haloed more brightly than usual. The clothes, shoes, even accessories—cufflinks, watch, even the three diamond earrings winking from each ear—represented a certain kind of image: the success and sexual magnetism of Rémi Bouchard, owner and manager of Gillespie's Jazz and Martini Bar. It was part of the show that people expected when they came, and it was what she gave them. They expected to come to Gillespie's and see the life-sized version of the androgynous demigod on the billboards hovering above the city. And that's exactly who she gave them. In the club she flirted with men and women alike, smiling, charming, and seemingly available.

The cool AC combined with the lazily turning ceiling fans churned the air in the club. Rémi felt the thick waves of her hair begin to loosen from the mousse she'd put through it earlier. The short curls tickled the tops of her ears and the back of her neck, telling her it was time for her to get a haircut. The trim she'd had just before Dez's wedding was already grown out, leaving her hair in loose black curls around her head. If she wasn't careful, she'd soon start looking like a butch Shirley Temple with a tan. Not the impression she was going for.

Rémi wove her way through the crowd as Candy Dulfer reigned on the stage, lulling the audience into an ecstatic stupor. Those not captivated by the saxophone watched Rémi. She felt their eyes on her, and she acknowledged those she could. Her eyes licked over them: the cool widow who'd lured Rémi into her bed a few months ago and wanted an encore, a stranger with friendly green eyes, the waitress walking by with the flirtatious saunter. Rémi turned and walked away from the need in their faces. Not tonight. She slipped quietly through the tables and the darkness and jazz-perfumed air to find her office.

Light peeked from beneath the not quite closed door. Rémi heard noises and smelled a familiar combination of scents. Jaw clenched in irritation, she shoved the door open.

They had barely made it inside the office before they started fucking. Sage's pants lay discarded on the floor beside her shirt and Phil's purse. Her shirt was unbuttoned and pushed aside to show her heaving breasts. The carpet must have been scraping her back as she took the pressure of Phil's hand filling up her pussy, thrusting three fingers deep and grunting as Phil, still wearing her frilly peach polka-dot dress with her forehead dripping sweat and her lips skinned back to show clenched white teeth, fucked the cum right out of her girlfriend.

One of the tattooed woman's legs pointed toward the ceiling, a sleekly muscled calf grasped tightly in Phil's hand.

"I love you," Sage hissed between her clenched teeth. "I love you."

The sound of their frantic fucking expanded in the room until it was just Sage's snaking breath, Phil's fingers plunging in and out of the dripping pussy, Phil's panting excitement. The two women were swallowed by it. Arousal gnawed at Rémi's skin. Suddenly it felt like years since she'd shared pleasure that powerful with a woman.

The two lovers only saw each other and only heard the sound of their shared passion. Although she knew that they wouldn't mind if she stayed to watch, Rémi backed out of her office and closed the door firmly on her friends. She wanted a smoke. The bite of her seven-year-long nicotine habit sharply made itself known. Her lips suddenly longed to feel the stroke of a Marlboro Light. She even missed the sting of the smoke in her eyes and the heavy scent it left on her clothes. But cold turkey or not, she'd quit and was determined to stick by that decision. She didn't want to pollute Claudia's air with it.

Rémi leaned back against the wall near her office door and took out a piece of peppermint gum. It wasn't ideal, but it would do. With a powerful act of will, she carefully emptied her mind of anything to do with Claudia or sex or what was going on behind her office door.

Nearly an hour passed before Phil and Sage emerged from the other side. The two women, pleasantly rumpled and smelling of mouthwash and sex, didn't notice her at all as they came out. Phillida slowly walked backwards down the small flight of stairs leading from Rémi's office, and Sage followed, chasing the other woman's lips with her own. Phil giggled and tangled her fingers in her girlfriend's shirt.

Rémi rolled the peppermint gum around on her tongue.

"Does this mean I can have my office back now?"

Her friends barely looked away from each other.

"Yeah," Sage muttered between kisses. "Thanks for the loan."

Phil laughed and passed by Rémi, brushing a hand over the tall woman's belly clothed in the pressed white shirt. She watched them drift into the darkened club with the music of Candy Dulfer the soundtrack to their graceful escape. Envy tugged at her skin, and she looked away as if from a too-bright light.

Chapter
12

Rémi left Gillespie's for her first night off in too many days. She left the club in the pseudocapable hands of her assistant manager, Gerard, with instructions to call her if he needed anything at all. Anything.

The night seemed as if it would be a trouble-free one, just like the past two weeks. Whatever trouble Anderson seemed intent on stirring up was dormant, and Rémi was grateful. It was hard enough for her to manage the club and remain socially available to her patrons plus maintain a life of her own. Her attentions were stretched and her nights of sleep were getting fewer, but it was nothing she couldn't handle.

Tonight all she wanted to do was stretch out on the sand and watch the moon overhead. But another part of her, the more responsible, less selfish part wanted to go home and talk with Yvette. Her sister seemed wounded even with all her bravado and charm. Like Rémi sometimes felt on the inside. But . . .

The bike growled under her as she coasted down Biscayne under the slivered moon and too-bright streetlights. Strip malls. Roti shops. Tanning salons. The eerie glow of the twenty-four-hour McDonald's. She passed them all, stripping everything from her mind but the essentials of navigating the bike, keeping out of the way of reckless drivers.

It had been days since she'd seen Claudia. Those days felt like a yawning gap of time. Before it would have been nothing to go a few days without seeing her. Even with Dez out of town, she had felt no hesitation about dropping in on her former professor, whether it was to talk for a few minutes or an hour about the events of the day or sit in her kitchen or on her deck while Claudia took care of her own business. Now, things were different.

She rode down the pier, past trendier shops, Starbucks instead of Mickey D's. Surf shops and the smell of salt water. As she rumbled past a cigar shop, a familiar flash of legs caught her eye. Rémi looked past the legs to the beloved face. The mouth turned down with boredom and eyes listlessly watching passing traffic. Rémi pulled up to the curb in front of a parked car and felt the familiar falling sensation in her belly when she looked into Claudia's face. She pulled off her helmet and raked fingers through her hair.

She felt Claudia's eyes on her as she dismounted from the bike. Her muscles stretched under the dark jeans and dress shirt and leather jacket, self-consciously. For the hundredth time in her life she wondered what the other woman saw when she looked at her. A child with a pathetic crush? Or a woman whose desires couldn't be ignored? Rémi's eyes skittered to the ground before she found something in her to look at Claudia again.

The decision she'd made to stop trying to become Claudia's lover abruptly unmade itself.

It was an eternity under the unreadable eyes as she pocketed the keys and her booted legs took her across the pavement to sit on the bench beside Claudia.

"You look like a gift."

"That's always been my life's ambition," she said.

Rémi flushed and dropped her eyes again. "I meant—"

Claudia lightly touched her arm, smiling. "I know what you meant. Just teasing."

Rémi should have known that. She pursed her lips and adjusted the helmet on her lap.

"Your hair is growing out," Claudia said in the silence. "I like it." She touched a curl looped around the edge of Rémi's ear, stroked it, and Rémi held her breath, savoring the echoes of the unintentional caress through her body. Claudia drew her hand away and Rémi almost groaned from its loss.

She looked at Claudia again. The woman was definitely on a date. Pale yellow halter dress. Dark gold bag with matching heels that punctuated legs bobbing to a private rhythm. The only thing missing was the guy.

"He went in to see about a reservation," she said, reading Rémi's look. Claudia gestured behind her to the second-floor seafood restaurant with its wide glass windows, gold velvet rope, and view of the bay. "They were booked when he called, but Kincaid is intent on using his powers of persuasion."

Rémi doubted more than his power of persuasion—his sense maybe—for leaving his date sitting on a bench waiting for something that probably wouldn't materialize. The Blue Egg was a fantastic restaurant, well-known in most circles, but one of the things that made the place so beloved among its clientele was its egalitarian treatment of everyone. You were well taken care of at Blue's whether you were a movie star or just liked to watch them in your spare time. No one's reservation got bumped in favor of somebody flashing a wad of cash or a high-society profile.

"Don't get that look. I told him that I wanted to wait out here. It's a beautiful night."

Rémi sighed. It *was* a beautiful night. That perfect mix of early fall heat and cooling ocean breeze. The evening's darkness was held at bay by scattered street lamps and light from the storefronts. This hidden part of Miami that was more like a New Orleans or Savannah bay front had long been a favorite of Rémi's. Everything seemed suspended in time here. Years ago, she imagined bringing Claudia here and showing her some of the things she loved.

"Do you want to go somewhere with me?"

The words seemed to startle them both and Rémi felt her face grow warm. But she didn't take them back. They seemed suddenly important. And very, very urgent. Rémi flicked her gaze behind her to the doors of the restaurant that opened to a steady stream of customers.

Claudia raised an eyebrow. "You do realize I'm here with some-one else, right?" A smile hovered at her lips.

"I don't see anyone but you and me out here on this bench." Her hand rested on the back of the bench, only a few centimeters from the naked curve of Claudia's shoulder. "Besides, it'll take him a while to get a table in there. You can come back later. Just call and tell him."

Was she really trying to do this? Yes, she was. The strange mix of lethargy and restlessness she'd felt before was gone. Now all she wanted was to share this dark, moist night with Claudia, to pull her into the world that she knew and let her feel what it was like for just a few moments. To seduce her with it.

"It won't take long."

After Claudia made the call to her date, Rémi cruised away from the restaurant with the small hands clasped around her belly and possibilities roaring in her head. Claudia fit on the bike like she was meant to be there. Belly and breasts flat against Rémi's back. The long thighs hugging hers from behind.

Her favorite stretch of beach was deserted. The surfers and sun-bathers had long gone home to their dinners and beds, leaving the beach glowing pale under the half-moon. Rémi turned off the en-gine and rolled the bike across the hard-packed sand. The beach stretched on for miles with only the occasional shadowy presence letting her know that they weren't completely alone.

"I haven't been out here in a long time," Claudia said as Rémi helped her to dismount.

"Warrick used to bring you out here?"

"He wasn't the only man I dated, you know." Claudia slipped off her shoes.

"He wasn't?" Rémi grinned and stepped back from the tempta-tion of Claudia's skin. She pulled the folded blanket from the saddle-bag and held out her hand for Claudia to take it.

"He was my first lover, but others before him tried."

"Lucky man. He must have done something right."

"Right at the time."

Rémi tugged Claudia across the sand, not far from the bike, to sit down on the blanket.

"So is this new guy the right one?"

Claudia adjusted her dress under demurely folded legs. "I doubt it. Something to do. There's probably nothing left for me out there anymore."

"So you're going to take whatever is out there just to occupy your time?"

"Yes. Isn't that what you're doing?"

With her jacket folded under her head for a pillow, Rémi looked past Claudia's calm face to the star-scattered sky above. "No. I'm going after what I know will make me happy."

Claudia's face looked startled. "Really?"

"Yes." Rémi looked at her.

"Rémi. I . . ." She paused as if considering her words carefully. "We don't fit together. I'm not able to give you what you want."

"Why are you so sure?"

"For heaven's sake, Rémi, I'm old enough to be your mother."

"And *I'm* old enough to be your lover. What's your point?" She sat up, bringing herself even closer to Claudia. The other woman didn't move back. She sat, dress rustling in the ocean-scented breeze, lips held in a soft line. Her breasts moved gently with each breath. "Do you want me?"

The breaths stopped.

"If you don't want me, I'll stop this. I swear I will." Rémi held herself back from touching Claudia, but just barely. The heat of her was so close. She was so close. This scented, beloved creature that turned Rémi's thoughts to salt blowing away on a breeze.

"You're too young to be focused on me like this."

"That's not what I asked you." And she threw her willpower aside. Inhaled the warmth of the one she wanted to be her lover, drifted her open palms up Claudia's arms, slowly closed her hands around the delicate skin. "Do you want me?" The question was more breath than sound.

The heat from Claudia's mouth tickled her throat. "I think only a stone wouldn't want what you have to offer," she said.

Rémi's pulse drummed in her ears. "And you're not a stone, are you?"

"No." Her eyes dropped to Rémi's lips. "I'm not."

Rémi didn't know who moved closer first, only that the lips under hers were even softer than she'd imagined. Her heart slammed against her chest. Everything inside her was drowning, senses blocked to everything but the feel of Claudia's skin, the mouth opening like a new world against hers. The breasts pressed to her chest.

"Let go of my hands."

The command shook her out of her stupor, and Rémi pulled her hands away quickly and drew back. But Claudia followed, mouth still open and wet against hers, body rising up to straddle Rémi until she was at a taller height and her palms pressed against Rémi's face, tongue sweeping into her mouth. Her hands dove down the back of Rémi's jacket and shirt, fingers splayed as far as they could go, over the scar on her shoulder blade, fighting to go lower. My god. My god. My god. The trembling started in her boots, worked its way up her body until all of her shook against Claudia. Tiny tremor after tremor. But that didn't stop her body from knowing what to do. Her hands fell to Claudia's thighs spread over hers. She grasped Claudia's back, her hips, pulled her closer, pressed against the yielding flesh.

"You don't kiss me like that anymore."

The alien words penetrated Rémi's heated haze, yet she paid them little attention. A couple walked by them, too closely, with the woman who'd spoken watching them. Claudia pulled back, trying to drag her succulent lips away. Rémi held on, sucking on the soft flesh, nipping, trying to coax her back. Claudia pushed at her shoulders. And Rémi drew back, finally, breathing heavily through parted lips.

"I have to go, I think." Claudia's eyelids drooped heavily over passion-black eyes. She licked her lips.

"Yeah." She forced her breath to a steadier pace. "Your date is waiting."

"Shit!" Claudia pulled abruptly away from Rémi, fumbling on

the blanket for her purse. The phone's electronic blue light pierced their intimate darkness as she opened it. "Damn. He called me three times."

"Come on. Let me take you back." Rémi folded up the blanket while she called Kincaid, only half listening to Claudia's lukewarm apologies to the man. Claudia wanted her. Claudia wanted *her*. A fierce smile hijacked Rémi's mouth. With the blanket folded under one arm she turned to the woman who would soon be hers.

"You ready?"

Chapter

13

"Some lady is here to see you."

Yvette's voice pulled Rémi from a dream of strawberries. The fruit was succulent, wet and red, and her teeth were just about to sink into the plump skin. She rolled over in the bed, groaning.

"What?" Rémi brushed away the fog of sleep, blinking in the shrouded darkness of her bedroom.

"I told the concierge to let her up. She's coming."

"What the fuck . . . ?"

"She sounds like she knows you." Yvette's head disappeared from the doorway.

"They all think they know me," Rémi mumbled, sitting up in the bed. She scraped a weary hand over her face and glanced at the clock. Now she was awake enough to be irritated.

"Tell whoever it is to go away," she croaked. *Dire celui qui qu'il est de partir.* "I'm not up. And I'm not in the mood."

Rémi sagged back against the wrought iron headboard, muttering. "It's too fucking early for this."

"I keep forgetting that you work late at the club these days." Claudia stood in the doorway. "Sorry."

A bolt of awareness shot through Rémi. And instantly, she was awake.

"The other night was nothing," Claudia said. "My date with Kincaid didn't go anywhere."

Her crisp white pantsuit gleamed in the darkness of Rémi's bedroom. The jacket with its single button clasped her small waist and revealed a V of something dark underneath. A camisole?

"That's good to know." So they weren't pretending anymore. "I wish you had left him and come home with me."

The open door allowed in a slice of the golden day, but that was all. Rémi suspected that while she could see Claudia, the older woman couldn't see her at all. She slid out of the bed on the side opposite Claudia.

"Oh!"

She heard the low gasp but only spared the surprised face a brief look before taking her robe from the hook just inside the closet and pulling it on. When she turned around, Claudia's back was to her.

"I didn't realize you were naked," she said.

"I'm not anymore," Rémi said. "Come in."

She brushed past Claudia, deliberately, and closed the bedroom door. A scent of fresh apples lingered around the older woman and Rémi fought the urge to reach for Claudia and sink her face into her throat, run her fingers through that pale hair. Instead, she returned to the bed, her back once again against the scrolled headboard.

"Please sit," she said.

There weren't many options in the large room, but Rémi liked to think that Claudia knew what she was doing when she sat on the bed, only a few feet from her. The crisp scent of apples touched her face again.

"I hadn't heard from you," Claudia said, eyes finding Rémi's. "Is something wrong?"

"No. I was just waiting for you to finish with your friend, Kincaid." The scrolled headboard felt solid and cool at her back. Rémi took a deep breath to deepen its comforting contact.

"Ah." Claudia said. She exhaled her understanding in that single breath. "Your sister seems like a sweet girl."

"Is she? I don't know her very well."

"I see some of you in her."

"Your eyesight must be especially good because I don't see any of that. She ran away from home and came here. I don't even know what to do with her."

"I'm sure you'll figure it out. She's family and she's here to be with you. That's a great place to start."

"Yeah . . ." she tapered off into silence.

Claudia's eyes rested on her face. "She didn't have anything to do with your parents' decisions from all those years ago. I hope you're not trying to blame her for the past."

"I'm not that far gone yet. What I am worried about . . . it's not her precisely." She sucked on the inside of her cheek. "I want you, but I don't want to lose what we had before. You and your family mean a lot to me. I don't want to throw that away because of what I want from you now." Rémi's breath shuddered in her chest. She felt like a fumbling teenager. None of this was turning out the way she had imagined. And now with Yvette here . . .

"We can't go back to the way that things were."

The words put a fist in Rémi's throat.

"I'll always remember with fondness the times you spent in my house as a teenager and later as a young woman. But if I'm to be honest with myself, I can tell you that I've enjoyed our . . . interactions these past few weeks." Claudia smiled. "I can see why the ladies find it nearly impossible to resist you." Rémi opened her mouth, but Claudia raised a hand, laughing. "Don't deny what I've said. I've heard the stories and seen the effect you have on women. It's all right." Her face grew serious again. "We can stop now before things get any more complicated. But like I said. We can never go back."

"Do you want to stop?" Rémi asked. She swallowed and kept her hands perfectly still on her thighs.

"I don't know." Claudia shifted on the bed. "I'm not very comfortable with this. But I've been entirely too comfortable for a lot of my life. I was comfortable with Warrick, and he left me for someone else. I thought I was comfortable being a mother and a teacher, but then this cancer came and made me realize that's not everything.

After it left my body, I felt that the reason I had been spared was to live a more daring life than the one I had before. I don't regret anything I've done so far. Not my children, not my marriage to Warrick, not my job at the university. But now I'm realizing that I want more. So while I'm not comfortable—this may be the least comfortable I've ever been, actually—I want more. And I feel selfish for wanting that because I know what being welcomed and loved by my family has meant to you."

Breath left Rémi's mouth in an explosion of sound. The breath she didn't even know she had been holding. Claudia understood. She understood. But . . .

"I know I'm risking a lot with this," Rémi said. "I've been toying with the idea of pursuing you for years now. For long enough that us being together seemed inevitable."

"No pressure or anything," Claudia murmured with a wry smile.

"None at all." Rémi sat up in the bed, moved until Claudia was close enough to touch. "This I'm serious about. If there's ever any point where you want me stop, just say it. I'm a big girl. I can handle it."

"And big girls don't cry?" It was Claudia's turn to slide closer.

"So the song goes."

She palmed the linen-covered calf. The white material, her dark hand, Claudia's warmth beneath them both. The knee bent beneath her fingers and she used that anchor to pull the older woman even closer. Her thigh. The plump heat of her bottom. Their breaths mingled.

"I won't hurt you," Rémi murmured, pushing her breath against the lips barely an inch from hers.

"Don't lie to me." Claudia hooked her hand at the back of Rémi's head and tugged her in.

Their lips met. Perfectly. An electrical current. Understanding. Then mouths opened. Rémi wanted it so badly, she trembled. Fingers digging into the linen-covered backside. Heart galloping in her chest. Their tongues tangled. Sigh drank sigh. The realization of all those years of longing unwrapped inside Rémi. Was this a dream? Her hands clutched at Claudia's skin. She wanted to open her mouth and devour her, to drink from her mouth until she was wet from head to foot. Until Claudia weakened enough to fall into the sheets and allow Rémi to feast on her skin, nibble on her flesh, enjoy every single morsel of her. She bit Claudia's lip.

Something buzzed at her ear but she ignored it, turning her head away to listen for important sounds. Like Claudia's soft moans. But Claudia was pushing her away.

"Your sister," she whispered against Rémi's mouth.

Rémi opened her eyes. At the door, Yvette stood blinking owlishly at them. "Mama is on the phone," she said.

Rémi's breath jerked in her chest. "Later. Take a message."

"Umm—"

"You might want to take that," Claudia murmured. "It could be important." She pulled away, wiping at her lipstick.

Yvette glanced at them, making sure that Rémi was going to get the phone, then disappeared from the doorway.

"Don't move," Rémi said. She smoothed trembling fingers over Claudia's thigh then reached for the phone near the bed.

"Kelia. This really isn't a good time."

Before her, Claudia's eyelashes fluttered in surprise. Rémi turned away to pay better attention to her mother. "What can I do for you?"

"I'm sorry I reacted badly the other day to the news about Yvette being with you."

Even now, it was still a shock to hear her mother's voice. Almost two years ago, the low words over the phone telling her Auguste was dead had rocked Rémi where she stood. Her brief stay in Maine during her father's funeral hadn't lessened the impact of the voice that had comforted her through childhood. The voice she'd relied on to keep her safe.

"I'm sorry too," Rémi said. "I would have preferred another reaction. She's too young to have your indifference."

A flinching silence. "That's not fair of you to say."

"Life isn't fair. Isn't that what Auguste used to say? Sometimes you get what you want, but most times you get shit."

"Don't quote your father to me. The last thing I want to hear is one of his cynicisms." Kelia's voice bristled with impatience. Rémi imagined her leaning over the desk in the office, irritably brushing aside an innocent bit of paper, another one of those "to-do" lists that she was so fond of making. "The reason I called was to talk about Yvette. I agree that she needs to come home, but I don't want her to come back to the way things were when she left."

"Then change how you interact with her."

"I've tried." Kelia sighed. "She's furious with me, and with your father, for the way things turned out with you."

"Why, after all these years?"

"I don't know. I—" Paper rustled in the background. "Please tell her that your life hasn't been that bad. That you don't hate us like she does."

"I don't want to lie to her."

An explosive gasp came from the other end of the line. "Rémi!" She waited.

"I took care of you. I made sure you didn't starve. You were better off after I left than when I was with you down in that awful city."

"Do you really think that?"

The silence spoke for itself.

"Listen, Kelia. I have to go. Yvette and I will talk and I'll let you know how things go." Before her mother could say anything, Rémi hung up the phone.

She breathed the tightness out of her chest then turned back to Claudia. "I think it's safe to say that the mood has been broken."

"Do you want to talk about it?"

"No." She nibbled on the inside of her cheek. "Maybe." Rémi glanced around her bed at the darkness, and Claudia stretched out like an engraved invitation in her bed. "I'm going to take a shower. Stay, please, until I get back."

"Okay."

After a quick shower, Rémi came back into the bedroom modestly dressed in a robe, toweling her hair dry, but Claudia wasn't there. She grabbed her cell phone.

"I thought you were going to stay?" she asked when Claudia picked up.

"I was, but then I thought better of it." A gentle rush of sound came through the line as if Claudia brushed her hand over her face. She lowered her voice. "You're naked now." Rémi didn't bother to correct her. "I'm not ready to see you like that."

"You saw me 'like that' earlier." Rémi briskly moved the towel through her hair one last time then dropped it to the bed.

"But that was a surprise. The next time I want it to be on purpose and very intentional on both our parts."

Rémi tongued her lower lip, paused reaching for her closet door. "I'm very much filled with intent right now."

Claudia laughed outright. "Just come downstairs when you're ready. Yvette and I are getting to know each other while you labor over your beauty regimen."

So Claudia didn't want to play. "You're no fun."

Downstairs she found them sitting around the kitchen island over a platter of fresh-cut vegetables and iced tea.

"Yvette is making me feel at home," Claudia said, chewing on a sliver of red bell pepper. Her eyes lingered on Rémi. The faded jeans and vintage T-shirt advertising the virtues of cow roping. Her bare feet. The smile widened. "You look nice. I feel like I haven't seen you in casual clothes since college. They suit you." Then she blushed, looking sideways at Yvette as if she'd said something too intimate in front of a child.

"Thanks. I'll remember that." Rémi walked past her sister and lightly squeezed her shoulder. A breath of cool hit her as she opened the fridge and pulled out the pitcher of iced tea.

"Claudia was telling me that you two just started dating."

Tea from the pitcher missed the cup and splashed over Rémi's hand and the speckled granite surface of the kitchen island. "Really?"

"Yeah." Yvette looked at them. "No offense, Claudia, but I didn't think Rémi was the type to go out with older women."

"No offense taken."

Yvette fingered a slice of red pepper. "I've never met an older lesbian before."

"Claudia isn't—"

"Well now you have," Claudia said.

Their eyes met over Yvette's head, and Rémi swallowed in the face of Claudia's certainty. This was going to be interesting.

Claudia left an hour later, but not before asking Rémi out to dinner. The older woman had smiled her pleasure when Rémi accepted her invitation, throwing a flirtatious wave as she sailed out the door.

Yvette bounced out of the kitchen. "Whoa! She is hot. Where did you find her?"

"You wouldn't believe me if I told you." Rémi grabbed a beer from the fridge and sat on the couch.

"I probably would. She looks so classy. What does she want with you?"

"My luscious body?" Rémi's eyebrow rose, making the words a question.

"It looks like she wants more." Yvette sat beside Rémi, knees curled under her chin, arms wrapped around her legs. Her nosy pose.

"You think so?" Rémi looked at the door as if she could still see Claudia standing there in her elegant white fitted capri pants and matching light jacket with the peeking lace camisole that made Rémi's fingers long to wander.

"Duh." Yvette rolled her eyes.

Chapter

14

One knock and she came in. Frosted hair gleaming even in the faint darkness, dressed in her university clothes that somehow in the dim light looked tighter. The white button-down shirt clung to her slim torso, the cuffs like razors below her wrists. Black pencil skirt. Black high heels. High, high heels.

"You're in bed awfully late," she murmured, her voice a low purr that Rémi almost had to sit up in bed to hear.

Under the white sheet she was naked. Nothing new since she rarely slept in clothes. But Claudia's presence in her bedroom made her want to clutch the sheet to her chest like a Victorian virgin. She didn't. Instead she adjusted the pillow under her head and turned on her side, allowing the white cotton to fall naturally at her waist. In the doorway, Claudia's eyebrow rose.

"It *is* late," Rémi agreed. "Are you going to discipline me for my laziness?"

"That's an idea." A smile cut across Claudia's face.

She left the door open and came all the way into the bedroom. Her eyes seemed to miss nothing. Not the tightly drawn shades, or the way Rémi's nipples tightened. Certainly not the clothes that Rémi had carelessly left on the floor last night before falling into bed. Claudia bent and picked up the black slacks, not taking her eyes off Rémi. She slowly pulled the black leather belt from its loops. The rasp of leather against cotton was loud in Rémi's ears.

"Turn over. Onto your stomach."

The whip of command in her voice instantly dried Rémi's mouth. She stared at the other woman, disbelieving.

"Don't make me say it again."

Rémi turned over.

"You have a lovely ass." Fabric whispered against flesh as she came closer. "I've always admired it. Don't think I don't notice how you flaunt it in front of me. In your slacks. Tight jeans. The way you cock it up in the air on your motorcycle."

Claudia came closer until her low voice breathed against the back of Rémi's neck. She flinched when she felt the other woman reach out. But it was only to rip the sheet, with the sound of a caress, from her body.

"Don't tense up, love. I like it when you're relaxed. Yes, like that. Now there's my beautiful ass. Relax. I'm not going to do anything that you won't enjoy."

Rémi's heart thudded heavily in her ears. Sweat prickled beneath her underarms, but the sheet under her breasts, belly, and thighs felt cool.

"You look perfect like this. This sumptuous body of yours tame and waiting for me to do whatever I please."

Rémi felt Claudia's gaze over every inch of her flesh, sending a prickling sensation over her back, ass, thighs. Even the soles of her feet tingled from the visual caress. As if she were staking a claim. A cool touch glided over her ass, trailing the dividing line between the cheeks, and she flinched.

Claudia chuckled. "And I haven't even gotten started yet."

The mattress dipped as she crouched next to Rémi. The skirt was pulled taut against her thighs, and from that position Rémi could smell the interested heat of Claudia's pussy. The creeping wetness between her lower lips.

Leather whistled through the air. And only tapped at Rémi's skin. Her calf responded to the unexpected gentleness with small hairs prickling up, wanting more. A breath of relief exploded from her mouth. It was nothing. But that nothing thought came too soon. The next slap of leather wasn't so light. Nor was the next. Or the next after that. The leather against her calves, the backs of her legs. Her ass. The soles of her feet. Stinging heat and slap! The smell of the leather. An awareness of sweat, Claudia's, as she wielded the leather with growing firmness, arm swinging over Rémi, biting pain into her back. Her shoulders. Her arms. Sweet heat burning over her skin. Slap! Her own hissing breath. Claudia's deepening breathing.

Each stroke of the leather against her flesh brought heat seeping beneath Rémi's skin. It sank into her muscles, which she felt rippling with arousal across her back. The thick mounds of her ass. Down into the skin, into her pussy. Her fingers clenched around the scrolled ironwork headboard. Between her legs, her clit throbbed. It pressed into the bed, a groaning, aching need, with each lash of the belt. Her pussy felt thick with wet.

The leather belt stopped.

"You're such a good girl. Not moving. Not saying a word. I should have done this long before now." Breath kissed the back of Rémi's neck again. And she couldn't help it. She really couldn't. She pushed her aching clit into the mattress, hunting for relief.

"Don't worry, darling. I'm not finished yet."

The leather landed again. Pain began to fall down on her again. Slaps on top of slaps. Hurt on top of hurt. Her mind swam in it, then beyond to a place of glowing gold edges, a sharpening and dulling of sensation at once. Until all of Rémi's body was a pulsing mass of heat, most of it focused between her thighs.

"Open your legs."

Claudia's fingers teased her dripping slit, and Rémi made the first sound. A gasp of near relief. Spreading her. Baring her hole to the cool air. Something thick, not fingers this time, probed at the entrance to her pussy. This was not something she wanted. Rémi's mind squirmed away from the penetration but her cunt knew something she didn't. It opened. Widened. Ass tilted up to receive whatever Claudia had to give.

"Good girl," Claudia murmured and sank the dildo deep into Rémi.

It glided thickly into her, sliding inch by inch inside her tight pussy. The tightness was unfamiliar. She hadn't felt such fullness in a long time. A long time. But it felt good. Especially with the fingers on her clit as the dildo moved wetly in and out. Fucking her. Stroking her deeply on the inside, pushing pleasure irrevocably into her body until a scream hovered at the back of her throat. Waiting.

"I know you want to make noise, my darling. I know you want to come."

The dildo glided inside her. Massaging. Pressing. Fucking. The angle was perfect. Perfect.

"You have my permission."

Rémi loosened her howl. Her body broke apart, abruptly. Shattering in painful, precious pieces all over the bed and Claudia's hand. Her eyes flew open.

And Rémi woke up. She blinked at the ceiling, panting. Sweat dripped into her eyes and her mouth. Her pussy felt thick enough to burst. Between her legs was a still-dripping fountain that added to the wet spot under her ass. For the first time in her life, she had come in her sleep.

Chapter

15

This time she kept it light. No flirtation. This was no ridiculously romantic place where all she would be able to think about was creeping up under the table to nuzzle under Claudia's skirt and staying there until the waiter brought the check. Claudia looked beautiful in black slacks and a pale blue silk blouse that shimmered over her breasts as she moved. Beyond the terrace where they sat, water lapped gracefully at the sand, winking in the silver and dark of the distant half-moon.

Despite her exhaustion from a long night at the club and a restless day of not-quite-sleep, Rémi was glad to be out. The dream from this morning lay heavily on her mind and between her legs, but she tried not to let it distract her. Be calm. Be cool. Claudia wanted to try this thing with them, and it probably wouldn't get Rémi very far to invite her to a quiet corner so they could fuck each other's brains out. She tried to think of the least sexy thing she knew of.

"Remember the other evening when I came to your barbeque?" Rémi cleared her throat.

The gold bangles on Claudia's wrist tinkled as she reached for her chocolate martini and sipped. "How could I forget? You had some trouble with someone that night. That's all you said about it."

Rémi nodded then looked away from the face across the table, suddenly uncertain. She'd managed to push aside her worry about

Anderson for so long. Did she really want to bring him up now? Her eyes floated around the room.

The restaurant, attached to a five-star hotel on Miami Beach, had a vague country club feel to it with its efficient but available looking waitstaff, cream and gold furnishings, and embossed napkins and cutlery. Muted conversation and the noise of sedately handled knives and forks rang through the nearly full restaurant. The food, Claudia had assured her earlier, was amazing.

Rémi faced Claudia again. "Yeah, there's this guy, *un cochon*, trying to take away my business. That night before I came to see you, he threatened me."

"Oh my god! Are you—is everything okay?" Claudia abandoned her drink and reached across the table for Rémi's hand.

"Everything's fine. There hasn't been any sign of Anderson or his dirty tricks for weeks now."

"Why don't you call the police? I'm sure they could do something to protect you."

Rémi shrugged. "I think his threat against me was just a bluff. Something to do. What he really wants is Gillespie's, and there's no restraining order I can take out for that."

"That's true." Claudia's voice trailed off, brow wrinkling in concern as she squeezed Rémi's hand.

"I didn't tell you this to worry you. Just to share. Understand?" Rémi lightly grasped her companion's fingers, looked meaningfully into her eyes. "I can handle this asshole by myself."

"Can you?" Claudia's look was doubtful.

"Yes. I just wanted to let you know what's happening with me. Sometimes I feel like you're the only person I can talk to about important things."

Rémi realized that she had wanted to tell Claudia about this for days now. Her shoulders immediately felt lighter, as if she'd shrugged off some great weight.

"I'm glad that you trust me. Just promise if things get worse with this Anderson character, you'll go to the authorities. I don't want you to get hurt."

Rémi nodded and offered a smile. "I'll make sure to get the professionals involved."

Claudia pulled her hand away, frowning. "Why do I feel you're just saying that so I can feel better?"

"I'm not." Rémi's drew the slender fingers back between hers, brushed their knuckles with her thumb, then her lips. "I'm not."

A reluctant smile claimed Claudia's mouth. She shook her head. The serious mood at their table collapsed into dust and blew away on the scented ocean breeze beyond the terrace.

"You're just too good at this," Claudia said, her lashes low as she watched Rémi.

"At what?"

"This." She indicated her fingers still clasped in Rémi's hand. The way she leaned in close on the table, chin propped up on her fist as if she didn't want to miss a word of what would pass Rémi's lips. "Have you seduced many virgins before?"

Rémi dipped her head to answer her question, then slowly released the fingers that had begun to scratch delicate hieroglyphics in her palm. This morning's dream was beginning to come back to her again. "Seduced? I wouldn't say that. But I've had my share."

"I mean virgins to being with women, you know. Not to sex."

Rémi loved it that Claudia didn't lower her voice and duck her head as if they were talking about something dirty. "Like I said"— she smiled, allowing the tease to show—"I've had my share."

Claudia took a sip of her martini, but not before Rémi saw her answering smile. There was still something surreal about being in this place with the woman she'd wanted for as long as she knew what want was.

"I've never been with a woman. But I guess you knew that."

Rémi nodded. Her glass of wine lay near her fist, untouched. "I suspected but I didn't know for sure. There was always something about your friendship with Eden that I thought was very . . . intimate."

"Oh, shut up!" Claudia laughed, nearly spilling her drink. "Eden and I have been friends since before Warrick and I met. I've never met a straighter woman."

"I'm sure some could say the same thing about you." She rubbed the stem of the wineglass with her index finger. "Do you worry about what your friends will say when they find out you've been"— she grinned—"dining at the Y?"

"What's th—? Oh! I haven't done that yet."

The "yet" made Rémi's pussy sit up in her pants and take notice. "We'll have to fix that soon," she said, finally picking up her wine to drink. Her throat was suddenly very dry.

When the food came, they lingered over it, putting their conversation on hold to savor bites from each other's plates. Claudia's grilled trout was buttery soft on Rémi's tongue while her own lobster tasted so-so. She pushed the barely touched plate aside, but Claudia laughingly pulled it towards her, making the comment that the food from someone else's plate always tasted sweeter.

"Hm. Sounds like we're talking about sex now."

"Well, I wasn't."

"Why don't we just pretend we were?" She leaned forward with barely concealed eagerness.

Claudia rolled her eyes, but she smiled back at Rémi, looking relaxed and replete in her chair. Classical music hummed from the restaurant's hidden speakers. The sound was not at all soothing. The cello sawed in the air, buzzing in Rémi's ear like a bee she'd like to kill. But for Claudia, she ignored it.

"Eating from other people's plates . . ." Rémi paused. "Does that mean you like rimming?"

"What?" Claudia laughed loudly, attracting the glance of nearby diners. She clapped her hand over her mouth. "That's so random." The corners of her eyes crinkled as she laughed again.

"Claudia." A slightly raised male voice fell between them. "I thought that was you."

Rémi felt more than saw Claudia flinch and pull away, dropping her hand from the table where it had been playing with Rémi's.

The man was only a few feet away, but he might as well have been sitting at their table, his gaze was so focused on them. Dark slacks, cable-knit sweater with the collar of a white dress shirt sitting in its V-neck, no wedding ring, and a too-pleased smile aimed at Claudia. An annoying Brooks Brothers ad with a pretty face complete with sophisticated gray hair to match. His eyes crinkled at the corners when she stood up to greet him.

"Kincaid. Good to see you."

He kissed her cheek and held her to him for just a trifle too long. Claudia gently pulled away. Her smile drew Rémi to her feet as she introduced them.

The banker shook Rémi's hand. She remembered him now, from a night at the club almost a year ago when he was Claudia's date. "More exciting than he looked," Rémi recalled her saying.

"Good to meet you." She shook his hand.

He said something then turned back to Claudia. "If I'd known you were here earlier I would have invited you and your friend to join my party at our table.

"That's all right." Rémi spoke up as if he'd addressed her. "This is a private party."

Kincaid looked puzzled; then he peered at Rémi as if seeing her apart from Claudia for the first time. Her man-tailored shirt and blazer, the loose slacks, the possessive hand she laid on the small of Claudia's back. She could almost see the wheels turning in his head. He turned a look of surprise to Claudia.

He opened his mouth to say something, then seemed to think better of it.

Claudia lightly clasped his arm. "It was good to see you, Caid. As always."

"Ah . . . sure. I'll call you later on in the week. Maybe we can check out the opera again sometime soon." His narrowed eyes seemed to challenge Rémi. But she shrugged, smiled.

"You didn't have to do that, you know." Claudia turned to Rémi.

"What?"

"Be possessive like that. This isn't a cock fight—"

"If it was, I'd win."

Claudia rolled her eyes. "No. Seriously. I don't think that was appropriate. It wasn't flattering when Warrick did it, and it's not flattering now. Machismo was never a turn-on for me."

Rémi's lips tightened. "Sorry." She blew out a tense breath. "Does that mean we're ready for the check?"

"I think so. We can continue this conversation somewhere else."
They sat in silence until the waiter came with their check. Before
he could leave again, Claudia pulled out her purse and gave him the
bill plus tip in cash. In Claudia's car, they endured a painfully quiet
ride for several miles before Rémi, tapping her fingers impatiently
against her thigh, decisively broke it.

"I'm sorry if I offended you. Sometimes my jealousy gets the better of me." She fingered the curls at the nape of her own neck.
"Strangely enough, only when you're involved."

"Is that supposed to make me feel good?"

"No. It's supposed to end this weird tension. I want to get back to
having a good time with you. Can I?"

Claudia, neatly maneuvering the silver Audi TT through the
sparse traffic on South Bayshore Drive, glanced quickly at her before refocusing on the road. Her hand tightened on the steering
wheel, and the small muscles in her arms jumped. Rémi watched
them, mesmerized.

"Warrick used to do that all the time. But it didn't mean anything." She changed gears and the car sped up. "He'd pretend jealousy when we were out with other people or even when we got
home. But there was no affection for me behind it. I was a possession
he wanted to have all to himself." Her eyes slanted at Rémi. "After a
while he didn't even take me out of the box to play with me."

Rémi felt the shock of Claudia's words settle into her chest. "I
didn't know."

"It's okay. How could you?" Her hand drifted down to Rémi's
thigh and squeezed. "By the way." The hand moved higher up, settling on Rémi's hip, just under her jacket. "Rimming is not quite my
scene. I've had it done to me before and it's not bad. I mean, you're
cleaning my bottom. I could have done that with a piece of tissue."

Rémi glanced at her with a surprised smile. "I'll remember that."

By the time they arrived at the house, tension had all but disappeared between them. Claudia unlocked the door and walked in
ahead of her.

"Can I get you a drink?"

She turned back to look at Rémi as she walked down the short hallway leading into the living room.

"No thanks." Rémi wasn't quite sure what to do with herself at this point. If it had been anyone else, there would have been no hesitation on her part. But . . .

Claudia cocked a hand on her hip. "You sure? Don't you know that it's required to drink whatever your date offers you at the end of the evening?"

Rémi's footsteps slowed on the way to the couch. "Oh? In that case I'll have some of whatever you have cold in the fridge."

"Good girl." Claudia smiled.

Rémi took off her jacket and lay back on the couch, dropped her head back, closing her eyes. Warrick hadn't taken her out of the box to play in a long time. Surprising. And cruel. How long had it been since Claudia felt someone else's passionate touch? Had it been that bourgie fucker at the restaurant?

Something cold and wet fell against her cheek. Rémi opened her eyes. Above her, Claudia held a sweating bottle of gold liquid. Sol. A Mexican beer she'd mentioned in passing was her favorite. Rémi smiled. Claudia never failed to make her feel special, no matter how simple the gesture. Another droplet from the beer bottle fell near her mouth. She reached for it.

"Again, sorry about what happened in the restaurant." Claudia sat beside Rémi on the couch. "I shouldn't have reacted like that. You don't deserve any of the anger I have left for Warrick." Claudia's fingers teased Rémi's throat, tracing the path the beer took as she drank.

"I know about leftover resentment. Consider earlier forgotten"—Rémi closed her eyes to savor Claudia's touch on her skin—"except the good parts, of course."

"Oh yes. The good parts. My favorite." Claudia gently tugged the beer from Rémi's hand and tasted it. The face she made surprised a laugh from Rémi. She returned the bottle and reached for her glass, sparkling with white wine on the low coffee table.

"Mine too." She put the beer on the table and reached for Claudia. "Do you think we can continue where we left off?"

The seductive warmth came, draped over her lap, straddled Rémi with temptation in her smile.

"I'm sure we could," Claudia said. "Maybe even a little farther." With one hand, she deftly undid the top button of Rémi's shirt. Then another. She sipped the wine, then, holding the glass delicately, she leaned in to kiss Rémi.

The slim body pressed against hers, a barely there warmth, soft lips, and the cool trickle of wine into Rémi's mouth. Sweet. The wine was sweet with a hint of raspberries and the lingering flavor of trout from Claudia's tongue. Rémi swallowed. Dropped her head back against the couch. Was it possible that Claudia wanted it as badly as Rémi did? Did she spend nights imagining their sex, fingers between her thighs, a yawning explosion bubbling up in her belly? Rémi's hands settled on Claudia's back, just above her bottom.

"I—"

They both flinched when the doorbell rang.

"What were you going to say?"

Rémi smiled. "Nothing that can't wait."

Claudia looked down at her with doubt, pecked her briefly on the mouth before pulling away. "Some things aren't meant to wait," she said.

"Like what?"

But the other woman was already padding barefoot across the cherry hardwood toward the door. Rémi sipped her beer. If Claudia meant what Rémi thought. . . . She paused with the bottle halfway to her mouth at the sound of the masculine voice that answered in response to Claudia's musical, "Who is it?"

Rémi refastened the top two buttons on her shirt as the front door opened.

"Is this a bad time?"

"I am busy at the moment, yes."

Warrick—Rémi recognized his voice now—didn't seem put off by his ex-wife's tone. If anything, it seemed to amuse him. When he walked into the living room just ahead of Claudia, his eyes gleaming with curiosity, Rémi didn't bother to stand up. His eyes widened when he saw her sitting on the couch.

"It's just you, Rémi." His smile spread wide. "From the way Claudia sounded I thought she had a man in here or something. Nice to see you, by the way. You look good. Prosperous."

Rémi wanted to ask him what he thought the "or something" was. "Thank you," she said.

"What can I do for you, Warrick? I didn't expect to see you tonight."

Something drifted across his face before he turned to Claudia. "I finished my conference a little early and I thought I might come by and say hello."

"Calling first would have been the polite thing to do."

"There's too much between us for it to all boil down to politeness, Claude." His glance flickered to Rémi again. "I thought you'd have time to have a drink with me tonight."

"I'm already having drinks."

"I see that."

A shadow passed over his brow again as he looked at the coffee table with the glass of wine and Rémi's beer. Claudia's black high heels lying beneath it. Rémi forced herself not to wipe at her mouth to get rid of the lipstick stains she suspected lay there.

A muscle in his jaw flexed. "In that case, can I get that case I left when I came to see you last time? I'll just get it and go."

"Oh—ah yes. Sure." Claudia glanced at him, wide-eyed, as if surprised he was giving in so easily. "I think I remember where I put it. Give me a second."

He and Rémi both watched Claudia disappear up the stairs.

Warrick turned to Rémi. "The last time I saw you, you were in high school. And you had long hair."

"That's true."

"Now here you are." The blade in his glance was out in the open now.

"Here I am."

He dropped his hands in his pockets. "Are you fucking my wife?"

My wife? Rémi's eyebrow rose. "I haven't been to California in a long time, so I doubt that."

"Don't be stupid. You know what I mean."

Rémi revealed part of a smile. "I don't think anything I do is any of your business."

Pulling his hands from his pockets, Warrick stepped closer. "Didn't your daddy tell you not to play with men's things?"

All of her smile burst out and Rémi relaxed even deeper in the chair. "I can see that your mama didn't teach you any manners. Ladies deserve respect. I think we can both agree that Claudia is a lady not a *thing.*"

Bare footsteps slapping against the stairs warned them both of Claudia's impending return. Warrick put his hands back into his pockets and walked past the sofa, stopping at the window, seeming to stare at the garden hidden in darkness outside.

"Here is the case, Warrick." Claudia slipped back into the room, a cool smile on her lips.

She passed Rémi, brushing a hand along the back of the sofa, to give her ex-husband the brown leather case. An inaudible rumble came from Warrick.

"There's nothing for us to talk about privately. Especially not now. Call me later if you have something to say."

Rémi couldn't hold back her smile. A real one this time. As Warrick walked past her, his back a stiff line under the dark blue blazer, she called out, "Nice to see you again, Mr. Nichols." His lack of response didn't surprise her.

Claudia walked in from the hallway after Warrick left, looking at Rémi with a puzzled frown. "What was that about?"

"He asked me if I was fucking his wife."

"He did what?" Claudia stopped in her tracks, stared at Rémi to see if she was telling the truth, then seeing the lack of a lie in her face, turned around and flew toward the door and her ex-husband.

"No, no, it's okay." Rémi said, not bothering to rush to Claudia's side and prevent her from going after Warrick.

He was already gone. "What was his purpose in asking you that question?" Claudia came back into the living room, hand on her hip.

"To make sure the Ethiopian beauty wasn't cheating on him?" Months ago, Dez told Rémi about her father's new wife and how hot she was. How Rémi would have enjoyed playing with her.

A smile trembled and fell off Claudia's face. As if it suddenly occurred to her what his knowing about them really meant.

"Do you think he'll tell Derrick?"

"Do you think your son will love you any less if he knows you're fucking me?"

"Maybe."

"No." Rémi pulled Claudia down into her lap. "He can be a prick but he's not that hopeless."

"You're probably right." Claudia crossed her arms behind Rémi's head and pressed herself closer. "Let's not talk about my son. I'll have to deal with him and Desiree soon enough."

And that was all right with Rémi. Claudia's anger at her earlier show of jealousy had cut through her like lightning, frying her senses with its uncharacteristic intensity and leaving her insides shuddering from the aftershocks. But the anger hadn't come because of Rémi, but rather from Claudia's ex. And then Warrick himself walked through the door, interrupting what might have gone on despite the mini explosion at the restaurant. Women with baggage. She'd always warned her friends to stay away from those, and now here she was. Her mouth tightened at the irony. And Claudia licked it, chasing the curves with her tongue.

"Forget about everything. Except for us."

Claudia's hands cupped the back of Rémi's head, fingers sliding through the curls and raking shudders up Rémi's back. The scent of apples pressed into her senses, and she sighed. Sweet kisses glided across her mouth, her jaw, down to her throat, and she gave into them, gladly. The slight back flared with heat under her palms. Claudia kissed her, teased her lips with small bites and licks, controlling every movement of Rémi's body as she bit, pulled away, teasing with her warm breath and hot mouth until Rémi leaned forward with each retreat of Claudia's mouth, reaching for more of the warmth, the flicking tongue.

Claudia's back was firm under her palms. Firm and hot. A fine tremor began inside Rémi when slim fingers dropped to her belt and began to unbuckle it. Hot breath licked at her ear.

"I think I'm ready for my dessert now."

The whisper touched Rémi like a caress. Her clit bucked inside her pants, and a hot itch, wetness flooding over her pussy lips, made her press her legs together and bite back a moan. She grabbed Claudia's arms. Unbuckled now, her belt gaped open, Claudia's fingers slid past the waistband of her briefs, skimmed through her pussy hairs, cupped her clit.

Sweet Jesus! When Claudia moved down Rémi's body, her intent clear in the way she eyed Rémi's swollen clit framed in the V of her zipper, her brain went into overload. Time stopped.

The doorbell rang.

Don't answer it! "Please don't answer it," she rasped.

Hot breath misted her clit. Her eyelashes fluttered. Fingers dug into Claudia's shoulder.

The ringing came again. Then whoever it was started to bang on the door. Someone shouted. Warrick. Claudia catapulted from Rémi's lap as if someone had yanked a string inside her.

Rémi hissed. "Fuck!"

"I'm sorry," Claudia said. She stood up and backed away, her eyes wide with annoyance, and perhaps, Rémi thought, a little relief. She padded toward the front door.

Rémi squeezed her eyes shut. Breathed slowly from parted lips, stood up, zipped and buckled her pants, pulled her jacket on. Anger and thwarted arousal warred equally for the tremor in her limbs. She scraped a hand across her face and breathed deeply again. With a quick glance toward the hallway where Claudia had just disappeared, she considered leaving through the back door.

Claudia's ex-husband stood in the doorway, bristling in his suit, the briefcase he'd come for earlier nowhere in sight.

"Mr. Nichols," Rémi bared her teeth at him as she came up behind Claudia. "What a pleasant surprise."

"I doubt it," he said, greeting her smile with a dismissive glance at her hastily tucked-in shirt.

She lightly touched the small of Claudia's back. "I have to go."

"I thought it might be a bit past your bedtime. Isn't it a school night?"

Rémi didn't bother responding to Warrick's taunts. "We can finish our conversation another time, Claudia. Call me."

Then, brushing the other woman's cheek with her own, Rémi stepped past Warrick Nichols and left the house.

Chapter

16

Despite leaving Warrick behind at Claudia's house, Rémi still managed to take him with her on the ride home. She couldn't stop thinking about him and his two appearances at Claudia's door. What was it that made a man who'd walked out on his family come back again? Not to reclaim that family but to prevent someone else from . . . from doing what? Did he think that Rémi would hurt Claudia, or was it more primitive than that? He just didn't want another cock—and Rémi did think of herself as one in this instance—slipping into the henhouse he had once called his home. Even though he'd been in California for over ten years, remarried for most of them, and replaced his old set of twins with a new child, Warrick still thought of Claudia as his.

Home. No matter how we move on, Rémi thought, the old home lingers in all of us, affecting our present day actions, warping reflections, turning our footsteps again and again toward the past.

She knew all too well that bittersweet ache when faced with familiar voices, people, even hurts that had played a large part in your life and helped define who and what you are. Rémi understood being an exile from those familiar things, but Warrick had exiled himself.

Despite his appearance at the house and her hostility toward him, Rémi wasn't jealous; she'd felt more jealousy toward that Kincaid fool. Claudia would never go back to Warrick. He had hurt her so badly in the past that Rémi wasn't worried about him being any real competition for the older woman's affections. And if the past wasn't enough to make Claudia stay away from him, his ex-wife at least had recent lovers—Kincaid, Rémi, even a tweed-coated professor type with the look of a seasoned pervert who Rémi had once seen her with—that had given her a taste of happiness and made her feel special as a woman. No. Warrick wasn't a threat, simply an annoyance.

At the condo, Yvette was still up and watching a *Project Runway* rerun. In the otherwise dark apartment, the acid gray light flickered over her sister's form curled under a blanket on the couch, palm cupped under her cheek, head propped up on a cushion.

"Hey," Yvette greeted, barely moving.

"Hey."

Rémi dropped her keys into the bowl on the shelf and sat on the couch near her sister's feet. Yvette curled up even more to make room for her, looking briefly at her face before turning back to the TV. On the screen, the designers were being criticized by the judges, their hard work ravaged in front of a salivating TV audience.

"Everything okay?"

"Mostly," Rémi answered.

She stared at the television, eyes blind to everything on the screen. The idea of exile still echoed in her head.

Rémi reached out, put her hand on her sister's feet. "Tell me about home," she said.

Yvette looked at her in surprise. She sat up, and the blanket fell away from her shoulders and pooled at her waist. Yvette opened her mouth as if to ask why. Then closed it. In the gray almost-darkness, her eyes sought out Rémi's face before she reached for the remote and turned off the television. Silence, darkness blanketed the room.

"Except for Daddy not being home, things are mostly the same," she said with sadness tucked into the corners of her voice. "Mama works in the garden a lot. René is really into astronomy."

Their life came to Rémi as clearly as if she'd been there. The house on a hill in Boothbay Harbor, with the rippling blue ribbon of the bay stretching out behind it. In the garden outside, exploding with roses and peonies, Kelia knelt in the dirt and pulled at weeds with her gloved hands while a jean-clad child sat on the back porch, legs swinging over its edge as she occasionally looked up from her book to glance at her mother. Another girl, younger, lay on the porch swing, eyes trained on the painful blue of the sky. In the kitchen, Auguste moved between the stove and counters, steam rising up from multiple pots to dampen the edges of the light brown hair that he kept military short. There were few things he hated worse than hair in food. But wait, that was before. Before he left. Before *they* left for Miami and became the splintered thing that Rémi knew now.

Rémi breathed easily through her mouth. Yes, home was an irresistible place. Difficult to escape, impossible to go back to.

Chapter
17

"I'm glad you were able to come to dinner with me tonight."

"You made it hard to refuse. Dinner, music, the pleasure of your company." Claudia smiled up at Rémi as she walked past her and through the office door with the hem of her dark blue dress fluttering at her calves like a mermaid's tail. "Privacy to do as I like without interruption."

Rémi's mouth tightened at that reminder of her ex's visit the last time they were together. She had made sure to clean up the office before inviting Claudia to come up and spend the evening with her, putting all the paperwork, clothes, and toys out of the way. The large room looked almost empty with the large double doors at its rear leading to the bedroom firmly closed. Before leaving to pick up Claudia, she set up a small dining table before the smoked glass wall with its view of the stage and the restaurant's main room below.

Tonight it was a local group, the Sonia Hui Trio. The mellow sounds of the piano and violin, background to Sonia's vocals, barely trickled into the office through the soundproof walls.

"This is very nice, Rémi. The view is even better than I'd imagined. I knew there was something interesting up here, but never imagined this." Her eyes seemed to swallow up the crowded restaurant below and the perfect view of the stage. The spotlighted Sonia crooned to the respectfully quiet crowd while the waitstaff moved unobtrusively between tables, dropping off food and seeing to the customers' comfort. "Things certainly look different from up here."

The office stood high up and jutted out slightly above the main floor of the club, affording an even more intimate view of the stage. From out there, no one could see into the dark office, even when the curtains lay open as they were now, and Claudia stood with her nose practically pressed against the glass. Only reflections of the club's interior showed in the two-way mirrored surface.

Rémi stepped close to the other woman and pressed a button on the other side of Claudia's hand. Their quiet disappeared. The sound from the stage instantly filled the room—Sonia's gravelly voice, the hushed seduction of the violin. With the speakers now on, she didn't bother to step back. The proximity felt too good.

"It feels very right to be here." Claudia slowly dropped her head back, making more of Rémi's accidental contact.

Rémi's skin jumped. Although she'd been the one to step closer, to tempt herself when she knew she wasn't ready, she realized abruptly that she couldn't handle it. Claudia's pale hair smelled of shampoo. The contact scorched Rémi's belly and thighs. Helplessly, she brushed her hands up Claudia's arms stretched wide along the ledge. Hot silk. She took in a deep breath of scent, then abruptly drew back.

Claudia nearly stumbled at the sudden withdrawal and looked back at Rémi, her eyes dark pools of maybes. Her fingers gripped Rémi's tie, deep green silk against a fine-boned hand. Then she changed her mind about whatever she was going to do, released Rémi, and turned her gaze back to the view beyond the glass.

"Thank you for inviting me into your inner sanctum," she said. "I'm honored."

Rémi forced her mind from what she really wanted to dwell on, what she really wanted to do. Her hands were like an empty pot still on the fire, waiting for something to fill it. She focused on what Claudia just said. The truth was that too many women had been allowed into the set of rooms. Invitations to join Rémi behind the glass wall weren't as rare as they should have been. But that wasn't something that she wanted to think about. Claudia was here. For the first time.

And that was what made the evening special. Still, Rémi had no plans on taking her behind the double doors to the large bedroom beyond. That place was too common for Claudia.

"I'm working tonight," Rémi said abruptly. "Things could get busy. But I still wanted to see you."

"Does that mean there will be many interruptions?"

"Not necessarily. It could be a pretty calm night, but on the other hand . . ." She shrugged.

"I see." Before the glass, Claudia slowly unwound the black lace wrap from her neck and shoulders while Rémi watched, mesmerized. The spaghetti strap dress, royal blue and cowl-necked, dipped low in the front, its loose neckline treating Rémi to a vision of the wide valley between her breasts. She wasn't wearing a bra. The skin, lightly dusted with what looked to Rémi like gold flecks, winked under the soft lighting, inviting touches. Kisses.

A knock at the office door shook her concentration from that strip of flesh. And she cleared her throat before moving away, surreptitiously wiping moist palms against her thighs, to answer it.

"Come in."

Monique slid through the door Rémi held open for her. The waitress held a wide silver platter in strong arms and, after only the barest glance at Claudia, set it on the rectangular table already dressed with a white tablecloth and four unlit candles at its edges. As if she were presenting herself as well as the food.

While Rémi watched, Monique carefully unloaded two beautifully arranged plates, bending over to show the sleek line of her backside in the pinstriped black skirt and her spine straight under the tuxedo-style vest and starched white shirt. Claudia caught Rémi's eye. She looked away, flushing with irrational guilt. The plates, fragrant with their burdens of black quinoa flavored with golden raisins and slivers of almonds, seeded olives and sweet carrots simmered in maple syrup and olive oil, gently kissed the table before Monique straightened. She turned, nodded slightly, eyes on the floor, belly breathing gently under the pearlescent buttons of her shirt. The smile lay across her face like a purple stain.

"Thank you," Rémi said.

And the woman turned from them to quietly leave the office. Her pouting footsteps muffled in the thick carpet. Then the quiet click of the door closing.

"Is she one of your girlfriends?" Claudia asked, peering down at the plates.

Rémi shrugged off her jacket and draped it over the back of one of the chairs. How to handle this one? She pulled a bottle of merlot from the wine rack built into a cubby in the wall. "I don't have girlfriends."

"Make sure you tell her next time you sleep with her. Just so her eyes won't look so . . . helpless next time they see us together."

Next time. Rémi smiled, setting the bottle along with two glasses on the table. "I'll make sure to do that." She lit the candles.

Claudia's eyes danced wickedly in the soft light. She glanced around the room. "This is a pretty stage for a seduction."

"Hardly that. Just dinner. Music. A little conversation."

"Really? That's a pity." Without waiting for Rémi to pull out her chair, she sat at the table and kicked off her shoes. "Maybe after a good meal and a few glasses of wine, you'll change your mind."

Rémi laughed, clamping down on the nervous edge that crept into her voice. "You never know."

She stood above Claudia, pouring the wine in their glasses like a maître d'. "Although I like to think I know what your normal tastes are, I took a chance that you might like this. Rochelle has not failed me yet. I told her what you like to eat, and she whipped this up for us. I hope you enjoy it."

"I'm sure I will. Sit. You're making me nervous with all that hovering."

Rémi sat. "That's the last thing I'd ever want to do."

"I know." Claudia reached across the table and palmed Rémi's cheek. "I'm just teasing you, darling."

Her blush was immediate. *Darling?* Claudia peeked at her from between short, spiky lashes. *Oh, yes you are,* her eyes said.

"You are such a delight. On the best of days you make this old fool feel desired again."

"There's never been anything old or foolish about you."

"Some would disagree. Especially now."

"Fuck them." Rémi picked up her fork, inviting Claudia to do the same.

"That's what I'm starting to think now, too."

She pressed the firm grains of quinoa between her tongue and palate, keeping her eyes on Claudia. "Good. You can't live for anyone but yourself." A raisin coated her tongue with sweetness.

Claudia nodded and bit into a maple-sweetened baby carrot. She made a noise of surprised pleasure and reached for another carrot. "Rochelle is an angel. You must do whatever you need to keep her." Her fork glinted in the candlelight as it came back empty from between her lips. "How she keeps turning out this heavenly food is a mystery."

"My theory is that her husband keeps her very happy. Once you're happy at home everything else seems like a breeze." Rémi smiled. "Again, only a theory."

"One that I might have to dispute. When Warrick and I were married and everything was falling apart, I spent a lot of time outside of the house doing nearly everything—sometimes very well—just so I wouldn't have to come home too soon."

"Really? You always seemed so happy to me. All I remember about the divorce was that you were so quiet. Then again, I had just really met you."

"I kept the tears locked in my bedroom in those days."

"And now?"

"Now there are only a few tears and they are very occasional."

Rémi watched her face, remembering its cold lines when Warrick had come back to the house on Friday night.

"What did Warrick want when he came back to see you the other night?"

"I wondered when, or if, you would ask."

"I've been thinking about it. A lot. But trying not to."

"It was nothing," Claudia said. "He was trying to piss on his territory again; he just needed to be reminded that his wife is in California, not here." She paused. "I'm sorry you had to go."

With that, Rémi was prepared to be generous. "Maybe he's just surprised about us."

"He doesn't want me to be happy and that's the truth of it. Whether it's you or Kincaid, it doesn't matter." Claudia waved her fork in the air. "I told him to go back to his wife and leave me in peace."

"Hopefully then, that'll be the end of that."

Claudia made a dismissive noise, shrugging her shoulders.

Rémi wanted to tell Claudia that she would never put her in a box, would never leave her lust unsatisfied, would always play with her and be there for her as long as Claudia wanted. Instead, Rémi reached across the table and wiped a grain of quinoa from the corner of Claudia's mouth.

Everything stopped. They breathed together, carefully. They picked at their food, watching each other over forks and the muted sounds of chewing. With the candlelight around her, Claudia glowed bronze and sphinx-like, a creature from another world. A world Rémi very much wanted to be apart of.

Rémi's phone rang, effectively breaking the mood. She answered the gently voiced question from the hostess downstairs at Gillespie's front door.

"No, if he doesn't have a reservation he can't jump in line in front of people who do. Please extend my regrets."

The girl murmured her assent and thanks. Rémi hung up the phone.

"Sorry about that."

Claudia smiled. "It's okay."

Rémi picked up her wineglass. "Now, where were we?"

Neither could remember, but they swam back into the depths of conversation. Nothing serious. Their words edged around the thick issue of their attraction to each other, meandering along the safe routes of Claudia's students, her teaching, how it felt for her to be back in the classroom again after a year's leave and illness. Then Rémi got tired of being safe.

"You know, the first time I saw you, I thought I was dreaming."

Claudia bit into an olive, eyebrows slanted in question. After all, weren't they just talking about school? She chewed the olive, and Rémi followed the motion of her lips around the green fruit.

"When you came to our house for dinner that first night after school?"

"Oh, no." Rémi gently touched the rim of her glass, wiped her finger along the smear of wine left by her mouth. "It was weeks before that."

She remembered the day vividly. Like most memories she had of Claudia, it was as clear as cut glass. That day, waiting for her mother to come pick her up after a school field trip to Surfside, Rémi sat on a low wall, halfheartedly reading a book she had a test on in class later that week. Rémi hardly recalled what the novel was about, only that when she looked up toward the roundabout in front of the school, a woman stood next to a car, looking as if she'd stepped out of a book: black kinks cut close to her head, elfin features, wearing what Rémi recognized now as an A-line dress, sleeveless and white vintage 1950s, with high-heeled shoes.

She walked around to the passenger side of the car and reached for something through the open window before going back to stand by the front bumper. With her gaze hidden behind dark glasses, the woman seemed to be watching for someone to come through the high school's front doors. She put something to her mouth, and in that moment Rémi thought it was a cigarette, but as the woman put one slender hand in her pocket and turned her head in the haloing sunlight, she realized it was a carrot stick.

After the carrots were finished—Rémi watched, enthralled with each movement of her mouth—the woman raised a hand to shield her eyes from the sun and continued to watch the school doors. What struck Rémi then was that Claudia's mouth was so relaxed, and even while waiting in repose, seemed to have just the smallest hint of a smile. And when she spotted the people she was waiting for, a girl and boy, obviously hers, the suggestion of a smile became more. Teeth flashed. The hand left her pocket to wave at and to receive her children. Everything about her shouted love.

"I never saw you," Claudia said.

"I know."

It was a happy coincidence that Dez and Rémi became friends not long after. The first time she walked into her friend's house and saw Claudia, she tripped over her own feet. Claudia's smile turned on her with a gently voiced, "Careful," and Rémi couldn't imagine anywhere else she'd rather be.

Rémi cleared her throat and reached for the wine bottle. "It was a long time ago. I've changed a lot since then."

Claudia pursed her lips, watching Rémi refill her glass. "And change is a good thing."

"Why, Mrs. Nichols, are you saying that you prefer me chasing after you instead of mooning from afar?"

"Absolutely. I prefer directness."

"In that case," Rémi murmured. "Come here."

Claudia's eyebrow went up. Their eyes dueled for control from across the table with the candlelight flickering over Claudia's tamarind skin and curved mouth. Rémi waited. When Claudia finally pushed her chair back, she sighed inside. With shaking hands, she pushed her own chair back, stood up, moved the chair away from the table, then sat back down.

"Sit in my lap." The voice felt rough in her throat. "Please."

Claudia sat, perched sideways in her respectable dress that Rémi longed to get under. The dark blue spill of cloth over Rémi's black slacks pulled her stomach tight. It was the most erotic thing she'd ever seen.

"Now that I'm here, what do you need?"

Rémi smiled without humor. "I want to touch you."

She wanted to take it slow. There was something she wanted more. To gaze in appreciation of Claudia's dress draped like a piece of loose silk over her small breasts, the sighing softness of the strip of flesh between, the texture of her shoulder under Rémi's fingers. But the moment she lifted her hands to Claudia's waist, felt the waiting anticipation in the other woman, she was lost. A groan pulled itself from the soles of Rémi's feet, scraping through her thighs, her pussy, beneath her nipples, and out of her mouth.

"Claudia."

Her mouth was spiced heat. Quinoa and passion. Wine and salva-
tion. Claudia kissed Rémi back as if she were drowning. As if she
wanted this connection of flesh more than anything. More than
Rémi wanted it. Hands gripped Rémi's hair, tongue slid wetly
against hers. Panting breaths. Claudia groaned too, pushed her skirt
up higher on her thighs and swung around to straddle Rémi in the
chair. The smell of her pussy breathed into Rémi's nose.

"You taste so good!" Claudia gasped in wonder.

Rémi shoved her hands away to get at the dress. The straps fell
into her hands, scraped down Claudia's arms to reveal her. Rémi
stopped. Breath hitching in her throat. Panting small, disbelieving
breaths. So perfect. The dress pooled at Claudia's waist, framing the
most perfect breasts she had ever seen. Small with tips like dark
chocolate kisses. They moved gently with each breath Claudia took,
lifting and falling above her curving ribs. Rémi licked her lips.

"If you don't touch me soon," Claudia rasped, pressing her fingers to Rémi's head, "I'm going to do something drastic."

"I—"

But Claudia pushed Rémi's mouth against the hard nipple and
she sighed, opened her mouth over it, and was lost again. The desire
in her body, warring with everything else, took over. It was just a
woman's breast. But it wasn't. Her tongue cupped the rough nipple,
licked it. Sucked until Claudia sighed. Rémi trembled, forcing herself to slow. The dizzying smell of Claudia's pussy, the soft gasps
above her head, the squirming femaleness on her lap. Her senses
went up in flames. Still she was careful. She cupped Claudia's ass,
pulled her closer, kneaded the soft flesh. Shaking, shaking on the inside.

"You touch me like I'm going to break." Claudia pressed her finger against Rémi's mouth. "I won't, you know."

But Rémi didn't know. She wanted to ravage her. Eat her up,
drink and fuck and take until they were both a trembling mass on
the floor, but she didn't want to hurt Claudia. Didn't want to damage
this precious thing.

"Fuck me."

The hot whisper exploded inside Rémi like a flare.

Rémi's mouth immediately reclaimed a nipple, covering the small breast with her hot and thirsty mouth. Her teeth scraped them. Claudia hissed. She wet two fingers and slipped them inside Claudia, her forearm shaking with restraint.

"Deeper." Claudia gasped softly. "Please."

Whatever she wanted. Whatever she needed. That's what Rémi would give.

She went deeper and the pussy swallowed her fingers, squeezing them. Beautiful. She was so beautiful. The moment swirled in Rémi's head. She heard the chair groan with their movements, felt the air move as Claudia flung her head back.

Music from the stage still poured in through the speakers, weaving jazz and magic through the other music of Claudia's groans. Her legs widened over Rémi's thighs. Her fingers dug into Rémi's shoulder. Soft "oh"s tumbled from her mouth with each dive and shallow of fingers, each slide of Rémi's thumb over her thick clit. The smell of her cunt made Rémi's mouth water. Claudia was close. Her breath hitching in her throat, sweat coating the graceful lines of her face. She wanted to touch her more. Wanted to get access to all of her skin, all of her passion. Rémi glanced quickly around. Not the desk. Or the table. But the floor . . .

Still fucking Claudia with her fingers, Rémi lifted them both out of the chair to the floor. Her clit ached to feel Claudia's against it. To feel anything but this frustrating lack of contact. But as soon as Claudia's back met the carpet, Rémi growled, forgetting about her own needs. Her mouth swam, anticipating the taste of wet pussy. She shoved the dress up, sweeping her thighs wider apart. The pussy smell, hot, salty, and intoxicating, made her dizzy.

"Open your legs wider for me. I want to see you."

They fell wider still, and Rémi almost cried. So fucking hot. Her entire body shook with want. How could she need something this much and not die without it? She opened her mouth hungrily over Claudia's pussy. Something in her pounded, knocked hard at the rightness of now, holding her thighs open as she fed on the steaming cunt. Plunged her tongue into the salty, wet hole. As the fingers resting against her head urged her on.

But Claudia tugged at her hair, pulling away from the streaming fount. No, that wasn't the way to do it. She wanted to tell Claudia, but her mouth was full.

"The door!" Claudia whispered hoarsely. "There's someone at the door."

They could wait. Everything could wait but this. She vaguely heard someone else call her name, but since it wasn't Claudia, they didn't matter. Nothing else mattered.

"Emergency—it sounds—oh!" Her thighs trembled around Rémi's ears. "Important!"

Rémi pulled her ears away from the sounds of Claudia's voice. Her moans. The suck and release of her pussy around Rémi's tongue. The knock on the door came. Harder. "Fuck." She pulled away from the heady smell of the pussy. Stood up panting and helped Claudia to her feet. Her own pussy twitched. With a low growl, she grabbed the napkin off the table and wiped her mouth before going to the door.

"Yes?"

Tamika, one of the waitresses, stood in the doorway looking as if she wanted to sink into the floor. "I'm sorry, Rémi, but we have a situation downstairs." She swallowed. "There's a guy, he—can you please come?"

She looked quickly behind her to Claudia, who smoothed her dress down over her thighs.

"I'll be right back," she said to Claudia.

But "right back" wasn't the way it turned out. A hulking football player and tourist had decided that he wanted one of the waitresses even though she told him more than once that she wasn't going to give it to him for free or otherwise. The six-foot-six musclehead insisted, and when the bouncers forced him to see the error of his ways, spraining his wrist in the process, the hulk started to shout about suing the club and everyone connected to it.

By the time Rémi soothed him, brought him into Elena's office for a private discussion and consultation from a staff member with knowledge of first aid, then sent him on his way, over two hours had passed. Rémi went upstairs expecting to find Claudia gone, but instead, when she walked into her darkened office, the other woman lay curled up on the black velvet couch, her lace scarf draped over her throat and her bare feet curled up on the sofa.

She crouched down. "Claudia." When the other woman opened her eyes, Rémi smoothed a thumb down her silky jawline. "Sorry about that. I didn't think it would take that long."

Claudia blinked the sleep out of her eyes. Smiled groggily. "It's all right, honey. You're doing your job."

"Still . . ." Rémi sighed. She had wanted so much to make love with her. But they say everything happens for a reason, right? "Come, let me take you home. It's late."

Claudia looked into her face. Whatever she saw there made her nod. "Okay."

She sat up, found her purse, and slid her feet in her shoes. Before she could do anything else, Rémi scooped her into her arms, holding her close, sank her nose into the fragrant curve of her neck. She took her down the back stairs that led directly to the parking lot. With some tricky maneuvering, she got the truck door open and gently put Claudia in the passenger seat.

"I'll make it up to you," she said.

Claudia snuggled into the leather seat. "You certainly will."

Rémi smiled. Moments later, she dropped Claudia off with a soft kiss before driving back to the club. Walking into her office, she sighed and rubbed the back of her neck. Managing the club was turning out to be much more intrusive in her life than she first thought. Maybe it was time to hire someone else. Or give Elena a raise when she came back to work.

"You look a little tense."

Rémi stiffened at the low voice that uncoiled from the darkness. On the couch, stretched out in the exact spot Claudia just left, lay Monique. The waitress had fully unbuttoned her top to show off the lace-edged black bra and the breasts overflowing it.

"What are you doing in here?"

Monique adjusted her bare legs against the leather, thighs sprawled to pull her skirt up even higher, showing that she wore nothing underneath. "To see if I can do anything for you."

Hands on hips, Rémi straightened, feeling her vertebrae pop one after the other, and took a deep breath. It was almost three o'clock. Beyond the glass wall, the club still hummed with activity although the stage was clear and shut down for the night and only the piano on the second floor still pumped music into the low-lit space. At this time of the evening, only those who intended to make Gillespie's their last stop remained. People still ate, the conversation still flowed, but on a much lower key. Romance sat between couples under the dim lights, comfortable singles entertained themselves with the bartenders. It was a lull that Rémi often enjoyed by herself long after her friends had gone on to less leisurely pursuits.

Sometimes it was good to sit in her darkened office, hearing Magnus on the piano while she settled into her bones. Into the quiet of the place that she owned. A place no one could expel her from. Tonight wasn't one of those nights. She turned to Monique.

"Get up."

The blood still throbbed inside her veins for Claudia. The pulse still beat thickly between her thighs. It was subdued before, but at the sight of Monique, it began raging again. The waitress, confident and sexy in the high heels, white shirt unbuttoned, the skirt already halfway pulled up her thighs, breasts offered up like fruit to Rémi's eyes and hands. But she didn't want anything so obvious. Not right now. Her eyes glittered with what looked like triumph in the darkened room. Rémi relit the candles from the aborted dinner with Claudia, scraped the plates, food and all, into the waste bin; she shoved the bin away.

"Here."

The word puffed from her mouth, a bull's hot breath.

Monique came and Rémi shoved her roughly forward over the table. The candles shuddered on its surface. The waitress gasped, grabbed the edge of the table, her ass a thick curve under her skirt. Rémi could already feel her excited breath, the way the skin already trembled beneath its clothes in anticipation of Rémi's hard touch.

"Pull down your skirt."

The last word was barely past her lips before Monique fumbled back, undid her skirt, and tugged it down past her ass to let it drop around her ankles and shoes. She kicked it away and stood, legs apart, breath coming harder. With a strong tug, Rémi pulled the white blouse from her back, unhooked the bra, leaving Monique bare, just the smooth expanse of back and her ass in the tiny lace panties. Thwarted lust swam in Rémi's veins. Claudia. Claudia. Claudia. That was who she wanted, but Monique's body flexed against the table, ass pushing back against Rémi again, reminding her what was close rather than desired. The thick pussy lips opened even more under the dark lace, sucking wetly at the fabric.

She'd wanted to make love to Claudia in this room, show her what fifteen years of pent-up lust could do. But instead she was here. Monique was here. The waitress's back twitched when the first drip of wax hit. She hissed. The white wax dipped into the hills and valleys of her back, forming a lake swimming toward the trough of her spine. The flame flickered over Monique's skin, the beautiful dark and light of wax and flesh. With one hand Rémi poured the wax, holding the thick candle like a cup over the undulating skin. And with the other . . .

Monique was wet. Under the panties, she was a river, eagerly soaking Rémi's fingers, pussy lips thick, the juicy entrance to her cunt flushed pink and eager. The waitress hissed again, pushed back harder. Wax splashed against her skin.

The table squeaked under Monique's body, jerking against the floor as Rémi fucked her gently, then not so gently, coating her fingers with the essence of her cunt, needing to feel the hot kiss of the woman's pussy around her fingers, her hand. Reaching past Monique, Rémi put the candle on the table and shoved it out of the way. Monique gasped when Rémi twisted, pushed, fit her entire hand, her fist into her pussy.

Her god. Monique groaned out his name, pushing back on Rémi's hand, her pretty back undulating and lined with sweat, the wax coming off in flakes as she moved. Rémi pumped her fist, feeling the strain in her arm, the burn that climbed into her shoulder, into the rest of her body, settling into her groin, her pussy, moving her fist faster inside the woman who swallowed it up, bucked against her, her every motion begging for more. Orgasm. Her cum crushed down on Rémi's fist. A vice that wrenched her arm the way her gut-tural screams wrenched into the air. Sweat rippling down her back, Rémi's fist buried into her. Ass round and full, jiggling and hot. Ripe and wet.

"Good," Rémi murmured. "So good."

But she wasn't finished. She was slow about pulling her fist back, careful the way she needed to be, but with the same hand, she stroked Monique's clit and the woman gasped again, laughed deeply in her throat. "Yes," she moaned, "yes." She wanted more. And Rémi gave it.

She jerked down her zipper, her pants, fabric gathering around her ankles as she leaned. Clit finding merciful contact against the full curve of Monique's ass. God! Rémi pulled off her tie and lashed it around Monique's throat, caressed the skin with the green silk while she rode the full curve of that ass, rubbing her clit, her breasts against Monique even as she used the other hand to play with the waitress's cunt, pulled back the thick pussy lips, slid her fuck finger deep into the dripping center of her, then out to caress, to nudge, to agitate the fat clit. Monique grunted again, speeding her move-ments, and Rémi sped her own movements on the thick and juicy ass, her clit coming into perfect contact with that flesh. Monique moaned.

"Close," she gasped.

Rémi pulled the silk tight. Squeezed it in her fist until the wait-ress was breathless, gasping for air. A river of sensation flooded her. Against the table, Monique panted. Rémi's world burst into flames. The table scraped against the floor, rocked, then stood still as they both gasped. Sweating. She loosened her grip on the tie at Monique's throat. Dropped her head into the heated valley of Monique's back, her breath coming quickly. Then slowing. Slow.

She pushed herself away from Monique. The waitress lay against the table, her breath still coming quickly, treating Rémi to her up-turned backside, the drip at her sex, wetness coating the insides of her thighs. She turned and looked over her shoulder at Rémi. Licked her lips.

Rémi acknowledged the look and the invitation to a marathon

fuck session with a dip of her lashes, but that was all. She turned away. In the bathroom, she washed her hands and straightened her clothes. By the time she walked back into her office, Monique was dressed and standing still by the table, shirt buttoned, skirt on, hair in perfect order. Rémi looked at her until she finally smiled in cool understanding and walked toward the door.

Rémi knotted her tie and smoothed down the collar of her shirt. "By the way, Monique."

The waitress turned to look at her.

"I don't ever want you in my office again without my invitation. Understand?"

Monique's face froze and her eyes darted to the side. She looked down at the floor. "Yes, Rémi."

"Good."

Rémi blew out the candles and waited until Monique walked through the door before closing herself inside the darkened office. A lonely melody from Magnus's piano trickled over her skin. Rémi sighed, climbed the small steps to the back bedroom. *Tomorrow,* she thought, opening the door, *I need to air this place out.*

Chapter

18

"Are you home to rest this time?" Yvette called out from the kitchen as Rémi walked into the condo.

"Something like that."

For once, the television wasn't on. Just a moody violin from the speakers. Sun poured in through the open windows, highlighting the small changes that had taken place since Yvette moved in. The fashion magazine on the coffee table. A rumpled blanket in the middle of the sofa instead of being neatly folded over its back. A bright pink cell phone and a physics textbook on the floor in front of the blank TV.

Her sister came into the living room drinking a glass of water. "Is all that busy-ness to do with the club, or do the ladies have your attentions that much?"

"None of your *busy-ness*."

"That answers my question then." Yvette giggled as she flopped onto the couch, shoving the blanket out of her way. "For an old chick, Claudia can hang. I thought for sure she didn't keep these crazy hours."

"I wasn't with Claudia."

"Oh."

Rémi sat on the couch and dropped her head back. The nap she'd had at the club after sending Monique away did her good. It left her mind clear and her body a few levels above functioning.

"Do you want me to make breakfast?"

She opened one eye to look at her sister in surprise. Yvette hadn't made a move toward the stove in Rémi's presence the entire time she'd been here. "Sure. Eggs and waffles."

"How did I know you'd say that?"

"You're psychic?" Rémi shut her eyes. "Not to mention that's the only thing in the fridge that's not takeout."

"Hm." Rémi heard the sound of her drinking the water, her throat gulping down the fluid. Yvette breathing after each swallow.

"You'll have to make the eggs yourself. But the waffles I can definitely do."

Rémi smiled, tilting up the corner of her mouth. "Sure, why not?"

In the kitchen, she pulled the gray carton of eggs from the fridge, checking to make sure that the expiration date hadn't passed. Her finger skated over the bumpy ridges of the carton. Claudia's eggs probably never got the chance to expire. She smiled and stepped around her sister.

"So." Yvette closed the freezer door. "Do you consider yourself one of those Aggressives or AGs that I keep hearing about?"

"What?" Rémi looked up from the stove. "What are you talking about?"

"You know, those lesbians who are mostly in their twenties. They act like guys but still consider themselves female and feminine." Yvette paused. "You seem like that type."

"Why do you want to know?"

"I'm curious about you. We're complete strangers to each other. I want to change that."

"That's a strange way to get to know me, asking if I'm an AG or whatever."

"Aggressive. They even made a movie about those girls." She paused in the act of pulling two plates from the cupboard. "Bois. I think most of them call themselves bois." Yvette closed the cupboard and took the plates to the kitchen island.

"You finding out what kind of lesbian I am"—Rémi chuckled at the thought—"is not going to lead to knowing me better." She broke an egg in the oil swimming with heat, and it splashed, immediately curling up at the sides and turning brown. "I'm just the daughter Auguste and Kelia threw away." With a cool twist of her lips, Rémi tossed the eggshells in the trash can under the sink.

Yvette looked up from pulling waffles from their yellow box. "What our parents did doesn't make you who you are." The freezer exhaled cool mist as she put the box back inside. "I'd like to think of you as one of these AGs. Kinda strong and making their own rules." At the counter, she pressed the lever on the toaster, submerging two waffles into the depths of the machine.

Rémi glanced at her sister. "Maybe one day I'll get to that place where what Mama did won't matter much anymore." She nodded. "That would be real nice."

Side by side, they finished making their respective breakfasts. Rémi didn't even ask where Yvette found the vegetarian sausages she quickly heated up in the saucepan while Rémi plucked her eggs out of the oil and took down glasses for both of them. They sat at the kitchen table across from each other with a bottle of maple syrup and the crystal butter dish between them.

Rémi pinched off the crispy brown curve from her egg and bit into it, sighing at the small pleasure, the crisped and lightly salted egg white saturating her tongue with flavor. Suddenly, it felt like she hadn't eaten in days. She tore off a bigger piece.

"How can you eat those little aborted chickens?"

Rémi continued chewing. "They're a little taste of heaven."

"If you think heaven is an abortion."

"Eat your veggie sausage and shut up. The day you have an abortion is the day you can talk to me about eating it on my plate."

"I've had one."

"What?" Rémi nearly choked on her food.

"Well, not really," Yvette muttered, looking down at her plate. "But I thought about what it would feel like."

Rémi cut her glance over her sister, the hair caught up in a single bushy ponytail, a red tank top, and yoga pants pushed down to show her belly button.

"Mama is a drama queen too, if I remember things correctly," Rémi said.

Yvette's mouth snapped shut around her waffle, and her eyes narrowed. Before she could open her mouth again, Rémi held up her hand. "Don't say it. Just let me eat my breakfast in peace. Please." She shook her head. "No wonder Mama is having a heart attack about you."

Yvette smiled, impish and unrepentant. "Speaking of Mama, she called yesterday."

Rémi sliced into the thick yolk with her fork. It burst, sticky yellow, exploding over her plate and up the tines of her fork. "What does she want?"

"Me. Back home."

"That was a fast turnaround."

"Tell me about it. Maybe she was looking at my old baby pictures and realized just how cute I am." Her smile flashed. "Deep down."

"Ha! Real deep down."

Yvette's smile faded. "So, if I go back to Maine, will you come with me?"

The waffle, heavy with the golden maple syrup, squished between Rémi's fingers as she tore off a piece to put in her mouth. "Okay."

Her sister grinned. "Really?"

"Sure. Why not? I can't stay long, maybe a long weekend. A holiday weekend."

She'd never been invited home before. After she'd left Auguste's house, not once did she receive an invitation back. When he died last year, Kelia called, leaving a simple sentence on Rémi's voice mail. "Your father is dead." Within twenty-four hours she was in Maine, checking into a hotel five miles from the Boothbay Harbor house where she spent the first fourteen years of her life. And while Rémi stood there at the funeral, drowning in memories of a man who'd shown nothing but contempt for her once he found out that she was gay, Kelia never once invited her back home.

"That's so awesome," Yvette said, leaning toward Rémi with a greasy hand extended. "I can definitely deal with that."

Rémi took her sister's hand and returned the squeeze. "Cool."

Chapter

19

"You look good." Dez threw Rémi a smile from her chair in the middle of the bustling café. She briefly stood up from the table to exchange hugs.

Do I? "Thanks." Rémi pulled out a heavy wrought iron chair across from her friend and sat down.

When she'd gotten the call from Dez saying that she was back in town from her honeymoon and wanted to see her, Rémi froze, feeling as if she'd gotten caught with her hand in the proverbial cookie jar. Guilt led her to a bottle of Scotch much too early, then to the kitchen for caffeine to clear her head before finally heading out to Victoriana's to meet Dez. Sitting across from her, alcohol and caffeine warred in Rémi's body with nauseating results.

The last time they'd been together at Victoriana's, the bookstore and café owned by Dez's new wife, Rémi and Dez had been wasted. It was after a sleepless night of fucking, smoking, and drinking. They'd been nearly comatose from their night of debauchery but Dez still found enough strength to go after Victoria.

"Back to the scene of the crime?" Rémi murmured.

She toyed with a glass of water on the table, turning it idly between her hands. Nerves. She was showing her nerves. Rémi consciously bit off a sigh, left the water alone, and leaned back in her chair. Dez's smile wouldn't be that big if she knew about the relationship with Claudia. *But what will I do when she does find out?* Rémi ignored the nagging question and focused on acting blameless.

"Not a crime," Dez said. "The best decision of my life."

"I'm glad you still think so. Forty-five days alone on a rocking boat with one other person isn't always a good thing."

Dez grinned and leaned toward her as if sharing a secret. "It was the *best*. Incredible."

And it obviously had been. Dez looked happier and more relaxed than Rémi had seen her in a long time. Maybe ever. On the long boat trip, her pecan skin had tanned to a darker brown. Her lean body looked fit, even a bit more muscular in the loose designer jeans and thin long-sleeved white shirt rolled up at the elbows.

"I guess you didn't miss your friends, then?"

"I missed you, all of you, but not the things we used to do." Dez's eyes flashed as if remembering all the things they'd gotten into together. The women. The drugs. The over-the-top parties. "Part of me thought that I would—I mean shit! It's been over a year since I slept with anyone else. But Victoria has been the perfect lover and the perfect partner. There's nothing else I want."

Rémi didn't doubt it. Before touching Claudia, the other experiences had been to pass the time. To temporarily fill the space that her need for the older woman had left in her. Now she was fulfilled. Rémi reached for the glass of water, thinking, with a savage twist of her mouth, that Dez would probably not appreciate her sharing that piece of news.

"You deserve it," she said instead. And meant it.

"What does my darling deserve?"

Rémi turned her head to look at Victoria as she approached their table. In a peach floral print dress belted high beneath her full breasts and fluttering around her dimpled knees, she glowed in the early afternoon light.

"Only the best." Rémi stood up to greet the new bride with a kiss on the cheek. "Which is why she has you."

Victoria laughed and squeezed her arm. "You always know just the thing to say, Ms. Bouchard."

"When it comes to pleasing women, I like to think I know what I'm doing." Rémi teased her, enjoying the riotous spill of curls around Victoria's face and shoulders, her ripe cleavage, and disarming smile.

"Lay off. That's my woman," Dez growled.

Rémi and Victoria exchanged another smile.

"I think she knows that," Rémi said.

She spent another hour with the couple in the café, graduating her drink to chamomile tea over the PG-13 details of their honeymoon. The fish they caught. How beautiful the stretch of sea between the Dominican Republic and Jamaica was this time of year. How they couldn't wait to get away from it all again.

But their exchanged smiles and lingering touches eventually drove her away, made her want to seek out Claudia and bask in the warm glow of her presence. In the stinging heat of her kisses. Rémi didn't get what she wanted, though. Instead, she had to go back to Gillespie's and tend to some minor emergency that thankfully had none of Anderson's fingerprints on it.

Chapter

20

"**S**luts need love too," Nuria pouted, her chin propped up on a loose fist.

Her friends laughed. At Gillespie's, the night's performance was over and the stage lay bare of everything except a few instruments and a dimmed spotlight. At three in the morning, dinnertime was long gone. People drank. Laughed. Gestured more broadly under the influence of the club's endless supply of alcohol.

"No one is saying that they—you—don't," Rémi sipped her mineral water and raised an eyebrow at her friend. "I'm just asking people to stop calling it polyamory when all they want is the right to fuck anybody they want, whether or not they themselves are in a relationship."

"Then what is this polyamory if not that?" Nicoletta Nakamura leaned in toward the other women at the circular table, the silver bangles on her arm tinkling as she gestured emphatically. "People seem so confused about it. I know I am."

Across the table, her sister, Matsuko, laughed. "You're always confused, Letta."

"Shut up," Chance Nakamura said, her gravelly voice deep with affection.

The sisters had agreed to join Rémi and her friends at the club for dinner and drinks, gracing Gillespie's with their triple-threat beauty and causing Sage to lose her mind. Again. Rémi's friend sat next to Nicoletta, trying her best to get the triplets into her bed for the night. Phil had agreed to watch if Sage got what she wanted.

"You are one of these polyamorous ones, Nuria, yes?" Nicoletta asked.

"I've *never* claimed to be," Nuria murmured, her eyes twinkling like faraway stars. She was enjoying this conversation too much. "Sex is one of the greatest gifts that human beings have been given. I love to fuck and will happily claim the title of slut. That is until I find the one person for me. After that, I'm only fucking her. Or him."

"I'll jump in to defend polyamory," Sage said, pressing her shoulder against Nicoletta's. Her eyes dropped to the Japanese woman's cleavage.

"There's no reason to defend it," Rémi said. "From everything I've read it sounds great. Threes and fours being in a sexual and loving relationship together. Nice. But so far, everyone I know who claims to be polyamorous, again single or not, just seems to want to have license to fuck anything with a hole." She turned in her chair. "Isn't that right, Phil?"

Phillida sputtered, almost choking on her martini while her friends laughed. "Not funny," she said, wiping off the front of her dress. "I don't know about the rest of you bitches, but I'm a swinger. Sage will always be my baby, but if I see something hot and I can have them according to the rules our relationship, I'm taking it."

"Here, here." Chance raised her glass. "That is the kind of relationship I have with my lover, also. We do what we wish when apart, but when together it is just the two of us."

"I'll drink to whatever keeps you available." Sage raised her rum and Coke while her girlfriend rolled her eyes, not bothering to raise hers.

"Is this a celebration I should be a part of?"

Rémi froze at the sound of Matthias Anderson's voice.

"Quite the opposite, actually," she said, turning and raising her eyes to look at him.

He stood too close to her, his hair haloed by the amber lights suspended from the ceiling. Dressed all in white except for a red handkerchief neatly folded and peeking from the pocket of his blazer, he looked like a European aristocrat summering in a country not quite to his liking. With hands in the pockets of his slacks, Anderson's eyes roved over the women at the table. Taking note of her friends, Rémi thought.

She felt the muscle in her jaw begin to tick. She glanced at her friends, the smile flicking like a seizure across her face. "I'll be back in a second, guys."

"Everything all right?" Someone at the table asked the question but Rémi was too far from all right to answer.

She left the table, motioning ahead of her, on the surface saying "after you" but wanting to punch him in his smiling face. What the fuck was he doing here?

"I don't appreciate your presence here," she said when they had left the crush of the dining room and were walking toward a more quiet place that turned out to be her office. More than anything she hated public scenes, so whether or not Anderson was going to cause one, she wanted their talk to be private. Rémi opened the door to her office with its key and waited for Anderson and his bodyguard—not Frank or Todd—to come in before closing it firmly.

Rémi sat down behind her desk. "Why are you here?" she asked when they stood alone except for his bodyguard, who lurked by the door.

Anderson sat in the chair before Rémi's desk, though he hadn't been invited to, sprawled his legs in the creaseless white slacks and brushed a speck of invisible dirt from his knee. "To show you the same courtesy you showed me a few weeks ago when you paid me a visit."

He took a cigar from his breast pocket. Within moments his bodyguard was before him, half kneeling to clip off the end of the pale man's cigar then catch flame to it with a gold butane lighter. His cheeks sank in as he puffed, once. Twice. Then he squinted at Rémi through the smoke. The bodyguard moved back to his place by the door.

The bit of smoke drifting to her nose made Rémi inhale more deeply. Cigars. She missed them even more than cigarettes. "If it's all about reciprocity then it would be my turn to drop a load of rats and their shit in your place of business. Just to make it more lively."

He didn't bother to deny it, only smiled slightly as he puffed his cigar and took in the details of her office, lingering too long, Rémi thought, on the closed door to the bedroom behind her.

"At any rate, Ms. Bouchard, I was just passing through. About the incident at my club with Franklin and Todd, I let the more unfortunate part of my nature get the better of me. Regrettably."

The "unfortunate part of his nature." That's what he called almost killing her in the stinking alley behind his club? Her hand fisted against the desk.

"Don't take things too personally, Ms. Bouchard." He blew a smoke ring, and it traveled lazily upward, circling like a devilish halo above his head as he leaned forward. "I hear you're practically running this club on your own now." Anderson paused. An indecipherable look flashed across his face. "You're doing a good job."

Something clicked for Rémi then and suddenly she couldn't sit and listen anymore.

"Mr. Anderson. I'd like nothing more than for you to leave my place of business and never set foot in it again. I don't even want you to *think* about Gillespie's for any length of time. But"—she stood up, walked to the door, and held it open for him—"if you insist on being here, have a good time, spend a lot of money. And don't bother me again."

Anderson sat in the chair, not even turning around to face Rémi and the door. "You remind me of someone," he said, slowly rising, "I used to know a long time ago. And I'm not sure if that's a bad or good thing."

"Well, I'm sure that doesn't concern me."

He passed her, trailing the smell of cigar smoke behind him. The bodyguard followed. Rémi stood at the door, gripping the doorknob long after Anderson and his goon vanished from sight. Long after the remnants of the cigar smoke dissipated.

At the table with her friends, Nuria glanced at Rémi as she sat down. "Who was that guy?"

Rémi shrugged, dismissing Anderson from her mind for the rest of the night. "No one important," she said.

Chapter

21

"Are you ready to make things up to me from the other night?" Rémi laughed at the sound of Claudia's low voice on the other end of the phone. "Of course. I am at your mercy."

"Well, you're lucky I'm a merciful woman." She chuckled. "I need a ride from school this afternoon. Can you pick me up?"

"Sure. What time?"

"Around four. Just park in the visitor's lot near my office and come up. I should be finished by then."

Less than five hours later, Rémi left the nearly empty visitor's parking lot, heading to Claudia's office on the third floor of the humanities building. At ten minutes to four the campus still held most of its fifteen thousand students and ebbed and flowed with tight young bodies shown off in the skimpiest summer wear. A woman wearing what looked like a bikini top and tight jeans, lightly bumped her arm as she passed.

"Excuse me," Rémi said.

"No. Excuse *me.*" The girl looked at Rémi from curls to toes and smiled, flicking her tongue against her teeth.

Rémi laughed and kept walking. Back when she was a student, Rémi had treated the beautiful women on the campus as little more than gorgeous scenery while she went about her day, indulging in her infatuation with Claudia as she sat near the back of the class.

Only later, after forcing herself to realize the futility of lusting after her best friend's mother, did she begin to part take of the bounty of beauty around her. Sex became her aerobic activity. These girls made the blood race through her veins, but it was Claudia who was her reason to live. Rémi eventually found other reasons, but she never forgot about Claudia.

In front of the third-floor office with "Claudia Nichols, PhD" etched across a frosted glass door, Rémi knocked once and waited for Claudia's soft "come in" before opening the door. She almost stumbled back into the hallway.

Claudia crouched, knee on the windowsill, reaching up high to open the two-section window with its view of the lushly green campus. Her ass, pulled tight against the rust-colored skirt, wriggled at Rémi. Claudia looked over her shoulder.

"So punctual," she said, smiling. "I don't know why I forgot that about you."

Rémi swallowed hard and closed the office door. Her eyes skittered around the office, desperately looking anywhere but at Claudia's ass offered up too temptingly in that skirt. But the framed photographs of French and New Orleans street scenes didn't hold her attention. She turned around, putting her back to Claudia, and found herself staring at the wall behind the desk covered in cards, both handmade and not, welcoming her back to the classroom. On the desk itself sat a vase of dried pink roses sprinkled with baby's breath.

If it was anyone else, Rémi would have sworn that the woman asked her to come just now to see her ass in that alluring position. Just to tempt Rémi into reaching out for what she wanted. Her fingertips felt hot with the need to touch. Rémi knew that flesh would feel right under her hands. Perfect. That Claudia would squirm when Rémi bit a plump cheek, inviting the harder press of teeth. More intimate caresses. She turned back to look at Claudia.

With a slight grunt, the older woman shoved open the window, allowing a slight breeze into the office. She dropped back down into the chair, her improvised stepladder, flashing her bare feet at Rémi.

"That feels so much better. Now I don't have to worry about suf-
focating to death when I come back to work next week."

She sat in the chair and shoved her feet into black high-heeled
sandals. Pursing her lips, she took a good look at Rémi. "Don't you
look nice."

Rémi fought the urge to look down at her faded jeans, old T-shirt,
and boots. "Thank you."

Claudia leaned back in the chair. The white blouse and silver
chain sparkled against her twilight skin. Her slight breasts moved
under the cotton as she breathed.

"Come here."

"I—uh," Rémi paused. What was she about to say again? Oh
yeah. "I saw Dez the other day."

Claudia raised an eyebrow. "I know. She talked about you."

"What did she say?" Rémi held her breath. Had she somehow
given herself away during their conversation at Victoriana's?

"Nothing life altering. Only that you looked good. Happy. And
that she was happy too."

She swallowed her relief. One day she would have to face Dez
about this thing she had with Claudia. But not now. "Okay. Good."

"And now that I've satisfied your curiosity about my daughter,
will you come?" A naughty smile played around Claudia's mouth.

Rémi didn't hesitate this time. She came.

"I won't ask you what you did after I went home Sunday night.
By now, I have a pretty good idea how things work."

Rémi stopped with her knees pressed against the front of Claudia's chair. "If you want me to stop seeing other women, I'll stop."

Claudia curled her finger, beckoning Rémi closer. She pressed a
knee into the chair's lap, between Claudia's spread thighs. The
scent of her—green apples with a hint of L'Air du Temps—wrapped
around Rémi's senses, opened her mouth.

"Can you?" Claudia's breath tasted hers. She shivered as Claudia
grasped her hand, sucked two of Rémi's fingers in her mouth, then
guided them under her skirt. "Can you?"

Soft pussy opened up around her fingers. Something catapulted into Rémi's belly and she grunted. Claudia hissed, opening her legs wider.

"Yes. I can stop." Rémi pulled her fingers back, only slightly. Felt her body starting to shake harder. Forced herself to take it slow. She pulled back, teasing the moist opening of Claudia's pussy.

"I dreamed about you last night." Claudia's eyes trapped hers. "I dreamed about us finishing what we started on the floor of your office." She grabbed Rémi's hand, pushed the fingers deep. Deeper. "Did you mean to leave me wanting like that? Hmm?" She pulled Rémi's fingers back, fucking herself with Rémi's hand. "Did you mean to leave me to touch myself in my own bed, dreaming about you tasting me? About the way your tongue would feel on my clit? How you'd feel when I finally got the chance to taste you?"

Her hips rocked in the chair as she rode Rémi's fingers, breath becoming uneven. Ragged. She dragged her skirt up and pushed her thighs wider apart, mouth moist and open as her head dropped back against the chair. Claudia moved Rémi's hand faster and faster. Her nipples pressed hard against the white shirt. Her fingers tightened around Rémi's hand, nails sinking into the flesh, digging up pain. But Rémi swallowed against that pain. Her own pussy ran wet with arousal. Her belly tight with anticipation of Claudia's orgasm. She wouldn't leave this unfinished. Not this time.

When the strength in Claudia's hand faltered, Rémi took up the slack, thrusting into the hot, wet cunt, inciting the swollen clit with her thumb. Claudia's face glistened with sweat. Her mouth, moist and dark with lipstick, was parted and wet. Rémi couldn't resist. She kissed her. The hot mouth instantly responded. Latching on to hers, the tongue darting out to stroke, to lick, while Claudia's hips bucked in the chair. While her pussy swallowed Rémi's fingers. Squeezed them as she came, bucking fiercely under Rémi. She grasped Rémi's head with both hands and her fingers tangled in Rémi's hair, holding her close for one last slippery, grateful kiss.

Claudia pulled back, breath puffing against Rémi's face. "Take me home."

* * *

They stumbled through the door of the two-story in Coconut Grove joined at the lips. Rémi's heart pounded heavily in her chest and her fingertips burned hot, a delicious heat now that they pressed against Claudia's skin. The door slammed behind them and they tumbled back against it. Claudia's back to the wood and her legs climbing up and around Rémi's waist. The smaller woman panting into Rémi's mouth. Heat built over Rémi's skin and she groaned as Claudia's blouse slid to the floor, baring the soft breasts in a sheer brown bra. Desperation climbed between her thighs and she reached roughly for the skirt, desperate to get to the simmering heat she had her finger buried in less than an hour before. The skirt ripped. Rémi stopped.

"Shit! I'm sorry." She pulled back, breath catching at the back of her throat. "I didn't mean—"

"It's okay." Claudia legs tightened around her waist, holding her still. "It's nothing. Just a skirt. I can always buy more."

"No. I can't control myself. I need . . ." She pressed her forehead against Claudia's. Breath chuffed between her lips. Her heart raced. "I have to go."

It felt like her pussy was too thick to stay between her legs. It throbbed fat and wet in her jeans, begging for Claudia. Rémi panted, leaning away though Claudia still refused to let her go. She wanted to fuck. She wanted to push the older woman to her knees and ream her pussy until Claudia screamed from the pleasure of it. She wanted to lie on top of her, cover her, wring her dry of all her juices, and stop only when they were both too exhausted to continue.

Rémi grasped Claudia's waist, preparing to pull her off and drop her back to the floor. "I have to go." Her legs shook.

"No." Claudia pulled down the straps of her bra, exposing her breasts, their hard tips. "Stay."

The bedroom was a blur of kisses and moans, the wet sounds of their mouths meeting and remeeting, her tongue lapping at Claudia's bared breasts, her shirt falling away, hands tearing away her belt buckle, her jeans. The bed sighed as their bodies met it; she groaned when Claudia's entire body was bare and hot in the late afternoon light and reaching for her. Oh my god. Oh my *god*.

In bed, with the intention to fuck, their kisses burned Rémi's senses away. The heat of her mouth, the inside of that fevered place that Rémi had imagined for so long and only recently been allowed to visit. Naked. She was finally naked with her, between her thighs and wetter than she had ever been, her nipples scraping over Claudia's nipples, their moans rising together in a thick concert of sex that tightened and released the insides of her—her belly, pussy, throat, lungs—so fiercely that she thought she'd come right then and there.

She finally found her voice. "Is there anything that you don't— don't want me to do?" Rémi swallowed her panting breath. She could at least try to sound calm and in control.

"Nothing. Do anything you want." Claudia arched up against her, legs twining with Rémi's, teeth scraping against Rémi's throat. "Give me everything."

A banquet. Rémi was at a banquet with all of her life's desires on display for her to take at will, at her leisure. But this was not leisurely. It was urgent. She pushed Claudia down on her belly and licked her. The taut line of her neck, her shoulder blades, her back, the slight weight of her ass cheeks. Between them she was musky. A moaning, sticky mess pushing back into Rémi's face, as she sampled from the secret space from her lover's anus to her cunt, open and wet and delicious beyond belief.

The groans were coming as much from Claudia as from her; Rémi moved her hips against the bed, sought Claudia's clit with her tongue, found it, sucked it, worshipped it, wetness pouring over her face as Claudia came, hips bucking back.

"Rémi!" Her lover panted. "Rémi!"

Her mouth around my name. Fuck. Her mouth around my name. The spring in her belly loosened. Rémi bucked against the sheets as darkness and light spiraled behind her tightly closed eyelids. She gasped into Claudia's cunt.

It was like she hadn't had sex in weeks. Months. Her skin flinched everywhere it touched her lover's. Sensitive. Eager. The hunger rose up in her again, even as she pulled her mouth from Claudia's pussy to turn her over and kiss up the still-panting line of her belly, latch onto her nipples, and feast on them. Painting them with her mouth, sucking and licking and biting until Claudia writhed against the sheets, her mouth open, hands grasping at Rémi's back and shoulders. She'd never been this hungry for a woman in her life.

Rémi burned to be inside of her, to feel her heartbeat thudding. To know without a doubt that Claudia felt even a little of what she felt.

"Lube," Claudia fumbled into the bedside table and came up with a small clear bottle. "I'm going to need some."

Lube?

"I'm not as young as you, sweet. Especially if you're going to go inside."

Claudia lay back against the tangled sheets, long body glistening with sweat.

Had her intentions been that plain? Yes. Yes, they had been that plain. Rémi licked her lips, nerves in her fingers already pulsing with the seduction of Claudia's pussy so close. Not just two fingers. All of her.

"I want to be inside," she rasped.

Claudia smeared the cold liquid on Rémi's hand. With the rapidly warming lube covering her hand, she didn't hesitate. *Thank you.* She wasn't sure if she said the words, only that the gratitude sang through her veins as she slithered down between Claudia's thighs again, hand trembling and urgent. The brown thighs fell open, showing off pussy hairs tangled with cum and sweat and Rémi's saliva. Her clit stood up, firm and flushed, a thrusting pistil among glistening petals.

She was a miracle of responsiveness, holding herself loose and easy as Rémi dove inside her shallows, testing with two fingers then three then four. The fifth brought a gasp and Rémi paused.

"No, don't stop. Please." Claudia panted softly, thighs pressed open against the bed. She reached for Rémi's head, meshed her fingers in the damp hair until Rémi was breathing with her, harsh and deep, fighting the urge to shove deeply into her, to fuck like she really wanted. But, muscles shaking, the smell of her cunt mouth-watering and rich in her nostrils, Rémi forced herself to go slow. Her thumb slipped, gently, into the soft flesh, like a kiss. And she sighed. Claudia sighed.

"So full." Her fingers tightened in Rémi's hair.

Another gentle push and twist, her body liquid and greedy around Rémi's wrist. Perfect. She felt warm and solid, pulsing around her fist, a heartbeat.

Claudia's hips moving against the bed, thrust minutely up, pulled Rémi from her reverie. *Fuck me.* The unspoken demand she happily obeyed. She moved, began light butterfly movements inside that precious pussy, building speed until the wings of Claudia's thighs beat gently against the bed, gasps becoming moans, becoming deep-throated screams as Rémi reached deeper and deeper for that place inside her lover. Above her, Claudia pulled at her own nipples, pinching the dark buds between her fingers, her back arching up, her head lashing against the sheets as she tossed her head back and forth.

"Rémi!"

She answered with deeper thrusts, her own grunts rising.

"Rémi."

Claudia's fingers flew from her breasts to dig into the sheets.

"Yes."

The butterfly beat its wings faster.

"Rémi! Yes!"

The motion of Claudia's hips froze. But inside . . . inside she was a cyclone. Pulsating around Rémi's hand, relentlessly clutching until Rémi gasped as much from pain as desire. But her body was full. The heart pounded in her chest. Claudia wanted her. She desired her. The body didn't lie. The waves of Claudia's desire broke once again against Rémi's hand before she slowly began to withdraw it. She pressed her mouth to Claudia's still-trembling thighs, the curl of her sex, before her lover drew her up, kissing her face as she laughed breathlessly.

"Enough. My god! Is it possible to die from sex?" She kissed Rémi's mouth and nose. "You are an incredible lover, but I am an old, old woman."

Rémi's heart began to pound in her chest for a different reason. "Did I hurt you?"

"No, darling. No." Claudia touched her face. "You made me come about eight times in a row, but you never hurt me. Never." Her pulse slowed. She collapsed against her lover's damp breasts. Closed her eyes. With her breathing deep and even, Claudia trailed her fingers lightly down Rémi's back. The delicate touches lulled Rémi into a light drowse. But that didn't last long.

Soon enough, the trailing touches became caresses, easing down her ass. And Rémi's heartbeat took off again. Claudia sighed with welcome when she slipped a thigh heavily between hers, pressing the thick muscle against her pussy. They crashed against each other, rising with the wave of desire that took them. Sweat rushed over Claudia's skin and she gasped with each movement of Rémi's thigh. Their breasts, bellies, pussies slid together until both were gasping and washed in sweat. Claudia's fingers dug into her back. She slowed. Rémi slowed too.

"Can I touch you?" Claudia asked.

She blinked sweat from her eyes, arms shaking as she hovered above the woman she loved, holding off her weight. "Yes. Please."

Claudia's hand slid down her belly, over her pubes. Her belly flexed, jolted when the tentative fingers found the swollen pussy lips, slid over her clit. Her skin flushed hot, as if fevered. She gasped.

The look on Claudia's face. Of wonder. Of pleasure. Two fingers skated over Rémi's hypersensitive skin. They dipped inside her pussy. She gasped again.

"I don't—"

But her world fell apart. Ripped open by the orgasm that buckled her elbows, she was falling, falling.

Light came to her slowly, bleeding gradually between eyelashes until she was flooded in it. She moved her head, heard the rustle of cloth. Felt softness under cheek—a pillow. A pillow on Claudia's bed. Claudia.

"Hey, sleepy."

She sat propped up against the wall, knees pressed to her chest with burgundy covers framing her nakedness. Her feet lay near Rémi's hand. Light from the large arching window beside the bed surrounded her face with softness. Rémi's eyes fluttered closed as fingers drifted over her forehead, down her nose and lips. A dream. It had to be a dream. She kissed the fluttering fingers and felt the smile in Claudia's silence.

Her body felt light and angelic, as if she'd made a visit to heaven and returned a changed woman.

"Hey," Rémi murmured.

"I thought you'd sleep through the night."

"Can't. Have to go to work."

"Of course." The disappointment leaked into Claudia's voice.

She felt regret too. Wanted to spend the entire night in this wonderful bed, living a dream she'd had for longer than she could remember. The bones of Claudia's feet were delicate under her fingers, ankles that seemed too small to support anything, much less this amazing woman.

"Can you come to Maine with me to visit my family?"

The unexpected words tumbled from Rémi's mouth in a flood. Instantly, she wanted to call them back. She didn't want to be that clingy one.

"When?"

"I didn't—" The gentle look on Claudia's face stopped her. "In a few weeks. Maybe your spring break?"

"I think I can manage that. Desiree and Derrick can do without me for a few days."

Rémi's hand tightened on the ankle pulsing with warmth. "Thank you."

Claudia dropped the covers, slid down into the bed beside her. "I wouldn't have said anything else." Her mouth brushed Rémi's. Her tongue licked. Rémi's body woke fully, skin warming again. She reached for her lover, pulling the naked chest against hers and kissed her, hungrily claiming what she wanted.

* * *

Rémi found herself at Gillespie's hours later, staring out at the empty main room. The club ready for another night. Tables cleaned and gleaming under the low lights, the long-haired technician testing the mic, Norlene counting the till behind the second-floor bar. But Rémi's mind was full of Claudia. The silk-salt taste of her. How she chanted Rémi's name, held it at the back of her throat until the word exploded past her lips and Rémi couldn't think anymore. Could only feel the wonder of Claudia's skin under her hands. Feel her heart thudding in her chest against the other woman's. Feel finally, at home.

Her hand plucked the cell phone out of her jacket pocket and, seemingly with a mind of its own, dialed the familiar number. Claudia answered on the first ring.

"I wish you could have spent the night."

Rémi turned from the view of the club. "I wanted to."

They breathed gently together. Silently. The skin under Rémi's shirt felt hot and she shrugged out of her jacket, threw it somewhere, rubbed her stomach through the white cotton.

"Thank you for . . . everything," Rémi said.

"I should be the one thanking you. This evening was incredible. I never realized it could be like that."

"Me either." Rémi swallowed.

A knock at the door cut off her next words. She growled. *Who the hell was this now?* "Excuse me a sec," she said to Claudia. "Who is it?"

Monique stood at the threshold with a tall glass of iced coffee and a sandwich on a small tray. "May I come in?"

"Darling," Claudia's voice purred from the phone. "I'll let you get back to work. Come over when you're done. No matter what time it is."

Rémi's chest warmed at the invitation. "All right, I will."

She closed the phone then looked back at Monique, waiting quietly in the doorway to be invited in.

Chapter

22

She left Monique wanting. Rémi knew that. The need in the waitress's eyes had been as plain as the nipples pressing hard against her starched white blouse. But Rémi was through using her as a substitute. Hands moving restlessly at her side, she rang Claudia's doorbell.

"Hey."

It was just past four o'clock, an unforgivable time of the morning, even if Claudia had said to come by. But she had to come. And Claudia had been waiting.

She ignored Rémi's verbal greeting and kissed her instead, pulling her in and closing the door. Her robe, something silky and white, brushed against Rémi's arms and legs as Claudia pressed close. Underneath it, she was naked.

"I hope you're not tired."

Rémi laughed. "I was just going to say the same thing to you."

"Ah. When great minds think alike."

They didn't make it upstairs. Hunger met hunger on the living room floor, coffee table shoved out of the way, the rug burning their knees, Claudia gasping as Rémi nibbled at her naked back while fumbling for the belt buckle. Through her thin undershirt, her nipples rasped on Claudia's bare skin. The edges of her shirt, unbuttoned and open, brushed Claudia's sides, hiding her from any prying eyes beyond the clear glass windows leading to the garden or the pool.

"I've been thinking about you all night," Claudia whispered, reaching back for Rémi's face. Rémi leaned into the heated palm, kissed it, bit the skin. The noise Claudia made! Electric heat tripped through her legs, burning at the point where her new dick pressed against her clit.

"What exactly were you thinking?"

"About this."

Rémi freed her dick. Claudia's breasts trembled in her hands, the nipples already hard and ready for her mouth. But that was later. Right now, she shoved into Claudia, sighed at the full contact of the dick with her clit, the sudden pressure. Her lover gasped.

"Oh!"

She kept herself still, letting Claudia get used to the pressure of the dick inside her, its newness, its weight. She moved her hips.

"I'm not going to break, so don't hold back, I can feel you."

Rémi was going slow, so slow. The feel of Claudia under her skin was sending ferocious shocks to her clit. She wanted to move. She wanted to fuck. But . . . Claudia moved against her, tilted her gorgeous ass up, slid her pussy against Rémi.

"Fuck . . . !"

"Don't hold back, sweet. I won't break." Claudia grunted, pushing back. "I won't."

And that was all Rémi needed. She pushed voluptuously inside. Deep. Sweet. Hips stirring the hot molasses of Claudia's pussy. Dick hot. Breath churning. Claudia gasping and ready beneath her. Nipples hard, rasping against naked skin, jerking in time to the see-sawing motion of the dick, the liquid suck and release, the grunting grip of her hands on Claudia's hips.

"Yes. Fuck yes."

Claudia grunted in return, her ass up and pussy wide open to receive, to take, to swallow the thick length of Rémi's diving dick. Sweat washed down her back, cleaving the shirt to her skin.

"Yes."

Rémi fumbled down for Claudia's clit, met her lover's fingers instead, her touching herself around the insistent pressure of the dildo.

"Is this enough for you?" Rémi panted.

"Nothing is enough. Touch me. I wish you could touch me everywhere at once, touch my breasts, suck my clit, lick my breasts. I want you everywhere at once. Making love to me."

"Yes." Rémi pulled out, spun Claudia to face her. Pulled off her shirt and dropped it on the floor behind her. "I can do that for you. Maybe not today. Maybe not right now. But I can. I will. And you'll love it. You'll love it."

Claudia faced her. Rémi fucked her. Legs over her shoulder, Claudia's arms back, clutching the back of the sofa as Rémi fucked the wet hole of her, her skin a dripping, electric thing that wept for her touch. Claudia reached for her breasts, squeezed Rémi's nipples, and she threw her head back, her hips forward. The hands slid over her sweat-slick chest. Over her nipples and belly. Gripped her hips, pulling her fast. Faster.

"Fuck."

"Yes."

"I love it."

"More."

"Yes."

"Fuck me."

"Yes!"

The sofa jerked under them. Jerked across the hardwood. Slammed into the floor with each thrust of Rémi's hips.

Claudia's eyes were languid but fierce, her fingers gripping Rémi's arms. "More," she gasped. "More!"

Whatever she wanted, that was what Rémi would give. Her hips lunged. Sweat slid. Effort churned in her throat. She clutched Claudia's hips harder. Fucked her fast. Faster. Sensation, like a wave of fire, crashed into Rémi, fizzing up through her cunt and belly.

"Yes!" Claudia's lashes trembled. Eyes rolled back. And she screamed Rémi's name, her body trembling, trembling.

"I think," she panted against Rémi's mouth moments later, "I want food now." She twitched against Rémi. Lips parted and wet.

Sweat caught in the edges of her pale hair and along the slim line of her throat.

Still on her knees, Rémi shuddered. Her body hadn't yet made the transition from carnal to victual and found Claudia's words a puzzle impossible to sort out. Her lover solved the problem for her by pushing away, unwinding her body from Rémi's, and heading for the kitchen.

"Do you know what you want to eat?"

Rémi didn't answer. She probably didn't need to. With a full-bodied quiver, she sat back on her haunches, arms draped across her thighs, head thrown back and eyes closed. The remnants of her orgasm shuddered quietly through her, leaving lightning twitches between her thighs, on her skin. By the time she recovered, Claudia was walking from the kitchen with a tray of fruit and cheese in her hands. She blinked as if seeing her lover for the first time in days. Whatever Claudia saw in Rémi's face made her laugh.

"Let's eat in front of the fireplace."

Rémi assumed that meant that Claudia wanted her to start the fire. She did, thankfully a matter of the flip of a switch, and the gas heat brought flames to life around the logs sitting behind the grate.

"Thanks. You're a darling." She pressed her mouth briefly to Rémi's.

The full tray, several pillows from the sofa, and a heartfelt sigh later, they lay together on the thick white rug in front of the fireplace. Claudia on her belly, gloriously naked, her legs moving slowly back and forth in the air as she delicately tore a fat red grape from the bunch and bit into it. The flames from the fireplace warmed Rémi's naked back.

In the otherwise dark room, light from the fire danced over the lean brown flesh of Claudia's body, over the snowy hair curled like tiny cotton balls against her head, over the face settled into lines of contentment, and the slightly tilted eyes that drank Rémi in like hot cider. When Rémi first saw the house years ago with its fireplace, she wondered what occasion anyone in Miami would have to use one. For the first time she could see why: To lay on a rug, naked, after thick and delicious sex with the most amazing woman she'd ever known. Her pants and still-harnessed dildo lay discarded near the sofa.

"You really did grow up nicely, you know that?" Claudia's eyes flicked over Rémi's body. She reached for a pale slice of cheese.

Rémi chuckled, sipping her grapefruit juice. "So I've heard."

"The last thing I want to do is bore you sexually, you know," Claudia suddenly said.

"What?" Rémi looked at her in amazement. "That's the last thing you need to worry about." She traced the curve of Claudia's arm under the flickering light with her palm. "I get excited just by looking at you. Couldn't you tell from earlier? If not, I can show you again." She arched an eyebrow and reached for Claudia with deeper intent.

"Stop it." Claudia playfully slapped her hand away. "I know that you're still excited by me. It's early yet. But I know the things you're used to doing with other women."

"What have you heard?"

Her lover's look was faintly challenging. "Stories about nipple clamps and S&M. I've heard that you like to be in control."

Rémi felt the heat rise in her cheeks. And with her light skin, she knew the blush was plainly visible. And that only made her blush harder. "I like to be in control, but it's not a must for me. Besides, whatever you heard is—it's in the past." She couldn't stop herself from stammering.

"Oh no, sweetheart. I'm not saying that I want you to stop enjoying the kind of sex you do. I'm just saying that I've heard about it. Am actually a little curious."

Rémi's eyes widened. "Really?" The blood began to beat between her legs again.

"I don't want you to change your sex life just because I'm in it. I want to enjoy the kind of sex you enjoy. The only change to your lifestyle would be that I expect you to be faithful to me."

And Rémi's eyes widened even further because they'd never had this discussion before and she hadn't thought about it either. Any of it. She'd assumed fidelity, yes. But also that she'd curb her sexual appetite. Become a gentler and kinder lover. This was turning out to be even better than she'd imagined.

"Oh, my sweet darling. I didn't get with you to change who you are. If anything, I'd want you to help me get out of my own ruts." Claudia laughed. "You should see your face. You look positively devilish."

"Not devilish. Just excited." Her voice vibrated in her chest. She set aside the grapefruit juice to sip from Claudia's lips instead. "I won't hurt you," she said, senses already overcome by the second-hand taste of grapes and pepper jack cheese. "Promise."

"I know, darling." She licked the corners of Rémi's mouth, smiled as if whatever she tasted there sat well on her tongue. "I won't let you."

Chapter

23

"You look much happier these days," Yvette said as she pulled the door open for Rémi, who struggled in, loaded down with two paper bags full of groceries, her keys still dangling in the lock.

Rémi felt herself blush then looked self-consciously over her shoulder at Claudia, who smiled at her, jauntily swinging a cloth shopping bag with their bottle of wine for the evening. "Can you at least let me come in the door first before you tell the entire building my business?" she muttered to her sister.

Claudia's hand gently descended on Rémi's back, warm and steady. She chuckled. "I'd only be flattered if you were, darling." She winked at Yvette, who had a blush similar to Rémi's on her cheeks.

"I'm sorry." The girl coughed on a giggle, tugged at the hem of her snug yellow shirt. "I didn't know you were there."

"I am, Yvette, and it's all right. *Comment allez-vous?*"

Yvette stepped back from the door to allow Rémi to walk into the condo then on to the kitchen. "I'm well, thank you. *Et vous?*"

"I'm actually much happier these days, too."

Rémi smiled as the echoes of both women's giggles followed her into the kitchen. She carefully put the grocery bags on the center island, making sure that the eggs were still unbroken and the various bottles of sauces that her lover had picked up remained whole.

"All perishables are intact," she called out to Claudia in the living room. "Do you want me to do anything with them?"

"Just stand around looking cute. I told you I'll cook dinner, and I mean it." Claudia came in to put the bottle of white wine in the fridge.

"I can help," Yvette said, walking up behind Claudia. "Papa used to say I was the best sous chef he'd ever worked with."

Rémi glanced up at the mention of their father. "I hope you don't cook like he used to. All that rich French food gives me indigestion."

"That's not fair! I've not made anything like that the entire time I've been here."

"Everything but the dreaded French cuisine, right?" Claudia's smile teased Yvette.

The young girl began to unpack the grocery bags. "Exactly."

Rémi left the kitchen to look through the mail Yvette had left for her on the side table. Credit card offer. Bills. A sale circular. Rémi fingered a black envelope with her name written across it in silver calligraphy. Without opening the envelope, she knew what was inside. After a brief glance in Claudia's direction, she tossed the invitation to Odette's latest party into the copper bin under the table with the other papers to be shredded. Sage and Phil would probably go. Nuria too. Rémi mentally shrugged before wandering back into the kitchen.

"I'll be right back," Claudia said, passing by her with a quick smile.

"Oh my god!" Yvette said as soon as Claudia left the kitchen. "I'm so sorry. I had no idea that she was standing there."

"It's okay." Rémi said. "By now she knows that I've lost my mind over her." She gently tugged her sister's hair. "At least you didn't say anything dirty. That I wouldn't be quite so forgiving about."

"What dirty things could I possibly have to say?" She turned twinkling eyes over her shoulder as she moved to the sink, gushing water from the tap over a fistful of carrots.

"Ha! I'm sure you would have come up with something."

Rémi picked up Claudia's purse from the center island and wiped the granite surface clean while holding the fancy piece of black leather in her free hand. All the femmes she'd ever known always took their purses with them to the bathroom when they went, and she assumed that's where Claudia disappeared to.

"Gimme a second," she said to Yvette. "I'm going to give this little thing to Claudia in case she needs it."

"Okay." Yvette didn't bother looking up from the sink.

Upstairs in the bedroom, Claudia's thin cotton sweater—what some apparently called a "shrug"—was a splash of pale green across the black sheets on her bed.

"I brought your purse," Rémi called softly toward the bathroom.

She sat on the bed, picked up the little sweater with its three-quarter sleeves and tiny faux pearls stitched across the material that cradled her lover's breasts. It seemed miraculous that this tiny bit of femininity in her bedroom belonged to Claudia. It seemed miraculous, too, that right now Claudia was with her. Was loving her.

Her lover appeared at the bathroom door, her face covered in a fine foam, grinned her thanks then disappeared back into the small room. "I don't need it, love, but thank you."

And Rémi lost the memory of why she was in the bedroom in the first place. Instead she lost herself in the sounds that her lover made. The sounds of intimacy.

The gush of the faucet then the sounds of Claudia drying her face. A twist of the jar of face cream, Rémi guessed, and the soft patting noises of her applying the cream. The porcelain on porcelain sound of the toilet opening.

Rémi leaned back against the headboard, imagining Claudia's curved bottom against the white toilet, her small feet perched side by side in their high heels waiting for the sound of piss to hit the water. The image made her smile.

"You know I never understood people who could read while on the toilet," Claudia said.

"What's there to understand?" Rémi watched the bathroom's empty doorway, the stretch of black tile waiting for Claudia's feet to walk over them.

"It's distracting. I figure I'm here in the bathroom for one thing, maybe two." Laughter bubbled up like new wine from the back of her throat. "I don't want to be distracted from that with news of the latest goings on in Hollywood or"—papers ruffled as she apparently went through the pile of reading material on top of the small table by the toilet—"the next riveting chapter of *Art and Rage in Modern-Day America.*

"There are some things in there that I can only read when I'm forced to. Ergo toilet literature."

"That's pretty impressive. I can't multitask in here. See. I'm having a hard time just peeing while talking to you."

Rémi laughed. "Okay. I'll shut up."

"No, don't stop. I love the sound of your voice," Claudia hummed in pleasure. "It's like velvet, rough and soft at the same time. I just won't say anything back to you for the next forty seconds or so."

"All right. Just for you, I'll do that."

And Rémi talked. She didn't listen very closely to what came out of her mouth, only kept up the steady stream of one-sided conversation until Claudia emerged from the bathroom a few minutes later, smiling.

"I like a woman who can do as she's told." She leaned over to kiss Rémi, tug her to her feet. Her eyes searched Rémi's for a moment, the lashes flickering in a face held still with seriousness. "Thank you for being in my life," Claudia murmured, pressing a hand to Rémi's chest.

Rémi pulled her close until their breaths were the same and she could feel her lover's heart beating undeniably against hers. "My pleasure."

In the kitchen that had been barely used before Yvette arrived, the three women laughed, cooked, shared the bottle of white wine, and ate the meal that Claudia and Yvette prepared. Tender slices of duck, fragrantly spiced with coriander, cumin, and the fiery bite of whole peppercorns. Grilled tofu marinated in orange juice, garlic, and red pepper flakes. Earth black olives, steamed carrots, and perfect spoonfuls of red rice. Rémi couldn't remember the last time she had a meal this delicious at home. She went back to the stove for seconds, batting Yvette's hand away when her sister pinched her waist and told her to leave some for lunch tomorrow.

"I can make another batch," Claudia offered, but Yvette pouted, saying it wouldn't be the same. Rémi made a show of leaving two large pieces of tofu behind just for her.

After dinner, Rémi washed the dishes while the other two women watched most of a reality show before falling into a conversation about the nature of reality. Rémi joined them on the couch but only laid her head in Claudia's lap while the conversation flowed above her head, lulling her into a light doze. Yvette sat curled on the sofa, her body leaned slightly toward Claudia, her thin hand gesturing, occasionally plucking at the neckline of her shirt as she spoke.

"These people don't even know what reality is."

"But we, the voyeurs, don't care. As long as we don't have to deal with our own realities in the meantime."

Still talking, Claudia lightly raked her nails through Rémi's hair, and her hand, fragrant with the remnants of spices from cooking dinner, teased Rémi's nose with scent. Much later, the night ended where it should, with Claudia tucked into the crook of her arm, snoring softly while the darkness in Rémi's bedroom gently cradled them into the next day. Together.

Chapter

24

The crowd was like nothing Rémi had experienced before. Buttoned down, academic. Men in tweed jackets, oxford shirts, some smoking pipes. Women in flowing dresses and sensible shoes. A few gray-haired hippies in Birkenstocks.

Rémi stood back as yet another university colleague greeted Claudia with kisses and smiles. This time, a tall Asian woman in a brightly colored sarong and bangles clinking up both arms.

"I'm glad you could come to the party, Claudia. You look great." Her voice dipped low in surprise.

And that's what Claudia had confessed to Rémi as they lay in bed together nearly a week ago.

"Most of them see cancer as a death sentence," she said in the quiet hush of her bedroom, fingers light against Rémi's belly, head cradled on her chest. "Even though the cancer is gone, they probably expect me to show up looking skeletal and pathetic. They'll pity me. I don't want that."

So Rémi had agreed to be her date to the pre-spring break faculty party, although both Dez and Derrick had offered Claudia their company and support for the evening. With only a few exceptions, everyone seemed genuinely glad to see her, hugging the slight woman, laughing at her wry jokes. And their eyes lit up with speculation when she introduced Rémi.

"Thank you, Leah. I *feel* great," Claudia said to her colleague. She reached back for Rémi's hand. "I'd like you to meet a very good friend of mine, Rémi Bouchard."

Claudia smiled as Rémi leaned in to take Leah's hand. But Leah shook her head. "I only believe in hugs."

The other woman stood a foot taller than Claudia. Her lips brushed Rémi's ear as she squeezed enthusiastically before slowly letting go. "A pleasure to meet you," Leah said.

Rémi practiced her manners. "Same here."

Leah turned back to Claudia. "Everyone is so glad to see you. We all missed your presence last year."

"I wish I had been able to come." With another smile, Claudia squeezed Leah's hand. "And thank you for the flowers and the cards that you and Dennis sent. They meant a lot."

"You're absolutely welcome." Leah kissed her cheek again, said something to Claudia that Rémi didn't catch, then floated away to greet another guest.

From Leah they went to Melissa then Shanice then Ingrid, until Rémi's head spun with all the names and faces and facts of their positions at the university. While her lover talked at length with the lumbering but gentle professor of Russian language, she took herself off to find the snacks, weaving past eyes that latched onto her with obvious curiosity.

At the food table, she bit into a slice of the Havarti with caraway seeds, surprised by the creamy texture of the cheese and the burst of flavor the seeds left on her tongue. She made a mental note to look for it next time she went to the market.

"—and did you see that butch dyke she walked in here with?"

The voice hissing low from behind the big potted palm brought Rémi up short. She stopped chewing.

"I don't think anyone missed *that* entrance." The masculine voice was thick with scorn.

"Do you think that they're . . . you know?"

"It sure would be a waste if they weren't. That stud is hot. Did you check out her ass in those pants?"

"You whore. Sometimes I think you'd screw anything with a pulse."

"Is that why she never fucked you?"

Feminine laughter trickled from behind the plant. Rémi chewed, swallowed, stepped from her inadvertent hiding place behind the palm.

The man spoke up again. "I just never thought of Claudia as the type to go *that* way."

"Your jealousy is showing, Preston. She doesn't want you. Move on."

"I'm sure that stud is a much better bargain than you anyway, Pres. When was the last time you even went down on a woman?"

A chorus of laughter answered the obviously rhetorical question.

"Pardon me."

The group of four, some she'd met earlier in the evening, stared at her with startled eyes. Rémi nodded at them in cold-eyed acknowledgment as she walked past, barely holding back her smile at their obvious discomfort at being caught gossiping.

She found Claudia not far from where she left her, this time laughing with two men who stood much too close to her for Rémi's liking. The younger one, blond and closer to forty than his gray-haired friend, kept sneaking glances at Claudia's body. Rémi imagined him getting hard at the way the mint green dress outlined her taut shape, at the sight of the firm nipples pressed against her gathered neckline.

His type was probably more in line with what Claudia wanted—academic, male, and into tweed. A surge of jealousy squeezed her throat tight, making impossible for her to finish the small plate of cheese and crackers. In the kitchen, she tossed the food in the trash and poured herself a glass of white wine.

"Are you having a good time?" Leah appeared at her side, reaching with a tinkling of gold bangles for the merlot.

"Yes, thanks. This crowd is not quite what I'm used to. But it's all right."

Leah squeezed her elbow and leaned in with a smile. "Good. I'm sure Claudia appreciates you coming to the party with her even more."

No more than she appreciated her lover inviting her here into her world. It would have been very easy for Claudia to keep their relationship separate from everything else in her life, but she didn't. And as boring as this party was, Rémi was glad to be there.

"I hope so," she said in response to Leah's comment.

Wine in hand, Rémi left the kitchen to wander through the rest of the house. It was typical of places she'd seen only in the movies: bookshelves built into nearly every wall, some held books but others had knickknacks from other countries—Japanese fans, African statues, Venetian masks. Native American dream catchers in lulling shades of blue hung on the walls. The chairs in each room were thick and cozy, made for curling up during long conversations or for making love. She sank into one, feeling the leather conform to her ass and thighs. Very nice.

"I've been looking for you." Claudia stood in the doorway, a glass of something clear and sparkling in her hand. A woman in a brightly colored dressed walked past in the hall behind her.

"And now you've found me."

Claudia stepped into the study and closed the door behind her. "Lucky me." Her smile lay loose and relaxed across her red mouth.

Rémi chuckled. "And how lucky do you want to get?"

Claudia's low laughter joined hers and she allowed the door to take her weight. "I won't answer that right now on the grounds that my response will incriminate me."

"It's only me, baby. Anything you say to me will be kept in the *strictest* confidence."

Claudia licked her lips. "Really?"

A pulse leapt in Rémi's lap. She was trying to be good. But her lover was making it very hard. The way she leaned against the door, one foot flat against the wood, pushing her hips forward, the graceful curve of her belly, the nipples like batting eyelashes. How easy would it be to convince Claudia to let her fuck her in this house? Tonight? Right now?

"You look gorgeous in that dress."

Rémi imagined tearing it off Claudia, pushing her against the wall and fucking her from behind. The base of the dick she'd packed earlier—just in case—pressed against her clit. She sucked her bottom lip. Oh, the noises Claudia would make.

"Thank you."

Lured by the look in Rémi's eyes, Claudia pushed herself from the door. Came closer. "When I put it on, I thought of you taking it off me."

"Really?"

"No. But I like the sound of it." Her thigh pressed into the chair near Rémi's hand. The smell of green apples seduced Rémi's nose as she leaned closer.

They both looked up at the sound of the door opening. A couple, framed in the light from the hallway, stood in the threshold.

"Oh! Excuse us." The woman backed out and closed the door before her companion could say anything.

Rémi looked back at Claudia, smiling despite the fierce ache low in her belly. "I guess this room isn't the most private."

"I don't care." Claudia walked behind the chair and slid her hands down Rémi's shoulders. Her fingers grazed the already hard nipples. Rémi hissed. Claudia bent low and she could smell her perfume, the champagne on her breath.

"Yes, you do. Especially when you have to face most of them at school after break."

Claudia said nothing, only nibbled lightly on Rémi's ear. Flicked her tongue along the sensitive whorl until a flood of wetness pooled between Rémi's legs and she was near the point of not caring either. But that couldn't happen. She stood up.

"Come. I know a place."

It was a closet down the hall and away from most of the party. A walk-in with the scent of perfume and cologne and cedar hangers and their lust.

"I don't know why this feels like the kinkiest thing I've ever done," she said.

Claudia chuckled as their mouths came together with a hot, wet sound. Her breasts pressed against Rémi's chest and she forgot everything else. Claudia might have said, "It doesn't matter," but that might have been Rémi too. Hands clawed Rémi's shirt open and pressed against her chest, pinching the bare nipples until the fire flared all over her and she wanted nothing more than to sink into Claudia. Rémi gasped into her mouth. She was going crazy. But she felt like she'd waited all day for this, for Claudia's fingers raking down to her belly. They gentled, but only a little, when they found her thick clit, her wet lips, her heart beating heavily in Claudia's hands.

They panted into each other's mouths. Even in the dark, she wanted to experience all of Claudia. She pulled the dress down, baring the small breasts. Rémi growled with frustration at not being able to see them, but oh they felt good. The hard nipples, the satin skin, Claudia's breath trembling under her hands.

She turned quickly around, baring herself to Rémi, and the smell of pussy almost buckled Rémi's knees. The panties pulled aside and her pussy naked to Rémi's touch and imagination in the dark of the closet because she didn't dare turn on the light. To say her lover was wet was an understatement. Rémi could have drowned in her. Could have died in her heaven with no regrets.

It was a small closet, smaller than she expected to find in this big house. But it was deep. Deep enough for them to push past the hanging clothes and find a space big enough for them both, and sitting low like a bench, a shelf with what felt like pairs of shoes. There were coats and shoes, a cashmere sweater that smelled like the sea. Claudia held onto the bar that held the hangers; she gasped and her breath was like champagne. Rémi freed her dick and pushed into her, gasping too, drowning in her clinging wet pussy. She felt cotton and silk brush against her naked ass as she pumped her hips. Sensation tumbling inside of her, prickling heat all over her skin, under her clothes. Rémi wanted to be naked with her. She wanted to feel Claudia fully under her. But she would take what she could get now.

Claudia reached back, squeezing Rémi's ass; her hands slid in the sweat over her skin. *Love you.* Claudia's nipples scored her palm with their hardness, tempted her fingers to squeeze and pinch then move down the heaving belly, the tangled pussy hair around the clit that seemed to pulse to Rémi's heartbeat. *Love this.* They grunted together, quietly, the drowning pleasure of their sex filling the closet with heat and musk from their bodies. *Need this.* Rémi twisted her hips. Kept pressure on Claudia's clit until every thrust from her brought a grunt from Claudia, brought lightning behind her eyes, a saturating wetness under the dildo slamming into her clit. *Need you.*

Their bodies shimmered together. Slammed together and she felt the noise building inside Claudia, the sound roiling up from her clit, up into her belly, heaving with her chest, and bubbling up her throat. Rémi clamped a hand over her lover's mouth. But she couldn't slow herself, the push of her hips, the prickles of hot and cold over her skin as the cum rose up like a flattening wave. The muscles of her ass bunched and released. Fuck quick. Jackhammer heavy. The smells hidden in the clothes, in Claudia's hair pressed into her face. The smell of their sex pushed into her throat. Rémi's low shout caught her by surprise.

Too late, she tried to suppress it in the damp flesh of Claudia's back. But she couldn't retrieve the sound. Her heart thudded in her chest. A pulse pounded, thick and heavy, in her groin. Oh god. She shuddered, hips still moving in shallow thrusts inside Claudia. Her hand fell away from her lover's mouth and Claudia shivered too, carried in the hollow cup of Rémi's body. She laughed breathlessly and turned on Rémi with kisses.

"I love it when you fuck me," she whispered. And the scrape of her breasts, incredibly, stirred Rémi again. She felt ridiculous and wanting, her body already shrugging off its recent orgasm to stand in hungry attention, salivating for Claudia again.

"How much do you love it?" Her voice didn't rise above the press of breath against Claudia's ear.

Her lover's quiet laughter died. "Enough to let you do it again. Anytime. Anywhere."

"Here?"

"Yes. Anywhere."

That's all Rémi wanted to hear. "Turn around," she hissed. "Grab the rod again." She prayed it was sturdy enough to hold Claudia again.

Kneeling, she tugged Claudia's dress all the way off and shoved it behind her on the shelf. Her hands trembled and the only cure for it was to press them against her lover's skin. Against the pretty ankles and feet slipped into the high heels, the waiting weight of her ass just above Rémi's face. Claudia's skin gave off the most delicious scent. Even here in the closet with the clothes that had touched other flesh pressed against her face, brushing her shoulders and cheeks, Rémi smelled her. And her mouth watered.

Like a ripe pear, its flesh coated with the sap of its readiness, Claudia's body hung before Rémi. Tempting. Sweet. She reached into her pants pocket. When she'd picked these up at Claudia's house, she wasn't sure why. Then it had been something to occupy her hands with in case she got bored at the party. But deeper, in the scheming recesses of her mind she knew what she wanted them for. What she would use them for.

Rémi tested them. Squeezed them open and shut, then reached up. The blunt tips of her fingers scraped over Claudia's belly, the underside of her breasts. Among the strangers's clothes, her lover shivered. The nipples were already hard, anticipation turning them to pebbles, into heat that called Rémi's heat. She stroked them. Pulled them. Flicked her thumbs over the hot flesh until they stood up even more. Then she closed the clothespins on them. One after the other. Claudia jerked in surprise but didn't pull away. A soft sob left her mouth.

"If you won't be quiet, I'll make you quiet. Understand?"

She felt the movement of Claudia nodding.

Ever since she knew what sex was, Rémi had wanted Claudia. It was a fact. No exaggeration. No hyperbole. Every time she grew aroused, pussy wet with want, nipples tingling with ache for a wet mouth, hands itching to be buried inside wet warmth, it was for Claudia. That elemental spark to desire. Rémi wanted to take every bit of the woman inside her.

She sank her teeth into the solid flesh at her calf. Like passion and hot fruit trembling on the vine. That was her taste. Her smell. Her scent wove its way into Rémi's nose, into her body until everything in her wanted to taste. Did she taste as good as she smelled? Did she? Ah yes. She did. She does. The dick bobbed through the gap in Rémi's pants but she ignored its insistent thrust for the wicked pleasure of sinking her teeth into Claudia again and again. The backs of her knees. Smooth-fleshed thighs. Quivering bottom. Her lover flinched, breath hitching in her throat.

The more Rémi bit, openmouthed, tongue gently lashing the tattoos her teeth left against the skin, the more fragrant her lover became. Secreting hot sweat, thick juice from her cunt. Rémi's hand brushed that tender place once, then reluctantly moved on. The dimples in her back were delectable. Their flavor shook something deep in Rémi, something that made her teeth sink deeper than before. Claudia bucked. And Rémi breathed in the smell of her pain. Of blood just beneath the surface of the skin. She kissed the damp valley of her back in repentance. Then bit into the soft flesh around it, her own body singing in gratification at the tiny tremors moving up and down her lover, at Claudia's restraint as she held tight to the wooden closet rod, fingers clenched between the cedar hangers that added to the exotic perfume of their hiding place.

Curling over Claudia's back now, teeth pressing, tongue soothing, Rémi was saturated. The phallus still strapped to her hips slipped between Claudia's thighs, probing. Her lover thrust back against it. Widened her legs to receive it. But that wasn't what Rémi wanted. Under her palms, Claudia trembled like a flower in a brisk wind. Her petals were soft. Slick. Wet. A smothered groan left Claudia's throat.

The door clicked, opened, cutting a shaft of light through their darkness. Claudia squeaked. But Rémi held her still, not moving. Not breathing.

"No, that's not the bathroom," A male voice slurred some distance away. "It's farther down the hall." The door pulled shut and the voices disappeared. The darkness became theirs again. Claudia's body began to tremble in earnest now, fear of discovery and desire battling hard within her. It was time for Rémi to end it.

"Don't make a sound."

She dropped to her knees, shoved her face between the quivering ass cheeks. Sweetsop. Her tongue was covered in sweetness, running fresh and wet over her lips. Another noise bubbled from

Claudia but Rémi didn't have the time to punish her. She wanted this, too. Tongue diving into the marsh of her pussy. Clit tight between her lips and against her tongue as she sucked. The dripping slit moving against her face. Rémi reached up and pulled the clothespins from Claudia's nipples.

The roaring cum slammed hard through Claudia. Rémi felt it, felt its echo in her own pussy as her thighs trembled and wetness flooded between her thighs. The cunt under her mouth spasmed, squeezed its juice over Rémi's face. Claudia didn't make a sound.

"That's my girl," Rémi breathed softly. She pressed a kiss against a quivering thigh then stood up blindly in the dark.

"Oh my god!" Claudia sagged against her, shuddering, offering up her mouth. "Oh my good god!"

Rémi sucked on the soft lips, instinctively pressing her fingers to the wet pussy. Claudia's thighs opened. Her shaky laugh leaked into the dark space. "Not that I wouldn't mind." Her pussy opened up, wetly swallowed the seeking tips of Rémi's fingers. "But I think we should go home. Eventually someone's going to come looking."

Rémi agreed with a nod, sensation still tripping through her. She reached back into the darkness for Claudia's dress and helped her into it before tending to her own clothes. Claudia led them out of the closet.

In the sudden brightness of the hallway, Rémi blinked. Two dark-clad backs receded slowly down the hallway and they straightened just as a third person rounded the corner. The woman, pale skinned, goth, and dressed in a black corset and floor-length skirt, as if for a party much more interesting than this one, gave them a distracted smile before continuing past.

"Home," Claudia said, leaning close to bite Rémi's earlobe. "Now."

The renewed throbbing in Rémi's pussy couldn't agree with her fast enough. They said their goodbyes to Claudia's colleagues and not-quite-friends before jumping in the Escalade and pushing eighty all the way back to the house in Coconut Grove.

Chapter

25

"What are you doing with that child, Claude?" Rémi paused at what she thought was the sound of Eden's voice. *Claude? Claudia?*

"I'm not doing anything." Claudia's voice pushed through the speakers in Rémi's office like superheated cream. The forced nonchalance in her tone didn't fool anyone.

Rémi's eyes searched the sparse crowd in the restaurant below then up to the second level. The women sat at a window table with the falling light from the sun haloing them and their nearly empty martini glasses. Claudia, in pale slacks and her favorite periwinkle blouse, leaned back in her chair and gazed at her friend.

"You talk about her too much. Not to mention the other night I was passing by your house and I saw her motorcycle in your driveway." Eden leaned forward, her voice tight with emphasis. "It was almost two a.m."

The previous owner of the building had wired nearly every inch of it for sound and video. When Rémi had first found out, she was vaguely repelled. But over the years, being privy to certain conversations that took place in her club proved very useful to her, even when that eavesdropping hadn't been planned. Like now.

Eden looked ready to confront Claudia for being a liar. Her pose against the sun, head cocked in disbelief, palm up and open as if ready for her friend's confession, spoke of someone in possession of another's secret. It wasn't any of her business who Claudia had in her driveway late at night, anyway. What was she, her fucking keeper? A jealous lover? Rémi's hand hovered over the button to kill the feed. Inside, she squirmed listening to their conversation, but— her hand fell away from the remote—she wanted to hear more.

"So what?" Claudia asked. "Rémi has been like family for years now. She can come see me anytime she wants to."

"Is that how you two are still acting? Like family?"

Images of them together flooded Rémi. Claudia bent over and open, ready to be taken from behind. The damp, heaving line of her belly while Rémi feasted between her legs.

"Yes. Like family. How long have you known me? Do you think all of a sudden I'm going to turn into a lesbian?"

"I've seen how she looks at you. That girl has had a crush on you for years. Don't tell me you haven't noticed."

Claudia shook her head. "Let's not go over this anymore. This discussion is pointless."

"You're avoiding this discussion."

"There's nothing to discuss, Eden. Nothing is going on between Rémi and me." Her voice rose in desperation, negating her words. "That's it. Just leave things alone."

A knock sounded on the office door, and Rémi looked abruptly away from the two women. She killed the audio feed and glanced at the monitor, expecting to see Elena at the door, but her eyebrow rose at the figure that waited there instead.

"Come in."

Her cousin walked in and closed the door behind her. "Your chef does some really impressive things in that kitchen," Wynne said, nibbling from a small plate of hummus and pita crisps, another of Rochelle's specialties. "What's in this thing? Pieces of black olives? Pine nuts? That reviewer from the *Herald* was really onto something."

Her black-and-white tennis shoes were silent against the floor as she made her way to the sofa she'd taken last time she visited. In dark jeans and a sky-colored T-shirt with "Visit the Florida Keys" scrawled across the chest, she again looked like a college student. A hungry one, by the way she was eating Rochelle's hummus.

"Thanks," Rémi said for want of anything better to say. She was trying to get past the point of being surprised when her cousin showed up unexpectedly, but she wasn't there yet.

"I hear you're heading back home." Wynne dipped the pita too deeply in the hummus, smearing her fingers pale. She licked them off before biting into the crisped bread. "Say hello to Aunt Kelia for me when you see her."

It seemed like no piece of information ever got by her cousin. "I will." Rémi put away the stack of invoices she'd been about to take a look at before she was distracted by Claudia and Eden's conversation. "I don't suppose you've found out anything more about Matthias Anderson and why he seems to have it in for me?"

"Not directly. But I'm sure you will soon."

Rémi made a noise and stood up from behind her desk. "I'm glad you have such confidence in me."

Even with her tall cousin stretched out in the sofa, she was able to sit comfortably at its end, legs stretched out before her and crossed at the ankles. She blew a breath out between pursed lips. Wynne, always the quiet one and especially with food in front of her, said nothing else, and Rémi didn't press her. She'd managed to put this thing with Anderson at the back of her mind in favor of more pleasurable preoccupations but she felt that it was all coming to a head. And soon.

"You know, I'm not sure what you're doing here in the city, but you're always welcome to come over to my place for dinner or something."

Wynne looked at her over the plate. "You cook now?"

"Not exactly. But I can always ask Rochelle to make us something. Not to mention I pour a decent bottle of wine."

"Thank you. I just might take you up on that." She used her finger to wipe the last of the hummus from the plate. "If your chef can make this taste good, then the prospect of a proper meal..." Wynne's voice drifted away at her slight smile.

Although her cousin never talked about it, Rémi easily imagined the bleak isolation of the life she must have now. Her parents dead. Sister disappeared. And a dangerous job that fostered the opposite of intimacy. The loneliness must press down on her hard like an unexpected wave on a calm sea.

"I'm sure that—"

But a quick rap at the door interrupted what she was about to say. Rémi stood up to look at the monitor and felt Wynne do the same.

"I'll let you get back to business," her cousin said.

She opened the door to let Elena in and herself out. Over the manager's shoulder, their eyes met. "I'll be around," Wynne said.

"Good."

After the door closed behind her cousin, Rémi gestured for Elena to join her on the sofa. With her dark hair pinned up in a severe bun and dressed in slim-fitting dark jeans, a dark blouse, and black blazer, the manager looked ready for a funeral.

"Thanks for coming in, Elena. I know you have important matters to take care of at home."

The other woman nodded. She sat on the sofa and crossed her legs, throwing a guarded, almost fearful, glance at Rémi. That look told Rémi all she needed to know.

She decided to get to the heart of the matter. "There's a man named Matthias Anderson who's been giving me some trouble over the last few months."

Elena flinched.

"Do you know this man?"

"Yes. I do."

"Tell me about him."

Elena visibly swallowed and clasped her hands together on her knee. She opened her mouth. Then closed it. "Rémi," she said finally. "I think you know everything."

"Tell me anyway."

The skin around Elena's mouth was pinched tight. She looked like she'd rather be anywhere but in Rémi's office. In the month and a half since she'd been gone, she'd lost weight. Her once curvaceous body was now like a prepubescent child's, thin and awkwardly posed.

"My husband. He works for a man—a man who owns another restaurant in North Miami. This man threatened Guillermo. Told him that if I did not disappear from Gillespie's for a few months he would fire him and make sure that no one else employed him." Elena blinked frantically but her eyes still shone with tears when they looked up. "We have the children to worry about. The new house. We couldn't afford to say no." The manager trembled, her hands maintaining a stranglehold on each other on top of her dark-clad knee.

Rémi nodded. It was not as bad as she thought. But it was bad. Anderson had gotten to Elena. Someone she thought she could trust.

"I know you trusted me, Rémi," Elena said as if reading her mind. "You probably feel that this trust was misplaced. But please don't think of this as a betrayal. When that man forced me to leave, I knew that wasn't going to change anything. You could handle the business by yourself. He thought you would fail but he was wrong."

Rémi arched a sardonic brow. "Are you trying to flatter me to keep your job?"

"No. If you've made up your mind to fire me, then I'm gone. My small words won't change your mind. Still, I wanted to say them."

The women looked at each other. They had known one another for three years. It was three years of hard work, of working side by side to ensure the success of this business that they had both invested so much in. When Gillespie's first opened, Rémi had taken a chance on a woman who'd never managed a restaurant before, and she'd been rewarded with a tireless and exceptional employee.

"Come back to work tomorrow. Consider yourself on probation. If anything else happens with you that affects the club, you're fired. Permanently." Rémi stood up. "Okay?"

"Okay." Elena's voice broke. She got to her feet. "Thank you, Rémi. You won't regret this. I promise."

Rémi nodded once. "I hope not."

Chapter

26

When Rémi walked into the classroom, it grew quiet. The students, mostly young women, turned to look at her, some stares lingered but most merely gave her silent figure a cursory glance before turning their attentions once again to the professor. Rémi nodded at Claudia, seated in front of the class in a dark skirt and white blouse, legs crossed, a book face up on her lap.

"—*Les Guérillères* remarkable for its time," she continued, not faltering at the sight of Rémi, but a slight question wrinkled her otherwise smooth brow.

Claudia didn't sit behind a desk away from her students. Rémi remembered this from when she took French 101 in college. Instead, she sat in front of the desk in a plastic chair much like the ones her students inhabited, minus the attached desk, paying seductive attention to a class full of eager young minds.

Rémi put her paper bag on the desk in front of her. Crossed her booted feet and waited for Claudia to finish. Her spurs jingled.

"Remarkable, yes, but still very opaque in some ways," an Asian girl with a pixie haircut said. "And that's a barrier to her ideas finding their way to us, the very people she is trying to reach."

A girl who reminded her of Nuria, only with a shaven head and large hoop earrings, jumped in without raising their hand. "I disagree. We don't ask Faulkner for clarity, do we? No. We keep engaging with the text until its buried meaning emerges and we are ourselves richer for the experience."

The discussion continued, but Rémi focused on Claudia instead, content with watching her guide the students where she wanted them, her soft voice agreeing or disagreeing as she saw fit but always respectful. Insightful. A few minutes after three, with the discussion still going strong, Claudia closed the book on her lap.

"That's all we have time for today, class." she smiled, at once conveying regret and finality. "For next time, have your two-page reactions ready to hand in to me and come prepared to discuss the Maryse Condé novel."

The classroom erupted into disorganized sound as the students put their books away, started conversations among themselves, and began to leave. The Nuria look-alike picked up her shoulder bag and approached Claudia, academic curiosity all over her pretty face.

With her questions satisfactorily answered ten minutes later, she too left, sparing Rémi a polite smile as she passed.

"This is a nice surprise," Claudia said once they were alone.

She dropped a stack of papers into her briefcase, looking over her shoulder at Rémi. "To what do I owe the pleasure?"

"My stomach," Rémi said. She pulled her present from the paper bag. "I got hungry thinking about you."

A smile curved Claudia's mouth. She hitched the bag onto her shoulder. "Thank you, tummy." She lightly patted Rémi's stomach. "Because I'm hungry too."

"I figured as much. Here." She extended the apple. When Claudia reached out to take it, Rémi shook her head, pulled the fruit back.

Claudia tilted her head. Pursed her lips. "Really?"

"Your mouth."

She chuckled, a low vibration deep in her throat before leaning in to sink her teeth into the glistening green apple. The fruit crunched. A bit of juice squirted on Rémi's fingers. When Claudia drew back, Rémi sucked the juice from her hand and bit into the apple too.

"If you don't have any more campus commitments today, I'd like to take you to dinner."

"Oh. I thought this *was* dinner."

"Not hardly."

"In that case, I'd love to have dinner with you. I can just come in early tomorrow and finish up."

They left the classroom, walking through the wide hallways with their arms touching, the sound of their heels synchronized against the tiled floor. Rémi's boots. Claudia's far-from-sensible shoes.

"I know it's a school night, so I promise to get you in bed by ten"—when Claudia laughed, Rémi shook her head, smiling—"in your own bed and alone. Promise."

"What if I don't want to be in my bed, alone, by ten?"

"Then I'm open to renegotiation."

Outside, the sky simmered with light. Sunset was at least an hour away. Looking at her watch, Rémi suggested Claudia leave her car in the faculty parking lot and come with her on the back of the Harley. Traffic would be less of an issue that way. After only a moment's hesitation, Claudia agreed, dropping off her briefcase in the trunk of her little toy car before hopping on the bike.

Rémi kicked the engine to life. She couldn't resist reaching back to clasp the naked length of Claudia's thigh, once, with her gloved hand. The hiked-up skirt, and revealed brown skin, made Rémi's body vibrate nearly as viciously as the bike rumbling under them.

She waited until they had ridden through the campus, coasted past the backpacked students, lazily waving palm trees, and miles of parked cars before opening up the bike. Claudia gripped her belly tighter, pressed her helmeted face against the leather jacket covering Rémi's back. Laughed as they shot out onto Ponce de Leon Boulevard toward Highway 1.

When they got to their destination, a high-rise apartment building near Biscayne Bay, Claudia looked around. "I didn't know there was a restaurant around here."

"Normally there isn't, but for you, the world appears."

Rémi drew her close, inhaling the scent of fresh apples from her laughing mouth. After stopping by the concierge's desk to get the picnic basket and blanket—Claudia eyed them with an intrigued smile—they rode the glass elevator up, and up, away from the dense green below until a view of Biscayne Bay appeared, a dazzling blue canvas with dozens of boats floating on its jeweled surface. Birds, pale and graceful like small clouds, hovered over the water.

"This city is so beautiful," Claudia breathed, leaning back into Rémi.

"Yes, it is."

On the roof, Rémi spread the thick plaid blanket, unpacked the food while Claudia looked down at the bay on one side and Coconut Grove on the other. Unlike most rooftops in Miami, this one hadn't been converted into a city-view deck or set up with cabanas and a pool. Instead, the surface under their feet remained rough and unpainted, and the hip-high ledge separating them from certain death was blocked cement and utilitarian gray. Except for the steady hum of the building's main air conditioner unit, it was just them and wide open sky.

"I can almost see my house from here," Claudia said, peering toward the Grove and shielding her eyes against the lowering sun.

Rémi looked up from pulling a bottle of wine from the picnic basket. "Your eyesight must be amazing." In her high heels, black skirt, and simple white blouse, Claudia stood silhouetted against the brilliant blue sky. "Along with everything else," Rémi finished.

A mild breeze tugged at Claudia's sleeves as she turned. Her mouth curved up. A hand at the fluttering collar of her blouse.

"Come," Rémi said.

Claudia sat down on the blanket, tucking her legs under her. She looked at each dish Rémi had pulled from the picnic basket, premade and snugly tucked under plastic wrap. Curried chicken. Brown rice. Cabbage. "This is wonderful, darling. Did you make all this?"

Without waiting for an answer, she leaned in with parted lips, tangling fingers in the hair at Rémi's nape. Her mouth was dry but warm. Rémi licked it, turning the quick peck into something else. She could never get enough of kissing Claudia.

"You know better than that," she said once her lips were free. "Rochelle made dinner for us."

Claudia grinned. "Silly me. But brilliant you for coming up with this. The last thing I wanted to do at home tonight was cook."

The last thing Rémi wanted to do was go home alone tonight. At least one of them would get their wish. She turned a crooked smile to Claudia. "Eat up."

She uncovered the plates and, miraculously, everything was still warm. Faint trails of steam hovered over the thin slices of raisin-flavored curried chicken, bringing the spicy-sweet aroma to Rémi's nose. Her companion sighed with appreciation when she put the plate in her lap and poured her a glass of white wine.

"You are the most delicious human being in creation," she said, taking a bite of cabbage.

"Interesting choice of words." Rémi chuckled. "Don't get my mind started on that path, please. It will all come to no good." She picked up her own food and turned to fully face Claudia, who eagerly sampled everything on her plate. "Tell me about your day."

They talked while the sun drifted lower in the sky, ripening everything around them. Falling amber light tangled in the faint lines at the corner of Claudia's eyes, blinding Rémi to everything but her lover. Her ears shut to everything but the words Claudia spoke. Her libido floated away with everything that was extra, everything but the warmth swelling inside her chest for this woman. She refilled Claudia's glass, leaving hers for the most part untouched.

Their plates emptied and Claudia relaxed even more, speaking freely about her love of teaching and books in a way that Rémi had never heard before.

"Sometimes," she said, in the tone of a sinner at confessional, "I find it all unbearably sexy." Claudia swirled the wine in her glass, glanced up at Rémi through her lashes. "I've even masturbated to Toni Morrison."

Caught off guard, Rémi laughed. "Honestly? Which one? Please don't say *Beloved!* That would be too weird, even for me."

"No." Claudia laughed and threw her head back to look at the sky. "I can't believe I just told you that."

"You haven't told me anything yet." Rémi poured more wine into Claudia's glass. "Tell me how it happened. Unless it happened more than once, and then just tell me about the first time."

Claudia's eyes sparkled between curling lashes. She leaned toward Rémi on the blanket, fingers landing like butterflies on Rémi's knee. "Why?"

"Why do you think?"

She laughed again and withdrew her hand. "We were reading the novel in a class—"

In class? Rémi's body perked up.

"—and the eroticism of the scene just hit me. The character laying there, pressing her naked body into a seal skin coat. I had to look up to see if any of the students noticed me pressing my legs together."

But Rémi wasn't picturing Claudia's students or even anything to do with the Toni Morrison book. The image of Claudia touching herself came to her as clearly as if she had been watching from the other side of the classroom. The students disappeared and it was her, hiking up the pencil skirt, baring a glistening pussy. Fingers dancing over her clit. Disappearing into the wet pink hole. Rémi's fingers twitched against her thigh.

Claudia's gaze caught the movement like a fly. "Does that excite you, darling?"

"I'm not made of stone." Rémi adjusted the air in her throat.

The laughter died on Claudia's lips. She looked at Rémi, tapping a finger very lightly against her mouth. "I never thought you were."

With the slightest twist of her body, she put her wineglass down, far away from them, nearly off the blanket.

"Could you be like stone for me if I wanted?"

"Why would you want—" Something in Claudia's eyes stopped the rest of the words. "Yes, I could."

"And right now, can you be still for me?"

"Yes."

"Can you not touch?"

"Yes."

Rémi closed her eyes and leaned back, bracing herself on flattened palms, as Claudia reached over to unbutton her shirt, fingers barely tasting skin as they flicked each button loose from its cotton prison. If she didn't watch, she thought, she could have as much control as Claudia wanted. The breeze gently batted at her flesh, her breasts, her belly.

"I love that you don't wear a bra."

The words brushed against Rémi's throat and all her senses shuddered.

"All I have to do is peel aside one layer, and there you are. Mine." A cool palm against her skin. Claudia's hand surrounding her breast. Cupping it. Fingers biting gently into her nipples.

I don't think this is the place, love. That's what Rémi wanted to say. *Anyone can see.* But when Claudia's tongue found her nipples, she was lost. Rémi had never been affected either way when women touched her breasts, but with Claudia her entire body seemed to wake to all sensual possibilities. The lazy lash of tongue flooded moisture between her legs. Their blanket wrinkled under her clenched fingers. Her lashes trembled against her cheeks. A touch on her belly. The sound of her zipper releasing. Her slacks whispering as they gave way.

"No." She grabbed Claudia's hand, stopping their progress.

"I thought you said you could be still. Not touch."

Rémi trembled at the voice. Steel wrapped in silk. She withdrew her hand.

Tiny kisses circled her breast, moved up to her throat, her ear, while a touch, featherlight and inevitable, crept low, tangling in the hairs at her pussy. She hissed. Her clit, swollen to painful thickness by the whip in Claudia's voice, throbbed under the delicate touch. The touch. Rémi's head flew back as the touch pressed between her legs. She opened them as wide as the slacks would allow. Electric and perfect. Firm and slow. Claudia's fingers swirled around her clit, dove between her swollen pussy lips. Filled her. Rémi gasped. Good. So good.

"Do you know how much I love the feel of you around my fingers? The way you get wet for me, so easily. I envy that."

Shallow movements. Then deeper. Firmer. The shadows behind her tightly closed eyelids flickered. Went red. Wind rushing in and out of her mouth. Rémi's pussy opened up, rushing wet, clinging walls, as Claudia's fingers unerringly found that spot.

"Be still for me."

Claudia whispered it against her breast. Tongue darting. Mouth sucking. But Rémi couldn't help the movement of her hips. Lifting up. Eagerly swallowing the small fingers. Liquid lust. Her belly tight and tighter. Hands clenched in the blankets to hold on to something, anything, since her body was flying apart. Apart. A brilliant sunset that rippled through her body, ripped her eyes open, tore gasp after gasp, a sprinter's labored wheeze from her.

Arms trembling, she opened her eyes to Claudia's smiling face.

"You are so lovely." And she licked Rémi's juices from her fingers.

Rémi's hips bucked against the blanket. She was still as Claudia buttoned her shirt, zipped up her slacks, buckled her belt. Another shudder ran through her. Rémi's mouth felt dry. Wordless.

"I'm enjoying you so much." Claudia lifted her fingers to her nose and inhaled deeply, smiling.

Then the smile fell from her face. Her look became serious. Eyes flickered to Rémi's face then beyond to the fiery sky and dark clouds slipping between cracks in the light. Rémi leaned forward to ask what was wrong, but Claudia's voice stopped her.

"Have you thought about what a long-term relationship with me means?"

"Of course." Sometimes that was all she thought about. Dez's reaction. Her friends' comments. Would Claudia ever be able to come out to her friends and acknowledge their relationship without being ashamed. She thought about these things. Often.

"I'm going to die," Claudia said.

Rémi's stomach dropped. She jerked her hand away from her lover's. Then clutched at Claudia's arms. "What? Are you all right? I thought the cancer was gone." She felt encased in ice.

"I'm sorry. I didn't mean to say it like that. What I mean is, I'll die long before you. I'll lose my sex drive before you." Whatever she saw in Rémi's face made her shake her head, smile sadly. "That's about the same as death for someone like you."

"There are differences between us, yes. But don't talk about death." Rémi's voice broke and she had to clear her throat. Then dropped into the French of her childhood. *"S'il vous plaît. Je vous prie.* Don't ever do that. When it comes, it comes."

Her body lurched forward, uncontrolled, and gathered Claudia close. *And even then I don't want to be away from you.* Rémi didn't realize she was shaking until Claudia pulled away, pressed cool hands to her cheeks. A curl of her own hair trembled before her face as if caught in its own small earthquake.

"I'm sorry, baby. I didn't mean to frighten you."

Rémi didn't know what to say. The thought of losing her lover had ripped away her speech, made it impossible for her to do anything but hold her close and feel the ice inside her slowly dissolve with each small kiss Claudia pressed to her mouth.

"I'm sorry," Claudia said again. "Take me home. There will be other sunsets to see."

Chapter

27

The house stood high on the grass-brushed hill, with glass from its tall, rectangular windows winking in the late morning sun. It had been designed and built by some famous architect that her father had gone to school with in France. Clean modern lines, wheat-colored marble, and acres of reflective glass somehow made the structure fit perfectly with the crystal water and seasonal extremes of the Boothbay Harbor landscape. Because of its unique beauty, Auguste's house had been the subject of many photo spreads in home and garden magazines. In snow, Rémi remembered, the house was breathtaking, rising up out of the white like a jeweled crown. Now, at the height of spring, the lawn was its most vibrant green, and the roses on either side of the path leading up to the door exploded in vibrant shades of red, yellow, and lavender. A hint of winter's cool breath still lingered in the air.

Rémi turned from watching the taxi driver disappear around the circular driveway to walk up the marble steps to the thick, wooden front door. She put the key in the lock and turned it.

Behind her, Yvette shivered in her thin T-shirt. "I wonder why Mama didn't come out to meet us. I called her when you were paying the cabbie and getting the luggage."

She gently shouldered past Rémi and through the open front door with her backpack over one shoulder and a pillow pressed against her chest. She wasn't able to sleep on the plane without a pillow so Rémi had given her one from the guest room.

"Maybe she's busy." Rémi dropped her duffel bag on the floor and passed the house key back to her sister. She looked at her watch. It was barely two o'clock.

Yvette glanced toward the stairs. "I'm going to put this stuff in my room and find her." She turned to go.

Claudia sat on the wooden bench near the door, her small rolling suitcase at her feet. She still looked as refreshed as she had this morning when Rémi and Yvette came to get her in the truck. Long legs crossed in the salmon-colored trouser shorts and a white blouse tucked in neatly at the waist.

"Maybe we should call again to make sure that she's here."

"Hey." They both turned when a side door banged open and a breathless figure emerged. "Sorry I didn't come sooner. I got tied up outside in the garden."

Her mother looked old. Rémi blinked at the woman she'd barely seen ten months ago and felt the surprise burst in her chest. Kelia's permed hair lay in glossy salt-and-pepper waves around her face, falling inches well above her shoulders. There were lines in her face that weren't there at the funeral. Her mouth was pinched and narrow, and although the brisk spring breeze from the outdoors should have made her coco brown coloring more refreshed, she looked washed out and toothpick-thin instead. The black cardigan and jeans nearly swallowed her thin body whole. Rémi knew that Kelia and Claudia were around the same age, but with the two of them in the same room, her lover could easily pass for Kelia's much younger sister. Or daughter.

Kelia pulled off her gardening gloves and dropped them in an antique-looking copper pail by the door.

"Rémi, it's good to see you." Rémi stood stiffly as Kelia hugged her and stood up on tiptoe to kiss her cheek. "Don't stand there as if you hate me." The brown eyes looked into hers as if searching for something. Rémi gently disengaged herself from her mother's embrace.

"Mother, this is Claudia Nichols." Rémi nodded toward her lover while her mother still looked at her, wide-eyed and hurt. "Claudia, my mother, Kelia Walker-Bouchard."

"A pleasure." Claudia extended her hand and a cautious smile.

Kelia cleared her throat and lightly shook the offered hand. "I didn't realize Rémi was bringing someone else along."

"Of course you did, Mama. I told you." Yvette bounced in the room, looking more like a child than Rémi had seen these past few months. "I told you Rémi was bringing her girlfriend."

Rémi could feel Claudia's cringe at her side, but her lover met Kelia's surprised look with the same smile. Almost a dare.

"Ah. Okay. I didn't realize . . ." Her voice tapered off into silence.

"Yes, it caught me by surprise too." Claudia laughed.

"No big deal, Mama. We're all adults here."

Kelia shook her head. "My daughter, the grown-up." As if she couldn't prevent the comment from spilling from her lips. Life catching up with her fast. "Still, I don't—" she paused again, as if considering her words carefully.

"We don't mind staying in separate rooms," Claudia said before Rémi could jump in.

"Good."

Yvette rolled her eyes. "The house is big enough, I guess. By the way, is René out back? I looked all over upstairs and couldn't find him."

"He's at camp until Thursday."

"Really?" Yvette shuddered. "Poor baby. But better him than me."

Kelia shoved her hands in the pockets of her cardigan with a determined smile on her face. "Rémi, you know where your old room is. I'll show Claudia to hers."

She watched as Kelia led her lover away, feeling helplessness tug at her belly. Only God and Kelia knew what Claudia would be subjected to now. Behind Kelia, Claudia turned with a gentle smile and blew her a kiss. She could take care of herself.

"Come on," Yvette said. "Your room's been shut up for years. Mom tidied it up for you before the funeral. She didn't expect you to stay at the hotel."

Rémi's mouth twisted at the reminder of her last visit. "That was nice of her." She followed her sister up the stairs.

"Come on. This is your home, too."

That's not what Auguste Bouchard had said to her the last time she'd seen him. Her father has been adamant that there was no room for a dyke in his family and certainly not in his house.

"Papa, I'm gay."

She'd thought about saying the words for days, ever since her best girl friend at the time had kissed her, and she liked it. At age thirteen, the kiss was young Rémi's final proof of her queerness, since she'd long ago realized that she had no interest in the boys at school other than as playmates. At the time, she shared everything with her father, and to her this was just another facet of her bourgeoning self-identity that they could talk about and come to understand together.

"Papa, I'm gay."

She finally said the words to him in his office, the darkened old-world room where he did much of the paperwork and planning required of him as the owner and chef of three Michelin-starred restaurants.

Rémi never saw her father move. Only felt the stinging surprise of his palm across her face. That slivered fury in his eyes. She gasped in shock, pressing her suddenly cold hand against the betrayal burning into her cheek.

"Never say that to me again," he hissed. "Never."

Then he went back behind his desk and looked down at his paper-work, dismissing her like an unwanted employee. They never spoke of it again. Never actually spoke of anything beyond what was necessary for two people living in the same house. After that evening she felt the abrupt withdrawal of his affection, like winter settling in. Late that night, she woke to the sound of glass breaking, one crash after another until after the twenty-forth explosion of noise, silence. It wasn't until days later when she went down to the wine cellar to get her mother a bottle of white wine for dinner that she realized what she'd heard: her father destroying the case of 1986 Haut-Bages Libéral he'd been saving for her wedding.

Yvette pushed open the door to Rémi's old room, unlatched the windows to let in the crisp spring air. Home, she had said a few moments before.

"This place hasn't been my home for a very long time." Rémi let out a short bark of laughter. "You don't remember how it was with him and me."

"You're right. I don't. But I think he regretted it."

"Bullshit. If he had regrets, he knew where to find me."

She'd been in Miami, with her nose pressed to the window, gazing in at someone else's family. At someone else's father. At his best, Claudia's husband had been a good father to his twin children. He took them to museums, the beach, even trips to the annual strawberry festival where they stuffed themselves full until they could barely fold their bodies inside the car for the drive back home. Rémi watched all this with pale-eyed envy. Even after Warrick abandoned his lesbian daughter and focused his attentions on Derrick, she had admired his fatherhood. For Auguste, she'd never been the perfect daughter or child. He never showed her the love that he lavished on Yvette. Rémi shook her head to banish her father from her thoughts.

In the room, Yvette sat down on the bed, watching as Rémi unpacked her toiletries before putting the duffel bag away. "I never thought he was a bad man."

"I'm sure he never thought that either."

Yvette looked up at Rémi, eyes dark with confused pain. Her fingers plucked at the quilted bedspread.

After her sister left the room, Rémi waited barely ten minutes before leaving too. The large bedroom, an aching reminder of her childhood self and especially her last year in the house, made her want to slit her wrists. Or someone else's. It didn't take her long to find the room where her mother had stashed Claudia. At the sound of their low voices behind the door, she walked past to wait patiently behind the stairs until her mother went about her other business.

"Dinner is at eight," Claudia said with a mocking curve to her mouth when Rémi slipped through the door and shut it behind her.

She straightened from putting the last of her travel clothes in the bureau. "In case you hadn't heard while you were eavesdropping outside."

Rémi smirked. "I heard. But I came for mine a little early."

Claudia laughed, but Rémi was serious. She had come to Maine to be supportive of Yvette, but it seemed as if she was betraying herself. This place wasn't good for her. The very air she breathed in the house felt oppressive. This was her father's air. This was his house. Even with him dead and buried, it felt thick with his presence. He'd always preferred things dark and traditional. The somber and heavy wooden furniture. Old maps of Europe. Tiny ships trapped in bottles and resting on untouchable pedestals all over the house. Children trapped in roles they could never truly fill.

Here she always had to live by his rules. But she was tired of it. Her entire life had been dictated by his whims. By his hatred of what she was. And her mother, except for her single rebellious act of leaving him for those few months, had never stood up for her. The house was poison. And she needed an antidote for it.

When Claudia moved toward her empty suitcase on the bed, Rémi blocked her way. The minute brush of Claudia's skin against hers was a balm to Rémi's senses. She traced her finger along the steady pulse in her lover's throat.

"Come outside with me. As much as I'd love to fuck you in this bed, I want to get out of this house more."

"Let me put this away, then we can go." Her soft voice held a smile.

While she shut the case in an empty wardrobe, Rémi pulled a thick blanket from the closet. Then she led her out to the terrace. With their hands loosely clasped together, they crossed the neatly trimmed backyard then waded through the high, impossible-to-cut grass on the steep incline leading down to the rocky footpath and the bay. Boothbay Harbor was like the sky spread out at their feet. Seabirds coasted above its rippling surface, dancing between the sailboats floating serenely in the blue.

"It's beautiful here." Claudia slipped her arm around Rémi's waist and anchored herself close as they walked carefully down the grassy hill. "But it's probably no consolation to you."

The grass brushed against their arms with a sound like whispers.

"It's not. When I was younger, I used to sneak back here to my secret place."

"Like a secret garden?"

"Nothing that luxurious." Claudia's hip fit perfectly under Rémi's hand. The smooth curve. The gently rolling motion of her backside as she walked. She could easily walk with Claudia until the end of the earth and be content. But they didn't have to go that far to get to their destination. "Just this."

They stepped through the nearly waist-high grass and pale flowering weeds into a place that always allowed Rémi to breathe easier. Here, the view of the harbor was much more intimate. The eye could take in a wide stretch of blue water, rolling hills, clustered trees, and other scattered houses surrounding the water on three sides. Farther out, beyond sight, Rémi had always assumed, lay more of the same. An empty hammock rocked gently between two trees.

Rémi took off her boots and socks and curled her toes in the feathery moss on the ground. She moved her boots aside and sat down, gently tugging Claudia down to sit beside her. The other woman looked out at the water rocking with its pretty cargo of boats and sparkling under the sun.

"What's wrong?" Rémi asked.

"Something. Though I'm not sure what." She put a hand on Rémi's thigh. "All these years that I've known you I never asked about your life in Maine. And now, seeing you in this place, I deeply regret that."

"It was a painful past that I tried to forget. Who's to say that if you had asked me I would have told you anything."

Claudia nodded, pale hair glinting under the sun, eyes. "But this all seems so wrong. That scar on your shoulder. How you tremble sometimes in your sleep." Her lips pulled tight as she frowned. "I can only imagine the cause of these things, and the things I imagine make me sad."

"Don't feel sorry for me. That's the last thing that I want." Rémi squeezed her lover's hand. "My father hurt me. Then my mother hurt me. I'm just trying to survive that and have a happy life despite these things. The reason I'm here is to help my sister deal with whatever it is that's making her so miserable. It may be as simple as the reasons she gave me, but maybe not."

Claudia cupped Rémi's cheek with her palm. A simple offer of comfort. "Whatever happens on this trip, I'm here for you."

And she believed her. "Thank you." Rémi kissed her very serious mouth then stood up to spread out the blanket. She lay back against the thick cotton, inviting Claudia to do the same. "Right now I just want you to feel you beside me."

Her companion snuggled into the crook of her arm, laying her soft weight against Rémi's side, a hand on her belly.

"You know, I used to hate being one of the few black kids here."

"Really? I thought you'd love an experience like that. Being unique and all."

Rémi laughed. Bitterly. She rubbed Claudia's back through the thin blouse, breathed in the scent of crushed grass and warm woman, felt the solid ground through the blanket under her back. Felt contentment. And began to talk.

It was nothing to tell about her childhood. About growing up in the large hillside house with parents who were sometimes too smitten with each other to pay her any attention. At school, the other kids envied her for her tall French father with his thick sandy hair and infectious laughter. These kids and their parents often wondered in Rémi's presence what he was doing with the quiet black woman from Canada. But because Kelia and Auguste were happy, she ignored them. All over the house, she often heard them laughing, often caught her mother sitting in her father's lap, heard sounds of them making love in the afternoons.

Rémi had no certain memory of when everything changed. Only that her mother's look became less love-struck and more strained. Her face pinched and narrow and the lustrous brown skin faded to gray. The laughter stopped, but not the sex. Rémi began to tread more carefully around the house so she wouldn't walk in on them.

"Then Yvette came along and things returned to normal for a

while. They were perfect parents again. Lovers on a second honey-moon. I didn't mind babysitting as long as things in the house were good." Rémi shifted, uncomfortable at the memories bombarding her. "Maybe it was stress from work. Maybe it was just my father being bored with happiness. Whatever it was, it started up again. And things only got worse after I told him I was gay." Her father's cold face swam before her eyes. "Living here became unbearable."

Claudia's fingers spun gentle circles on her belly. The warm touch seeped into her body, gently burning away the acid her father's memory churned up.

"I'm glad that your mother at least took the step to get you out of his house and harm's way."

"Yeah. At least she did that much."

Rémi didn't bother to hide the sarcasm in her voice. There were days when she wasn't sure which hurt her worse, her mother's aban-donment or Auguste's indifference and abuse. With a quiet sigh, she pushed away her bleak mood. No more. Not today.

Rémi dipped her hand underneath the back of Claudia's shirt. "Enough about that," she murmured, consciously shifting her ca-resses from tender to arousing. Claudia wriggled as Rémi raked a path of pleasure along her spine. "The door to my less-than-pleasant past is now closed." Rémi deepened her voice. "Will you open *your* door for me?"

Claudia chuckled. "Who knew you were this cheesy?"

She sat up on the blanket to hover, light and fragrant, above Rémi. "But I'll play along." The sky was a sharp blue behind her, with wisps of clouds trailing its expanse. "My door is always open to you."

"Hm. That's the best thing I've heard all day."

Rémi lifted her head, stretching her neck to lightly kiss her lover on the mouth. "Now come down here. I want to play with you."

Claudia smiled, and came closer, her mouth hot with kisses. But Rémi gently and firmly pulled her down onto the blanket, switched places until she was the one on top and Claudia looked up at her, still smiling. Rémi wanted to lick that smile off her face.

Her lover must have read the intent in her eyes, because she shuddered. Rémi pressed a kiss into her palms, one after the other, finishing with a tender bite then stroke of tongue against the pale flesh. Claudia smelled like the sun. Her skin only slightly damp with spring dew. The scents in the arbor confused Rémi. Her thoughts spun with memories from her childhood spent there, wishing for better, but her body craved the immediate satisfaction of Claudia and her hungry look. Rémi drank her. Tasted her as she tried to separate her memories, senses, and thoughts from what was happening now. Back then, she yearned. Now she yearned too. The pulse in Claudia's wrist throbbed against her mouth. The skin burned between her teeth. Claudia's breath began to deepen.

Everything that she'd wanted as a teenager coalesced into Claudia then. Quietly panting breath. Nipples hard beneath her bra and shirt. Rémi pulled them off her. With her hands hovering at the zipper of Claudia's shorts, she paused. Claudia didn't say a word. *Perfect.* Rémi tugged off all her clothes, the virgin white underwear. Nothing else so beautiful existed under the sun.

Rémi began again. Tasting her fingertips, the faintly pink nails, that rounded flesh just beneath her belly button, every piece of her that fit under and into her mouth. Except where Claudia ached to be touched. She shivered under Rémi's caresses, breath coming heavily, eyes drowsy with desire.

"Did I tell you before how happy I am that you're here with me?" Rémi sipped at the sweat in the crook of Claudia's elbow. Sucked the skin.

"Yes." The word panted from her mouth and she shook her head. "No." Her eyes closed. "I can't remember."

And it was okay, because Rémi remembered for both of them. She felt the gratitude in her own bones, in the way her clit throbbed, the way her breasts felt swollen where they rubbed against her shirt. She was grateful to have her lover here. Her flesh sang with it, her pussy wept with it.

"I want to fuck you now," Rémi murmured, watching Claudia with hooded eyes. At the way her lover looked as if Rémi was the only thing that mattered. Face shimmering under the sun with sweat.

Dark body moving restlessly against the sage green blanket. Pussy bare and naked, exhaling its delicious scent. Legs sprawled in expectation though Rémi hadn't even touched her cunt yet. "May I?"

"Yes," Claudia breathed. "Yes."

She'd gotten into the habit of packing nearly every day with Claudia. Loving, even in the midst of the most innocuous conversation, the press of the cock's thick base against her clit. Knowing that any moment, if either of them wanted, she could be buried inside Claudia, fucking her into pleasure. Rémi unbuttoned her pants. Pulled them off. Then her shirt and boxers.

Claudia's pussy welcomed Rémi like she was born to be there. It swallowed Rémi's dick, and Rémi felt it swallow her clit too, the hot insides grasping her like a welcome and please don't leave. Naked, they lay belly to belly. Breath to breath under the cool spring sky. Rémi moved her hips, lazily. Firmly. Fucking with a gentleness that seeped from her skin and encompassed her lover. Their nipples kissed. A light breeze walked across her back, skimmed between her thighs. Claudia wrapped her legs around Rémi's waist and pulled her closer. Deeper. She groaned. Their mouths met. Held. Exchanged a rolling kiss of tongue and feelings and tenderness while their cunts came together, even through the silicone dick, in the spring breeze that seemed intent on cooling their sweat but couldn't. Couldn't.

Rémi pushed into Claudia. Again and again. Into the welcoming pussy that was like a dream of everything she'd ever wanted. The butter to her bread. The suck to her sweet. The gasp to her groan. The heaven to what she wasn't sure she had.

"You're perfect." Rémi gasped. The muscles of her back flexed. Sweat washed down the hills of her back. It gathered above her pumping buttocks, flowed between them. Rémi felt every movement of her flesh. Every response that Claudia made to it.

Claudia moved under her, beginning to move, frantically, toward her orgasm. But Rémi held her captive to the slow and firm movement of her hips. She built the pleasure deliberately, prolonging the

fuck until they were both drenched in sweat and panting. She an-
gled her thrusts for sweetness, dragging with shattering ease against
Claudia's clit with every movement.

Under her, Claudia's eyelashes fanned like a hummingbird. Her
lips parted as if in amazement. Her hands scrambled past the blanket, curling into the dirt. Digging. Soft animal gasps left her mouth.

"I feel like . . . I feel . . ." Whatever words Claudia wanted to say
washed off her tongue as she swallowed, stretched her neck under
the sun. "I had no idea." She trembled. "I had no idea. . . ."

Rémi felt the minute tremors that signaled the start of orgasm.
Claudia's. Her own body trembled in response. The heat climbed
higher in her belly. Her cheeks flushed.

"I want you to come for me now, baby." Rémi breathed the words
into Claudia's ear. Breathed them as her hips rocked and the ball of
light rolled inside her, exploding finally to incinerate her senses.

"Rémi!"

"Yes, love. Yes."

Water birds, spots of brilliant white against the blue sky, glided
over the water, calling passionately to each other. Waves lapping up
on the rocks. The wind caressed the high grass, whispered incoher-
ent love songs through the long limbs. Beneath Rémi, Claudia's
breath slowed to something like normal. Rémi kissed her parted
lips.

"I think you've put a spell on me," Claudia whispered. Then she
laughed, the sound ribboning up into the wind.

Chapter

28

"You two certainly looked refreshed," Kelia remarked, looking the couple up and down as they came through the back door.

Rémi closed it behind them and defiantly drew Claudia closer. "The view of the harbor is inspiring, as always."

Kelia's smile flattened. "I'm sure."

"If you'll excuse me," Claudia said, cutting into the uncomfortable quiet. She pulled away from Rémi and took the blanket. "I'll go upstairs to freshen up. Be right back."

Rémi watched her swaying backside disappear up the stairs, before turning back to her mother.

"I wish I found the harbor so invigorating these days," Kelia murmured, looking at her with an arched brow. "Some days I can barely tend to my garden and René without feeling drained."

"I think they have vitamins for that," Rémi said.

"But it's not so much fun to take them solo."

Caught off guard, Rémi laughed.

With an answering smile, Kelia led Rémi out of the hallway and into the den. She sank into the armchair near the darkened fireplace and sighed as she settled into its depths. Her slight figure almost disappeared into the large chair.

Kelia's body wasn't the only thing that had downsized since

Rémi's last visit. The den as well as other areas of the house had lost furniture and become less cluttered, less claustrophobic. And there were no maids. Her mother seemed to be taking care of the house all by herself.

"Thanks for inviting us to stay in the house."

Kelia pursed her lips, looking dismissive and insulted at once. "Where else would my child stay if not at home?"

Rémi raised a mocking eyebrow. "At the B and B down by the lake, like last time."

Kelia winced. "Rémi. Don't."

"Don't what, Mama?" Rémi's fingers tapped restlessly against her thigh. She fought the urge to walk out of the room. To leave her mother sitting there alone with her look of insulted parenthood. But she forced herself to sit still. "Please don't pretend that everything is fine between us. I don't have the energy for that right now. Things are complicated enough for me right now."

"With a new *older* woman, I can imagine how interesting life has become for you."

Was this how Kelia was going to welcome her back into the fold, by insulting her choice of girlfriend? Rémi clenched her teeth. "Please, don't judge what I do with my life."

"I'm not judging. Just be careful."

"My involvement with Claudia is nothing for me to be careful of. You're the one who hurt me. You're the one I should be careful of."

Kelia's hands burrowed into the pockets of her cardigan. "That's not fair. Or true."

At the light sound of approaching footsteps, Rémi turned. Claudia appeared in the doorway seconds later.

"Am I interrupting something?" she asked.

"No." Rémi glanced at her mother. "You're not."

After a brief, hesitating look at Kelia, Claudia came fully into the room. She sat on the sofa, stretching out her legs and dropping her sandaled feet in Rémi's lap. Rémi had a moment of déjà vu as Claudia gave her a gentling smile. That moment in Montréal came back to Rémi. The evening on the hotel balcony with the smell of the St. Lawrence River on the air and the drugs humming through her system like a low-grade fever. Claudia's compelling beauty and Rémi's irrevocable decision to get the older woman into her bed.

Kelia cleared her throat. "My daughter and I were just discussing why she hates me so much."

A look of surprise flitted across Claudia's face. She glanced first at Rémi then Kelia. "I don't think she hates you. If anything, she hates the life you abandoned her to." She paused as if carefully examining her next words. "Living without a mother is a hard thing. You left her to strangers. I'm sure she just feels that if you'd stayed in her life, she would have been a happier and better person."

"Do *you* feel that she would have been a better person?"

"I can't imagine her being better than she is now." A smile played briefly around Claudia's mouth before she sobered. "But happier, yes."

Kelia visibly swallowed. But she said nothing. Then: "We could all be happier with the hand that we were dealt in life."

Rémi wanted to howl in frustration. But she only shook her head. Why had she allowed herself to even hope that Kelia could see what she had done to her oldest child? As far as her mother was concerned, as long as Rémi hadn't ended up on the streets, starved, or molested by strangers, she did her job well. Claudia's foot intentionally grazed her arm but she couldn't look at her lover.

"And speaking of the hand that we were dealt, why are you with my daughter?"

Rémi stiffened and opened her mouth. "That's none—"

But Claudia sat up on the couch, put a gentling hand on Rémi's. "What do you mean by that? Doesn't Rémi deserve someone to love her?"

Love?

Kelia looked away briefly, as if embarrassed. The reason for her asking that question backfiring spectacularly in her face. "That's not what I meant."

"Then tell me please, what exactly do you mean?"

"You've had men in your life. A husband. You have grown children. Why are you with Rémi? You're still attractive. You can still get a man. Why are you with my child?"

Rémi swallowed. As much as she was insulted that Kelia, a virtual stranger to Claudia, would dare ask this question, she wanted to know the answer to it. They'd never talked directly about what had brought her into Rémi's bed. She could have said no when Rémi pressed her. She could have walked away. But Claudia had done neither of those things.

"Are you asking this as a concerned parent? Or are you trying to satisfy some kind of morbid curiosity?"

"I'm asking out of concern for my child." Kelia's voice was soft. "You have to admit this situation is a bit unusual."

"This concern you have is a little bit too late, don't you think?" Rémi sneered, unable to keep quiet.

Claudia squeezed her hand again. "Darling, please. Let your mother talk."

Kelia glanced at her gratefully before turning to Rémi. "I know you think that I don't care for you. Yvette thinks the same thing. But I wouldn't have done what I did fifteen years ago if I didn't love you."

"I'd hate to see what you'd do to someone you didn't give a shit about."

"I'm with Rémi because I want to be." Claudia spoke into the resulting silence. "And even though this is what I want and she is who I want, I admit to some nervousness about being involved with a woman for the first time. Sometimes I find myself worrying about what my friends will say, or even my ex-husband." Her eyes flickered to Rémi. "I'm not perfect. I don't even think I'm perfect for her. But I'm being selfish right now and taking every wonderful thing that she has given me. I was happy with my husband, and after that with other men. Now, I'm happy with her."

In her oversized chair, Kelia drew a deep breath. "That's hard for me to imagine, but you seem sincere enough."

"There's nothing for you to image, Kelia. Just know that I love your daughter and won't hurt her."

Rémi swallowed past the unexpected lump in her throat at Claudia's declaration. "I hope that answers your questions, Kelia."

"For now." Her mother looked at Claudia. "Thanks for sharing that with me. In spite of my misgivings, I appreciate your candor. Now"—she stood—"I'm going to see about dinner."

After Kelia walked out the door, Rémi pulled her lover into her arms. Kissed her unsmiling lips. "You said quite a mouthful just now."

"Yes, I know. Did that make you uncomfortable?"

"Just the opposite." She breathed in Claudia's clean smell. "I can't believe I waited so long for this."

"This is perfect timing. I wasn't ready for us before." The distance between them disappeared as their mouths met and their sighs tangled.

A cleared throat just outside the den's open door drew them apart.

"What's with all the smoochy-smoochy?" Yvette asked.

"What's with you calling kissing 'smoochy-smoochy'? How old are you, anyway?" Rémi absently smoothed her hand down Claudia's back, and she smiled when her lover shuddered beneath her casual caress.

"Whatever." Yvette laughed and shook her thick hair back from her face. "I came down to watch TV until dinner was ready, but if you're going to do that"—she waggled a hand at their close bodies and entwined hands—"I can go back up to my room."

"Oh shut up and come in here." Rémi waved her sister into the room. "If things were that serious we would've at least locked the door."

"You'd hope." Claudia smiled.

"You never know." Yvette shrugged and dropped her slim form into the chair Kelia'd just vacated. She grabbed the remote. "Is *Top Chef* okay?"

Rémi reached for the blanket draped over the back of the couch and pulled it over her legs and Claudia's. "Whatever you want to watch is fine. Right, love?" She turned to Claudia.

Her companion hummed in agreement and lay back into Rémi's chest. Moments later, the television flickered to life and washed them in a cool, soothing gray light.

Chapter

29

"Mama, you shouldn't have made all this food!" Yvette stared at the feast Kelia had prepared.

"But I did, sweetheart." Kelia leveled a dry look at her daughter.

Rémi sat down at the table. Despite the quantity of food, the meal at the table was thankfully plain. And light. Caesar salad in a large wooden bowl, a platter of spring vegetables tossed with red sesame seeds, a whole roasted chicken, brown rice, wheat rolls still steaming from the oven, and fresh bread pudding sprinkled with crushed almonds and sitting in its clear Pyrex dish. Although Rémi wasn't particularly hungry, she felt strangely pleased about the food on the table.

Growing up, she had gotten used to her father's monumental experiments in haute cuisine—dishes thick with butter, cream, and cheese that reminded him of the home he abandoned in Normandy. His endless versions of wine-laced boeuf bourguignon, meaty cassoulet, or canard à la Rouennaise all became too much for Rémi's stomach. Not even breakfast was safe from his extravagant touch. She grew sick of crepes and quiches. During the first few months of her exile in Miami with Yvette and Kelia, Rémi had delighted in scrambled eggs on wheat toast. The simpler the meal, the more she loved it.

Across the table, Claudia looked at the food with admiration.

"The food looks wonderful, Kelia. But"—she exchanged a glance with Rémi—"we couldn't begin to do this lovely meal justice."

"Don't apologize. Just eat what you can. But don't be surprised when you see the same thing on the table for lunch tomorrow."

"It'll be nice to have this tomorrow afternoon, Kelia," Rémi felt obligated to add. "Thanks for making it."

Her mother gave a strained smile. "I wish you'd stop calling me that."

"It is your name, isn't it?" Rémi folded a napkin over her lap and reached for her water glass.

"I'm your mother, damn you! Treat me like it."

Her sudden outburst brought all three pairs of eyes at the table swinging toward her.

"Mom, please!"

Kelia ignored Yvette, staring hard at Rémi. "I'm tired of this."

"Supporting someone financially doesn't make you their mother," Rémi said acidly, refusing to feel guilty.

"Mama, you *did* do something wrong," Yvette finally spoke up. "Please stop pretending that nothing was your fault. Daddy did terrible things, but you did too."

"I didn't ask you back here to blame me, Yvette."

"Then why am I back here?" Yvette clenched her fist on the table. Did not look at her mother. "I've talked with Rémi. She's not the bad person Papa made her out to be." Her face became flushed with indignant blood and she blinked quickly as if fighting tears. "She's pretty and she's kind and she's my sister. I still don't understand why he kept saying those bad things about her. Or why you never once came to her defense. It was like you cut her off from you, just so you could be with Daddy."

Rémi reached blindly for her water again. Swallowed the cool liquid past the sudden lump in her throat. It was just like she had imagined. Her mother and Yvette living a life in Maine as if she never existed. But to hear it from her sister's mouth . . . Nausea settled in the pit of her belly. She tore the napkin off her lap.

"Excuse me."

Upstairs in her old room, she gently closed the door behind her, willing the tide of sadness to subside. She'd known. Dammit, she'd known. *Shit!* Moisture slid past her tightly closed eyelids but she pressed her fingers against it, wiping the tears away. This was not worth crying about. Not after all these years.

Beyond the windows the bay glittered in the darkness. On the water's surface, lights from pleasure-bound boats bobbed gently in the inky black. Rémi flinched when the door opened behind her, but didn't turn around.

"Darling." Claudia's low voice curled against her ears but Rémi shook her head, knowing that she needed something but uncertain about what it was.

"Darling," her lover said again, but she couldn't look away from the comforting darkness beyond the window.

A light hand settled on her back, smoothed over the tense muscles that bunched and released under her shirt. "Fourteen years is too long to carry this pain," Claudia said. "Try to let it go."

Rémi rested her knee against the padded bench below the window and sagged against its frame. "I wish I could." Her fist clenched, banged once against the window, rattling it. Claudia's palm pressed against her spine.

"Don't hurt yourself over this." Hands slid around to press against her belly. She felt Claudia's cheek on her back, the delicate breath fanning her skin through the cotton shirt. "The time for pain is past, don't you think? Allow this visit to be about healing and forgiveness."

A rusty chuckle worked its way past Rémi's lips. "It's not that easy." Even now, her hand throbbed faintly with pain from its impact with the window. It felt good.

"It can be easy. Just open yourself and let it go."

The hands crawled slowly up her belly, unbuttoning the shirt as they went. Rémi drew in a deep breath. "I don't think—"

"Now isn't the time for you to think, my darling."

The shirt came away, then the white undershirt. From behind, Claudia grasped Rémi's belt buckle and pulled until they faced each other. Her hands skimmed over Rémi's belly, barely touched her skin. Her nipples. Goose pimples exploded over her arms. The fingers floated over her throat and settled gently around them as if to squeeze, but instead she reached up higher to grasp Rémi's jaw and pull her head down for a searing kiss of teeth and tongue that dragged a premature grunt from deep in Rémi's belly. The teeth yanked her mind from the pain of the last hour and settled her firmly in her lover's unflinching gaze. Claudia was serious.

Rémi licked her lips, willing now to be distracted. "I can see where you're going with this."

"Good. I'd hate to think that I was being unclear."

With a growl, Rémi lifted Claudia up until they were at mouth level, turned to sit her on the window seat, and kissed her. Sucked the last taste of roasted chicken from Claudia's tongue until all she drank in was the clean and intoxicating flavor of her lover, sipping her soft moans and feeling delicate arms around her neck.

"Perfect," Claudia murmured against her lips.

Rémi pushed up her skirt, up past her thighs, and grazed her fingers atop the crotch of damp panties over the press of her needy clit. Yes. This was perfect; *this* was what she needed. Claudia opened her legs wider, making inciting noises in her throat, fingers sinking into Rémi's shoulder and pulling her closer. She unbuckled Rémi's belt, and Rémi's belly jumped when her hand slid between cotton and flesh. The fingers effortlessly found Rémi's clit, and her knees almost buckled.

"Let me—" Ah! So good. Claudia's thighs opened for her and the velvet pussy purred under her fingers. "Let me get my . . ." what was it that she wanted again? Her mind went blank. All she wanted was to get inside. To feel that sweetness around her hand. The panties were no barrier to her fingers. Cotton tore easily and the hot cunt eagerly swallowed what Rémi had to give. She groaned. *So wet.*

With one hand, Rémi pulled off Claudia's blouse, pulled the green silk out of the way to get to the hard nipples, the soft skin.

"You taste like heaven," Rémi whispered. "You *feel* like heaven."

She sucked the nipple into her mouth, and Claudia's pussy greedily sucked her fingers in turn. Claudia fumbled up, her hands grasping for the window frame above her head, mouth parted, head thrown back, breasts even more in Rémi's face. *Yes.* Her lover's pleasure urged her on. The small noises she made in her throat. The way her hips thrust back against the fingers, hunting with frantic circling motions for pleasure. And she found it. Claudia groaned. Her fingers sank into the back of Rémi's head.

"Oh god," she whispered. "That's good. That's so good."

The orgasm tore through her in a low scream. She covered Claudia's mouth with hers, swallowing the noise, absorbing the tremors into her own skin. Rémi caught her as she sagged on the bench, body shuddering in her cum.

"The bed," Claudia said breathlessly. "I want to feel you properly."

"I need to get my . . . equipment." That's what Rémi wanted to say earlier, but the thought of her strap had flown out of her head.

They stumbled back, fell onto the mattress in a tight tangle of limbs and clinging mouths.

"We don't need it." Claudia shoved Rémi's pants and underwear down. "I want you to taste me." She pecked at Rémi's mouth, nibbled down her throat. "Fuck me with your tongue, not that fake penis you think I need. I only need you tonight, baby. You."

But Rémi was too slow and Claudia pressed *her* back in the sheets instead, shimmying quickly down to nuzzle between her thighs. At her first lick Rémi nearly jerked off the bed. Her fingers dug into the sheets.

"I've tasted myself before and this is similar." Claudia licked her again. "But not the same." The image of Claudia tasting herself, fucking her own pussy with her fingers then licking them off one by one, exploded before Rémi's eyes. A firestorm flashed through her, consuming her from clit to crown. Her toes clenched and water leaked from her eyes. Claudia's name tumbled up in her throat and she shut her teeth against it. This wasn't her house. Shit. This wasn't her house. Shudders wracked through her body as the sweet heat of orgasm diffused inside her before slowly, slowly dissipating.

Low on the bed, Claudia laughed. "And I'm not even done yet."

Claudia kept her mouth and fingers on Rémi's pussy all night. It was as if once she got a taste of the juice between Rémi's legs, she couldn't stop drinking it. One orgasm after another tore through

Rémi until she didn't know where one ended and the other began. An amateur but enthusiastic tongue swirled between her pussy lips, around her thick and throbbing clit, deep into her cunt again and again. Tears streamed down Rémi's face.

Her hands tightened in Claudia's hair. "Stop."

Fingers slid effortless inside Rémi, curling, calling sensation to the surface of her skin. Air wheezed in and out of her dry mouth. Sweat dripped down her face, her neck, over her breasts. "Don't stop."

The leisurely fuck gained momentum until the fingers became like a jackhammer inside her, hitting her sweet spot once, twice, and again. Again. The world exploded behind her tightly closed eyelids. Rémi was helpless to the scream that tore itself of her parched throat.

"Stop! Please. I'm finished. Not anymore."

And surprisingly, Claudia relented this time. Rémi was vaguely aware of her lover kissing up her body and collapsing against her sweat-soaked belly. Her pussy-spiced breath tickled Rémi's mouth as she breathed softly, said nothing, just lay her head in the curve of Rémi's throat. Their hearts knocked gently together through skin and sweat. Rémi blinked up at the ceiling, feeling eyelashes flutter, skin tingle, breathing begin to slow. Everything was sensation with no thoughts to cloud them. Just the feel of Claudia's skin against her own and the air moving cleanly in her lungs. The window, still flung open, let in a cooling night breeze and the smell of roses. Beyond, the sky was a canopy of winking stars.

Rémi slid her fingers through the damp hairs at the back of Claudia's neck. "Thank you."

Chapter

30

The clouds had burned away with the early morning hours, and the sun now lay, warm and golden, on the rolling grass surrounding the house and the rocks leading down to the water. Cool air pressed intimately against Rémi's face and bare arms. Without the distraction of Claudia, she realized that her hiding place was not much of one. Although out of sight from the house and past the untamed high grass, the widely spaced twin maple trees with the hammock swinging between them could have been any other backyard sanctuary. Across the mile or so of water and past the few white-sailed boats bobbing in the bay, there lay other houses. Other backyards. Anyone could see her swaying in her solitary hammock if they just raised their eyes.

When she was a teenager, the grasses had seemed higher and this place much more isolated. But Rémi saw evidence that others had found her hiding place. The patch of grass worn down to almost nothing near the hammock. A forgotten wooden picnic basket tattooed from rain and sun. Someone's blue hair ribbon.

Rémi raked her hair back from her eyes and felt the dark strands flutter around her face in the wind. *Everything changes*, she thought, sighing. For better or worse.

"I thought I would find you out here."

She half turned in surprise at her mother's distant shout from high up on the hill. This place *really* was no secret. Rémi leaned back against one of the maples and waited for Kelia to reach her. With her hands in the pockets of her jeans, Kelia walked toward Rémi, eyes nearly hidden by the gray-streaked locks whipped across her face. Her pink blouse flattened against her rounded stomach in the wind.

As her mother waded through the tall grass toward Rémi, a memory surfaced. She blinked against the glare of it, caught unaware.

The smells in their small dining room were wrong. Rémi paused in the doorway and watched her mother ladle soup into three small bowls then take the cover from a platter sitting in the middle of the dining table. Without seeing the food, she knew what it was. Leek and potato soup and coq au vin. Her father's favorite foods. She sat down at the dining table, hands folded stiffly in her lap.

"Is Papa coming to visit?" she asked.

"No."

Kelia Walker-Bouchard, permed hair scraped back in a messy ponytail and her pretty face wearing a smile for the first time in weeks, sat at the small dining table she often shared mournfully with her two daughters and looked up at Rémi who, at fourteen, was already tall for her age. "We're going home."

"I am home."

"My face is clean, Mama!" Yvette burst into the kitchen with a smile, showing off her newest missing tooth. Her long plaits flapped around her head as she rushed up to her mother. "Look!"

Kelia reached out for Yvette. "Much better, baby. I don't know how on earth you find the only mud hole to fall into in this entire godforsaken city."

She brushed the back of her hand over Yvette's cheek as the five-year-old slid into the chair next to hers. Rémi was still standing. The smile slipped off Kelia's face.

"You knew this was temporary while your father and I worked things out."

"*No.* You *knew this was temporary.* I'm *in school.*" *The last word rose and fell with dejection and disbelief. A whine that refused to be suppressed.*

"*I'm going to school next year,*" *Yvette said, swirling tendrils of linguine around her plastic orange fork. It was her favorite too.*

Kelia absently stroked one of Yvette's braids. The child sucked the pasta into her mouth and smacked her lips. "*Baby, you can just transfer. Kids do it all the time.*"

"*Why did you bring us all the way to Florida and put me in school if you knew we were going back to him?*"

"*I didn't know.*"

"*Yes, you did!*" *Rémi pounded her fist on the table. Winced at the pain that vibrated up her arm.* "*I don't want to go back there. He makes you cry. He wants me to be something else.*" *She backed away from the table and the food.* "*I'm not going.*"

"*Your father is different now. He won't ask you to do anything that you don't want to. All he wants is for you to be normal. That's all. He wants us to be a normal family again. What's wrong with that?*"

Rémi stared at her mother. When they ran away from Auguste Bouchard over a year ago, Kelia had sworn they would never go back. Crying and nearly weak with fatigue, she had woken the two girls from their beds one cold night in November and drove through the night and most of the day until they reached the winter warmth of North Miami Beach and the safety of Aunt Jackie's house. And now she wanted to take them back to Maine to squirm underneath Auguste Bouchard's iron fist.

"*It's not fair!*" *Rémi pushed her chair back from the table and it scraped across the linoleum like a scream.* "*You promised he wouldn't do that to us again. To me.*"

"*Rémi, baby . . .*"

"*No. You have to fix this.*" *Rémi turned, face crumbling with tears, and walked stiffly from the room.*

In that moment of betrayal, Rémi's love for Kelia began to dissipate.

She swallowed past her dry throat, willed away the fresh pain raked up by her memories.

"Is anything wrong?" she asked when Kelia drew close.

"Nothing's wrong. Must something be wrong for me to want to talk with my daughter?"

With this one, yes. The words hovered at the back of Rémi's tongue, but she didn't say them. "What's on your mind, Mama?"

"You."

Kelia sat with her back pressed against the neighboring tree, looking suddenly like she needed to be off her feet. She looked tired.

"That's a change."

"Don't be mean, Rémi. I don't deserve that."

"People don't always get what they deserve." She toyed with the grass between her boots, not looking at the face opposite hers.

"That's true. I don't think I deserve to have my children taken away from me." She looked up at Rémi. "And I didn't think you de-served what happened to you fourteen years ago."

Rémi couldn't hide her surprise at her mother's admission.

"Yvette won't talk to me." Kelia shook her head. "I had hoped with your father passing on that things would be good between us again. But if anything, they're worse. When I was her age I never thought I'd be a mother, much less one my daughters have nothing but contempt for."

"I don't feel contempt for you. Resentful. Sad. Furious. But not contemptuous. At my most self-pitying, I feel like my entire child-hood was lost because you chose Papa over me." Rémi split a blade of grass between her fingers then frowned at the green stain left under her nail. "You left me in Miami with *money.*" She spat the last word at her mother. "Aunt Jackie barely knew what to do with me when she stopped by once a month. I wanted my mother. I wanted someone who had the room in her heart to love me *and* her lover. But that wasn't you."

The words that she'd always wanted to say tumbled out of her mouth coldly, in concise syllables that held nothing of the pain she felt when Kelia left her in Miami to go back to a man who ruthlessly controlled her and her children. A man who physically abused his gay daughter just because he didn't see Rémi as his child anymore.

"Baby . . ." Kelia moved closer and reached out to touch Rémi's face. But she flinched back.

"Like I said, it's okay. I'm learning to live with your decision."

"Is that why you're involved with Claudia?"

Rémi looked at her sharply. "What do you mean by that?"

"Are you looking for a mother in her? Is that why she's allowed herself to become involved with you? She seems like such a kind woman, I can't imagine her saying no to you, especially knowing how you grew up. Without a mother."

Rémi felt the muscle in her jaw twitch. She counted silently past ten, then fifteen, before she spoke. "I'm not fucking Claudia as a way to fuck you. I'd like to think that I'm better than that."

Kelia's gaze jerked away from her face. "I'm not talking about . . . fucking me, I'm talking about—"

"I know what you're talking about. You're wrong on both counts. I've wanted her for years. Even before I knew she was somebody's mother. And before I accepted that you and Yvette were actually going to stay with Auguste."

"I'm not trying to excuse myself. By now, I realize that leaving you alone wasn't the best move I could have made." As Kelia turned from her contemplation of the bay, the wind flung her hair back into her eyes. With a thin hand, she impatiently scraped it back from her face. "Things were so different for me then. I knew that you would survive. The money was to help you through that survival. Living alone in Miami was better for you than living in this house with your father. He wasn't always a good person."

Rémi blinked at the last bit of understatement. She had the scar on her shoulder, a kiss from the business side of a blade, to prove that he wasn't the kind of man she would have picked to call Papa. Rémi didn't even remember what she had done wrong, only that she felt the first slap with the flat side of the knife before she knew that he was even standing there. Then she must have flinched and turned because the second blow brought more pain. And blood. Kelia stitched her up, and it was not long after that the two of them ran away with Yvette from Boothbay Harbor and Auguste Bouchard's petty cruelties.

"You're right," Rémi said. "He wasn't always a good person. But I thought you were."

Kelia flung out her hands as if to grab Rémi's arms. But she didn't. "I wish I could make you understand."

"Try then. Try to make me understand what all this is about. Because right now I'm still in the dark about what happened. I'm still pissed, and for some reason, you seem to think that I have no right to be."

"It's not that I don't think you have no right to be angry at me, Rémi. I just—" Kelia sighed. "Your father and I didn't have the healthiest relationship."

Rémi stared at her, waiting for something else besides what she already knew.

"We loved each other, I think sometimes too much. Looking at it from a distance now, we might have been obsessed with each other." Her eyes skittered to Rémi, then away. "I couldn't get enough of him. Even when I was angry at him, even when he had done the most awful and insane things, I wanted him. Badly. I know that's no excuse for my behavior, but I needed to give you that explanation."

Looking back, Rémi could now see the signs of her mother's unhealthy connection to Auguste. She'd felt the tug of that devil a few times, too. The one that forced her to ignore everything but the person under her hands and mouth. Nothing else mattered. Not sanity. Not friendship. But . . .

"If I hadn't come to Maine, would you have reached out to me in Miami to give that explanation?"

Rémi searched for the truth in her mother's face. Or whatever it was that she could decipher.

"I don't know," Kelia said very softly. "Your father's been dead for almost two years now. Sometimes the way he and I treated each other embarrassed me. It's hard acknowledging these things I let him do to me. Never mind confessing them to my child."

Rémi nodded, swallowing past the rock in her throat. Kelia carefully avoided any details of what she and Auguste had been to each other. But Rémi had both an imagination and a past to refer to.

"You have to forgive me sometime, Rémi Mathilde," Kelia murmured, forehead wrinkling as she squinted against the sun's glare. Her hair fluttered around her face in the breeze. "Can you start now?"

Chapter

31

"I don't think I can duplicate what you did to me that night of our first date, but I'll at least try to relax you." Claudia took Rémi's feet in her hands.

Rémi sighed and leaned back into the sofa. The other woman reclined at the other end, thighs fanned open to cradle Rémi's feet. "I'm already relaxed, actually. Mama and I had a talk today. It was better than the last one."

"That's good. I was worried that we'd have to run back to Miami and cross this trip off as a failure."

"Never that." Rémi shook her head. "Mama and I are on the way toward some kind of truce. As for Yvette, she needs a home. She needs her family. I don't want her to reject Mama and everything she's known here just because of me."

"I don't think she will. Because of you, she started to question what her parents have done. Their actions sparked her questions. Don't add this tension between Yvette and Kelia to the list of things that you're shouldering blame for."

"Hmm." She sighed into Claudia's amateur but effective touch. "Maybe."

"Maybe nothing."

Claudia's fingers slid between Rémi's toes, gently stroking the light webbing between them, and she shuddered.

Her lover smiled. "You like that?"

"What a question." The shudder traveled up through her feet into her thighs. Rémi's head fell back. "You're getting very good at this."

"Like I said, relaxation is my goal. For now." The smile Claudia gave was decidedly naughty.

She pressed Rémi's heels even more deeply between her thighs, leaning into the massage until the toes pressed into her breasts, creating subtle cleavage in her pale green blouse. Unable to help herself, Rémi skimmed her toe across Claudia's nipple, sighing at its delicate feel.

"Right." Rémi licked her lips. Pursed them. Then decided to let it go. They were in her mother's sitting room after all. "I'll need more of this pampering when I get back to town and have to deal with Anderson and his shit again."

"I thought all that was finished?"

"No. He wants something. Even though my cousin told me that it's not personal, I feel like it is. It doesn't make sense for him to come after me this hard when all he wants is the club."

Claudia winced. "I hope you'll be able to resolve this thing without any more violence. The last thing I want is for that man to hurt you, or for you to hurt him and end up in jail for it. You don't need to get into some sort of primitive battle with him. There are other ways to take care of men like Matthias Anderson."

"Matthias Anderson?" Rémi's mother stood at the entrance to the den. In a cream dress belted at the waist and her hair swept up and pinned to her head, she seemed more at ease than the day before. "How do you know him?" A frown wrinkled her brow.

"Unfortunately, he's someone in our lives in Miami," Claudia said before Rémi could object to her mother's demanding tone. "He's trying to take over Rémi's business, and maybe even hurt her as well."

"What?" Kelia came fully into the room and sat down hard in the armchair across from them. She touched her belly as if suddenly nauseous. "Are you sure it's the—what does he look like?"

Rémi described him, watching her mother's stunned face with growing curiosity and concern. "What's going on?"

"What is he doing?" Kelia whispered, as if to herself.

"Do you know this guy, Mama?" Rémi withdrew her feet from Claudia's lap and sat up in the couch.

"Yes. Yes, I do. He and your father were friends a long time ago. Something happened between them. I'm not sure what; Gus never told me." Kelia's low voice changed, became deeper as if giving way to secrets. "Whatever it was, was bad. They stopped speaking and it suddenly seemed like Matthias was trying to destroy Gus and whatever mattered to him." She swallowed and looked up at Rémi. "After your father died, I didn't hear any more from Matthias."

"You said that this rivalry was between Auguste and Anderson. Why would you have any reason to hear from him?"

Beside Rémi, Claudia made a low noise. Rémi looked at her but her lover watched her mother with understanding. And pity.

"What? What happened?"

"Over the years, my relationship with your father became very turbulent. We . . . fought. And I grew angry at the way that he sometimes treated me. The first time I did it I was so angry that I barely knew what I was doing."

"Did what?"

But Kelia didn't answer her.

"You don't have to tell us this if you don't want to," Claudia said gently.

"No. I have to. It's only fair. Especially with what Matthias is trying to do to Rémi's business."

Then it hit Rémi. "You fucked him."

Kelia flinched as if her daughter had slapped her. "If you have to put it that way, yes."

"Shit." Rémi sank back into the sofa.

This was the last thing she expected. Matthias Anderson and Kelia Walker-Bouchard? The image of her mother writhing beneath Anderson's cold hands came unbidden to her mind. "You must have been *really* mad at my father."

Kelia clasped her hands in her lap but did not look away from Rémi's cool stare. "I'm not proud of what I did."

"It seems like your relationship with Papa made you do a lot of things that you regret now."

"Yes." The flesh around Kelia's mouth was tight and drawn, her eyes bleak with worry. "I can't imagine why Matthias is doing this to you. You're not Gus. You have nothing to do with his business dealings."

"Are you sure what happened between them was business related? If he seduced you, there must have been something personal to it."

"He didn't seduce me. I went to him," Kelia said with the voice of a woman who'd lived with her own martyrdom for a long time.

Rémi shook her head. "I'm sure there was a build-up. I'm sure he sowed the seeds of it. And he could have said no. Anderson doesn't strike me as the kind of man to let things *happen* to him. He's an opportunist who takes what he wants, regardless of whether or not people around him realize he's the one doing the taking."

"You don't have to give me an excuse, Rémi."

"I'm not giving you an excuse, dammit!" Anger flared to life, suddenly, in Rémi's chest. "You were stupid. He took advantage of that."

"Rémi . . ."

But she shrugged off Claudia's cautioning hand.

"Don't you think I've already punished myself over this even more than you ever could?" Kelia stared at Rémi, the long line of her throat taut with emotion. "I regret everything that happened between me and Matthias. I wish I hadn't been so stupid, as you call it. I had other options, but I chose him. Just like I could have stayed with you in Miami but instead I came back here. I regret everything!"

"Did my father know?"

"I don't think so. He never said anything to me."

But Rémi knew that her father might not have told his wife all that he knew. Auguste could hide a boiling rage under the most pleasant of smiles. Even his contempt and disappointment in her,

Rémi was convinced, he hid from everyone else in the family until the day he slashed her with the knife.

Her fist squeezed and released in her lap, anger still thrumming through it. Why was she angry? She should have been thrilled that Kelia had managed to get some of her own back in the face of Auguste's abuse. But this just seemed too much. Her head spun. Kelia had slept with this man? This man who had tried to kill Rémi? This man who had tried to take everything she built over the last five years away from her? A muscle in her jaw ticked.

"Darling, this thing between your mother and that man is in the past."

"But isn't the past what's kicking us in the ass even now?"

Claudia said nothing, only leaned close to stroke Rémi's back, her eyes still watching Kelia with pity.

"I'm going to call Matthias," Kelia said, standing up. "I must have his number around here somewhere."

"Call him and say what? By your own admission you haven't spoken to him in years. What do you possibly have to say to him now that will change the course of whatever he has planned for me?"

Kelia sat back in the chair, deflated. "I guess you're right." She cupped a hand over her mouth, staring into space.

Claudia squeezed Rémi's arm. "Let's give your mother some space. I think she needs some time to digest what you just told her."

Alone with Rémi in her bedroom upstairs, Claudia was even more sympathetic.

"I can't imagine the kind of life she had with her husband that made sleeping with his worst enemy a possible choice to make."

Rémi couldn't imagine the kind of woman who would lie under that vermin, Anderson, and keep coming back for more just because of a tiff with her husband. She squeezed her eyes shut to banish the images that crowded into her head. Anderson's ash-white body moving like a snake over her mother's. Kelia clutching at him, not in pleasure but in bitter revenge for whatever her husband had done to her at home.

"I can't even imagine what—" Rémi pressed a fist to her forehead. The mattress dipped as Claudia sank into it next to her.

"Don't judge. What's done is done. Your mother is already beating herself up over this. Don't get in line to do your damage too. Put yourself in Kelia's shoes. She made choices. They were wrong. Let's just deal with this Anderson character and stop looking back at the past."

Rémi turned her head to look at her lover. "But the past is waiting in Miami, trying to take my livelihood away from me."

"And if anything, it's because of something your father did, not Kelia. Be reasonable and be fair. Think about it."

Claudia sat above her, an oblique line in the bed, face soft with concern. She took Rémi's fisted hand in hers. Long fingers roamed the back of Rémi's hand, dipping in the shallow valley between each finger, warm and undeniable until the fist released and Rémi felt a sigh take her entire body and release through her mouth.

"What are you doing to me?"

"Nothing you won't allow."

Claudia fed her a gentle smile. "Forgive her," she said. "Forget about what she did. Think about how to stop him when we get back."

Just that simply, it was done. Rémi nodded and closed her eyes. "You're right." She sighed again. "You're right."

Sunlight poured like honey over Rémi's bare legs and arms through the high windows of what had been her father's study. Even with the windows and the sun high and shining most of the days she'd been in the room, Rémi only remembered the study shrouded in darkness. The thick curtains drawn to keep out the cold. A fire crackling and popping sparks in the fireplace. Her father's brooding face behind the desk.

But now the room was a revelation of light. Kelia had apparently moved all the books into the darker adjoining room and made it into a library. Curtains still framed the windows, sentries at the ready to fight against seasonal chill, but that was all that remained of the old room. Bright purple and white orchids in porcelain pots sat on the window ledges, peeking out against a backdrop of deep green spring grass outside and the hedges of blooming lilac—thick and tall with their pale purple stalks like wheat—that rippled at the outer edges of the yard. Far beyond, white sails waved like flags from the bay's glittering blue surface. Compared to the view, the book face down on Rémi's thigh held little appeal.

"Mama, Mama! Look what I—"

She turned her head at the sound of the high-pitched voice bursting into the library. A boy who looked about eight years old stopped short just inside the room. His green eyes widened.

"You're not my mama."

A blue and white Transformers backpack hung heavily from both hands.

"That's true," Rémi said. "I think"—she paused, making the time to breathe as she took in the shape and shade of her brother's face— "you might have better luck outside. She's in the garden."

"Okay." He ran off, hip bouncing off the doorjamb, not even questioning who Rémi was and what she was doing in his house.

She abandoned her book on the sofa and walked after him, through the house with its shifting light and dark, beyond the kitchen and the radio warbling NPR news, and out into the backyard. The screen door banged shut after him. Beyond the mesh, his pale curls twisted in the midafternoon sun.

"Mama!" he called to Kelia, who was kneeling near an explosion of yellow roses. "Are you hiding out here again?" His voice rang high with laughter.

Beside her, Claudia looked up and at the boy. The automatic smile fell from her mouth as she got a proper look at René.

"Never from you, sweetie." Kelia pulled off her gloves and pulled her son into a long hug. "I think you grew taller while you were gone," she said, pressing his cheeks with her bare palms and dotting his forehead with kisses.

"Mama . . ." the boy protested, flicking an embarrassed gaze at Rémi and Claudia. But he leaned, greedy after so long from home, into his mother's touch.

"Oh, I'm being rude." Kelia stood up. "René." She turned her son to face Rémi. "This is your sister, Rémi. Remember, we talked about her."

He held out his hand, a grown-up in miniature, wearing jeans and a remarkably clean oversized white T-shirt. "Pleased to meet you." The weight of his hand was slight in Rémi's. A feather. He was eight years old. He could have been any child, blameless. But when he looked into her face, his father's eyes stared out at her. Vividly green and undeniable. Rémi's grip slackened and she dropped his hand.

"And her friend, Claudia."

She took his hand and smiled gently down into his face. The boy smiled back, cheeks coloring at her warmth. A new infatuation? Then his mother touched his shoulder and he turned away.

"I wasn't expecting them to drop you off until almost dinner-time," Kelia said, hugging his slight frame to hers. His wordless reply made her laugh and she took his hand in hers. "I'm going in to make lunch," she tossed over her shoulder as she and René walked toward the house.

"Sure." Rémi answered automatically. What else was she sup-posed to say?

"This is unexpected," Claudia murmured, moving close to slip an arm around Rémi's waist and lean in.

Rémi shook her head. Unexpected. Yes. This new development certainly was that. In the kitchen, Kelia fussed over her child, mak-ing a lunch of meatloaf sandwiches and salad that was enough for all of them, including the absent Yvette who was off with friends and had been since just after breakfast.

They sat down at the table and ate in an odd triangle of silence. René and Kelia chatted about the boy's camping trip while Rémi and Claudia could only look on in bewilderment. The awkward lunch couldn't end fast enough.

Afterwards, Rémi took Claudia sailing, coasting out onto the placid waters of the bay in the small boat that once belonged to her father. The sun pressed down on her shoulders and arms, which were bared in a white tank top that fluttered against her braless breasts in the breeze. In a pale yellow polo shirt tucked and belted into match-ing shorts, her companion sat back in the small sailboat, eyes shaded by sunglasses, face held up to the caressing wind.

Claudia hadn't questioned her sudden need to be on the water and away from the house, only said yes to Rémi's question and changed her clothes. Her silence in the rocking cradle of the boat said that she understood everything. Rémi was glad. For now, she didn't want to think, didn't want to question. That was for when they returned to shore. For now, it was just her lover, the breeze, and the water. The rest would come later.

Chapter

32

"**D**id Auguste know the child wasn't his?"
Rémi asked the question baldly as she stood with Kelia over a sink full of dirty dishes. Claudia, Yvette, and René had already fled the scene of the great American feast to watch the sunset, leaving the two women alone.

Ever since Rémi could remember, Kelia always preferred to hand wash the dishes then leave them to drip dry in the dishwasher. They set up a mini-assembly line, with Rémi rinsing the soapy dishes she took from her mother then sliding them down into the white insides of the underutilized machine. A white salad bowl clinked against a clear glass plate as she settled them side by side.

Earlier, after the few hours on the water, her mind had cleared enough for her to see past her shock at René's existence and her mother's nonchalance. At the dinner table, Yvette, René, Claudia, Kelia, and she chatted amicably about nothing in particular over another of Kelia's plain and delicious meals until it was time to disperse.

Now, up to her pink-gloved elbows in hot soapy water, Kelia stopped. The oval plate burped as it slid between her soapy hands and almost fell back into the water.

"What?"

Looking at her mother, Rémi felt stirrings of the same sympathy that Claudia had expressed. Here was a woman so caught up in the horrors of her own world that she missed the most obvious things. Or perhaps she just hoped others had missed them.

"Were you able to fool my father?"

"There's nothing to fool Auguste about, René is my—our son."

"You were right the first time. René is your son, but if Matthias Anderson walked in here right now, he'd say the same thing. That boy is his son too. He's the image of him. And there's no way that my father didn't know this." Rémi braced her wet hands against the granite counter. "There's no way that *you* didn't know this."

Kelia allowed the plate to fall back into the sink with a splash. "Is it that obvious?" Her face was a study in amazement.

"Mama, yes." Rémi stared at her mother. Not able to believe that this woman kept the child she bore from a man other than her husband. A revenge child. "Papa would have been blind not to notice that René is not his."

"But he never said anything." Kelia's voice hovered barely above a whisper.

At least not to you.

The thought of Auguste suffering in emotional agony while another man's child thrived in his wife's belly and then his home filled Rémi with a sudden and vicious satisfaction. She cleared her throat.

"I can't tell you anything about what my father may or may not have said. Obviously I'm the last one who'd know what was on his mind. But I do know if my woman got knocked up by my enemy, I wouldn't be able to keep on going as if nothing happened."

"But he never hurt me. At least no more than usual. And Gus was nothing but wonderful to René. All the way until the very end." Kelia's gaze fell into the soapy water, as if seeing the past eight years with the man she thought she knew.

"I don't know what to say, Mama. I really don't. But this definitely complicates things with Anderson. I don't even know what to say to this man the next time I see him."

"You shouldn't have to say anything to him. René is mine. He doesn't need to know about my son."

"But what if this has something to do with *your son?*"

Kelia pulled her gloved hands from the water and turned to Rémi, keeping a soapy grip on the edge of the sink. "What can this possibly have to do with René?" Her eyes bored into Rémi. "Nothing," she spat. "Absolutely nothing. I'll do whatever I can to help you in this situation with Matthias. The last thing I want is for something that your father or I did to come back and hurt you. But this has nothing to do with my baby. Just remember that."

Rémi ignored the pinch of jealousy that wished Kelia had felt the same way about her fourteen years ago. Possessive. Guarded.

"All right," she said then cleared her throat. "Do you want to switch with me? I can wash the plates while you put them in the dishwasher."

Kelia blinked as if waking from a startling dream, then nodded jerkily. "Okay."

They continued cleaning the dishes in silence until footsteps on the walkway made Rémi look up.

"Why do you both look like someone just died?" The screen door slid closed as Claudia walked into the house.

Rémi shrugged. Kelia continued to rinse the dishes and put them away.

"Anyway, it doesn't matter. René and Yvette sent me up to get you. The sunset is much too nice for the two of you to waste it cleaning dishes."

Rémi opened her mouth to protest, but Claudia gently squeezed her side. "Come on, you two. René and Yvette would enjoy some family time with you."

"You're probably right." Kelia dried her hands on a towel, face settling into lines of exhaustion. "I feel like it's been ages since I've sat down with my children." She looked at Rémi.

"Come on. The others are waiting down by the water. We even saved a place on the blanket for the two of you." Claudia wove her fingers through Rémi's and touched Kelia's shoulder. In the backyard, just as the grass began to slope, Yvette and René sat shoulder to shoulder on the blanket, their heads bent in laughter.

"I did *not* fart," René chortled.

"Whatever. You did. Like broccoli and green peas." Yvette nudged his shoulder, and both dissolved again into giggles.

Rémi sat down close to Yvette, wrinkling her nose. "Broccoli *and* green peas? Jesus!"

"I know, right?" Yvette laughed again.

Kelia pulled her son backwards into her lap and ruffled his curls.

"Mama!" he protested, but stayed where he was.

Yvette moved back to allow space for Claudia on the blanket. But Rémi tugged her lover close until Claudia sat in the juncture of her thighs and Rémi could bury her nose into the fragrant curve of her neck.

The setting sun drowned the world around them in darkening light. Soft orange. Amber. A curtain of approaching dusk. The wind picked up, sneaking into the spaces between Rémi's jacket, but Kelia's arm pressed against hers was warm. She didn't feel the cold.

Chapter

33

"I wish you didn't have to go so soon."

Yvette sat on the edge of Rémi's bed, watching as she packed. Her eyes bounced from Rémi's face to the black duffel bag slowly filling with clothes.

"Soon? We've been here a week." Rémi tucked her cell phone charger in the pocket of her bag and zipped it shut. Their cab would be at the front door in less than half an hour. Claudia had long since packed and was downstairs having one last round of coffee and croissants with Kelia.

"That's barely any time at all." Yvette frowned, folding and unfolding the cuff of her jeans.

In some ways Rémi had to agree. She had only just begun to understand her family as it was now, fractured but healing, the way Auguste had left it.

"I know," Rémi said. "But I'm glad for the time I had with you and Mama. If you hadn't come down to Miami she and I would still be fighting."

"And I would still be without a sister."

They exchanged cautious smiles, and Yvette bit her lip.

For Rémi, the past few days had been an unexpected blessing. She'd come to Maine to help Yvette work through her issues with their mother, but she was the one walking away with a better relationship with Kelia. Through her inability to simply accept things as they were, her sister had managed to accomplish what Rémi hadn't been able to because of her fourteen-year-long bout with resentment and fear. Things weren't perfect between her and Kelia, but they were better.

"I never thought I'd say this." Rémi zipped up her duffel bag and pushed it aside to sit on the bed next to her sister. "But thanks for running away from home and coming down to Miami to disrupt my life."

Yvette laughed quietly and tossed back her wild hair. The sun arching through the wide windows and over her face picked up chips of gold in her hazel eyes. "You're welcome." Some of the sadness leaked from her face.

Rémi squeezed her sister's hand. "Any time you want to come visit me, just come. I left you my spare key and you already have the alarm code."

"Do I get the same invitation?" Kelia walked through the bedroom's open door with Claudia in tow. Her look was tentative. Hopeful.

"Of course, Mama," Rémi said. She stood up to take her mother in a loose embrace. The scent of fresh coffee and pastries from Kelia's hair brushed her nose as her mother pressed a smiling mouth to Rémi's cheek.

"I'll try not to come unannounced," she chuckled.

"Unannounced guests are free to stay with me," Claudia said, laying a gentle hand on Kelia's back. She flicked a grin Rémi's way.

"Seeing how the two of you have been carrying on since you've been here, I'll make sure to call ahead." Kelia chuckled at her own joke while Rémi blushed helplessly.

Claudia only brushed the back of Rémi's scalding cheek with a cool hand and smiled. "We're still in the honeymoon phase," she murmured with curving lips, looking at Kelia. "I'm sure you understood."

Then it was Kelia's turn to look away with suspicious color in her cheeks, but she smiled back at Claudia. "I do."

The taxi honked its horn a few moments later while simultaneously the house phone rang. When Kelia answered it, the driver announced over the speakerphone that he was waiting in the circular drive.

"Okay," Rémi said and picked up her bag.

She and the others trooped down the stairs and out of the house to where the black taxi sat idling. The driver, sitting behind the steering wheel and reading a newspaper, looked up quickly as they came outside; then he tossed the flimsy pages in the passenger seat and got out to help Claudia with the luggage.

"Call us when your plane lands," Kelia said, her arm around Yvette's waist.

The young girl hugged herself through the thin sweater and leaned into her mother's shoulder as a crisp breeze whipped up to tug at their clothes and hair.

Rémi nodded. "We will. And give René another kiss for me when he gets back from his piano lessons."

She and Claudia briefly hugged the other two women again before getting into the cab. The door slammed shut. Rémi felt a lump in her throat as her sister and mother waved beyond the car's open window. Her lover squeezed her hand in sympathy before leaning forward to speak to the driver.

"Take us to the airport, please."

As the car pulled away, Rémi forced herself not to look back.

Chapter
34

Rémi dropped Claudia off at home with the promise that they would get together the next day for a quiet dinner at the condo. It felt strange leaving her lover standing on the doorstep, lips still tingling from their kiss and knowing that they wouldn't be spending the night together like they had for the last week. Too soon, she'd gotten used to domestic simplicity with Claudia. Much too soon.

She walked into the condo, dropping her duffel bag by the door with an exhausted sigh. The apartment felt quiet without Yvette. In the guest room, things were as they were before her sister arrived. Everything neatly put away, the television off, no clothes scattered all over the bed. Only the single pillow was missing, leaving its mate behind to rest in solitude in the middle of the bed. Rémi sat on the low bench before the window and looked at the garden below. The small cherry trees, in full blossoms of pink and white, trembled with restrained sensuality under the spring breeze. She pushed open the window. Having family around her, she realized, was something else she'd gotten used to.

Smiling, she pulled her cell phone out to call the bar and let them know she'd be in tonight. It rang just as she opened it. Claudia's number flashed on the screen.

"Missed me already?"

"Would you be offended if I said no?" Claudia said with a weak chuckle.

"Are you all right?" The hesitation on the other end of the line made her pause. "Sweetheart?"

Her lover cleared her throat. "I'm—I'll be okay. Just wanted to hear your voice."

Rémi walked quickly out of the room, grabbed her keys, and was out the door. "I'm coming over right now."

"No! No, you don't have to. I'm actually just a few minutes away." She paused. "Just open the door for me."

"Okay." Rémi stopped her progress down the hall and went slowly back into the condo. "Can I do anything for you now? Anything at all."

"Just stay on the phone with me. Be there when I get off the elevator."

"I'm already here waiting for you."

When Claudia walked out of the elevator barely twenty minutes later, Rémi wasn't sure what to expect. But it wasn't the coolly self-contained creature who glanced once at her before whisking past to go into the apartment. The woman she'd left in Coconut Grove had been relaxed and smiling, her face a warm invitation itself and her lean form draped in a floral sundress. This woman wasn't that. Black slacks, white blouse, closed face. That's what she wore now.

Claudia's features, ice-cold and devoid of emotion, chilled Rémi more even than her brushing past to disappear inside. Rémi closed the door. Claudia dropped her wisp of a purse on the sofa, gripped the back of the chair as she leaned forward. Her shoulders shook. Rémi came up behind her lover and pulled her backwards, bracing Claudia against her chest, clasping her hands over the tight belly.

"Love, what's wrong?"

Claudia relaxed against her. Minutely, slowly, until she was a fragile liquid weight. She began to talk. Warrick had been calling all week while they were in Maine, but she never answered the phone. Just after Rémi left the house, he called again. She answered.

"He called me a fool for being involved with you. Said I became a dyke because no real man would want me." Claudia turned to face Rémi, tears crawling down her face and between her lips. "Can you believe he said that shit to me?" She drew air between her teeth. Her body trembled in anger. "Why does he always make me feel like nothing?"

Rémi shook her head, feeling the helpless rage ripple through her. "I'm sorry, baby. His life must be really empty if he's coming after you like this." She tightened her arms around the other woman. "I know it's hard, but try to ignore him. He can't live your life for you. He's way the hell out there in California. A divorce ten years ago and he still wants to fuck up your life. What is he, the fucking IRS?" The tremor in the small body crept into hers.

"For the first time in forever," her lover said, "I'm happy again. And he makes one phone call, making me feel like a pedophile and a worthless old woman for loving you."

With a low sound, Rémi swept her up and carried her to the sofa, crooned softly and rubbed her back. Claudia slackened in her arms, trembling like a tuning fork. She pushed herself away.

"I don't want your pity." A pulse pounded in her throat. Rémi flinched when Claudia's fists clenched in her shirtfront. Then shook her. A button popped away. And another. "Make me feel better."

Rémi didn't have much experience in this arena. Usually women came to her for sex, not comfort. Their emotional states weren't what she was able to take care of with any degree of success. There was only one kind of comfort that she knew how to give to a woman. She dipped her head to kiss Claudia's mouth but the smaller woman turned her head away.

"No. I don't want that." Her face was hard again. Harder than when she'd first walked through the door.

A ball of ice slammed into Rémi's chest. Did this mean that Warrick's careless words had ruined what they had with each other? She slowly pulled back. But Claudia's fingers dug into the skin under Rémi's shirt.

"I want more." Claudia's eyes burned. "Do you understand?"

The ex-husband who had abandoned her bed for another— younger—woman's caresses just came back into her life accusing her of not being worthy of real pleasure. He denied her satisfaction as a woman. Denied her desires. Just like when they were together, he wanted to shut her off from pleasure. He wanted to make her need him and never satisfy that need.

Finally Rémi did understand.

"Are you sure you want this?" Rémi's voice grated in its lowest register.

Claudia leaned close, breath hissing against Rémi's throat. "Yes."

They took the bike. Claudia held on tight to Rémi's back as they blasted through the thick Miami night, city lights and car lights blurring on all sides as they passed. The Harley roared between Rémi's legs. At the door of Odette's, a new hostess carefully looked over Rémi and Claudia before scanning Rémi's membership card and waving them inside the two-story building that had once been a beachfront hotel. They walked down the carpeted stairs into the sunken main room. Tonight, the music hummed low and sweet, a sensual caress against the air, just loud enough to register against the skin. Trance music, straight out of the mid-1990s.

On three of the walls moved real-time images of sex. Three different films, all featuring women kissing and stroking each other, their mouths occasionally moving silently in some bit of irrelevant dialogue. Their corseted backs or bare breasts or open thighs moved seductively on the giant screens.

The windows covered with thick velvet curtains, darkness that saturated the intimate space, the twin semicircular bars on opposite sides of the room with their dark-clad and flirting bartenders. All this added to the atmosphere of anonymity and decadence of Odette's. Women, heavy shadows, moved around them, lightly touching, their scent animal and thick. Some smelled like sex, others of the outdoors and the ocean just outside. A woman walked past in nothing but strings—a scarlet thong and spider web fabric that emphasized the small and pert shape of her breasts.

At her side, Claudia took it all in, eyes alternately wide and shuttered. "What is this place?" she finally asked.

"A fun house," Rémi murmured against her ear, keeping a hand at the base of her lover's spine, gently guiding but ready to lift away at the slightest sign. "But tonight, you can call it therapy."

She moved them slowly through the crowd, giving Claudia a chance to take it all in, see properly the place that she had been brought to. Instead of going upstairs as she would have normally done, Rémi took her lover past the stairs and down a wide hallway. Here the only sound was the music of fucking. Doors remained slyly half opened for a voyeur to peek in or perhaps join. Gasps. Moans. The vicious slap of flesh against flesh. Hand against flesh. Leather against flesh. Grunts. Sighs.

Claudia stopped. Her hand grasped Rémi's. For the first time in hours, her face was hers again. Warm and beautiful. She looked like a woman waking up from a dream.

"Here?" Claudia asked.

"Yes. But only if you want." Rémi allowed herself to tease. "As the great lyricist Ricky Martin once said, we're at the age we don't have to behave."

A smile rippled briefly across Claudia's features.

They chose a room at random, walking past; Claudia pointed and Rémi stopped, opening the door on a scene of plenty. Three women playing together on a thick fur rug. Two mouths kissing around a full breast. The woman being pleasured leaned back, palms flat against the ground, elbows locked, mouth parted in pleasure. Her lovers licked her breasts, lovingly, treating her like a scoop of ice cream they were afraid would melt. Their tongues left trails of wetness on her brown skin.

When Rémi and Claudia came fully into the room, the three barely stirred from their play. Pleased murmurs bubbled from the two women with their mouths full, ecstatic praises on the taste of their lover's breasts. They fondled each other, fingers tangling and untangling in the thick dreadlocks of one and the pixie cut of the pale-skinned brunette.

Rémi sat down in the only chair in the room, avoiding the bed. Claudia sat on the edge of the bed to watch the women, her mouth slightly parted, nipples already hard against the white shirt.

"Is this the kind of thing you do all the time?" she asked after a long moment.

"Not quite all the time, but often enough. I love sex; you know that."

Claudia's ghost smile made another appearance. "Yes."

The women's play licked the flames of arousal in the seat of Rémi's body, but she made no move toward them. The one being tended to, though, watched Rémi through eyes slitted with pleasure. Then winked. She pressed her hands into the women's hair, pushed them harder against her breasts. Her hot gaze rested on Rémi.

"Do you want to join us?" the woman asked in a not-quite-steady voice.

"Not yet." Rémi glanced at Claudia. "What would you like, love? Anything you want, you can have."

Before coming to Odette's, Rémi wasn't sure what her lover would say when faced with the reality of the kind of life she had before, or the things Claudia could do tonight to assert her womanhood, to recognize the fact that she desired and deserved to be. Her gaze moved between Rémi and the naked women.

Claudia seemed to breathe Rémi's words in, palms flat against the bed, eyes flickering. Then she stood up.

"I want to touch your breasts."

Without asking, she unbuttoned Rémi's shirt, bared her to the other women in the room. Over Claudia's shoulder, Rémi watched the three women, saw them adjust their positions to see what Claudia was doing. The brown girl opened her thighs. That seemed to be the signal the other two were waiting for. They both dove down, and one began to lap eagerly at her pussy, eyes trained on Rémi and Claudia as her tongue worked through the dense pussy hairs and her fingers plunged into the wet nest. Behind her knees, the other one bent, dipping her head under the upturned ass. Claudia's mouth at her breast pulled Rémi's attention from the women.

Her lover kissed her breasts one after the other, then sighed as if the flavor of Rémi's skin made her swoon. She curled her tongue around the stiff nipples and tugged them slowly into her mouth again and again. The sensation shot straight to Rémi's pussy, but she held herself calm, didn't want to rush it. Her head fell back in the chair. Her eyes closed. The sounds. She lost herself in the sounds of Claudia licking her breasts, her eager sighs. The girls on the floor, lapping at each other's pussies, groaned and lost themselves finally in each other.

Claudia fingers fluttered down to unbutton Rémi's pants. A faint squeak sounded as someone opened the door and came in. Rémi felt them standing over the daisy chain of pussy eaters on the rug. She lifted her hips for Claudia to pull down her pants and underwear. Her lover moved low, sinking into the cradle of Rémi's hips. Her breath scorched Rémi's cunt. *Ah.*

Through her slitted vision, Rémi saw the couple who had entered. A woman, butch with a soft pink mouth and red hair clipped close to her head. And her friend, not so butch and with waist-length black hair loose and moving like a wave around dark and brutal features. The woman leaned back against the wall to take in the action of the room. One foot flat against the wall, hand diving into her pants. Her friend came up behind Claudia, cocked a questioning eyebrow. Claudia, whose mouth delicately licked Rémi's pussy, tucking her tongue into the slick folds of cunt lips, teasing the dripping hole with the tip of her tongue, just the way she knew Rémi liked. Claudia. Rémi allowed the groan past clenched teeth and told the woman to shut the door.

"There's someone who wants to fuck you," Rémi breathed to Claudia. "Should I let him?"

Her lover jumped at the pronoun, the motion of her mouth stopping for a naked moment. Then she nodded.

Etienne came closer, holding the long length of his dick in hands, stroking himself to Claudia's dark-clad form crouched between Rémi's legs. He was someone Rémi had shared with in the past and didn't mind too much. He was bi, trans, and very good. Her nostrils flared.

Rémi looked up at Etienne and nodded too. Quickly, he rolled on a condom and came toward Claudia.

"She likes to have her pussy eaten first. Do it slow. And then you can fuck her." Her voice rumbled deeply in her chest.

"Can we play too?" Two of the girls from the floor stood close, their naked bodies scented with desire and cum.

Her eyes moved over them. "Yes."

On either side of Rémi, they immediately leaned down to take her nipples in their hot mouths. Claudia ate her pussy with a rhythmic ease, but Rémi could sense the tension in her, a vibrating readiness, a waiting as Etienne settled in on his knees behind her. Rémi felt when his mouth touched Claudia. Her lover's mouth froze on her for a moment, then opened wider. Soft sounds of pleasure pulsed against Rémi as the tongue sought deeper entrance and the hands tightened on her thighs.

"Yes," Rémi murmured, watching the pale head move between her thighs. "That's good. Very good. You really know what you're do—" A gasp sucked away the rest of her words.

The girls' mouths on her breasts, Claudia ravenously eating her pussy, combined to push Rémi closer and closer to the edge, but she forced herself under control. One steadying breath. Then two. When the fingers began to sink even deeper into her skin, Rémi signaled Etienne with a movement of her head. He glided up and sank himself smoothly into Claudia's cunt. Her lover groaned against her flesh. His entrance into Claudia was like the click of the final piece of a puzzle.

Etienne's long hair brushed against his shoulders as he fucked Claudia, slowly, then built to a sawing rhythm that threw her mouth hard against Rémi's skin, raising groans and grunts from both women's mouths.

"Isn't she sweet, Etienne?" Rémi murmured as Claudia lapped at her pussy, as the girls sucked at her breasts and fucked themselves with their fingers. Their hair brushed over Rémi's chest. Thick dreads tumbled over her chest as the long-haired one jerked from the force of her own attentions.

"Yes," he said, clearly almost beyond speech. "So tight. So fresh." His hands gripped Claudia's hips. His thighs slapped against her ass. "She's so hot inside. She's burning me up." The muscles in his belly clenched as he worked at pleasing Claudia. "Sweet," he hissed past clenched teeth. "She's sweet."

"Oh yes." A gasp tore itself from Rémi's throat.

A scream of release muffled itself in Rémi's pussy. Behind Claudia, Etienne gave a hoarse shout, his face ugly with orgasm. After too many panting moments, he pulled limply from her, stripped off the condom, and stumbled back to lean his forehead against the wall next to his redheaded friend. She had finished too, fingers still in her unzipped jeans, eyes watching. Claudia panted, the breath rushing from her parted lips, hands quivering on Rémi's thighs. When she leaned in again to finish what she started, Rémi put a hand in her hair, shook her head. Her body was a tightly coiled spring. It wanted to come. But not this way.

With an equally gentle hand, she pushed away the women nibbling on her breasts. A hiss cleared her teeth. Tomorrow, she knew, her nipples would be sore from such concentrated attention. The women looked at her askance, then shrugged, going off to rejoin their friend on the rug.

Claudia looked up at her, eyes wide and unfocused, mouth wet with Rémi's juices. Rémi stroked her lover's jaw with her thumb, feeling the slight tremor in the muscles beneath her palm.

"How do you feel?"

When she didn't get an answer, Rémi reached down to pull Claudia's pants back up and her lover into her lap. She asked the question again, and instead of answering, Claudia crawled closer to rest her cheek against Rémi's chest. Tears streaked from between tightly closed eyelids, staining soft cheeks, quaking lips.

"I'm sorry," Rémi whispered, shutting out the moans of the three women fucking on the floor. Their noises now seemed obscene to her. Intrusive. "I shouldn't have brought you here."

But Claudia shook her head. "I'm not sorry for this," she finally said.

Her tears continued to rain down. They stained Rémi's shirt and burned her skin like acid.

They slipped out of Odette's just before midnight, barely avoiding being locked in the oceanside pleasure palace for the night. Claudia held tightly to Rémi's back as they rode back up Highway 1 toward the Miami Beach condo. Aside from those few words spoken in the comfort of Rémi's arms, Claudia had said nothing else, only clutched at Rémi as if she would never let go.

Once they got into the condo, she headed straight upstairs for the bedroom. By the time Rémi had put aside her jacket and helmet to join her, Claudia lay naked against the sheets, her pale hair and dark body only a vague impression of beauty in the womb-like darkness of the room.

"Thank you for taking me there tonight."

The words stopped Rémi's silent and penitent progress across the hardwood. Her jackhammer heartbeat seemed to slow. "You don't hate me for making you go through that?"

A hiss of surprise came from the bed. "No. Never that." The sheets rustled as Claudia moved against them. "Come to bed. I want to feel you."

Rémi quickly discarded her clothes and climbed into the bed, slipping close to her lover until they lay breast to breast, belly to belly, feet tangled together. The pulse thundered in her throat.

"What you did for me tonight was perfect. I wanted to be desired and I was. I needed to feel safe and you gave me that." Claudia shivered as if remembering the sensations from Odette's. "It's a form of therapy that I highly recommend." Rémi felt more than saw her smile in the darkness.

"I'm glad because I wouldn't—I didn't want to do anything that you weren't ready for. Anything that you'd regret."

"The only thing I regret is that I let Warrick's mean-spirited words affect me that much." Claudia's sigh fluttered against Rémi's throat. Her fingers clutched. "I still have some insecurities about loving you. He found them easily."

No, don't be insecure. This was meant to be. She wanted to say those words and wipe all her lover's fears away. She wanted to have the other woman dive courageously into their relationship and not worry about what others would think or how they would react. But from the conversation she'd overheard between Claudia and her friend Eden, Rémi knew that wasn't possible. She smoothed her fingers through Claudia's pale hair and down the back of her neck.

She had to ask. "Is there anything I can do to make those insecurities go away?"

"Just keep loving me. That's all I need right now."

"I can." Rémi kissed the warm mouth, the gentle slope of her jaw. "I will." The body beneath her hands sighed into her embrace and fingers tightened at the back of her neck. "I do."

The sheets whispered languidly as their flesh came together. In the darkness, velvety sighs began, gentle notes of passion rose and fell, continuing like music until the sun rose, finally, and burned the shadows away.

Chapter

35

"I like Rémi," Claudia said, playing with the straw in her glass of clear liquid. Probably a gin and tonic.

Eden looked at her from across the table, apparently waiting.

"And not as a friend, or Dez's playmate."

Staring at the monitor with the framed images of the two women, Rémi fidgeted. The sudden silence between the two friends made her hand tense against the desk. Claudia looked suddenly miserable, while her friend's mouth hung open in shock.

"Are you joking?" Eden finally asked.

"No, I'm not. I'm being honest." Whatever she saw in her friend's face made Claudia look down, fiddle with a curl of calamari on her plate before looking up again. "From the last time we talked, it seemed you already knew. I don't—I don't know why you're acting like this now."

"Then it was my paranoid delusions of you getting ass from someone besides yourself. Now, this is—" Eden made a vague gesture in the air, her fingers shaking like agitated leaves as she struggled for the right words.

"She's over twenty-one," Claudia said quietly.

"But you knew her when she was in high school. You practically babysat her." Eden sat back in her chair. "And *she* is a *she!*"

"Thanks for stating the obvious, Eden, because you know none of these things occurred to me before."

"Claudia, even you have to admit this is strange."

"It is unusual. But she makes me happy and some days I feel like she's everything I ever wanted."

Eden sipped her apple martini, wedding rings clicking against the glass.

"There was a time when I would have been ashamed to admit my feelings for Rémi."

"You mean like last month when I asked if you were involved with her?"

Claudia looked down at her plate again, but this time a small smile played with her mouth. "Then I wasn't ready to tell you. Now, I am."

Rémi pressed the mute button on the remote control, suppressing the voices at Claudia and Eden's table, but she kept the camera focused there, watching Claudia's mouth move, her friend's eventual nod of acceptance, the waiter bringing more drinks as the hours wore on. *She told Eden the truth.* Rémi leaned back in her chair, feeling the tension loosen in her chest. Claudia was really ready to be with her. On the monitor, Claudia laughed at something Eden said. Not her usual unrestrained laughter, but still a sign that said she was all right. And that everything else would be.

Whistling beneath her breath, Rémi switched on her desk lamp in her darkening office and turned her attention to the new sample menu that Rochelle had left for her the day before.

Chapter

36

"So, how was your trip up north to see the family? Same as last time?" Sage reached for another beer in the fridge and swung back to face Rémi.

At the bar, Rémi leaned onto her forearms and sipped her beer. "Not quite the same. Better." The satisfaction in that truth made her smile.

"That's surprising. But cool."

"I know, right?"

"Hey, handsome!" Nuria's throaty voice joined them in the kitchen before she did. Barely covered in a tight white tube dress, she radiated contentment that Rémi hadn't seen in a while.

"Who are you fucking? You look too good for this all to be from your own natural well-being."

"Oh, thanks." Nuria's sarcasm didn't faze Sage one bit. The muscular Jamaican leaned closer as if Nuria had agreed to tell who her latest fling was.

"I'm not telling you a damn thing." She kissed Rémi lightly on the mouth. "I brought you a present from my birthday party."

"Shouldn't it go the other way around?"

"You already gave me prezzies, I'm just returning the favor." She slid a DVD case on the bar. "Watch it at your leisure." She winked.

"Is it something to be enjoyed alone?"

"Or with a friend. Depends on what you're into these days."

"You know me," Rémi murmured, waggling her eyebrows. "I'm into everything."

"Whatever!" Nuria laughed, labret stud flashing under the lights. She paused at the counter, taking in the various platters of hors d'oeuvres that the caterer had dropped off barely half an hour before. Phillida chose that moment to come into the kitchen from her trip on the roof to soak solo in the Jacuzzi. Her shapely form in a red bikini and matching swim cap attracted her girlfriend's admiring wolf whistle.

Nuria rolled her eyes. "Hey, where are the casabes?" She plucked a sliver of fried ripe plantain from the platter and bit into it.

Rémi hopped down from the barstool to put her empty beer bottle in the recycling bin under the sink. "They didn't have cassava anything at that place. I found out too late. Sorry."

"No problem." Nuria flashed a smile. "At least you tried."

"I do try to take care of my girls." As Rémi passed by the marble-topped kitchen island for the living room, she slapped Nuria's white-clad ass.

Her friend wiggled her pert backside and laughed. "Yes you do, baby."

Rémi smiled. It felt good to have her friends at her side now. The week in Maine had laid her open in ways she never thought possible. And the trip with Claudia to the sex club. . . . She shook her head. Being with the girls rejuvenated her bruised soul, reminded her that even separate from Claudia, there were people out there who cared for her.

Nuria followed her into the living room, sitting close enough on the couch to tickle Rémi's nose with her dark perfume. "You look distracted." Nuria crossed her legs and draped a hand across her knee.

"Do I?" Rémi took her friend's hand in hers, smoothed the long bones under dark pecan skin. "Maybe it's because your intoxicating presence is just too close to me."

"Bullshit. Even I'm not going to buy that load of caca." Nuria's hair tumbled around her shoulders as she shook her head and tugged her hand back. Rémi chuckled ruefully. She wasn't about to lie to her friend. Not when she had so obviously given her so much support, so much love, even in the midst of her various crises.

"Having flashbacks. Missing someone."

"You? Missing someone? It must have really been a good fuck."

Leaning across the kitchen island, Sage teased Phillida with a cold shrimp, painting her lover's mouth with the cocktail sauce then pulling the pink and white flesh away from her at the last minute, before her lips could claim them.

"It was. She is."

"So you're heading the way that Dez did, then? Happily ever after and all that?"

Rémi winced at her friend's name. "It's not going to be that easy."

"It's always that easy if that's what makes you happy. The alternative is just too boring."

"You think so?"

"I know so."

The alternative to being with Claudia was misery. Rémi looked at Nuria, saw for the first time the light of real experience in her eyes, beyond the casual fucking and sometimes dangerous hedonism she invited into her life.

Nuria touched Rémi's knee. "The last few weeks I've realized that you have to go after what you want. Even if it hurts."

"Even if it hurts other people?"

"But would anyone really be hurt by your happiness? Or is it another emotion entirely they feel?"

Like pain. Rémi could feel the hurt already waiting just under the skin the way her desire for Claudia always sat. Waiting and never sated. She swallowed. Smiled. Nodded. "Who knows, really? Sometimes even we don't know how we feel."

Nuria made a sympathetic noise. "You must have it real bad, baby. If you weren't so precious to me I'd invite you into my parlor and make you forget all about that other broad."

Rémi laughed weakly. "Thanks. I think."

Nuria patted her knee then stood up, walking toward the kitchen to join Phil and Sage's game.

Although her friend didn't understand it, Rémi was glad to not be able to forget about Claudia. The fact that the older woman still sang in her bones even now made her restless and glad. There had never been anyone else in that place. Never. Suddenly Rémi had to see her.

She got to her feet. "I uh . . . I have to go. Stay if you want, just lock up if you leave."

"How are you going to step out on your own party?" Sage walked out of the kitchen, hands on her hips.

But Nuria only dipped her finger in the bowl of cocktail sauce and licked it. "Okay. Be careful on the road."

The ride to Claudia's house passed by in a blur of motion and sound. The bike thundered between her thighs, and wind tugged at her clothes as she shot down Biscayne toward Coconut Grove. Not soon enough she stood at Claudia's door, pressing the neat white bell.

Between Rémi's late nights at the club and Claudia's increased commitments at the university, they hadn't seen each other much since the night at Odette's. They'd only managed to spend a few nights together, but they spoke on the phone every day, several times a day. The night of abandon at the sex club had given Claudia the courage to call her ex-husband and curse him viciously for the things he'd said that drove her to Rémi's arms in tears. Rémi had taken particular pleasure in lying in her lover's bed and watching as Claudia paced naked, the phone pressed to her ear, as she told her ex-husband in no uncertain terms that he no longer had the right to interfere in or pass judgment on her life. Then she advised him to go fuck himself before slamming the cell phone shut. Their sex had been especially explosive that night, with Claudia riding Rémi to happy exhaustion until sunlight peeked past the curtains to flood over the rumpled bed and their sweat-soaked bodies.

"Did you know it was me or do you always answer the door in sexy outfits?" Rémi asked, smiling, when her lover appeared in the doorway.

Claudia grinned and tilted her pale head. The floor-length silk nightgown slithered over her skin. "I'm grading papers, so I need all the sexy I can get."

"Care to share some of that sexy with me?"

"Of course." The press of a warm mouth, bare of lipstick and sweet, licked an instant fire in Rémi.

She had come to Claudia's door simply wanting to see her lover, but now she just wanted to come. Claudia's nipples crested perfectly under the light blue silk. She turned and the rear view was no less inspiring. Hips swinging like a dinner bell. Rippling silk over the taut curves of her backside. The tide of long legs moving under the floor-length material as she walked away.

"Come. I'm out on the deck."

What could Rémi do but follow?

"You have to know that you look amazing in that," she said.

"Of course. I didn't buy it for warmth."

The deck flickered with candles. All along the railing and on the low table with its glass of white wine, a small electric lamp, and two uneven stacks of papers. Student papers. Among the flames, Claudia glowed, an iridescent butterfly against the backdrop of the deep green woods surrounding her house on all sides.

She glanced back over her shoulder at Rémi. "Because of your party—" Her mouth, a pretty red bow, opened and closed around the words as Rémi watched. "I didn't think you'd come."

"The party is still going on. I just wanted to see you."

"So now you've seen me." A smile teased her mouth again.

Rémi shrugged off her leather jacket—it scraped her sensitized skin like a cool tongue—and dropped it on the ground behind her. "And now I really, really want to touch."

Claudia came into her arms like she was meant to be there. No teasing, no coyness. Just her mouth, a hot spark, against Rémi's.

"I'm so glad you came."

"Hmm." Rémi chuckled. "I haven't come yet, but I was hoping you could help me out with that."

"Of course. Anything I can do to be of assistance."

In the aftermath of their kisses, Claudia pushed her into a lawn chair. She crouched over Rémi, quickly unbuckled her pants with its obvious bulge.

"I love it when my darling comes prepared." She pulled down Rémi's pants, jerking the denim roughly down her legs. "I've been preparing myself for you too." Biting her lip, she took Rémi's hand and pushed it under her gown and against her pussy. It was already wet, the curls soaked together and viscous with more than just her excitement from seeing Rémi. Claudia had been touching herself. "I've been thinking about you."

A groan quivered through Rémi's body. She imagined Claudia touching herself, sprawled on the deck, legs wide open for anyone to see. The vision set her thoughts aflame. Claudia's nipples scored the thin material of her gown, pressing against it to tempt Rémi's mouth. Rémi licked the cloth, gasped at the feel of silk over flesh and her lover's hands tearing away her shirt.

"My darling." Claudia grabbed the dick in her fist and crouched, slowly lowered herself, her hot and wet pussy, onto it. Her weight against Rémi's clit was miraculous.

"I love you." Rémi hissed the words between her teeth, eyes full of Claudia. The pretty breasts under the silk, her snaking weight pressing against the fire in Rémi's lap.

"Faster," she begged.

But Claudia ignored her. Took her time. Mouth licked wet as she undulated, her ass swirling in Rémi's palms. She reached up and pulled down the straps of her nightgown, freed her breasts. They jumped into Rémi's mouth, and she moaned around the hard nipples. Sucking their hot, hard tips until she was sure, sure she tasted milk. Her clit pounded under her lover's attentions. The lawn chair squeaked under them.

Claudia was a graceful grunting beast as she rode Rémi. Her breasts leaping in the night air, wet from Rémi's mouth. The nightgown bunched at her waist. The hot, liquid sounds of their fucking finally shattered Rémi's control. Heat exploded in her belly, shooting up into her chest and face until she had to close her eyes against it.

"Oh fuck!" she gasped. "Oh fuck!"

She came to herself with Claudia nibbling on her breasts. Her small fingers pulled at Rémi's nipples, plucking the skin taut and biting wickedly into it. The pain pulled her out of her orgasmic stupor. She gently pushed her lover away.

"Don't tell me you're done already?" Claudia's damp face was lean and hungry.

"If you're going to eat me alive, yes."

Claudia looked down at the teeth marks and blushed. But didn't apologize for them. Rémi's clit perked up again under the black dildo.

"All right then." She pulled herself away from Rémi's lap, the dildo withdrawing from her pussy with a soft liquid slide.

"No. Maybe a little bit more." Rémi found herself standing up abruptly, one hand grabbing at her pants, the other reaching out for her lover.

Claudia turned in a swirl of silk and sex scent. A smile bared her sharp white teeth. "One day you'll say no to me and mean it," she said.

Claudia grabbed the edges of Rémi's open shirt. Dragged her close. Sensation tripped through Rémi at their shared kiss. She hoped this feeling never went away. The surge of familiarity and gladness that shook her each time their flesh connected.

Her back met the deck's railing. Away from the flickering candles, thank god. Claudia chuckled against her mouth as if sensing her fear.

"It's only fire, darling."

Only. Rémi groaned. Claudia's lips burned a trail down her body. The agile tongue licked at her belly and the pale-haired woman shoved the hands away that would unbuckle the harness and make way for her mouth. She pushed Rémi's pants down.

"Watch carefully, my love. You might never see this again."

And she took the head of the wet dildo in her mouth. Rémi would have staggered back against the railing if her entire body wasn't pressed back against it. Claudia licked the smooth black silicone, swirled her tongue around its length, slurping as she sucked her own juices from it, enjoying it.

On her knees in front of Rémi, she enthusiastically worked the dick. She took it deep into her mouth until her cheeks hollowed, her eyes closed. Rémi's clit pulsed. The diving mouth nudged the base of the cock against her center until she too was groaning. Then Claudia touched her. The groan became a gasp when fingers slid against the soaked lips, trailing the slit of her pussy.

"Claudia." She grabbed her lover's hair. Her head fell back.

Rémi didn't know when Claudia got the harness and dildo off, but they were and she was slurping at Rémi's naked pussy, crouched in the wide V of Rémi's thighs, her hands digging into the solid muscles. Her barely muffled moans of delectation dropped like tiny explosions in Rémi's body. Her hips surged. Her hands fell down to Claudia's neck and tightened. The mouth hummed between Rémi's legs, tongue darting over her clit, into her soaking wet pussy.

"Oh my fuck—oh!"

Fingers. Claudia slipped fingers in. Rémi couldn't tell how many. Only that they were gliding against her inner walls, mouth latched to her clit, tongue beating against the distended bundle of nerves like a drum. The fingers! Rémi staggered. Pussy pulsing. Hips thrusting against Claudia's face. Her knees buckling like the last of her resistance to whatever Claudia was doing. She imploded. Died. And floated back to the heaven of Claudia's mouth. Tiny soothing kisses against her cunt gently lowered her back to earth.

"You have no idea how long I've been waiting to do that." Claudia licked her fingers.

Against the railing, Rémi dropped to her knees, her chest rapidly rising and falling. "If you get any better at this, you're going to kill me," she gasped.

Claudia kissed her mouth, laughing. "You aren't the only one allowed to blow minds around here, you know."

"Shit! *Now* I do."

Her lover laughed again.

When she could again, Rémi stood, bringing Claudia up with her.

She leaned back against the railing and Claudia pressed against her, lazily nibbled along her throat and collarbone as Rémi pulled up her pants and buttoned her shirt. She left the top two buttons loose to allow Claudia access to her skin. She could be generous. Claudia swayed in her arms to some internal music as she hummed. Her bottom's tantalizing curve warmed Rémi's palms.

"I love that your skin smells like Dove, even after all we've done." Claudia chuckled against her throat.

Rémi loved that Claudia knew what brand of soap she used. She pressed her lips to her lover's forehead. Over Claudia's shoulder, her eye caught the stack of papers underneath the laptop.

"I completely forgot that you're grading papers. I should go and let you get back to your work."

"No. You should stay." Claudia bit Rémi's lip, sucked it into her mouth. Cool hands moved against her back.

"You need to work," Rémi murmured against the teasing mouth, trying to mean it.

"I can grade these papers tomorrow. Wouldn't you like to be with me all night?" She pulled down the straps of her nightgown, baring her breasts. "Wouldn't that be nice?" The nipples pushed into the night, like Hershey kisses, begging Rémi to take them into her mouth. Her hands tightened on Claudia's arms. She bent her head, taking the dark nuggets into her mouth, one after the other. Claudia moaned and clutched at the back of Rémi's head.

"What the fuck is this?"

Dez's unexpected voice snapped into Rémi's spine and she stiffened, head rocketing up. Claudia's nipple slid from her mouth with a soft, obscene pop. And she felt more than heard her lover swallow a gasp then tug at the straps of her nightgown until it covered her breasts. Claudia's eyelashes fluttered rapidly, like butterflies caught in a storm.

"Tell me this is not what I'm seeing!"

With embarrassed heat prickling under her skin, Rémi turned to face Dez. Her best friend stood in the doorway, an intruder in their circle of candles, light flickering over the face tense with fury and disbelief.

"Mama?" Dez staggered a few steps toward Claudia. "What is this?"

This could be nothing other than what she saw. And Rémi saw the denial of it creep over her face. Not her mother, not her best friend. And although she had been dreading this moment, realizing that it would come as surely as the next sunrise, she didn't know what to say.

"Darling . . ." Claudia reached out to her daughter. "Let's talk about this inside."

Dez shrugged off her mother's hand as if it was unclean. "No. There's nothing to talk about." She drew an unsteady breath, then another, as if trying to calm herself down or wake herself up. "Please don't let there be anything to talk about."

Beyond her shoulder, still in the shadows of the house, her new wife stood back, eyes wide, hand to her throat.

The breathing apparently didn't work. "What are you doing?!" Dez's voice rose, wailing as she spun back to Rémi. "What did you do to my mother?"

Before Rémi could say anything, Claudia clutched her arm, looked at her with a plea in her eyes. "Please go. I'll talk with you later. Tomorrow."

Go? Why did she have to go? They had done nothing wrong. Claudia's hand pressed against her belly. Pushed her gently toward the door. The hand fell away, leaving a cold spot in its place.

"Yeah, go home, you fucking traitor!" Spit flew from Dez's mouth. "Parasite. Get the fuck out of here!"

More than anyone, Dez knew what Rémi did with her women. Knew what she liked. They'd fucked together enough for Dez to know how Rémi wanted her women to behave, what pleasure and pain she wanted them to take. The things she asked them to do, and how many of them did it without question. Again and again. The knowledge of these things twisted in her friend's poisonous gaze, in her sneering mouth.

Rémi shook her head. "It's not like that. I swear. This is different."

"Bullshit! I can't believe you're fucking doing this." Dez's mouth hardened then she turned abruptly away as if unable to stand the sight of Rémi's face. But in the next breath she twisted back, her body in a blur of motion. Rémi felt the pain in her face, the explosion of blood in her mouth, before it registered that Dez punched her.

"Stop!" Victoria ran out from the house but not before Claudia flew in front of her daughter.

She gripped Dez's tensed arms. "Stop this right now."

With a hissing sigh, she looked over her shoulder at Rémi. "Tomorrow. Please?"

Rémi looked at her best friend then at her lover. Both stared at each other, leaving her outside their snap-tight circle of family. She nodded once, put one foot carefully ahead of the other and walked out. Images somersaulted through her mind. Claudia's mouth on her dick. Fingers curved inside her pussy, the hot mouth tugging at her clit. Her lover's stricken face. Rémi stumbled and nearly fell, catching herself with flattened palms against the paved walkway. The scraping pain in her hands jolted her out of frozen disbelief. She let herself fall, tip over and drop ass-first into the damp grass laying flat next to the walkway.

"Fuck!" She gripped her hair, elbows propped up on her shaking knees. "Fuck. Fuck. Fuck!"

She didn't know how long she sat there with the dampness from the grass sinking into her jeans. Very faint sounds came the house, but she wouldn't go back there. She couldn't. Rémi pulled herself to her feet and stumbled to her bike. The thick rubber grips of her handlebars felt foreign under her hands, as if she didn't need to touch them. What she wanted to touch was Claudia's face. To tell her that everything would work out. For her lover to tell her the same thing. Her hand convulsed on the bike and she let go. She backed away. Away from the bike, from the house. At this time of night, the narrow, tree-lined street was quiet. No dogs barking. No passionate arguments bleeding past the thick walls of foliage and palm trees. Just quiet.

This quiet was thick enough for her to hear her pounding heartbeat. To feel the tightening in her chest as the world she'd known for the past fourteen years collapsed around her. She should've expected it, but no amount of preparation could have steeled her against this. Breath ran ragged in her chest.

She walked until she was too tired to walk anymore. She walked until the swaying Spanish moss and night-blooming jasmine guided her across a wide expanse of grass, a jogging path, and the salt-sour scent of the bay. Tired. She was so tired. Heart sounds still blinded her ears to everything but her own pain. Claudia told her to go. Dez called her a parasite. This was worse than anything she could have expected. Was it so wrong to want someone to love her?

In the dark she found a park bench to ease her tired body onto. The jasmine scent pressed into her, distracted her nose from the drip of tears.

"Looks like you're in a bad way, cousin."

"You think?" The words squeezed without bite past Rémi's dry lips. She closed her eyes and leaned back against the bench, not even wanting to know how Wynne knew she was here. Air shifted beside her and Rémi felt the brush of cloth against her leg as her cousin sat in the grass at her feet.

"I should have warned you. Sorry."

Rémi laughed, a dead, rusted sound. "It wasn't your business to *warn* me. I was careless, end of story."

"This isn't the worst thing that could happen."

"Is this your way of cheering me up?"

"You mean it's not working?" The laughter in Wynne's voice was strangely comforting. "I think your friend will forgive you."

"She won't. I knew it before I started this." Some part of her had known.

Wynne was silent. Rémi sighed and put her feet up on the bench, stretched out as much as it would allow.

"I'm so fucking stupid sometimes." She dropped a tired arm over her eyes and prayed for sleep.

Chapter

37

"You look like you slept in your clothes."
Rémi glanced up at Nuria as she threw her keys into the bowl by the door. Her friend sat up on the couch, the blanket over her falling down to reveal bare shoulders.

"I did." The words croaked from between Rémi's dry lips, surprising her with the pain they carried. "Now I'm going upstairs for a proper night's sleep."

Her body ached from the night spent on the park bench in Coconut Grove. She remembered huddling into her jacket to keep warm, shivering at the memory of Claudia's cool touch against her skin, her dismissal. Facing her friends who were sure to still be at her apartment wasn't an option, and so she'd huddled in her own misery. Rémi was lucky that cops didn't wander by and cart her ass off to jail. But maybe that was why Wynne had spent the night by her side, only wandering off after Rémi had opened her eyes to a piercing sun. She sighed and walked past her friend, ignoring the curious eyes that followed her across the living room and up the stairs.

Merciful blackness came with the closing of her bedroom door. But it didn't last long. A knock came, then Nuria with the blanket wrapped around her like a sarong.

"I was worried," she said.

"No need. I'm fine."

Rémi pulled off the jacket, her shirt, shoes, pants, all without looking at her friend and climbed between the cool sheets. She felt filthy and used up, but the comfort of her bed took precedence over a shower. All she wanted to do was lay down and rest.

"Bullshit. You look like something the leper's dog squeezed out of its asshole." She climbed into the bed next to Rémi. "What's wrong, amiga? Were you at the club last night?"

Rémi shook her head. "I don't feel like talking right now, Ria. Let's do this later, okay?"

She felt the shadowy brush of a hand over her hair. Then a warm touch at the back of her neck.

"Okay. When you're ready, just know you can talk to me."

"I know."

She drifted into sleep with Nuria's presence beside her in the bed. Unusual, but comforting. In what felt like moments later, the sound of her cell phone jolted Rémi out of her uneasy slumber. With a low groan, she fumbled for it on the bedside table, but another hand met hers, pushed the phone in her palm.

"Here." Nuria's voice was rough from sleep.

Grunting her thanks, Rémi answered the phone.

"Sorry to wake you. I didn't think you'd still be asleep."

Rémi pushed aside the sense of déjà vu and sat up in the bed. "I'm not. What happened after I left? Is everything all right?"

"No." Claudia sighed. "Yes. It's good to hear your voice."

"You don't sound like everything is all right."

Again that sigh and a long pause. Unease scuttled over Rémi's skin.

"I don't think—we shouldn't . . ." More words stopped and started, none of them emerging in complete sentences. Rémi swallowed. This wasn't like her lover at all. Even after what happened last night, Claudia shouldn't sound so hesitant, so unsure of herself.

Rémi swallowed her rising panic. "Tell me what's wrong."

"We need to take a break. It wasn't a good idea to start this. I'm sorry." The words emerged from the other end of the telephone in a breathless rush.

Rémi's hand spasmed around the phone. "What?"

Claudia spoke again. Suddenly, Rémi couldn't see. Her lashes felt wet, and her throat was thick with something she didn't want to swallow. She blinked. Once. Twice. And her eyes became dry again, but the muscles around them were pulled tight.

"Are you saying you don't want to see me anymore?" Her voice scraped her throat like sandpaper.

"Yes."

"Okay." She closed the phone.

Beside her, Nuria sat heavily in her silence, as if afraid to disturb Rémi with even her breathing. Cold settled over her like a blanket. She rolled onto her side away from her friend and closed her eyes.

"Will you be okay?"

"Yes." But she felt a tear drip across the bridge of her nose and into the other eye. "I'll be fine."

Chapter

38

We need to take a break. It wasn't a good idea to start this. I'm sorry.
The words echoed in Rémi's head, loud and jarring as a bell under her pillow. Rémi gave the bike more gas and it growled under her, ratcheting up to ninety miles an hour. Closer and closer to her destination. Instead of turning left onto Tiger Lily Drive, she continued farther up until her bike slowed to a stop in front of the converted church with the enormous red double doors. She punched in the security code at the gate and rode in as the gate swung open onto the quiet driveway.

The lights were on, illuminating the stained glass windows that made up nearly the entire front façade. Rémi pressed the doorbell and stepped back.

"What the fuck are you doing here?"

Dez stood in the doorway in tight jeans, T-shirt, and bare feet. The bones of her face stood out sharply, as if she'd been fasting.

"Who is it, babe?" Victoria's voice called out from behind her in the house.

"Nobody." Dez's lips barely moved.

"Did you tell her to leave me?" Rémi braced herself against the door frame, spreading her arms and sinking her fingers into the wood like an innocent at crucifixion.

Her friend crossed bare arms, a muscle twitching in her jaw. Her eyes held the cold of a winter chill. "Yes. As if she had a choice." She thrust out her chin at Rémi. "She knows what you're doing is disgusting."

"You're not the only one who deserves happiness, Dez," she said quietly, despite the pulse galloping in her throat.

"Mama practically raised you."

"But there's no blood between us. I love her."

Dez shoved her back out of the doorway. "Shut up!"

Rémi stumbled and almost fell. Her chest stung from the force of Dez's push but it was nothing to the agony already tearing her insides apart.

Victoria's head appeared behind Dez. "Darling, what's going on?"

"Just getting this filth out of my front yard."

But Victoria came to the door, stepped into its mouth, and grabbed Dez's arm. "Stop being unreasonable, she's your friend. Invite her in so you two can work this out."

"This bitch isn't setting foot in my house again."

"It's *our* house now."

Dez froze then swung to face Victoria. But her wife ignored her.

"Rémi, come in." Her voice was low with tenderness. In the knee-length copper robe showing plainly that she had nothing on underneath, she reached for Rémi's hand and drew her into the house. "Please."

In their living room, Dez avoided touching Rémi. She stood as far from her as possible, as if a disease lingered on her former friend and threatened to infect her.

She stood before the darkened fireplace with her arms laced across her chest. "I'm only going to ask you this one more time. Why are you here?"

"To make you understand."

"There's nothing to understand. You're fucking my mother." Dez sucked in a breath. "Jesus! Even as I'm saying this I can't believe it!" She paced the length of the sitting room.

Victoria sat down next to Rémi on the sofa, gathering her legs beneath her and arranging the cotton robe modestly over her thighs. "Calm down, Dez. You reacting like this isn't making things better."

"I don't want this better. I want it gone." She turned her head, a reptilian motion independent from the rest of her body, and looked at Rémi. "What did I ever do to you to deserve this?"

Rémi braced her legs apart, linked her fingers together and leaned forward. *Be cool. Be cool.* Maybe if Dez could understand about her and Claudia then she and her lover would get back together. Maybe—"This isn't about you, Dez."

Her friend stopped pacing. "You're right. Because you sure as shit didn't think about how I would feel."

"I thought about your feelings. A lot. And I thought about how happy you are with Victoria." Rémi glanced at the woman by her side, at Victoria's sympathetic smile, the wild curls and red mouth that her friend had been unable to resist. "You know what that's like, to want someone so badly that nothing else matters."

Dez catapulted across the room, fists raised. "Don't compare—!"

Rémi kept her seat, refusing to flinch.

"Is this your way of keeping Mom in your life forever and finally getting a family of your own?" Dez towered over Rémi, body vibrating with violence.

Rémi forced her voice to remain calm. She hadn't come here to fight. "Before I would have said that I don't know. Now, I can tell you no. That's not at all what's happening."

"I hope you realize that *nothing* is happening now. My mother doesn't want you anymore. She told me she made that phone call."

That ache, familiar to Rémi since that early morning call, throbbed even more viciously in her chest.

"Yes, she told me. But I wanted—"

"No. Nothing you want matters here. Leave. Nobody wants you."

The words hammered at Rémi, striking with painful accuracy at her most vulnerable places. In a daze, she stood up. She nodded once at Dez and Victoria then found her way, step by painful step, out of their house and back to her own. It was the hardest journey of her life.

Chapter
39

Now she knew. Rémi dressed for the club, hidden from herself in the mirrored walk-in closet with the scent of cedar lingering in the air. She pulled on slacks, tucked in the crisp white shirt, buckled her belt, arranged her face away from lines of grief. Then she went to Gillespie's earlier than she needed to. Her steel watch and her wrist were the same temperature.

Later, much later, Rémi sat in her office—the only place in the club not wired for sound, not infested with cameras. She closed herself into its silence, turned off the speakers feeding her music from the stage, and watched everything below.

A jazz quartet pantomimed music on the stage. The bass player tapping his feet to the rhythm he was helping to create. Sax player blowing his cheeks into balloons while the drummer brought the deepest sound for their singer, a brown-skinned pixie in tight slacks, to rock her hips to. The audience sat enthralled, fingers snapping over the remnants of their dinner.

It was all Rémi's. The only thing she had left.

In the crowd that moved through the club, swaying back and forth to the music like stalks of wheat in a friendly breeze, a familiar figure intruded. Pale dress. Dark skin. Rémi's heart in her fist.

Elena walked in front, leading the one behind her toward Rémi's office. Rémi didn't want to notice the proud lift of the small head. The diamond earrings catching light and throwing it on the bare throat and shoulders shimmering above the white tube dress. Her jaw, a firm line of stubbornness below the wine-red mouth pulled tight at its corners. Rémi forced the breath inside her to move more slowly, expanding the rib cage beneath her starched shirt and vest. The air conditioner hummed cool and quiet from the vents above her, ruffling the curls she still hadn't cut.

Rémi took out her phone. "Elena."

She watched her manager pull the tiny cell from her pocket.

"I'm on my way to your office," Elena said. "You have a visitor."

"That's what I wanted to talk to you about. I'm not seeing anyone today. No exceptions."

Elena's steps faltered on the stairs only a few feet from the door. She knew about the cameras. Knew that Rémi had to be watching. Her eyes darted up to the tiny camera above the door.

"Ah." She paused. "Okay. I'll make sure the rest of the staff knows."

And she turned to Claudia, opened her mouth to relay the message. Rémi hung up before she could hear Claudia's voice. She slid the phone into her breast pocket and pressed a button on the remote to slide the bank of monitors back into the recessed cabinet.

A shipment of wine from the day before had come up over a dozen bottles short. That had to be dealt with before she turned the business of paperwork back over to Elena. Rémi picked up the invoice and her pen. The phone over her heart vibrated in three short bursts, paused then vibrated again. She ignored it, reaching instead for the cordless on her desk.

A knock came at her office door.

"Yes?"

Monique walked in with a tray of food held before her like an offering. She had taken off the long-sleeved white shirt that went under the cropped tuxedo top of her waitress's uniform. Her breasts plumped above the low neckline, and her belly button played hide-and-seek with the cloth for every step she took. When she turned to close the door behind her, Rémi shook her head.

"Don't bother," she said.

Monique stopped, her breasts hovering just above the tray. "You haven't eaten today."

"And I don't plan on it." The food on the tray—penne pasta, red peppers and fat curls of pink shrimp glistening with olive oil—made Rémi's throat clench with revulsion. "Take it away. I'm not interested."

Monique opened her mouth to say something else, but Rémi shook her head again. "Leave."

The waitress's eyes fell briefly to the floor. She waited a few seconds, perhaps hoping for Rémi to change her mind, before she turned, making her way through the open door. Rémi didn't look up when she heard it close.

Hours later, with the sun chasing any lingering traces of the night's coolness from the air, Rémi pushed open the door to her condo. Hushed quiet. The air conditioner's toothless bite at the back of her neck. Keys by the door. Helmet on the shelf. Then a beer in her hand. The bottle's cold sweat against her palm. Rémi stood in the middle of the kitchen, breathing in the silence that before had been a balm to her spirit, the perfect antidote after a night of work or a day of pleasure. And now was not. Rémi breathed deeply and felt the tight band of misery around her chest. In the quiet. In the desolation. She knew. She knew what it was like not to have Claudia in her life. It hurt.

Chapter

40

It was worse knowing. The thought plagued Rémi while she played manager during Elena's periodic absences, dealt with time sheets and deliveries and people requesting vacation days. It was worse.

At least twice a week she and Yvette talked on the phone, her sister giving her the dirt about the goings on at school now that she was back in Rhode Island and enrolled for the summer semester. The girls were boring, her sister said. And the boys even more so. As she rambled on about Brown and the teachers she was dealing with, occasionally pausing to allow Rémi a grunt or a comment, Rémi allowed her mind to wander to another university campus not too far from where she sat. On one of these occasions, Yvette paused her riot of words.

"You should call her. I'm sure she misses you. It's obvious you miss her."

"It's more complicated than that," Rémi said. *She doesn't want me in her life in that way anymore. If she asks me to go back to the way things were before, I'll fall apart.*

Yvette didn't press her, only segued smoothly into a less prickly topic until Rémi was lulled once again into the mindless rhythm of their mostly one-sided conversation.

Alone in her office, with the emptiness of daylight enfolding the bar on all sides, Rémi leafed through a pile of receipts she'd wrestled from Elena. Her mind was a focused blade as she studied the numbers. But try as she might, she could find nothing wrong with them. Anderson seemed to have lost interest in sabotaging her business. Their days of finding rats in the kitchen and moles in the office seemed to be over, and Rémi hadn't had a sign of the man since his visit three weeks ago. Still, she waited for the other shoe to drop.

At her elbow, the office phone rang. She almost slammed it back down when she heard the voice on the other end of the line.

"I was just thinking about you," Rémi said.

Anderson laughed. "I'm flattered."

"Don't be," she snarled. "What do you want?"

"You." The mockery remained in his voice. "I'd like you come to my office for a chat."

"I have nothing to talk with you about."

"How about your mother? Do you have anything to say to her?"

Rémi felt the question all the way down her spine. Her toes clenched in their boots. "Where is she?"

"Here. In my office."

Rémi hung up and grabbed her jacket.

With the sun firmly in the sky's center and the lunch crowd going about its frantic business, Rémi was surprised to find Anderson's place open. On the way into the building, she thought she saw Wynne, a sly shadow, huddled next to a boy playing a handheld video game. *René?* But she looked again and the vision disappeared. No one stopped her progress through the nearly empty club and to his office at the rear of the building. The two bulky men, smoking and chatting easily with each other in French as they stood guard on either side of the door, barely glanced at her as she strode past and flung the door open.

"Where is she?"

Rémi stopped short, prepared to see Anderson behind his desk or even holding a knife to her mother's neck as she hung suspended from the ceiling in chains. Instead he sat, civilized and calm, on the sofa facing . . . no one. The office was clothed in darkness, the shades drawn over the windows and with only a small banker's lamp glowing a deep blue to provide light.

"Where's my mother?" She slammed the door shut behind her.

"Not here. I lied." There was something in Anderson's face, a cool irrationality that froze the blood in Rémi's veins. "She called me. She's coming down here to rescue you." He stood up. "You, who split her apart coming out the way that Auguste"—he spat the name as if he couldn't get if off his tongue fast enough—"split her going in."

Rémi didn't bother to hide her confusion. She braced her hands on her hips, shaking her head. "What is this really about? Really. I'm tired of playing cat and mouse with you. I'm finished."

"You're finished when I say you are." He pulled a gun out of his coat pocket, pointed the silenced 9mm Beretta in Rémi's direction.

Fuck. The blood froze under Rémi's skin. Not this bullshit again. Anderson reached over, too casually, and pressed a button on the small table near the couch. As soon as he sat back, one of his body-guards walked into the office, wrenched Rémi's arms behind her back, and slipped handcuffs—tight—around her wrists. She staggered as he released her. Without uttering a word, the muscle-bound blond left the office, closing the door firmly behind him. She twitched in the cuffs, feeling metal cut even deeper into her wrists.

"You dickless motherfucker," she snarled, although her heart slammed out of control in her chest. "Does it make you feel good to tie up an unarmed woman?" She loosened her shoulders, tried to steady her breathing. "Is that how you prove to yourself that you're a real man?"

"I don't have to prove anything to anyone, Rémi." On his lips, her name became a curse. "Not to you or that father of yours who couldn't care for the precious things he had."

"That's what this whole thing has been about? My father?" De-flated, she sagged in her binds and dropped to her knees. "This is so fucked." Even now Auguste was poisoning her life. She turned slitted eyes to Anderson. "What did he do to you that he didn't do to me? Do you think that you're special somehow? Auguste fucked everyone over."

"What are you talking about? You were his prize. The one he always talked about in those damn interviews."

Anderson's look was maniacal. Gone was the urbane, vaguely sinister man who'd made Rémi's insides crawl with fear. Now he just looked crazy.

"Wrong daughter," she growled.

"No, I don't think so. You have every look of Auguste." Spit flew from his mouth, and his face contorted with real hatred. The gun in his hand shook as he stood up and stepped closer to Rémi. "And all his petty cruelties and ego too, I'm sure. That's why he thought so well of you."

Rémi jerked with revulsion at the idea. Her and Auguste being the same? Never. "You don't know a damn thing about me!"

"I don't need to know you to see the kind of person you are. You live a life of waste and idleness. You and your friends screw your way through Miami as if the city was your personal harem. And for most people you're nothing more than a meal ticket. No one can love a creature like you."

Rémi's chin wrenched up. The backs of her eyes stung. She sprang up and, before he could react, knocked the gun out of Anderson's grasp with her shoulder, swung her cuffed arms from behind her back and up above her head. Around his neck. The chains of the handcuffs yanked at the skin below his Adam's apple. Anderson choked, gasped, tried to jerk away, clawing at her arms. But she held him fast. Rémi pulled the cuffs tighter around his neck. She heard him fight for air. She felt the breath struggling to get past her fisted hands. And she didn't care.

He sagged in her arms, but she kept the pressure hard, sinking with a jarring thud to her knees as he fell forward, sprawled full length under her on the carpeted floor. His hands grappled for the tightening handcuffs.

"You won't be able to run the club from behind bars, you know."

Rémi jerked upright, scattering her gaze around the office, breath huffing from her open mouth. Wynne stood in the doorway. Anderson's goons lay discarded at her feet like mown grass. Behind her, Kelia stood silently plucking at the neck of her pink blouse, her face a mask of concern.

"It's not worth it, darling," her mother said. "Let him go."

"He said that he had you." Rémi stared at Kelia, her chest fluttering with relief to see her mother safe. Under her, Anderson's head hit the floor as she released his throat.

"He was obviously wrong. I would never foolishly come here by myself."

From the doorway, Wynne laughed silently. "I'm glad to see you in one piece, cousin."

She leaned down to unlock Rémi's handcuffs, squeeze her shoulder in brief comfort. Then went back to the unconscious bodyguards, pulled plastic handcuffs tight around their wrists, and dragged them off, one by one, to stuff in a closet across the hall. Wynne was very efficient. And stronger than she looked.

Rémi rubbed at her wrists and stood up from her sprawl on top of Anderson. Unthinking, she reached for her mother. *She was safe. She was safe.* Kelia's warmth slowly penetrated her icy body. In her mother's arms, she gradually stopped trembling. Kelia pulled back and looked into her face.

"I need to speak with Matthias privately, sweetheart."

"But—"

"I need to. This business has continued long enough." Her glance dropped to Anderson, who still lay on the floor gasping quietly and clutching at his throat. "I don't think he's in any position to do anything right now."

Wynne stepped back into the office holding out one of her plastic orange cuffs. "But just to be safe, I can—"

"No, Bronwynne. It'll be fine. Wait just outside the door. I won't be long."

Rémi looked at her cousin. Wynne shrugged, but pressed the cuffs and a tiny pistol pulled from her leg holster into Kelia's hands anyway. The two of them left the office and stood outside the door. Kelia closed it behind them.

When the older woman emerged nearly half an hour later, Rémi had stopped shaking, though she badly wanted a cigarette. And a *bottle* of Scotch. As the door handle clicked, she turned, not knowing what to expect. But Anderson's face, shell-shocked and staring empty-eyed at Kelia's back stopped her cold.

"I'm ready now," her mother said.

Rémi and Wynne had no choice but to follow after her.

"I met Matthias first." Rémi's mother said. "He was the one who introduced me to your father."

That was how Kelia Walker-Bouchard's story began in the cool comfort of Rémi's house, with her slight frame propped up against the pillows in the guest room, Rémi curled at the foot of the bed watching her face, and Wynne, for once not a ghost but a solid presence, her legs tucked under her as she leaned against the footboard, drinking the hot chocolate that Kelia had made.

The story was a typical one, variations on a theme that Rémi had seen all too often. Two men, one woman, a business partnership shattered by jealousy, and Auguste Bouchard's inability to take care of the precious things entrusted to him.

"Matthias was angry with the way Gus treated me in the later years of our marriage. When I became angry about that too, I turned to Matthias. I shouldn't have, but he was convenient. He always had the right words to make me feel good about myself."

But he'd wanted more. When Kelia told him she would never leave her husband, Anderson broke off all contact with her and seemed to disappear from the face of the earth. Then at Auguste's funeral, a delivery of two dozen scarlet roses arrived with a note that simply said, "Regrets."

"That was the last I'd heard from him until today." Kelia sipped her hot chocolate then settled the mug carefully in her lap, palms curled around the white ceramic.

In the privacy of his closed office, she had confronted him. Bludgeoned him with details of how Auguste had treated Rémi, that he was continuing the work of his dead enemy by trying to destroy her daughter and everything she had built in Miami. Then Kelia shocked him with news of their son. He literally stumbled back as if she'd shoved him. His office chair squeaked and bounced as his dead weight dropped into it.

"You're lying," he said.

But she offered proof he couldn't ignore. And a chance to be a part of René's life as long as he left her daughter alone. He agreed.

Rémi listened to Kelia's story in amazement. At the end of it, she felt something like respect stirring in her chest for Kelia. And gratitude.

"Thank you for coming here for me, Mama. I didn't expect you to. But I really appreciate it."

Kelia waved aside Rémi's words with a thin hand. "When Yvette told me everything that was happening with you, I had no choice. I had to come. Are you and Claudia—?"

Rémi had to blink and look away. "We're nothing."

Next to her, Wynne made a low noise. Her cousin and mother exchanged a look. Then Kelia put her hot chocolate on the bedside table and slid down in the bed. Her hand brushed over Rémi's head, navigating a new geography of comfort.

"Things will work out, darling."

Rémi swallowed the denial of her mother's words. And nodded anyway.

Chapter

41

"And that's it? The guy isn't going to bother you anymore?" Phil aimed her questions at Rémi.

"Nope. Thanks to my mother."

"*Fabuloso, mija.*" Nuria leaned over to squeeze Rémi's arm. "I'd hate to see you lose this place. I know how much you love it."

Rémi grinned. "And need it."

"We need it too, baby," Sage offered. "Where else in this town can we go blow off steam, have a fantastic meal, and see some of the finest ass in the world?"

"Besides Rémi's house?" Phil chuckled.

Sage glanced over Rémi's shoulder. "I haven't seen her in a while. I hope everything's all right."

Dez? But when Rémi turned to look it wasn't her old friend that she saw. Sage was right. It had been a long time. She'd almost forgotten—no, that wasn't right, because she could never forget—she'd *underestimated* Claudia's effect on her senses. It had been three weeks, five days, and eighteen hours since she'd last seen her. And longer. Much, much longer since she'd touched her skin.

She was wearing that red dress. The same one she'd worn on their first real date when Rémi had tasted her for the first time. Felt the blood rushing through Claudia's feet. Smelled her desire. Rémi's fingertips slid against the textured surface of the table as her hand curled into a loose fist. The familiar scent of apples settled around her shoulders as Claudia drew closer.

"Mrs. Nichols." She forced a smile. Felt Nuria's curious eyes flicker to her face.

"Hi, girls. It's good to see you." Claudia's voice trailed like teasing fingernails around Rémi's ear.

Her friends said their hellos, though Rémi couldn't distinguish between what one said over the other. Only that Claudia smiled at each, before resting her eyes on Rémi.

Please don't ask me anything. Please.

"May I speak with you privately?"

"No." The word came out harshly, but she tried to gentle it. "I'm sorry. I'm"—she waved her arm to indicate the table full of food, her friends, the bar with its jostling Friday evening crowd—"busy." Rémi felt her friends' disbelieving looks, but she refused to meet them, only glanced down at the table, over Claudia's shoulder. Anywhere.

"All right. Then I'll speak with you publicly." Claudia took a deep breath, as if diving off a cliff even though she wasn't sure there was water below to save her. "I was wrong the last time we spoke. I—shouldn't have said what I did. I don't want us to end. There has to be another way."

Stop this. Rémi wanted to stop. To halt the flow of Claudia's words and take her somewhere else other than the humiliation of the dining room where her friends could hear every word and judge. But she couldn't stop herself.

Rémi shook her head. "No. You were right before. We were just fooling ourselves that there could be anything between us. Now there's nothing more to talk about. You can go home now."

"I didn't mean to betray your trust."

The loose fist on the table became a tight one. *Yes. That's what it had been, a betrayal.*

"You said you wouldn't abandon me." The words came out against her will.

"Rémi." Nuria's hand settled lightly on her fist. "I think you should take this somewhere else. Now."

Phil's eyes were wide and horrified as they darted between Rémi and Claudia. Sage only stared at Rémi, her gaze narrow with speculation. Other people in the dining room were beginning to stare, whisper behind cupped hands. Rémi got woodenly to her feet, straightened the tie that didn't need straightening, and walked out of the club, brushing past customers, waiters, anyone in her way. Night absorbed the burning heat of her face, her body, as soon as she walked out of Gillespie's doors. *Oh god! What did I just do?* She shoved her hands in the pockets of her slacks and joined the stream of people meandering down Ocean Drive.

"I'm not going to beg you."

Claudia's voice came from just behind her, the click of her heels keeping time with Rémi's boots. "But I need for you to understand."

She was crumbling inside. Crumbling. Any moment now her gut would pour onto the sidewalk. Liquefied by Claudia's presence. Then her heart. Her lungs. Then everything that held her together. Rémi's trembling fingers begged for a cigarette to calm them.

"Claudia, please!"

Was that raw voice hers? Rémi's breathing was going out of control, coming out in gasps. She stopped, ignoring the curious stares, veered away from the crowd into a smaller stream of midweek pedestrians. The footsteps remained behind her. They followed her into the quiet isolation of the narrow street bracketed by low-rise condos with windows intermittently lit with lights and shadows of people moving behind them. Claudia drew closer and Rémi couldn't stop herself any more. Her hands on Claudia's arms, rough, she jerked the older woman from the main sidewalk, slammed her back against the building's muted white brick.

"Please!"

Rémi tasted tears. Her own. "Don't do this to me. I can't take it. I really can't."

The breath hiccupped out of her.

Claudia's fingers in her curls, raking across her scalp. "I'm sorry, baby. I'm sorry. I didn't realize. I just didn't realize."

"Oh god!"

And she tasted like the first time. Claudia's mouth. Open and coming closer. Claudia said other words, but Rémi swallowed them, made them her own. The *Sorry* and *Please* and *What are you doing* and *Oh my god!* They clung, like starfish, to each other with Claudia's legs locked around Rémi's waist. Her hand pressed to Claudia's bare pussy, the clit that thrust against her palm firmly, slowly, their mouths hot against each other, hearts thudding, tongues dueling, and their smells built in the small alley, and Rémi's tears still didn't stop flowing. Claudia trembled against her, hips bucking, her fingernails like perfect daggers sinking into the back of Rémi's neck.

"I need you," Claudia gasped between kisses. "I tried to give you up, but it didn't work. Everything was so hard with you away from me."

She unwound her legs from around Rémi's waist, and Rémi held the warm weight of her bottom, still not believing it. She squeezed the soft flesh. Closed her eyes and released the low moan of relief she'd kept trapped behind her teeth. Claudia staggered against the wall as Rémi eased her to her feet.

Rémi slowly became aware of where they were, of the public display of their sex and her emotions. She drew in a trembling breath and pulled Claudia against her. "You're right, we should talk."

Her condo sighed with Claudia's returned presence. Rémi felt it. She'd left the windows open and the salt-edged ocean breeze flowed through the fifth-floor apartment like a healing elixir. At the bottom of the stairs leading to her bedroom, Rémi swayed. She grabbed the banister and closed her eyes against the sudden dizziness.

"Are you all right?" Claudia pressed a hand to Rémi's forehead.

"I'm okay." She gently lowered her lover's hand, kissed its palm. "It's been a long few weeks, that's all."

"You look like you've lost weight. Have you been eating?"

"No. You're all the food I need." Rémi grinned.

"Foolish woman."

Claudia pulled her away from the banister, tugged her down to the floor to sit on the thick green rug that covered the blond hardwood in front of the floor-to-ceiling windows overlooking the city.

"You're too big for me to drag upstairs so we might as well stay here."

"Okay." Rémi leaned back against the wall, watching her prodigal lover through half-closed eyes. Outside, the Miami landscape was little more than a series of climbing lights spread around a blanket of darkness that was the Atlantic Ocean.

"I'll be right back."

Before Rémi could protest, Claudia was gone. But moments later she was back with a blanket and pillows from the sofa, and a small glass of lychees soaking in their own juices.

"Your refrigerator is a wasteland," Claudia murmured. "I almost forgot that I left a can of these in your pantry." Her eyebrow rose in a teasing arch. "Apparently you forgot, too."

"Very funny."

Claudia reached into the glass and caught a floating pale fruit between two fingers. She lifted it to Rémi's mouth. "Shut up and eat."

Sweetness exploded on her tongue, a sudden pleasure that made her eyes fall completely closed. Rémi couldn't remember the last time she'd eaten anything substantial. At the club, her friends had ordered all their favorites on the menu and encouraged Rémi to take whatever she wanted. Instead she'd barely sipped from her glass of ginger ale, not wanting to deal with any demands of her body.

Claudia's eyes didn't leave her as she chewed, slowly despite her sudden hunger, then opened her mouth for another bite. Her lover slipped the tender-fleshed fruit, open and slack from its lack of seed, between her lips and onto her tongue. Although Rémi hadn't realized she wasn't well before, suddenly she felt worlds better. She ate every morsel Claudia fed her and, on the last bite, took the long fingers into her mouth, sucked them clean of juice until Claudia's own lips parted and her lashes dropped low to pay attention to what Rémi's tongue was doing.

"You must be feeling much better," Claudia said, her voice a low rasp.

"I am."

And to prove it, Rémi reached for her. Claudia didn't protest when her hands found the zipper at the side of the red dress and slowly drew it down, slowly unveiling the tender skin. Ah, so the bra was built in. The tiny panties were next. Then the stilettos hooked to her heels with a delicate strap. Claudia's eyes watched, unblinking. Her face hard with desire.

The smell of their sex still lingered on Rémi's hand. It flavored the reintroduction to Claudia's body—it felt like so long—and made her anticipate their lovemaking with a painful pleasure that cramped her belly and made her mouth dry with the need to taste.

"I missed you," she said, nose skimming up Claudia's foot, the long leg, and the faintly trembling thigh. The hair at the top of her thighs was musky, tempting, and still damp. But she moved on. To nuzzle the belly, float up between her small breasts, to kiss her throat, her lips, the eyes that finally closed. Then she did a difficult thing. Rémi used the blanket to cover Claudia's nakedness and drew back to lay her head on one of the pillows, her body curled like the yin to Claudia's yang.

"Tell me what this is," she said.

Claudia didn't pretend to misunderstand. "I don't want to be without you." She sat up and adjusted the blanket, tucking the top edge under her arms and leaning back against the window's thick glass. "Even if it means making my children angry."

"Derrick too?"

"Desiree told him."

Christ! Rémi could imagine how that conversion went.

"He was . . . surprisingly understanding. Said that we can't always choose who we love. That love doesn't always make sense. Or make everyone happy."

In a low voice, she told Rémi about every day since the conversation that had sent Rémi into a deep freeze.

After Rémi left Dez and Claudia together on the deck that night of discovery, her best friend cried. Dez was horrified that her mother had allowed Rémi to touch her that way. She cried, asking why. Why did this happen? Why Rémi? Why another woman? How could she let Rémi use her like that? Dez never said how she thought her mother had been used, but Claudia was too caught up in her shame to ask that question then, or even the next morning when she and her daughter sat down at the breakfast table over tea and uneaten toast. All Claudia could imagine was how her daughter had seen her, in lust with someone young enough to be her other child. Claudia felt ashamed. She wanted to do anything to make her daughter's tears disappear. Before making that call to Rémi, she and Dez sat across from each other in the kitchen, helpless tears streaming down their faces. Their hearts broken by different things.

"It felt like pulling out a part of myself." Claudia's fingers smoothed the blanket over her thighs. "Dez watched me call you. She listened to every word. And she seemed to feel better afterwards."

But Claudia felt worse. Dez went back to her life with Victoria and their post-honeymoon bliss, while she had nothing but regret and an empty bed. After he got news of the relationship from Dez, Derrick called to understand what was going on, and Claudia told him. He didn't judge but she sensed he was glad that it was over. As time passed, the reality of what she had done—to herself and to Rémi—broke through her notions of parental self-sacrifice. And that led to the day she dropped by Gillespie's. She had put on her best, knowing that Rémi liked her in white, liked her shoulders bare. She went to the club to beg Rémi to take her back.

"But you wouldn't see me. I called. I tried everything I could think of."

Rémi clasped Claudia's ankle and gently squeezed it.

The pain from that day was a weeping wound. A throbbing sore Claudia couldn't stand to look at. Finally, she went back to her daughter. On a bright Sunday afternoon, she presented herself at Dez's house, wearing the grief on her face. Dez immediately sagged in the doorway, knowing what her mother was there to say. Claudia couldn't live without Rémi and didn't want to. She was her own woman. A grown woman whose children had their own lives. She needed hers too.

Victoria sat with them as they talked, as Dez tried to talk Claudia out of her decision, tears carved into her face like scars. But Claudia remained firm. She forced her daughter to remember how unhappy she had been in the last years of her marriage with Warrick, how everything in their household had crumpled nearly beyond repair. And in those weeks with Rémi, she had been at her happiest in years.

"I just wanted to let you know what I'm going to do," she'd said to her daughter. "So when you see us together, you won't be surprised. Try to understand. Please. I know it's hard. But I need her in my life."

Throughout the conversation, Victoria said nothing, only held her new wife's hand, eyes shining with understanding at what Claudia was saying. Then at the door, just before Claudia left, Victoria kissed her on both cheeks and murmured a husky, "Good luck." That small act of kindness endeared her even more to the older woman.

"I think it was only after I was able to face Desiree," Claudia said to Rémi in the cool wash of darkness, "that I could finally get what I need. You."

She sat up, holding the blanket to her breasts. "Even with all that, I'm sorry it seemed like I abandoned you. It was a hard time. And since you haven't said much of anything since I started talking, it's still a hard time for me."

Rémi took Claudia's hand and drew her close and closer, until, off balance, she tumbled into Rémi. "If you're saying that you want to be with me, then I'm saying yes."

Claudia, her eyes bright and focused, stared unblinkingly at Rémi.

"I feel like I've waited all my adult life for you," Rémi said. The blanket slipped, and she set it to rights, pulling it up to cover Claudia's body. "I love you," she said. "I want you. And if you'll truly have me, I'm yours for always."

Claudia's cry was a sound of laughing relief. "Yes," she said with tears anointing her cheeks. "Yes."

And Rémi believed her.

Epilogue

"**D**o you think they'll come?"

Rémi rearranged the wineglasses on the dining table one more time, desperately needing something to do with her hands. There were four place settings. Would they need them all tonight?

"They have to come," Rémi said, answering her own question. "It would just be rude to accept our invitation then not show up."

But it was seven forty-eight. Twelve minutes until Dez and Victoria were supposed to join them for dinner in Rémi's condo. Claudia, seemingly unconcerned, moved gracefully through the kitchen, turning down the flame under pots and sliding the freshly baked honey wheat bread in the oven to keep it warm.

"Sit down, darling." She brushed a kiss against Rémi's neck on her way to the dining room with the butter dish. "You're making yourself a nervous wreck."

"I'm fine," Rémi said, but she went into the living room and sat down anyway.

She picked up the remote. Then discarded it without turning on the TV. A magazine Yvette had left behind, *Essence* from last November, caught Rémi's eye from the coffee table, but she didn't bother to open it. Her fingers rapped nervously against her thigh.

Warm breath whispered against her neck a moment before Claudia's hands slid down her chest from behind.

"Whatever happens, we're going to be okay."

Over the last eight months, their lives had come together firmly. Cleanly. All their family, friends, even former lovers now knew about them and either approved or seemed determined not to interfere. As Claudia's lover, Rémi had met Eden and endured the older woman's speculative looks, even her not-so-subtle warning that she better handle Claudia's heart with care. Dez remained the only loose end.

Claudia seemed to have made peace with the fact that her daughter had problems with her and Rémi's relationship and always would. She and Dez maintained their close mother/daughter bond, but they never spoke about Rémi. Never. A few nights before, when Rémi had suggested that they invite Dez and Victoria for dinner in an effort to put an end to the lingering awkwardness, her lover had actually stopped in her tracks as they made their way down Collins Avenue toward Gillespie's. Then Claudia had nodded.

"That's a wonderful idea," she said with the slightest of smiles, the look on her face saying she wished she'd thought of it first.

Claudia called her daughter the next day to issue the invitation and, to Rémi's happy surprise, it was accepted.

And now they waited.

"They'll come," Claudia murmured against her cheek, the scent of curried chicken still caught in her pale hair.

Rémi nodded and rubbed her palms over the soft flesh of her lover's arms. *They'll come.*

"Sit with me," she said.

Claudia came and sat in her lap, dangling bare feet over the arm of the sofa.

In her dark capri pants and a plum-colored camisole beneath one of Rémi's shirts she'd rolled up at the elbows, Claudia was the epitome of sexy and relaxed.

"Just think of it this way," she said. "If they don't come we'll have plenty of leftovers for our picnic tomorrow." Her fingers teased open the top button of Rémi's shirt.

Rémi leaned back in the sofa, consciously trying to relax beneath her woman's slight weight. "Not even I can eat that much food."

"Don't delude yourself, love." Claudia snuck her fingers between the shirt's buttons, gently raking her short fingernails over Rémi's skin until a quiet purr vibrated beneath her palm. "Your big appetite is one of my favorite things about you."

Rémi chuckled softly, soothed by her lover's caress. "Maybe I should enter a hot dog eating contest next time one rolls into town. To further secure your favor."

"No, no. Your appetite in the bedroom is enough to tie me to your side. Keep that up and I'll remain suitably impressed, and enslaved."

The laughter burst out of Rémi full force this time and her lover smiled, pressing even closer and offering her deep red lips to kiss.

"Thank you," Rémi murmured against that soft mouth.

"For what?"

But the doorbell rang before she could answer. They both froze; then Claudia carefully got up from her lap and walked toward the front door. But she didn't open it. Instead, with her hand on the doorknob, she turned back to Rémi. Suddenly Rémi realized that the other woman wasn't as nonchalant as she acted. Claudia's face was tight with sudden tension, her mouth a trembling line. She got to her feet.

At the door, she pressed a kiss to Claudia's cool cheek then covered the hand on the doorknob with her own. Claudia nodded, and they opened the door together.

Dez stood in the doorway, her arm linked with Victoria's and a bottle of wine in one hand. Her look was cautious, as if she didn't quite know what to expect.

"Come in," Claudia said.

Rémi glanced at her then, at her best friend and a gently smiling Victoria. "We're glad you were able to make it," she said, and opened the door wide to welcome them in.